Reframing the Urban Challenge in Africa

This book explores the changing dynamics and challenges behind the rapid expanse of Africa's urban population.

Africa's urban age is underway. With the world's fastest growing urban population, the continent is rapidly transforming from one that is largely rural, to one that is largely urban. Often facing limited budgets, those tasked with managing African cities require empirical evidence on the nature of demands for infrastructure, escalating environmental hazards, and ever-expanding informal settlements. Drawing on the work of the African Urban Research Initiative, this book brings together contributions from local researchers investigating key themes and challenges within their own contexts. An important example of urban knowledge co-production, the book demonstrates the regional diversity that can be seen as the main feature of African urbanism, with even well-accepted concepts such as informality manifesting in markedly different ways from place to place.

Providing an important nuanced perspective on the heterogeneity of African cities and the challenges they face, this book will be an important resource for researchers across development studies, African studies, and urban studies.

Ntombini Marrengane is the Manager of the Secretariat for the African Urban Research Initiative (AURI), a Pan African, interdisciplinary applied urban research network, based at the African Centre for Cities at the University of Cape Town, South Africa.

Sylvia Croese is a research associate with the African Centre for Cities, University of Cape Town and a senior researcher with the University of the Witwatersrand (South African Research Chair in Spatial Analysis and City Planning) in Johannesburg, South Africa.

Routledge Studies in Cities and Development

The series features innovative and original research on cities in the global South, aiming to explore urban settings through the lens of international development. The series particularly promotes comparative and interdisciplinary research targeted at a global readership.

In terms of theory and method, rather than basing itself on any one orthodoxy, the series draws on a broad toolkit taken from across social sciences and built environment studies, emphasizing comparison, the analysis of the structure and processes, and the application of qualitative and quantitative methods.

The series welcomes submissions from established and junior authors on cutting-edge and high-level research on key topics that feature in global news and public debate.

The Politics of Slums in the Global South
Urban Informality in Brazil, India, South Africa and Peru
Edited by Véronique Dupont, David Jordhus-Lier, Catherine Sutherland and Einar Braathen

Social Theories of Urban Violence in the Global South
Towards Safe and Inclusive Cities
Edited by Jennifer Erin Salahub, Markus Gottsbacher and John de Boer

Reducing Urban Violence in the Global South
Towards Safe and Inclusive Cities
Edited by Jennifer Erin Salahub, Markus Gottsbacher, John de Boer and Mayssam D. Zaaroura

Sustainable Urban Tourism in Sub-Saharan Africa
Risk and Resilience
Edited by Llewellyn Leonard, Regis Musavengane and Pius Siakwah

Reframing the Urban Challenge in Africa
Knowledge Co-production from the South
Edited by Ntombini Marrengane and Sylvia Croese

For a full list of available titles please visit: www.routledge.com/

Reframing the Urban Challenge in Africa

Knowledge Co-production from the South

**Edited by Ntombini Marrengane
and Sylvia Croese**

Routledge
Taylor & Francis Group
LONDON AND NEW YORK

First published 2021
by Routledge
2 Park Square, Milton Park, Abingdon, Oxon OX14 4RN

and by Routledge
52 Vanderbilt Avenue, New York, NY 10017

Routledge is an imprint of the Taylor & Francis Group, an informa business

British Library Cataloguing-in-Publication Data
A catalogue record for this book is available from the British Library

Library of Congress Cataloging-in-Publication Data
A catalog record for this book has been requested

ISBN: 978-0-367-44220-0 (hbk)
ISBN: 978-1-003-00838-5 (ebk)

Typeset in Times New Roman
By Apex CoVantage, LLC

To Phila, Sfiso, and Lunga, and Lucas and Oscar
and the next generation of urban scholars in Africa

Contents

Figures

Tables

Contributors

Divine Ahadzie, BSc, MSc, PhD, MGIOC, CMCIH (UK), is Associate Professor at the Kwame Nkrumah University of Science and Technology (KNUST), Kumasi, Ghana. Divine has in the past provided support to GHK Consulting Ltd (UK) in developing an Urban Flooding Risk Management Handbook for Developing Countries. He was an outstanding reviewer awardee in 2017 for the *International Journal of Project Management*. He has published on flood-related issues in the *International Journal of Safety and Security Engineering*.

Allan Cain O.C. is an architect. He is also a specialist in project planning and urban development, and is the Director of Development Workshop (DW). Allan has worked as a consultant and lead on research projects for the World Bank and UN-Habitat, and lectured at universities in China, Angola, Norway, USA, South Africa, UK, and Canada. His articles and papers have been published widely in international journals.

Douty Chibamba holds a PhD in geography. He is a lecturer in the School of Natural Sciences, Department of Geography and Environmental Studies at the University of Zambia. He teaches a number of courses in spatial planning, natural resources management, geo-information, and urban geography. He is a seasoned climate change negotiator, and has negotiated for Zambia at several conferences of parties (COPs). His research interests are in land use and land cover change detection, climate change and sustainable development, and renewable energy and sustainable growth.

Sylvia Croese is an urban sociologist with a PhD from the University of Stellenbosch in South Africa. Her research interests, experience, and publications include work on urban politics and governance through the lens of housing, land, urban infrastructure, and mobility, with a focus on Southern and Lusophone Africa. Her current research examines the implementation of global urban policy in African cities, particularly the Sustainable Development Goals.

Irene-Nora Dinye is Assistant Research Fellow at the Centre for Settlements Studies, KNUST. Irene's research interests include business enabling development in urban areas, financial literacy, and local economic development. Recently

Irene's research has focused on identifying flood-risk solutions through community participation. Irene holds a BA in economics from KNUST and an MPhil in development studies from the University of Cape Coast.

Wiza Kabaghe holds an MSc in urban management and development from Erasmus University in Rotterdam in the Netherlands, and a BArch. His research interests and specialization include, among others, urban policy and planning, housing and land development strategies, urban social development, urban environmental management, sustainable cities and climate change, urban governance, and urban and regional development. He also lectures at the University of Zambia in the School of Natural Sciences, and is a participant of the Centre for Urban Research and Planning (CURP) Project.

Deena Khalil is currently Research and Advocacy Unit Manager at Takween Integrated Community Development, an urban development consultancy focusing on underserved communities and urban issues in Egypt. She is also a PhD candidate at University College London (UCL), where she is studying the politics of access to potable water and infrastructure in Cairo's informal areas. Prior to this, she obtained her MA in economics of international development at the American University in Cairo.

Rudith Sylvana King, BSc, MSc, PhD, is Associate Professor at the Kwame Nkrumah University of Science and Technology, Kumasi, Ghana. Her research work covers energy, activities in the informal sector, and settlements in the urban space, as well as gender. She has a number of publications in these areas to her credit, and has served as a reviewer for a number of local and international journals, including the *Commonwealth Journal for Local Governance* (UK).

Ntombini Marrengane is a geographer with specializations in urban development and management of African cities. She holds an MA from Clark Atlanta University in international affairs and development. Her research interests include traditional authorities in African cities and comparative politics. She has lectured at the University of the Western Cape, and manages the secretariat for the African Urban Research Initiative (AURI) at the African Centre for Cities at the University of Cape Town.

Garikai Membele holds an MSc in geo-information and earth observation from the University of Twente in the Netherlands and is Programme Coordinator for the Geo-information and Earth Observation Programme at the University of Zambia. Current research interests are in GIS and remote sensing, volunteered geographical information (VGI), land use/land cover change, web mapping, urban planning, land administration, land governance, and population modelling.

Peter Mulambia has an MSc in spatial planning and a BA in geography from the University of Zambia. He is a researcher at the Centre for Urban Research and Planning (CURP) at the University of Zambia, with research interests including urban water governance, urban service delivery, city and regional planning, urban informality, urban food security, and climate change impacts in cities.

Beverly Musonda Mushili is a lecturer and researcher at the University of Zambia, Department of Geography and Environmental Studies. She holds an MA and BA from the University of Pretoria and the University of Zambia, respectively. Her research interests and recent publications include climate change and fisheries management, climate change vulnerability and adaptation assessments, urban informality, waste management, statistical analysis, livelihood, and gender analysis. Beverly is also a Nuffic Scholar (awarded by Maastricht University in Netherlands).

Brenda Mwalukanga is a socioeconomic planner with an MA in urban management and development from Erasmus University in Rotterdam and a BA in development studies from the University of Zambia. For over ten years she has worked on community development projects, disaster risk reduction projects, as well as other climate change projects, including those using climate information for decision-making.

Omar Nagati is the cofounder and Principal of the Cairo Laboratory for Urban Studies, Training and Environmental Research (CLUSTER). He is a practising architect and urban planner, with over 25 years of experience working in Cairo, and has been the recipient of a number of honours and awards, including representing Egypt in the 6th Architectural Design Exhibition, Venice Biennale. He studied at UBC, Vancouver, and UC Berkeley, and is currently a visiting professor at the University of Sheffield, UK.

Wilma S. Nchito (PhD, MScWEM, MSc, BaEd), is a senior lecturer in the Department of Geography and Environmental Studies in the School of Natural Sciences at the University of Zambia. She is an urban geographer, specialized in planning in transition. Her research interests are small towns, tourism geography, urban water supply and sanitation, waste management, and urban informality in Zambia. She is also interested in transdisciplinary research methods.

Dorothy Ndhlovu is a final year student in the MSc in the Spatial Planning programme at the University of Zambia and holds a BA degree in geography from the University of Zambia. She is a researcher and assistant at the Centre for Urban Research and Planning (CURP) at the University of Zambia, where she has participated in various research projects. Dorothy's current research interests are in urban governance, climate change and cities, urban water security, the food-water-energy nexus, and urban informality.

Peter Ngau is an urban planner and professor in the Department of Urban and Regional Planning, University of Nairobi. He has a PhD in urban planning and over 20 years of university teaching and research experience. His research interests include informal settlements, urban transformation, and peri-urban land governance. He serves as part of the secretariat for the Centre for Urban

Research and Innovations at the University of Nairobi, and is Managing Editor of the journal *Regional Development Studies*.

Progress H. Nyanga, PhD is a senior lecturer at the University of Zambia, Department of Geography and Environmental Studies. He is Assistant Dean for Research in the School of Natural Sciences. His research interests include corruption and land administration; project planning, monitoring, and evaluation; agriculture; food systems; development aid effectiveness; sustainable natural resource management; gender; social-ecological systems analysis; participatory action research; political ecology; and mixed research methodology.

Philip Olale holds an MA in environmental law and an honours undergraduate degree in urban and regional planning from the University of Nairobi. He is currently pursuing a PhD in environmental law, specializing in coastal and marine spatial planning. His professional and research interests are in marine spatial planning, land use planning, physical planning law, land tenure, informal settlement planning and regularization, natural resource planning, and environmental law. He also lectures at the Department of Urban and Regional Planning at the University of Nairobi, and is an associate researcher at the Centre for Urban Research and Innovations (CURI).

Margot Rubin is a senior researcher and faculty member at the University of the Witwatersrand (South African Research Chair in Spatial Analysis and City Planning) in Johannesburg. She holds a PhD in urban politics from the University of the Witwatersrand, and since 2002 she has worked as a researcher and policy and development consultant focusing on housing and urban development issues. Of late, Margot has been writing about inner-city regeneration and housing policy, and also is currently engaged in work around mega-housing projects and issues of gender and the city.

Gilbert Siame holds an MA and a PhD in city and regional planning from the University of Cape Town in South Africa. He is the convener of the MSc in spatial planning programme in the Department of Geography and Environmental Studies at the University of Zambia, where he is also a cofounder and current Coordinator of the Centre for Urban Research and Planning (CURP). Gilbert's research interests and projects include, among others, urban informality, urban sustainability, urban governance, climate change and cities, urban knowledge co-production, and the interface of planning theory and practice in the global South.

Beth Stryker holds a BA from Columbia University and an MA from Princeton University. She has curated exhibitions and programmes for the Downtown Contemporary Arts Festival in Cairo, Beirut Art Center, Leslie Tonkonow Artworks + Projects, the AIA/Center for Architecture in New York (where she held the position of Director of Programs), and the Museum of Contemporary Art in Chicago, among other venues. She is currently the Executive Director of ArteEast in New York.

Preface

The works contained in this edited volume represent the culmination of eight years of effort to plant and develop the foundation of an interdisciplinary African urban research network anchored in African institutions. With initial support from the Rockefeller Foundation and the Cities Alliance, the creation of the African Urban Research Initiative (AURI) network was subsequently fortified by the Ford Foundation's call for scholarship oriented towards urbanism in the global South. Based at the African Centre for Cities at the University of Cape Town in South Africa, AURI was thus designed to support and, where needed, strengthen existing urban research centres on the African continent to produce credible and robust new knowledge on urban conditions in African cities.

The main purpose of AURI's work – both generally and in the research contained in the following volume – is to give space to explore and demonstrate the value of two core principles within the context of scholarship on African cities. The first core principle is the value of knowledge co-production as a vehicle for scholarship that seeks to disrupt the notion that the only source of knowledge and expertise is the academy. Rather, in the co-production context, it is the deliberate and careful building of partnerships – between researchers interested in urban dynamics, communities living within the urban environments under examination, and government officials tasked with managing those environments as well as the services that influence urban systems – that renders essential new knowledges and invaluable perspectives.

The second core principle asserts the need for African institutions to be at the forefront of research concerning the interconnected dynamics at work in cities around the continent, taking into account the heterogeneity of the geography, politics, and economic systems in place. This necessary repositioning of African experts and their institutions as principal researchers and authors of scholarship on African cities is a critical part of enabling an examination of urban dynamics in ways that prioritize local knowledge. This approach aims to disrupt the longstanding power relationships that have governed urban research historically, and to elevate the lived experiences of urban dwellers. In doing so, AURI serves as a conduit for empirical research that can support the formulation of both innovative urban management policies and urban theory. This approach directly challenges the ways knowledge about the 'African city' has previously been (and often still is) constructed. Moreover, this work enables scholarship from the global South to surpass geographic commentary, and rather serve as a space where different perspectives on urban conditions and opportunities can be articulated from close proximity.

Since its establishment, AURI network members have worked incrementally to find ways to engage with one another over significant linguistic and spatial divides. While sometimes painstaking, this important work has connected an organic and growing network of knowledge institutions working across the disciplines that make up the urban. *Reframing the Urban Challenge in Africa: Knowledge Co-production from the South* is the first collaborative knowledge outcome of that process-driven and often hard-to-measure effort. Providing a lens into the major urban challenges facing residents and policymakers in eight African cities and six countries, the chapters in this volume thus give a sense of the range of actors, resources, and institutional stakeholders influencing urban development around the continent. As such, *Reframing the Urban Challenge in Africa: Knowledge Co-production from the South* challenges the notion of an 'African' urban narrative, and provokes the reconsideration of a single set of solutions for a continent where the often-shared conditions of rapid urbanization are surfacing in very particular and distinct ways.

Looking ahead, AURI remains committed to facilitating and supporting research at a city scale and on a comparative basis, with the aim of using research to contribute to local urban policy agendas, and promoting and disseminating quality, multilingual publications that shape and inform the urban development agenda in Africa.

Ntombini Marrengane

Acknowledgements

The editors and authors would like to acknowledge the Ford Foundation for its sustained and generous support of the African Urban Research Initiative.[1] The foundation has been instrumental in facilitating the growth of this pan-African urban research network and supporting AURI members within their respective geographic regions.

The work presented in this volume is the result of deliberate collaboration by researchers, local government officials, and communities in the six cases documented. Specifically, the editors would like to thank the research team based at the Centre for Urban Research and Planning at the University of Zambia, the Lusaka City Council, and stakeholders at the Soweto Food Market (Zambia). They would also like to extend thanks to the research team at the Centre for Settlement Studies, Kwame Nkrumah University of Science and Technology, Kumasi Metropolitan Assembly, the National Disaster Management Organization (Ghana), and the traditional leaders representing Sepe-Buokrom (Ghana). In addition, the editors would like to highlight the contribution from the team of researchers at the Centre for Urban Research and Innovations at the University of Nairobi, officials from Thika municipality, and members of the Kiandutu Residents Association and Muungano wa Wanavijiji (the federation of slum dwellers) (Kenya). In Luanda, the editors are indebted to the research team at Development Workshop Angola, the Belas, Cazenga, and Luanda Municipalities, as well as the Ministry of Urbanization (Angola). The editors would like to acknowledge the team of researchers at the Cairo Lab for Urban Studies, Training and Environmental Research (CLUSTER) for their collective efforts in delivering research across three Egyptian cities. Lastly, the contribution of Reitumetse Selepe is acknowledged for the production of maps on Johannesburg. Without the generous and sustained participation and contributions of community members in all of the cities, this work would not have been possible.

This publication represents three years of continuous effort, and would not have been possible without the commitment of all participating AURI member research centres, which include those just mentioned, as well as in Ouagadougou, Dar es Salaam, and Maputo. We would also like to acknowledge the support of the AURI Scientific Committee, Professor Marie Huchzermeyer, Professor Peter Ngau, Allan Cain, Omar Nagati, and Malick Gaye. The editors would also like to thank

Dr Jane Battersby-Lennard and Dr Warren Smit for their critical input, as well as Alison Pulker and Kevin Mutia for editorial support at the African Centre for Cities, University of Cape Town. Finally, the editors wish to express thanks to Lee Middleton, whose attention to detail helped transform this collection of academic papers into AURI's first collaborative knowledge product.

Note

1 For more information on the AURI network, visit www.africanurbanresearchinitiative.net.

Acronyms

CH 1

African Centre for Cities (ACC)
African Urban Research Initiative (AURI)
Cairo Laboratory for Urban Studies, Training and Environmental Research (CLUSTER)
Centre for Settlement Studies (CSS)
Centre for Urbanism and Built Environment Studies (CUBES)
Centre for Urban Research and Innovations (CURI)
Centre for Urban Research and Planning (CURP)
Community Resilience Framework (CRF)
Development Workshop (DW)
New Urban Agenda (NUA)
Sustainable Development Goals (SDGs)

CH 2

African Urban Research Initiative (AURI)
Central Business District (CBD)
Centre for Urban Research and Planning (CURP)
International Labour Organization (ILO)
Lusaka City Council (LCC)
Market Advisory Committee (MAC)
Movement for Multi-Party Democracy (MMD)
Patents and Companies Registration Agency (PACRA)
Patriotic Front (PF)
People's Process on Housing and Poverty in Zambia (PPHPZ)
Slum Dwellers International (SDI)
Social Solidarity Economy (SSE)
Socio-Economic Rights Institute of South Africa (SERI)
United National Independence Party (UNIP)

Ward Development Committees (WDC)
Zambian Kwacha (ZMW)

CH 3

Agence Française de Développement (AFD)
Cairo Laboratory for Urban Studies, Training and Environmental Research (CLUSTER)
Central Agency for Public Mobilization and Statistics (CAPMAS)
Deutsche Gesellschaft für Internationale Zusammenarbeit (GIZ)
Egyptian Pound (EGP)
Greater Cairo Region (GCR)
Informal Settlement Development Facility (ISDF)

CH 4

Association of Africa Planning Schools (AAPS)
Centre for Urban Research Innovations (CURI)
Global Land Tools Network (GLTN)
Government of Kenya (GoK)
Kenya National Bureau of Statistics (KNBS)
Muungano Support Trust (MuST)
Slum Dwellers International (SDI)
Sustainable Development Goals (SDGs)
Thika Water and Sewerage Company (THIWASCO)
Urban Innovations Project (UIP)

CH 5

Central Agency for Public Mobilization and Statistics (CAPMAS)
Central Business District (CBD)
City of Johannesburg (COJ)
East Madinat Nasr (EMN)
Egyptian Environmental Affairs Agency (EEAA)
General Organization for Physical Planning (GOPP)
Greater Cairo Region (GCR)
Greater Cairo Water and Wastewater Company (GCWWC)
Informal Settlement Development Facility (ISDF)
Ministry of Environmental Affairs (MEA)
Ministry of Housing, Utilities and Urban Development (MHUUD)
Ministry of Planning (MoP)
Muncipal-owned entities (MOE)

Reconstruction and Development Programme (RDP)
Socio-Economic Rights Institute of South Africa (SERI)
South Western Townships (SOWETO)

CH 6

Africa Climate Resilient Infrastructure Summit (ACRIS II)
Centre for Settlements Studies (CSS)
Community Resilience Framework (CRF)
Disaster Resilience of Place (DROP)
District Assembly Common Fund (DACF)
Environmental Protection Agency (EPA)
Focus Group Discussions (FGDs)
Government of Ghana (GoG)
Intergovernmental Panel on Climate Change (IPPC)
Kumasi Metropolitan Assembly (KMA)
Kwame Nkrumah University of Science and Technology (KNUST)
Metropolitan Chief Executive (MCE)
Metropolitan/Municipal/District Assemblies (MMDAs)
Millennium Development Goals (MDGs)
National Disaster Management Organization (NADMO)
Population and Demographics, Environmental/Ecosystem, Organized Governmental Services, Physical Infrastructure, Lifestyle and Community Competence, Economic Development, and Social-Cultural Capital (PEOPLE's model)
Qualitative data analysis (QDA)
Stakeholder Meetings (SMs)
Sub-Saharan Africa (SSA)
Sustainable Development Goals (SDGs)
Unit Committee (UC)

CH 7

Angolan National Institute of Territorial and Urban Planning (INOTU)
Development workshop (DW)
Office of Urban Reconversion of the Cazenga Municipality and both Sambizanga and Rangel Districts (GTRUCS)
Global Urban Observatory (GUO)
Government of Angola (GoA)
Housing Development Fund (FFH)
Millennium Development Goals (MDGs)
National Bank of Angola (BNA)
New Urban Agenda (NUA)
Overseas Direct Investment (ODI)
Sustainable Development Goals (SDGs)
Urbanization and Housing Programme (PNUH)

CH 8

Association of Africa Planning Schools (AAPS)
Community Resilience Framework (CRF)
New Urban Agenda (NUA)
Sustainable Development Goals (SDGs)

1 Introduction

Africa's urban challenge

Sylvia Croese

With the world's fastest growing rates of urbanization, Africa's urban population has doubled in the last decade, and is predicted to increase threefold between 2010 and 2050 (UN-Habitat, 2014). Already home to seven megacities as well as a rapidly multiplying number of secondary cities, the transformation of this continent formerly regarded as rural to one that is largely urban is undeniable (UNDESA, 2018).

Over the past two decades, a growing body of work examining Africa's 'urban revolution' has emerged (Parnell & Pieterse, 2014). An important strand of this work distinguishes itself from traditional and conventional urban research and theory by recognizing that the drivers, scale, pace, and nature of urban growth in Africa are vastly different from the experience and historical patterns of urbanization in the North (Parnell & Robinson, 2012; Fox, 2014). Urbanization without industrialization, high natural growth rates, and housing, employment, and basic services that are predominantly generated without government intervention or regulation are only some of the many characteristics of African urbanisms (Pieterse, 2011; Cobbinah et al., 2015).

This means that many of the concepts, models, and logics traditionally associated with urban growth and development – and related to the role of the state, economy, and society – either do not apply, or operate in very different ways, and therefore need to be rethought, reformulated, or simply considered in their own right (Robinson, 2006; Bekker & Fourchard, 2013; Myers, 2011). The growing scholarship on African cities recognizes that this reality is part of a wider geographical realignment occurring in urban studies over the past years, in which southern perspectives are representing new points of departure for theorizing the city and urban governance, development, and planning (Edensor & Jayne, 2012; Caldeira, 2017; Simone, 2010; Roy, 2009, 2011; Parnell & Oldfield, 2014; Bhan et al., 2018; Watson, 2009; Satgé & Watson, 2018).

The need to better understand African cities in order to shape the continent's urban future is also increasingly recognized in the policy sphere (UN-Habitat & UNECA, 2015), reflecting a global shift acknowledging the role cities will need to play if global development agendas such as the Sustainable Development Goals and the New Urban Agenda, as well as agreements such as the Paris Climate

Agreement, are to be realized. High-level support for these global agendas by African governments, and the adoption of continental policies such as Agenda 2063 and national development plans with an urban focus, mark an important watershed, and a departure from policies predominantly focused on the rural. However, in spite of this discursive turn, there remains a disjuncture between urban policies and practice (Pieterse, 2018). National governments across the continent often remain unresponsive to the needs of urban citizens, while local governments continue to lack the political, administrative, and fiscal means and resources to adequately plan, govern, and manage sustainable and inclusive cities and human settlements (Silva, 2016; UN-Habitat, 2014).

As a result, few African countries are on track to meeting global goals by 2030 (UNECA, 2018; SDG Center for Africa & SDSN, 2019). While a lack of financial and technical resources represents an important barrier to the implementation of plans and policies for more sustainable development, a shortage of the data and knowledge that can adequately guide and monitor progress and implementation of such plans and policies is just as obstructive. Indeed, much of the knowledge that is produced in and on urban Africa does not speak concretely to the challenges that are experienced by those who govern and are governed on the ground.

This edited volume seeks to address the disjuncture between urban research, policy, and practice, with a particular focus on African cities. It brings together contributions from various members of the African Urban Research Initiative (AURI), a pan-African interdisciplinary and applied urban research network that comprises universities, think tanks, research institutions, and practitioner agencies concerned with urbanization and its impacts across various scales on the African continent. As such, the following chapters present research entirely conducted by researchers and practitioners working in and on Africa, most of which is also applied, and was conducted in collaboration with local communities, governments, and other relevant stakeholders on issues that directly relate to local challenges.

This introductory chapter provides an overview of Africa's urban challenge, and emerging modes and methods – expanded on in subsequent chapters – to reframe this challenge through knowledge co-production.

Africa's urban challenge

The challenges of rapid urban growth, poverty, unemployment, mounting social, economic, and spatial inequality, and vulnerability to climate change in globalizing and urban Africa, and the systems of exclusion these challenges produce are increasingly well-known and documented by researchers, international organizations, and development institutions alike. However, solutions to address these issues too often continue to be shaped by external or outdated perceptions of development, and implemented in top-down, isolated ways that do not respond to the complexity of local dynamics, needs, and priorities.

This is partly because – in spite of growing interest and scholarship – there is still not enough research conducted in and on urban Africa. In this context, researchers have pointed to the geopolitics of urban data production: 'If 21% of the world's urban population will be living in African cities in 2050, this part of the world is still largely overlooked by existing global urban databases . . . partly due to capacity issues, as the technical and human resources needed to collect, process, and analyse urban data is often lacking in municipal departments' (Robin & Acuto, 2018, p. 79). Moreover, existing global urban databases often do not include the full range of stakeholders producing urban data, such as local research institutes, civil society, or even national governments (Robin et al., 2017).

When looking at research on urban sustainability, most of the influential and mainstream academic scholarship also continues to largely emanate from the global North (Nagendra et al., 2018). A lack of research funding represents a major impediment to local research output and knowledge creation. The decline in research funding in Africa due to a combination of factors can be traced back to the 1990s. These factors include the destabilizing influence of political events and civil wars, the impact of a change in the policies of the World Bank and other international agencies on higher education, and continued low investment in science by African governments. These factors in turn affected research infrastructure and research management and support within higher education institutions, further hindering robust data production (Mouton, 2018). These research challenges have also been exacerbated by rising student numbers and the mushrooming of private higher education institutions, often of dubious quality and standards (Mahlubi et al., 2007; Banya, 2008).

But the deficit is not just about the lack of sufficient research; it is also about the kind of research that is being produced. The hegemony of western thought in education and knowledge production is still reflected in many African universities, where teaching programmes premised on colonial models of knowledge production and taught in colonial languages continue to reproduce themselves (Mamdani, 1993; Jensen et al., 2015). Nevertheless, most of the calls for the decolonization of higher education remain limited to South Africa (Crossman, 2004). In some cases, calls for decolonization ironically are the result of changing international donor agendas, which are increasingly beginning to support local or endogenous knowledge production (Shizha, 2010). The sum result is that most of the research produced in and on Africa continues to be disconnected from local issues.

According to the Kenyan scholar Nyanchoga:

The process of decolonizing education system has been slow. Many times universities in Africa are indifferent to the social climate in which they operate in because they are alien to it. University education fails to integrate the multicultural traditions of the society in which they operate largely because many of them had their roots in the colonial order. They simply manifest lack of a social responsibility to society. Consequently they are unable to mediate between cultural diversity and nation building, ethnic contours and political disjuncture.

(Nyanchoga, 2014, p. 64)

Due to the ways in which much research on or in Africa is funded and conducted, it often does not find its way back to prospective users, whether policymakers or local communities. This lack of reciprocity also reflects the power dynamics between researchers and the communities they study. While this is not just an African problem, it is one that requires urgent attention in an environment where the value of research goes far beyond academic curiosity and can inform innovative and inclusive policy.

As noted by the international expert panel 'Science and the Future of Cities' (an independent, international effort to assess the state of the urban science-policy interface for global sustainability):

> Cities need better science-policy connections. To harness the global efforts around these agendas, we urgently need to address two key matters: forge new knowledge that responds to complex urban challenges, and accelerate uptake of scientific urban information by practitioners.
>
> (*Science and the Future of Cities*, 2018, p. 3)

This assessment illustrates an emerging call for more applied work that bridges the gap between science/research and policy, especially in the field of cities and urban sustainability, as well as adequate support for such work (e.g., Mauser et al., 2013). Building on this call, this book identifies Africa's overarching challenge as the need for new knowledge production, through the use of methodologies and approaches that bridge the science-policy gap with an explicit intention to adequately, sustainably, and inclusively respond to the continent's development challenges.

As such, the questions underpinning this book's rationale are: what modes of knowledge production are needed to fill the knowledge gaps in/on African cities? And how can different ways of producing knowledge contribute not only to knowing more about Africa's urban challenges, but also to reframing the challenges themselves?

Reframing through knowledge co-production

There is growing interest and an expanding body of work around the notion of 'co-production'. Many still use this term in the way it was first introduced in the 1980s, from work on street policing in the US that argued that security was not delivered solely by the police, but rather was the product of relationships, negotiation, and collaboration between police officers and local residents (Brudney & England, 1983, cited in Mitlin & Bartlett, 2018). In their review of the concept in a special issue of the journal *Environment and Urbanization*, Mitlin and Bartlett (2018) outline how the concept moved to the global South in the mid-1990s, but still retained a focus on service delivery (Ostrom, 1996; Evans, 1996). As such, the primary emphasis of the contributions published in that special issue is on the co-production of public services such as water and sanitation, informal settlement upgrading, or post-disaster reconstruction, with each contributor using a different definition to describe the nature of the collaborations involved.

Another strand of work instead focuses on the co-production of *knowledge*, with a view to bridging the gap between science and society (Gibbons et al., 1994; Jasanoff, 2004). In more recent years, this work has increasingly moved into the field of sustainable development, emphasizing the need to produce 'usable' knowledge not just *on* but *with*, as well as *for*, society (Polk, 2015; Clark et al., 2016). This kind of work is also referred to as 'transdisciplinary' research, in the sense that it represents a 'reflexive, integrative and method driven' way of doing research aimed at the solution or transition of societal problems . . . by differentiating and integrating knowledge from various scientific and societal bodies of knowledge' (Lang et al., 2012, pp. 26–27; see also Jahn, 2008; Lawrence, 2015).

In an attempt to synthesize this growing body of work, a large group of researchers have collectively defined knowledge co-production in the context of sustainability research as: "Iterative and collaborative processes involving diverse types of expertise, knowledge and actors to produce context-specific knowledge and pathways towards a sustainable future"(Norström et al., 2020).
Norström et al. also distinguish four principles that can contribute to high-quality knowledge co-production for sustainability. Specifically, they suggest that processes should be:

1   Context-based: situated in a particular context, place, or issue.
2   Pluralistic: explicitly recognizing the multiple ways of knowing and doing.
3   Goal-oriented: articulating clearly defined, shared, and meaningful goals that are related to the challenge at hand.
4   Interactive: allowing for ongoing learning among actors, active engagement, and frequent interactions (Norström et al., 2020).

The chapters in this book demonstrate that knowledge co-production is an appropriate approach to conduct urban research in the context-specific manner demanded by the challenges facing Africa's cities. This imperative stems from the fact that while key urban trends can be discerned across the continent, local dynamics, needs, systems, actors, and priorities remain highly specific to local contexts, mostly undocumented, and often contested and in flux. Knowledge co-production represents a way to include voices typically absent in research, and in the process, to foster new relationships between key stakeholders. Such an approach not only generates new knowledge concerning societal problems, but also renders actionable knowledge for problem-solving. While still incipient, the use of knowledge co-production by researchers in and on Africa is growing, especially with reference to (urban) sustainability challenges related to slum upgrading, coastal flooding, and waste management (Buyana, 2019). Much of the work done so far has been concentrated in South Africa, where experiments with knowledge co-production can be seen as having emerged in the post-apartheid era as a way for researchers to call for more reflexive approaches to policy deliberation (Swilling, 2014).

At the African Centre for Cities (ACC) at the University of Cape Town in South Africa, knowledge co-production has become ingrained in the ACC's DNA through its work over the past decade as part of Mistra Urban Futures, a network of researchers using co-production processes for achieving sustainable urban futures and realizing just cities (Mistra Urban Futures, 2016). The network is part of a number of multi-country, multidisciplinary, and multi-partner research consortia across the global North and South engaged in research for urban sustainability and equality (Osuteye et al., 2019).

Central to ACC's work has been the CityLab programme, which started in 2008 with the aim of brokering 'interdisciplinary engagement, both across academic disciplines and between the academy and broader society, towards new knowledge generation and knowledge sharing, and the creation of working partnerships to engage with the issues pertinent to the African urban situation' (Anderson et al., 2013, p. 2). CityLabs can have different meeting formats, ranging from seminar series to the establishment of a think tank or collaborative research projects. In Cape Town, they have been both place- and theme-based, concentrating on particular parts of the city or on topics ranging from healthy cities and sustainable human settlements, to climate change, urban violence, safety, and governance, and have resulted in a variety of outputs from academic journal articles, book chapters, and edited book volumes, to popular publications and policy documents (Cartwright et al., 2012; Brown-Luthango, 2015; Cirolia et al., 2016).

Altogether, the ACC CityLabs can be seen not just in the literal sense as referring to places of work or 'labour' (Anderson et al., 2013, p. 2), but also as laboratories or sites representing 'experimentations with knowledge co-production' (Culwick et al., 2019, p. 9). As such, they fit into a broader body of work on 'urban experimentation' (Bulkeley & Castán Broto, 2013; Karvonen & van Heur, 2014; Evans, 2016; Patel et al., 2017).

While important and needed, knowledge co-production – through CityLabs or other research methods – is not without its difficulties. Based on their experiences as sustainability researchers in research projects in Kenya, Switzerland, Bolivia, and Nepal, Pohl et al. (2010) point to three specific challenges. The first is the challenge of addressing power relations and ensuring that no single actor or viewpoint is privileged over others. The second concerns the challenge of integrating and interrelating different perspectives on the issues at stake in order to achieve a more comprehensive or balanced understanding of the issue and its corresponding solutions. The third has to do with the challenge of working with the concept of sustainable development as a framework that is normative and contested and therefore requires negotiation around its use as 'a starting point and key motor of the co-production process' (Pohl et al., 2010, p. 272). Dealing with these various challenges requires a set of practical skills – often acquired in past experiences as practitioners – to enable researchers to let go of their own viewpoints and assumptions as academics, and assume roles that can vary from reflective scientists to intermediaries or facilitators (Pohl et al., 2010, pp. 277–279).

Experiences from the ACC CityLab programme further highlight challenges around knowledge co-production, including micro-politics, getting people to move out of their disciplinary and practice biases (and related norms, values, and ethics), the difficulties of writing and producing knowledge in interdisciplinary groups, and the fact that this type of work is more time-consuming than standard research (Anderson et al., 2013; Smit et al., 2015). Culwick et al. (2019, p. 4) therefore conclude that 'the CityLab model is not suited to all contexts or objectives. They require commitment and joint goals, and a willingness to engage and rethink current practices and ways of knowing'.

Indeed, knowledge co-production is inherently complex, time-consuming, and often unpredictable in terms of outcomes (Simon et al., 2018). In order for such research to feed into the formulation, implementation, and monitoring of urban policy – and ultimately changed practices – there is a need to find sustained modes of collaboration between government, researchers, practitioners, and communities.

The African Urban Research Initiative

The AURI network emerged in 2013 at the ACC at the University of Cape Town in South Africa out of a sustained engagement with policy actors and Africa-based research centres seeking to reach a shared understanding of the scope and implications of the urban transition in Africa. The project is driven by the premise that unless an active network of durable knowledge institutions, focused on applied urban research and capacity-building, is urgently established, the decision-makers for the continent's rapidly growing urban centres will not be in a position to understand their urban development dynamics, let alone address them effectively.

AURI is distinct not just because its contributions come from researchers and practitioners who live and work on the ground, but also in its methodological focus on knowledge co-production. ACC cofounders Susan Parnell and Edgar Pieterse point to the need for appropriate understandings of urbanization in Africa to go beyond theoretical, dogmatic, and dichotomous approaches, and to focus instead on 'endogenous readings of the urban' (2014, p. ix), firmly grounded in the complex local realities of African cities. Such efforts require different theoretical and methodological practices to generate the kind of urban research and knowledge that is needed to understand and inform Africa's urban transformation. In other work, Parnell and Pieterse call this 'translational research': a method that is, at least initially, primarily descriptive, and which builds on 'the co-construction of a knowledge base to provide a legitimate and shared understanding of the state of the city and its needs' (Parnell & Pieterse, 2016, p. 241). Parnell and Pieterse see translational research as a method that is not just practically suited to and needed in light of the constraints of doing research in Africa, but also as a deeply political practice that aims to enable urban transformation.

Members of AURI recognize the necessity for research centres in Africa to be networked, in order to exchange knowledge, know-how, and expertise, and thereby foster a foundation of credible and resilient knowledge institutions on the continent that are at once rooted in local realities and engaged with broader trends.

AURI currently consists of 21 interdisciplinary applied urban research centres. These institutions include university-based research centres, think tanks, and civil society organizations. The basis for membership is voluntary, requiring only an active participation in the urban research agenda, and a commitment to building and strengthening local knowledge networks. AURI's core objective is to develop a collaborative pan-African network that relies upon and actively nurtures African expertise and research agendas. This network is intended to serve as a platform for both innovation and strategic thinking for Africa's urban challenges and opportunities. At present, the membership of AURI is as per Table 1.1.

Contributions: outline of the book

This book includes a selection of research undertaken by AURI members as part of the 2017–2019 work programme on 'Spatial Inequality in African Cities:

Table 1.1 AURI member institutions

Institution	City, Country
Centre for Urban Research and Innovations	Nairobi, Kenya
Institute for Urban Development Studies, Ethiopian Civil Service University	Addis Ababa, Ethiopia
Development Workshop Angola	Luanda, Angola
Takween Integrated Community Development	Cairo, Egypt
Lagos Urban Research Network, University of Lagos	Lagos, Nigeria
Ecole Africaine des Métiers de l'Architecture et de l'Urbanisme	Lomé, Togo
Laboratoire Citoyennetés	Ouagadougou, Burkina Faso
Environnement et Développement du Tiers Monde	Dakar, Sénégal
Centre for Urbanism and Built Environment Studies, University of the Witwatersrand	Johannesburg, South Africa
Cairo Laboratory for Urban Studies, Training and Environmental Research	Cairo, Egypt
Sierra Leone Urban Research Centre	Freetown, Sierra Leone
Laboratoire d'Etudes et de Recherche sur les Dynamiques Sociales et le Développement Local	Niamey, Niger
Urban Research and Advocacy Centre Malawi	Mzuzu, Malawi
Centre for Urban Research and Planning, University of Zambia	Lusaka, Zambia
Centro de Análise de Políticas, Universidade Eduardo Mondlane	Maputo, Mozambique
Institute for Human Settlement Studies, Ardhi University	Dar es Salaam, Tanzania
College of African and Oriental Studies, Addis Ababa University	Addis Ababa, Ethiopia
Faculty for the Built Environment, Arts and Science, Ba Isago University	Gaborone, Botswana
African Centre for Cities, University of Cape Town	Cape Town, South Africa
Institute for Development Studies, University of Nairobi	Nairobi, Kenya
Centre for Settlement Studies, Kwame Nkrumah University of Science and Technology	Kumasi, Ghana

Source: AURI

Research and Practice'. AURI members responded to a call for proposals for contemporary applied research to be carried out over a 12-month period with the support of the Ford Foundation.

There were three broad themes:

- Urban governance.
- Infrastructure and service delivery.
- Dynamics and nature of informality in African cities.

Researchers were asked to respond with proposals for research that included knowledge co-production methodologies as well as critical comparative analysis. The result is this new body of research that makes three important contributions. First, it demonstrates the depth of contemporary urban research being undertaken by African knowledge institutions across the continent. Second, it allows the reader to examine a selection of African cities beyond the (traditional) frame of city classification as measured by criteria such as population size, global competitiveness, or economic productivity. Third, the collection of work contained in this volume provides important perspectives on how ideas such as knowledge co-production travel across boundaries and, in particular, differentiate across diverse African contexts.

The six chapters are grouped together under the two broad themes of (in) formality and infrastructure, with issues of urban governance underpinning all of them. While an attempt has been made to include contributions from across the continent, not all linguistic or geographical regions, such as Francophone Africa, East Africa, or the islands of Africa, are equally represented. However, by covering large metropolitan areas (Cairo, Johannesburg, Luanda), mid-sized cities (Kumasi, Lusaka, and Alexandria), small cities (Minya), and peri-urban spaces (Thika) alike, different urban environments are represented. Moreover, the chapters collectively cover some of the issues most pertinent to African cities – from urban inequality to climate change, the urban food economy, and land and housing – as entry points into wider discussions on urban governance and development in Africa. In addition, all chapters have sought to adopt innovative mixed methods and research approaches to knowledge co-production, as well as comparative experimentation.

(In)formality

The book's first three chapters are concerned with the governance and different manifestations of urban informality. In spite of the importance of the informal economy across the continent, government actions continue to be, at worst, aimed at eliminating informality and, at best, formalizing it. The Zimbabwean scholar Kamete (2013) explains this urge by discussing African city authorities' 'fetish about formality', which he sees as 'fuelled by an obsession with urban modernity and Western notions of the "desired city"' (p. 24). However, as Indian scholar Ananya Roy (2005) has persuasively argued in the context of urban India, in the process of denying informality, states often play an important role in (re-)producing informal practice. The chapters in this first part of the book provide insight into the different actors and practices involved in producing informality, and the particular, complex, and interwoven nature of the ways in which these interactions manifest in the African urban context.

Chapter 2 presents the Centre for Urban Research and Planning (CURP) at the University of Zambia's research investigating the 'everyday' in Zambia's largest urban food market, with the goal of better understanding the formal-informal continuum, and thus grounding policy to support more inclusive and sustainable urban development in the global South. Conducted together with policy officials from Lusaka City Council as well as a range of food actors from the Soweto Market, the research process included round-table meetings, multi-stakeholder meetings, learning labs, and a policy dialogue on the Soweto Food Market. Through this collaborative process, the team gained insight into the ways in which formal rules and regulations are used and contested by multiple actors and practices in ways that are neither fully formal nor informal, but rather a constantly negotiated hybrid, structured by 'multiple sites' of power and control.

Chapter 3 comes from practitioners at the Cairo Laboratory for Urban Studies, Training and Environmental Research (CLUSTER), who have been undertaking urban research and design interventions in Egypt's post-uprising era since 2011. In a multi-scalar study across three different Egyptian cities, the researchers developed a comparative framework that utilizes the variables of borders, crossings, activities, and flows to explore the nature of the interconnections between the informal and formal. Working with practitioners, academics, community leaders, and experts in each city to examine different physical, social, and economic variables that have often emerged as responses to policies seeking to combat informality, the chapter proposes a redefined understanding of informal spaces and activities as central nodes of urban integration and connection, with the aim of illuminating larger questions around how to promote integrated urban policy.

Chapter 4 is written by researchers from the Centre for Urban Research and Innovations (CURI) at the University of Nairobi. Through a series of CityLabs bringing together community members, nongovernmental organizations (NGO), and city officials in the informal settlement of Kiandutu in the peri-urban municipality of Thika on the outskirts of Nairobi, the research team explored prospects for land sharing as an approach to resolving long-standing local conflicts and contestations around land tenure. Based on this experience, the chapter offers useful insights into the challenges and opportunities for community engagement and negotiations around land tenure and slum upgrading, exploring land sharing not only as a potential solution to a housing problem, but also as a rights-based model that may illuminate new ways of teaching, conceptualizing, and implementing urban planning in contested and fragmented spaces on the continent.

Infrastructure

An important link connects informality and infrastructure. As Pieterse (2018, p. 40) puts it: 'infrastructure systems . . . reveal most clearly the coexistence of formal and informal systems of social and economic reproduction'. We can see this in areas from energy to transport and housing, but also in their social manifestation, as urban scholar AbdouMaliq Simone describes, using his notion of 'people as infrastructure' (Simone, 2004). In both their social and physical dimensions, studies of infrastructure offer useful insight and critique on the extent to which global agendas such as the Sustainable Development Goals can be monitored and achieved in African cities (Pieterse et al., 2018).

Chapter 5 brings together contributions from researchers at the Takween Integrated Community Development practice in Cairo and the Centre for Urbanism and Built Environment Studies (CUBES) at Wits University in Johannesburg. Mapping and comparing the locations and levels of access to basic services and infrastructure, the chapter shows how inequality is manifested differently both between as well as within the two cities. It further argues that there is a recursive relationship between service provision and inequality: that lack of public services is not only a manifestation or measure of inequality, but also a producer of social inequality, and that these inequalities are often disguised by scale. In doing so, the chapter highlights the importance of spatial analysis and localized measures that reflect the local nature and diverse characteristics of urban inequality as they are manifested on the ground.

Chapter 6 reflects on a study conducted by researchers from the Centre for Settlement Studies (CSS) at Kwame Nkrumah University of Science and Technology in Kumasi, Ghana. Addressing the increasing devastation caused by recurrent floods, the research team conducted a series of CityLabs in the flood-prone settlement of Sepe-Buokrom in the city of Kumasi. Through focus group discussions and stakeholder meetings, the team brought together local community members and leaders, as well as city and national government officials to explore the potential for developing a community resilience framework (CRF) for flood-risk management. In the process, the role and importance of different levels of leadership sharing a common vision – and existing impediments to a spirit of collaboration – emerged as a key enabling factor for the successful development of community-based approaches to flood-risk management. The research further concluded that a shift in methodological approach to co-production is vital if the gap between research and policy in Africa is to be bridged.

Chapter 7 presents findings from research conducted by the NGO Development Workshop (DW) in Angola. This work builds on decades of action research conducted by DW among peri-urban communities and informal settlements as well as the monitoring of the implementation of global agendas at the Angolan government's request, bearing in mind the goal of building sustainable and equitable cities that leave no one behind. Based on a combined set of mixed and participatory research tools, the research shows the limited impact of the Angolan government's ambitious Urbanization and Housing Programme, launched in 2009 with the aim of building 1,000,000 houses, and suggests a more inclusive approach to rebuilding Angola's war-torn cities that builds on and supports self-built 'social production of housing'.

Knowledge co-production

Taken together, the chapters in this book represent the diverse set of actors, practices, and experiences involved in urban governance and development across the continent. In their work the researchers affirm a heterogeneous concept of knowledge co-production (van der Hel, 2016) by giving concrete examples of how difference can play out at the city, neighbourhood, and settlement levels. As such, they offer useful learnings on the localization, monitoring, and implementation of global and local urban policy agendas, and importance of recognizing urban difference and complexity (Parnell & Robinson, 2017).

In their collective pursuit to adopt innovative and more inclusive approaches to knowledge production, one of the major learnings that comes through from the chapters in this volume is the importance of close relationships between researchers and representatives from local governance structures, which in most of the cases have been fostered and built over long periods of time. In a context where levels of trust – both in public institutions as well as among different members of urban communities – are generally low, the importance of such relations cannot be underestimated. However, even with such relationships in place, the chapters also demonstrate the challenges of working with those local leadership structures – including traditional authorities or local party cadres – which are vital for access to local communities, but also function as gatekeepers. Often, day-to-day cultural and political practices and dynamics, as well as 'conflicting rationalities' (Watson, 2003), determine the scope, availability, and willingness of local leaders and communities to participate in research projects and knowledge co-production, even when these projects are aimed at community participation. Overcoming such challenges requires a deep understanding of the complexity and workings of local governance structures, as well as the factors, systems, and dynamics that can contribute to building trust and collective action.

This volume contributes to the growing literature on urban research, and specifically offers a view from the ground that provides insight into the wide spectrum of actors, systems, processes, and modes of governance that constitute African cities. Rather than offering and replicating a standard research approach across the case cities, the collection demonstrates the fluidity of urban themes and concepts, as examined across six African cities. Most importantly, the work contained in this book amplifies the need for urban research in African cities to be viewed beyond its ability to conform to or defy northern typologies. The output of this research collective demonstrates that indeed there are other understandings and knowledges of urbanization that require different terms of engagement. We offer this work from AURI – a nascent pan-African collaborative network – as a contribution to both new forms and methods of knowledge production.

References

Anderson, P.M.L., Brown-Luthango, M., Cartwright, A., Farouk, I. & Smit, W. (2013). Brokering communities of knowledge and practice: reflections on the African centre for cities' citylab programme. *Cities*, 32, pp. 1–10. DOI: http://dx.doi.org/10.1016/j.cities.2013.02.002

Banya, K. (2008). Globalization, knowledge economy and the emergence of private universities in Sub-Saharan Africa. In: Hopson, R., Camp Yeakey, C. & Musa Boakari, F. (Eds.), *Power, voice and the public good: schooling and education in global societies (advances in education in diverse communities, vol. 6)*. Bingley: Emerald Group Publishing Limited, pp. 231–259.

Bekker, S. & Fourchard, L. (Eds.). (2013). *Politics and policies: governing cities in Africa.* Cape Town: HSRC Press.

Bhan, G., Srinivas, S. & Watson, V. (Eds.). (2018). *The Routledge companion to planning in the global South.* Abingdon and New York: Routledge.

Brown-Luthango, M. (2015). *State/society synergy in Philippi, Cape Town.* Cape Town: University of Cape Town.

Brudney, J.L. & England, R.E. (1983). Towards a definition of the co-production concept. *Public Administration Review*, 43(1), pp. 59–65.

Bulkeley, H. & Castán Broto, V. (2013). Government by experiment? Global cities and the governing of climate change. *Transactions of the Institute of British Geographers*, 38, pp. 361–375. DOI: https://doi.org/10.1111/j.1475-5661.2012.00535.x

Buyana, K. (2019). Keeping the doors open: experimenting science-policy-practice interfaces in Africa for sustainable urban development. *Journal of Housing and the Built Environment.* DOI: https://doi.org/10.1007/s10901-019-09699-3

Caldeira, T. (2017). Peripheral urbanization: autoconstruction, transversal logics, and politics in cities of the global South. *Environment and Planning D: Society and Space*, 35(1), pp. 3–20. DOI: https://doi.org/10.1177/0263775816658479

Cartwright, A., Oelofse, G., Parnell, S. & Ward, S. (2012). Climate at the city scale: the Cape Town climate think tank. In: Cartwright, A., Oelofse, G., Parnell, S. & Ward, S. (Eds.), *Climate change at the city scale: impacts, mitigation and adaptation in Cape Town.* Abingdon: Routledge.

Cirolia, L., Görgens, T., van Donk, M., Smit, W. & Drimie, S. (2016). *Upgrading informal settlements in South Africa: a partnership-based approach.* Claremont: UCT Press.

Clark, W.C., van Kerkhoff, L., Lebel, L. & Gallopin, G.C. (2016). Crafting usable knowledge for sustainable development. *Proceedings of the National Academy of Sciences*, 113(17), pp. 4570–4578. DOI: https://doi.org/10.1073/pnas.1601266113

Cobbinah, P.B., Erdiaw-Kwasie, M.O. & Amoateng, P. (2015). Africa's urbanization: implications for sustainable development. *Cities*, 47, pp. 62–72. DOI: https://doi.org/10.1016/j.cities.2015.03.013

Crossman, P. (2004). Perceptions of 'Africanisation' or 'endogenisation' at African universities: issues and recommendations. In: Zeleza, P.T. & Olukoshi, A. (Eds.), *African universities in the twenty-first century.* Dakar, Senegal: CODESRIA, pp. 319–340.

Culwick, C., Washbourne, C.L., Anderson, P.M.L., Cartwright, A., Patel, Z. & Smit, W. (2019). Citylab reflections and evolutions: nurturing knowledge and learning for urban sustainability through co-production experimentation. *Current Opinion in Environmental Sustainability*, 39(9), pp. 9–16. DOI: https://doi.org/10.1016/j.cosust.2019.05.008

Edensor, T. & Jayne, M. (Eds.). (2012). *Urban theory beyond the West: a world of cities.* New York and London: Routledge.

Evans, J. (2016). Trials and tribulations: problematizing the city through/as urban experimentation. *Geography Compass*, 10(10), pp. 429–443.

Evans, P. (1996). Government action, social capital and development: reviewing the action on synergy. *World Development*, 24(6), pp. 1119–1132.

Fox, S. (2014). The political economy of slums: theory and evidence from sub-Saharan Africa. *World Development*, 54, pp. 191–203. DOI: https://doi.org/10.1016/j.world dev.2013.08.005

Gibbons, M., Limoges, C., Nowotny, H., Schwartzman, S., Scott, P. & Trow, M. (1994). *The new production of knowledge: the dynamics of science and research in contemporary society*. London: Sage.

Jahn, T. (2008). Transdisciplinarity in the practice of research. In: Bergmann, M. & Schramm, E. (Hgs.), *Transdisziplinäre Forschung: integrative for – schungsprozesse verstehen und bewerten*. Frankfurt and New York: Campus Verlag, pp. 21–37 (English translation, not yet published).

Jasanoff, S. (2004). *States of knowledge: the co-production of science and social order*. London: Routledge.

Jensen, S., Adriansen, H.K. & Madsen, L.M. (2015). Do 'African' universities exist? Setting the scene. In: Adriansen, H.K., Madsen, L.M. & Jensen, S. (Eds.), *Higher education and capacity building in Africa: the geography and power of knowledge under changing conditions*. London: Routledge, pp. 12–35.

Kamete, A.Y. (2013). On handling urban informality in southern Africa. *Geografiska Annaler: Series B, Human Geography*, 95(1), pp. 17–31. DOI: https://doi.org/10.1111/geob.12007

Karvonen, A. & van Heur, B. (2014). Urban laboratories: experiments in reworking cities. *International Journal of Urban and Regional Research*, 38(2), pp. 379–392.

Lang, D.L., Wiek, A., Bergmann, M., Stauffacher, M., Martens, P., Moll, P., Swilling, M. & Thomas, C.J. (2012). Transdisciplinary research in sustainability science: practice, principles, and challenges. *Sustainability Science*, 7(Supplement 1), pp. 25–43. DOI: https://doi.org/10.1007/s11625-011-0149-x

Lawrence, R. (2015). Advances in transdisciplinarity: epistemologies, methodologies and processes. *Futures*, 65, pp. 1–9. DOI: https://doi.org/10.1016/j.futures.2014.11.007

Mahlubi, M., Levy, D. & Otieno, W. (2007). Special issue: private surge amid public dominance: dynamics in the private provision of higher education in Africa. *Journal of Higher Education in Africa*, 5(2–3).

Mamdani, M. (1993). University crisis and reform: a reflection on the African experience. *Review of African Political Economy*, 20(58), pp. 7–19.

Mauser, W., Klepper, G., Rice, M., Schmalzbauer, B.S., Hackmann, H., Leemans, R. & Moore, H. (2013). Transdisciplinary global change research: the co-creation of knowledge for sustainability. *Current Opinion in Environmental Sustainability*, 5, pp. 420–431. DOI: http://dx.doi.org/10.1016/j.cosust.2013.07.001

Mistra Urban Futures. (2016). *Co-production in action: towards realizing just cities*. Gothenburg. Retrieved: www.mistraurbanfutures.org/sites/mistraurbanfutures.org/files/co-production_in_action_towards_realising_just_cities.pdf

Mitlin, D. & Bartlett, S. (2018). Editorial: co-production – key ideas. *Environment & Urbanization*, 30(2), pp. 355–366. DOI: https://doi.org/10.1177/0956247818791931

Mouton, J. (2018). African science: a diagnosis. In: Beaudry, C., Mouton, J. & Prozesky, H. (Eds.), *The next generation of scientists in Africa*. Cape Town: African Minds, pp. 3–25.

Myers, G. (2011). *African cities: alternative visions of urban theory and practice*. London and New York: Zed Books.

Nagendra, H., Bai, X., Brondizio, E.S. & Lwasa, S. (2018). The urban South and the predicament of global sustainability. *Nature Sustainability*, 1, pp. 341–349. DOI: https://doi.org/10.1038/s41893-018-0101-5

Norström, A.V., Cvitanovic, C. & Löf, M.F. (2020). Principles for knowledge co-production in sustainability research. *Nature Sustainability*. DOI: https://doi.org/10.1038/s41893-019-0448-2

Nyanchoga, S.A. (2014). Politics of knowledge production in Africa: a critical reflection on the idea of an African university in sustainable development. *Developing Country Studies*, 4(18), pp. 57–66.

Ostrom, E. (1996). Crossing the great divide: coproduction, synergy and development. *World Development*, 24(6), pp. 1073–1087.

Osuteye, E., Ortiz, C., Lipietz, B, Castán Broto, V., Johnson, C. & Kombe, W. (2019 May 1). *Knowledge co-production for urban equality*. KNOW Working Paper Series. Retrieved: www.ucl.ac.uk/bartlett/development/sites/bartlett/files/know_workingpaper-no1_vf.pdf

Parnell, S. & Oldfield, S. (2014). *The Routledge handbook on cities of the global South*. London: Routledge.

Parnell, S. & Pieterse, E. (2014). *Africa's urban revolution*. Cape Town: UCT Press.

Parnell, S. & Pieterse, E. (2016). Translational global praxis: rethinking methods and modes of African urban research. *International Journal of Urban and Regional Research*, 40(1), pp. 236–246. DOI: https://doi.org/10.1111/1468-2427.12278

Parnell, S. & Robinson, J. (2012). (Re)theorizing cities from the global South: looking beyond neoliberalism. *Urban Geography*, 33(4), pp. 593–617. DOI: https://doi.org/10.2747/0272-3638.33.4.593

Parnell, S. & Robinson, J. (2017). The global urban: difference and complexity in urban studies and the science of cities. In: Hall, S. & Burdett, R. (Eds.), *The Sage handbook of the 21st century city*. London: Sage, pp. 13–31.

Patel, Z., Greyling, S., Simon, D., Arfvidsson, H., Moodley, N., Primo, N. & Wright, C. (2017). Local responses to global sustainability agendas: learning from experimenting with the urban sustainable development goal in Cape Town. *Sustainability Science*, 12, pp. 785–797. DOI: https://doi.org/10.1007/s11625-017-0500-y

Pieterse, E. (2011). Grasping the unknowable: coming to grips with African urbanisms. *Social Dynamics*, 37(1), pp. 5–23. DOI: 10.1080/02533952.2011.569994

Pieterse, E. (2018). The politics of governing African urban spaces. In: *African cities and the development conundrum, international development policy, vol. 10*. Leiden, The Netherlands: Brill, Nijhoff, pp. 26–52. DOI: https://doi.org/10.1163/9789004387942_003

Pieterse, E., Parnell, S. & Haysom, G. (2018). African dreams: locating urban infrastructure in the 2030 sustainable developmental agenda. *Area Development and Policy*, 3(2), pp. 149–169. DOI: https://doi.org/10.1080/23792949.2018.1428111

Pohl, C., Rist, S., Zimmermann, A., Fry, P., Gurung, G., Schneider, F., Speranza, C.I., Kiteme, B., Boillat, S., Serrano, E., Hadorn, G.H. & Wiesmann, U. (2010). Researchers' roles in knowledge co-production: experience from sustainability research in Kenya, Switzerland, Bolivia and Nepal. *Science and Public Policy*, 37(4), pp. 267–281. DOI: https://doi.org/10.3152/030234210X496628

Polk, M. (2015). *Co-producing knowledge for sustainable cities: joining forces for change*. Abingdon and New York: Routledge.

Robin, E. & Acuto, M. (2018). Global urban policy and the geopolitics of urban data. *Political Geography*, 66, pp. 76–87. DOI: https://doi.org/10.1016/j.polgeo.2018.08.013

Robin, E., Steenmans, K. & Acuto, M. (2017). Harnessing inclusive urban knowledge for the implementation of the new urban agenda. *Urban Research & Practice*, 12(2), pp. 137–155. DOI: https://doi.org/10.1080/17535069.2017.1414870

Robinson, J. (2006). *Ordinary cities: between modernity and development.* London: Routledge.

Roy, A. (2005). Urban informality: toward an epistemology of planning. *Journal of the American Planning Association,* 71(2), pp. 147–158. DOI: https://doi.org/10.1080/01944360508976689

Roy, A. (2009). The 21st century metropolis: new geographies of theory. *Regional Studies,* 43(6), pp. 819–830.

Roy, A. (2011). Slumdog cities: rethinking subaltern urbanism. *International Journal of Urban and Regional Research,* 35(2), pp. 223–238. DOI: https://doi.org/10.1111/j.1468-2427.2011.01051.x

Satgé, R.D. & Watson, V. (2018). *Urban planning in the global South: conflicting rationalities in contested urban space.* Cham: Springer International Publishing.

Science and the Future of Cities (Expert Panel). (2018). *Science and the future of cities: report on the global state of the urban science-policy interface.* London and Melbourne: International Expert Panel on Science and the Future of Cities. DOI: https://doi.org/10.13140/RG.2.2.27706.64969

SDG Center for Africa and Sustainable Development Solutions Network. (2019). *Africa SDG index and dashboards report 2019.* Kigali and New York: SDG Center for Africa and Sustainable Development Solutions Network.

Shizha, E. (2010). The interface of neoliberal globalization, science education and indigenous African knowledges in Africa. *Journal of Alternative Perspectives in the Social Sciences,* 2(1), pp. 27–57.

Silva, C.N. (Ed.). (2016). *Governing urban Africa.* London: Palgrave Macmillan.

Simon, D., Palmer, H., Riise, J., Smit, W. & Valencia, S. (2018). The challenges of transdisciplinary knowledge production: from unilocal to comparative research. *Environment and Urbanization,* 30(2), pp. 481–500. DOI: https://doi.org/10.1177/0956247818787177

Simone, A. (2004). People as infrastructure: intersecting fragments in Johannesburg. *Public Culture,* 16(3), pp. 407–429.

Simone, A. (2010). *City life from Jakarta to Dakar. Movements at the crossroads.* New York and London: Routledge.

Smit, W., Lawhon, M. & Patel, Z. (2015). Co-producing knowledge for whom, and to what end? Reflections from the African centre for cities in Cape Town. In: Polk, M. (Ed.), *Co-producing knowledge for sustainable cities: joining forces for change.* Oxon and New York: Routledge, pp. 47–69.

Swilling, M. (2014). Rethinking the science – policy interface in South Africa: experiments in knowledge co-production. *South African Journal of Science,* 110(5–6). DOI: http://dx.doi.org/10.1590/sajs.2014/20130265

UNDESA. (2018). *2018 revision of world urbanization prospects.* Retrieved: https://www.un.org/development/desa/publications/2018-revision-of-world-urbanization-prospects.html

UNECA. (2018). *Africa sustainable development report: towards a transformed and resilient continent.* Addis Ababa: African Union, Economic Commission for Africa, African Development Bank and United Nations Development Programme.

UN-Habitat. (2014). *The state of African cities: re-imagining sustainable urban transitions.* Nairobi: UN-Habitat.

UN-Habitat & UNECA. (2015). *Towards an African urban agenda.* Nairobi: UN-Habitat.

Van der Hel, S. (2016). New Science for global sustainability? The institutionalisation of knowledge co-production in future earth. *Environmental Science & Policy,* 61, pp. 165–175.

Watson, V. (2003). Conflicting rationalities: implications for planning theory and ethics. *Planning Theory & Practice*, 4(4), pp. 395–407. DOI: https://doi.org/10.1080/1464935032000146318

Watson, V. (2009). Seeing from the South: refocusing urban planning on the globe's central urban issues. *Urban Studies*, 46(11), pp. 2259–2275. DOI: https://doi.org/10.1177/0042098009342598

2 The formal-informal interface through the lens of urban food systems

The Soweto food market in Lusaka, Zambia

Gilbert Siame, Douty Chibamba, Progress H. Nyanga, Brenda Mwalukanga, Beverly Musonda Mushili, Wiza Kabaghe, Garikai Membele, Wilma S. Nchito, Peter Mulambia, and Dorothy Ndhlovu

Introduction

Although it is widely recognized that informal-sector activities heavily characterize urban systems in Africa, debates around African urbanization, urban development, and urban planning still fail to usefully conceptualize and characterize informality and its interface with formal actors, practices, and interactions in African cities. Based on a one-year research project implemented by the Centre for Urban Research and Planning (CURP) at the University of Zambia on the operations of the Soweto Retail and Wholesale Food Market (a large urban wholesale and retail market in Lusaka, the capital of Zambia), this chapter takes urban food systems as an entry point to understanding the workings and complexity of the formal-informal continuum in an African city (Jones, 2017). The study had two goals: firstly, to use co-production research methodologies to achieve a nuanced understanding of the formal-informal interface in an African city through the lens of food systems; and secondly, using this understanding, to ground and explore policy and other interventions that could make Lusaka's urban food markets more inclusive and sustainable spaces.

By critically evaluating market interactions and processes by and with food actors (in production, transport, storage, wholesaling, retailing, and waste management), we found that groups and individuals from the state, private sector, and society engage in creative and often manipulative interpretations of formal market regulations and laws to achieve maximum gain, resulting in both exclusion and inclusion. These multiple practices, relations, and systems are interwoven, interdependent, and exist between and within state and society – creating a new urban operational space that cannot be categorized as either formal or informal, and which exemplifies the wider workings of a society operating in the absence of a democratically functioning state.

Policy interventions and intellectual discourses in and on urban Africa need to engage with the complexity of urban governance dynamics and the ways in which they relate to and manifest themselves in formal and informal practices, power relations, and urban systems (Satterthwaite, 2016; Jones, 2017). We argue that urban studies and planning research need to set clear intellectual and policy goals for Africa and, by extension, the global South. Such studies need to delve into the policy space, critically analysing how the state and society interact, how these interactions are configured by power, and how they territorialize over geo-temporal scales. In other words, urban scholarship needs to transcend traditional urban studies and planning methodologies, and critically interrogate how urban contexts of the global South function in order to better understand why they remain so resistant to policies or interventions that are developed with different systems in mind.

The first section of this chapter provides the study's conceptual framing (which uses urban food systems as an entry point into debates on informality), and relevant context and background about urban markets and local governance in Zambia. Next we present our methodology and findings, which provide a granular understanding of the relationships and systems in Lusaka's Soweto Food Market, and point to the necessity of understanding the formal and informal as an interface or continuum. Finally, we present the study's conceptual implications, followed by conclusions and policy recommendations.

Conceptual framing

Urban food systems, governance, and informality in African cities

While global demand for food is rapidly growing, sustainably and equitably producing and distributing sufficient, nutritious food is becoming ever more challenging (Knorr et al., 2018). Meanwhile, with the impact of rising global food insecurity increasingly felt in cities, access to food – like that to clean water, sanitation, energy, and income-generating opportunities – has become a major urban issue (Crush & Riley, 2017), as well as one increasingly determined by income levels. On top of climate change and shifting patterns in small-scale farming, the rise of supermarkets, shopping centres, and wholesale retail chains further add to the complexity of a global food system that has led to poverty, unemployment, education, and city planning impacting hunger and malnutrition as much as agricultural yields and environmental conditions. Despite all of this, the urban dimensions of contemporary food systems are often overlooked, as are the ways in which these systems are governed, especially in the African context (Crush & Frayne, 2011; Battersby & Watson, 2018).

While there are many gaps in the existing knowledge about urban governance and urban food systems in Africa, one of the main deficits concerns the role of food actors in ensuring an inclusive and sustainable urban food system (Smit, 2016). Although much work has been done concerning potential improvements to the governance of urban food systems in African cities, there is surprisingly little research examining existing processes through which urban food systems are governed (Battersby, 2013). As Porter et al. (2007) suggest, complex processes and rules shaping food systems and food marketing in Africa exist, and there is a need to know more about how these formal and informal regulatory systems and norms operate, and how they influence urban food dynamics and the broader urban livelihood systems.

The governance of urban food systems in Africa is complex and includes a range of formal and informal actors and economies, between whom a growing body of work shows many points of intersection and interdependence (Battersby et al., 2016). That said, Skinner (2016) argues that the majority of food retail and wholesale sectors in most African cities are located at the 'informal' end of the formal-informal continuum, and indeed, a wide variety of informal food outlets are evident in most African cities – from traditional, large public market spaces, to a variety of shops and kiosks, to street food vendors.

Like their formal counterparts, informal food traders are impacted by urban governance in various ways, from processes allocating trading space, to infrastructure and service provision (e.g., water, security, energy, and waste removal). Additionally, the regulatory environment, which can include 'land-use planning and retail sites, shopping hours laws, labour-market regulations, and advertising codes, health claims legislation and consumer protection' has a significant impact on urban food systems (Dixon, 1999, p. 155). Such regulations, which can be formal or informal (or a combination of the two), can impact on where food is (or is not) produced or processed, where and when retail is allowed, what types of food can be sold, and who is involved in producing, distributing, and selling food.

While this chapter argues that formal and informal systems are inextricably interwoven, it is also true that the often-contested nature of who is able to access ownership to spaces and opportunities, and who is excluded, is highlighted in informal spaces (Roy, 2005). For example, concerning the informal nature of marketplace governance in Maputo, Mozambique, Lindell (2008, p. 1896) notes: 'governance appears to lack any semblance of coherence and to be more fragmented, disjointed and split by deep antagonisms'. In other words, key actors continuously challenge each other's legitimacy to govern, and this contest is invariably more pronounced in informal spaces. As such, the examination of bottom-up, market-based, urban-space governance systems and tools (such as levies and planning regulations, among others) can offer new perspectives on the use of surveillance, peer pressure, and control of physical space (Lyon, 2003) as modes of governance. But bottom-up approaches to food governance rarely exist in a vacuum, and often interlock with top-down state apparatuses, creating select, aggressive groups that conquer and control others in urban market spaces. However, the details and nuances of how the formal-informal continuum is governed – and how these groups interact – remain largely unexamined.

In spite of advances in the literature, 'the African city' often remains depicted in policy circles as a dualistic space made of formal and informal activities, systems, actors, and processes.[1] Such a dualistic understanding perpetuates views of the informal as illegal and impermanent, negates the complexity and interdependence of the actual relationship between the two, and reinforces the state's perception that the informal economy should be eradicated (SERI, 2015). The reality, however, is that urban space in Africa is formed and structured by an interwoven and interdependent continuum of both formal and informal practices, power relations, and infrastructural systems, which are in turn characterized by various concepts, urban management dynamics, and urban development outcomes (Lindell, 2008). Chief among these is Resnick's (2014) argument that the urbanization and governance processes and dynamics in sub-Saharan Africa have direct implications on livelihoods and service delivery, and that understanding the 'everyday' – and the survival tactics required to get through it – is key to critical African urban studies. As such, this study seeks to contribute to debates on what Pieterse (2011a) calls the 'vein of postcolonial theorization', opened up by de Boeck and Plissart (2014), Diouf (2003), Mbembé and Nuttall (2004), Simone and Simone (1994), and many others, who argue that theorizing the urban post-colony requires nuanced insertion of theoretical discourses in grounded reality.

Achieving a deeper appreciation of urban reality in contested food market spaces requires deployment of a pedagogical approach that can unravel the complex urban food systems found in African cities. This requires digging deep into the reality of relations; that is, how actors deploy various governance tactics to dominate and control what we call 'dense food markets'. As such, this study is mindful of the imperative to know what is happening on the ground before proceeding to interpret how citizens understand, experience, navigate, transcend, resist, admit, or reinterpret the psychosocial experiences that are affected by 'tough material conditions' (Biehl & McKay, 2012; Pieterse, 2010).[2]

But to understand relationships on the ground, a broader view of governance in the African urban context must also be considered. Swyngedouw (2005) draws on neo-Foucauldian theories of governmentality and technologies of government to discuss a 'democratic deficit', or a lack of governance that raises questions about who is allowed and enabled to participate, and who is excluded. Such a deficit underscores ill-defined systems of representation, accountability, and legitimacy, and the state's role in organizing and 'legitimating' urban governance networks systems. Urban spaces characterized by such deficits tend to be governed by creative and manipulative relations between state and society, and aspects of clientelism, fear of the politically powerful, patronage, utter theft, and corruption become the structuring elements of such urban governance. Thus while policymakers extol the virtues of democratic citizenship and participation, in reality 'existing forms of participation in many parts of the global South do not conform to these idealized governance models' (Robins et al., 2008, p. 1070). That the nature of democratic practices in countries with political and historical contexts marked by disenfranchisement, poverty, and clientelism differ from those found in countries of the global North (Robins et al., 2008) must be acknowledged. Robins et al. (2008, p. 1071) further argue that the relations between the state and people in such 'political and historical contexts' are punctuated by disenfranchisement, authoritarianism, and clientelism, and do not align with normative versions of citizenship and the virtues of a functional democracy.

Using the lens of food systems, this study thus investigates the 'everyday' in the 'ways of doing business and existing' in Zambia's largest urban food market. By uncovering and critically interrogating inter-actor relations (between food traders, market managers, political party cadres, and national state operations), this chapter attempts to capture the granular reality of Soweto Market's governance, and through this, arrive at a better understanding of the formal-informal continuum.

Context and background

Urban markets – history and governance

Though Zambia does not have a long history of urban market activity (Nchito, 2007), markets exist in every urban settlement today, where they serve a dual purpose of providing employment for people not in the formal labour structure, as well as goods and services to the majority of urban households. The Markets and Bus Stations Act of 2007 sets out two ways of establishing and managing a public market in Zambia. The first is the formal, top-down process, where a city council establishes a market with on-the-ground administration through the market master (a city council employee), and a Market Advisory Committee (MAC) overseeing functionality and management (see the section on Local Governance for more detail).

The second type – known as cooperative markets – is a response to a governance void in areas of the city that are yet to be formally sanctioned through the city council. Cooperative markets, constituting about half of Lusaka's marketplaces (Blekking et al., 2017), are governed through independent market committees comprised of people elected from the market's vendors. Official channels point to the market committee, but everyday access to markets relies on negotiating with a number of actors, includes political cadres, the city council, the traders themselves, the food suppliers, and the commodity association(s), all of which have a core interest in the running of the market.

While access to trading spaces in both formal and informal marketplaces is guided by rules and regulations, the reality is that these rules are relaxed, suspended, or simply contravened when 'political party cadres' take charge of market management. Indeed, most markets in Zambia serve as strongholds of the ruling political party. Political party cadres in Zambia refer to party loyalists who use their political affiliation or association with the ruling party principles to influence and control access to the markets.[3] The allocation of market trading spaces by party cadres has a long history, dating from the UNIP era (1964–1992) through to the MMD (1992–2011) and PF (2011-todate) eras.[4] Traders, who can always be threatened with eviction, continue to be easily manipulated and organized for political gain, making marketplaces indispensable to politicians (Nchito, 2007).

Lusaka's Soweto Food Market

Lusaka is Zambia's capital and largest city, with a population of over 2.5 million people. Located near Lusaka's Central Business District (CBD), Soweto Food Market (henceforth referred to in this chapter as Soweto Market) is Zambia's largest formal, council-managed, open-air urban market that serves as both a wholesale and retail space for various food products farmed and manufactured from within and outside Lusaka (Hampwaye et al., 2016, p. 46; Wragg & Lim, 2015). According to Blekking et al. (2017, p. 7), 'Soweto Market is the central node of Lusaka's food system . . . supplying both cooperative and city council markets with fresh produce daily'. Acting as the largest landing site for food from farms and traders in the Lusaka City region and beyond, the Market is also an important contributor to food security in Lusaka (Hampwaye et al., 2016). Soweto Market's core role in influencing urban food systems, and the obvious financial flows in Lusaka's food value chain, mean the stakes here are high, causing a broad range of actors to be interested in the Market's activities and functioning.

Local governance

The Constitution of Zambia, as amended by Act No. 2 of 2016, has devolved powers to the local authorities (called city councils) in a quest to decentralize government operations, with all government departments and institutions intended to eventually be managed at the local authority level. Lusaka City Council (LCC) is the largest local authority in Zambia, and its primary responsibility, like that of all city councils, is public service delivery (e.g., garbage collection, construction of drainage systems, management of public markets, etc.). A representative form of local government, the LCC is formed of elected local leaders who serve as community representatives (councillors). The LCC encompasses 33 wards, which are smaller geographical demarcations in the seven larger constituencies that constitute the broader boundary jurisdiction of greater Lusaka City (LCC, 2019).

The Markets and Bus Stations Act of 2007, which, as noted earlier, governs market function in Zambia, names the city council as the body responsible for market management. In Lusaka, the LCC 'formally' interacts with market traders through the MAC, which is the committee responsible for administering and managing a market's affairs on behalf of the city council. MACs are comprised of seven members: the chair (the local councillor), secretary (the market master), tax collector (a council employee), council police officer, and three elected vendors from the local market. Some of the listed responsibilities of MAC include enforcement of council bylaws, provision of security in a market, revenue collection, monitoring standards of hygiene, and general cleanliness and allocation of market stalls.

Officially, access to formal market trading spaces like those in Soweto Market is based on merit-application to the MAC as an agent for the LCC, where applicants must meet minimum requirements, including the capacity to pay council-approved levies. While Soweto Market has a MAC in place, actual management of the market – including the allocation of trading spaces – is dynamic and contested among various forces and actors. As is further discussed next, de facto governance systems differ sharply from those prescribed by law, and rules are more often than not relaxed, suspended, or simply contravened, particularly in the face of political party cadre interference, as is discussed in our findings.

It is important to note here the overarching role that political cadres have played in city council governance in Zambia since the early 1970s with the passage of the Village Registration and Development Act No. 30 of 1971. Seeking to actualize one-party state governance, this Act integrated city councils, ward development committees (WDC), and ruling party functionaries in the governance of local councils (Mukwena & Lolojih, 2002). Over the 1970s, the supremacy of the ruling party over local governance was further consolidated (Chikulo, 1993), until multiparty democracy in 1990 led to the scrapping of the one-party state (Chikulo, 1993). The promulgation of the Constitution of Zambia Act No.1 and Local Government Act No.22 (1991) delinked the ruling party from the civil service and state apparatus, reintroducing the distinction between the ruling party, the central government, and local government. However, implementation of subsequent Acts and decentralization policies have fallen short of depoliticizing local government, and national laws and Lusaka city bylaws have not been used effectively to ensure markets are not overtaken and managed by political party supporters. As a result, political party cadres continue to exert a strong influence in Lusaka city's governance and operations.

Methodology

Studying the market

The method applied in the study of Soweto Market was informed by the African Centre for Cities CityLab Programme[5] supporting co-production of policy-relevant knowledge for African cities. One of ten CityLab studies funded at urban research centre members of the African Urban Research Initiative (AURI), this research, framed as a case study, follows the principles of case study methods in urban studies and planning literature (Flyvbjerg, 2011, 2004; Duminy et al., 2014). Using qualitative methods, our research sought to study the 'everyday practices' (Horelli et al., 2013) in food transactions in Soweto Market, a response to Robins et al.'s (2008, p. 1069) call for 'more attention to contextual understandings of the politics of everyday urban life, and to locating state, civil society, and donor rhetorics and programmes promoting "active citizenship" and "participatory governance"' in the urban South.

In doing so, our research also responds to Parnell and Robinson's (2012) post-neoliberal call for a need to re-engage with the state as a 'complex set of institutions, open to diverse political and policy agendas' (Parnell & Robinson, 2012). That is, Parnell and Robinson (2012) argue that traditional critiques of urban neoliberalism that may have salience in the global North are inappropriately applied to interpret contexts that do not reflect this context, for example, in cities in the global South. To move beyond this approach requires more than understanding that neoliberalism is produced in different ways in different contexts, and indeed demands a geographical repositioning of urban theory (ibid.). As such, we argue that research such as this, which highlights the complexity of dynamics and economies as they actually operate in cities of the global South, are contributing to the need for more relevant ideas and concepts to emerge.

Focusing on the 'everyday' in Soweto Market, we collected and analysed data on transactions, engagements, and relations in food merchandizing, including a wide range of sociopolitical actors and infrastructural technologies of food flows both in Soweto Market and the wider City of Lusaka. We zoomed in on the detail of the food business in a growing city, examining specific instances of how actors engage with food merchandizing in Soweto. Responding to Flyvbjerg's (2004, p. 283) call for a return to 'concrete things' of the urban (Pieterse, 2011b), we sat down with food retailers, food middlemen, farmers, political leaders, and state agents, examining how all these actors engage with both formal and informal food systems in Soweto. Given the complexity of Soweto's food systems, a nuanced study of these systems required active involvement from all relevant actors. As such, the study was transdisciplinary and collaborative in nature, with our research team including scholars from different disciplines, as well as non-academic stakeholders, who together could address the challenge of food system governance with a view to developing solutions (Lang et al., 2012).

Research consisted primarily of personal interviews, focus group discussions, round-table discussions, and observations by all project researchers to generate primary data. We selected research participants using a purposive sampling approach, which sought to achieve data collection based on level of actor engagement in the activities and processes in Soweto Market. Research participants included: officials and senior managers at LCC, researchers at CURP, members of the People's Process on Housing and Poverty in Zambia (PPHPZ), a local branch of the Slum Dwellers International (SDI) in Zambia, and relevant groups from Soweto Market (e.g., political party representatives, produce associations and alliances, individual traders, consumers, and market managers).

As per the co-production methodology, our team worked together with policy officials from LCC and food actors from the Soweto Market to frame the research questions for the study, collect and analyse the data, and produce research findings. Stakeholders grouped the data in themes and presented the data in the form of narratives; this happened in round-table meetings, multi-stakeholder meetings, learning labs, and a policy dialogue on Soweto Food Market.

The two CityLabs that we held enabled us to collaboratively analyse the data and share the research findings in the form of policy briefs. A city learning lab is a multi-stakeholder social meeting that seeks to collaboratively explore city development problems and frame possible actions by stakeholders. Allowing for deep conceptual analysis and exploration of material for policy innovation to improve systems relevant to a complex and contested issue such as equal access to Soweto Market (Steynor et al., 2016). Intended to create an open space for thinking, debating, and engaging with the research process and outcomes, the labs proved a key innovation in our knowledge of co-production process, and we endeavoured to make them neutral or 'safe spaces' for all stakeholders. In some cases, creating a safe space can be done by choosing a venue that is both convenient and unfamiliar, in the sense that it is outside of people's day-to-day 'functional' environments (Culwick et al., 2019, p. 13). In our case, we chose to separate political party leaders from the administrative staff of the LCC during the two CityLabs held on Soweto Market, in order for them to engage more freely.

Findings

This section identifies the actors present in the Soweto Market and shows how relationships are organized and structured; that is, the various ways multiple actors in the market use and interpret rules and regulations, and command control to change the outlook of market operations from a supposedly top-down market to a seemingly cooperative market.

The actors and regulations

As discussed in earlier sections, Soweto Market is officially a formal market. However, daily activities at Soweto show that its operations tilt towards those of an informal or cooperative market managed under non-state approved rules. For example, the ability to secure trading rights is not a clear process, but rather considered a privilege that is dependent on the nature of one's relations with either LCC, one or more of the many commodity associations, or political party representatives. These agents or actors, all of whom compete for visibility and 'job' security, control all activities in Soweto Market. Thus, to win a food trading space in Soweto, one must show allegiance and loyalty to one or all of these actors. Findings around these actors and how they engage both formally and informally follow next.

Lusaka City Council

The most 'formal' mechanism around access to trade in Soweto Market is the LCC, which has established a daily 2 Zambian Kwacha (ZMW) citywide levy for all traders using public markets in Lusaka. While the LCC argues that this levy is used for service provision (e.g., security, waste removal), this was hard to prove on the ground. And although the LCC claims the fee is uniform and citywide, the reality we observed is that the amount varies according to the size, location, and quality of trading space (i.e., accessibility and convenience for doing business).

The LCC is also responsible for health and sanitation regulations at the Market, and fees are intended to improve the delivery of these services.

Although health inspectors carry out routine inspections, the maintenance of stipulated health and hygiene standards is never certain, and Market services are mostly provided by traders and political party representatives. Limitations around services such as poor public health, poor water and sanitation conditions, and waste management, among others, came to the fore in 2017, when a cholera crisis forced the Market to shut down nearly completely from November–December.

Produce associations

Produce associations are formally registered with the Registrar of Societies, the LCC, the Zambia Revenue Authority, and the Patents and Companies Registration Agency (PACRA), implying that they pay some statutory taxes, and can be said to be formal entities. In addition to paying the LCC's required levy (providing access to trading spaces), food traders are pressured to register with produce associations (e.g., Banana, Beans, Tomatoes), which membership enables them to deal in the associated commodity.

Each association has its own procedures for joining, as well as rules and regulations governing association operations and, to some extent, transactions in the trade of products. Transaction regulations include things like only allowing registered commodity traders to deal in the associated commodities, and enforcing separate produce trading spaces (e.g., bananas from potatoes). It is worth noting that all produce designated spaces in the Market are owned by various associations, and as such, traders must register with an association to acquire produce trading rights. Only bona fide members of an association can trade on the premises belonging to associations.

Association membership does come with benefits, including social protection, access to capital, the aforementioned right to trade, as well as discounted rates for trading spaces depending on market forces of demand and supply. Associations sometimes provide small loans to members at a widely used 20% interest rate, or act as guarantor when members need to borrow from micro-financial lending institutions found in the Market, thus increasing opportunities for business growth. Most produce associations also have storage facilities where member traders can keep their goods at the close of business for a reduced fee. Most associations require a universal association joining fee of ZMW55, and monthly or annual contributions to the funeral committee, which pays out ZMW2,000 to cover funeral expenses.

Political parties

As discussed in the previous sections on context and local governance, the Market is dominated by 'party cadres', through whom national politics operate, and who – according to traders, LCC market staff, and LCC head office actors alike – are the Market's most feared actor.

The study established that the easiest guaranteed way to obtain a good trading space in the Market is to pay party cadres, with amounts varying from ZMW2 to ZMW20 per month (in addition to the daily LCC levy of ZMW2). The fees to party cadres include what both traders and party cadres refer to as an 'operations fee' (ZMW5), required by all traders every Wednesday, as well as the daily ZMW2 LCC trading levy. No one could say what the operation fee is for. While these levies cannot be 'questioned' by the traders, party cadres promise traders physical security and potential loans from government. Party cadres justify the levies on the basis that they provide material support in the form of improved security, access to capital, and guaranteed trading rights. While access to trading rights is verifiable, it is hard to prove that complying with party cadre demands creates opportunities for physical security, and/or increased access to financial capital.

Because both the LCC and party cadres allocate trading spaces, traders often pay twice for the same trading space (personal interview, Soweto trader, November 2018). Such levies for trading spaces, registration, and commodity licences mean that traders often pay at least twice and sometimes three times (overlap of LCC, association, and party-cadre levies) for the same thing. Traders also must pay offloading fees of ZMW30–40 per load to party cadres, which maintain ultimate control of space in Soweto Market. Loading fees also differ from one trading space to another, with trucks coming from out of town taken advantage of and required to pay offloading fees of no less than ZMW100, while those from within Lusaka pay a maximum of ZMW40.

When it comes to security, while official rules governing actors' behaviour in the market do exist, an informal arrangement between the LCC and party cadres allows cadres to play a larger security role at Soweto Market than the officially and legally mandated actors:

> The police and party cadres jointly maintain law and order in the market. When an offender is caught, he or she is first taken to the cadres who assess the gravity of the offence before deciding whether they deal with the case conclusively or refer it to the police. Offenders with smaller offences are fined and released, while those with serious offences are handed over to the police where the due process of the law is purportedly followed.
>
> (Personal interview, November 2017)

This quote illustrates how informal and formal actors and systems meld to the extent that it is impossible to separate one from the other, and how power is maintained through a constantly negotiated process and sharing of benefits among them. Law and order in the Market is a product of both formal and informal systems, symbiotically intertwined on mutually agreed aspects of the Market. For example, the police use cadres as fronts to enforce the law, while the cadres gain monetary benefit by engaging in this collaboration.

Meanwhile, our findings also reveal that multiple actors in Soweto Market express political identity – in order to gain influence and power in the

Market – through various means, including displaying party regalia, expressing verbal allegiance to senior political party leaders and individuals, and promoting and enforcing clientelism between food traders and the party in power by means of rule relaxation. It should also be noted that within the cadres there are many individuals who merely claim to be members of the ruling party, but in fact are just thieves. Pickpocketing and beating of Market patrons (especially traders and consumers) by the cadres is rife, and often carried out by people who purport to act in the name of a ruling political party. In sum, it is very hard to delineate genuine from non-genuine party cadre members in Soweto. As such, the study's findings show that the relations and interdependences between formal and informal systems and actors create a non-sovereign, urban market space that belongs to no single actor exclusively.

Social solidarity economy

It is notable that the study found an absence of a strong farmer or food producer association in Soweto Market. This lack works against the interest of market farmers and food suppliers, inhibiting their ability to harness the potentials of a social solidarity economy (SSE). The International Labour Organization (ILO) explains SSE as enterprises and organizations (cooperatives, mutual benefit societies, associations, foundations, and social enterprises) that produce goods, services, and knowledge that meet the needs of the community served, through the pursuit of specific social and environmental objectives and the fostering of solidarity (ILO, n.d.). Given that all actors have power and a sphere of influence, if the governed masses in Soweto Market could find a way to overtly assert their influence on those in power, they could redirect actor relations to safeguard the public good, which would serve to protect the food traders and consumers, and ensure that the Market's politics work for the good of all.

In fact, some of the Market's produce associations have begun to create SSE for their members, setting objectives to improve their own operations and make the market more enabling to their members. Providing members with things like social protection through funeral grants, access to capital at lower interest rates, and protection of their businesses (through restrictions on nonmembers to engage in certain activities), these produce associations have also made efforts to increase production through collective entrepreneurship. Such collaborative efforts endeavour to create and sustain the social solidarity economy (Jolly & Raven, 2015) in Soweto Market.

However, the current overwhelming relationship between Soweto Market food producers can best be described as disjointed and uncoordinated, undermining the potential of SSE, and creating sociopolitical spaces for manipulative acts by 'local political elites' to continue. In other words, there is no farmer or food producer association that seeks to protect and champion the interests of food producers in this dynamic and contested food market space.

Balance of power

Examining the various actors managing Soweto Market,[6] the study revealed constant contestations over ownership and control of space, as well as implementation of norms and practices.

Pros and cons of 'belonging'

Despite clear benefits of association membership, some traders do not belong to any association, having withdrawn membership because they feel the associations do not meet their expectations of providing loans or boosting their business. These traders typically register only with the LCC for permission to trade. LCC-only registration allows one to trade with limited rights in a shop or established stand, and not on open spaces, which are largely controlled by party cadres. Thus, while incurring lower costs, such traders remain confined to the shops, and argue that they have less visibility (and limited market rights). While LCC-only traders may escape commodity association affiliation fees, they still must pay the party cadres' other fees, as described earlier.

Some traders have neither association membership nor LCC permission to trade, and rather acquire trading spaces or rent trading stands solely from political party cadres and/or those who have opted to sublet their trading spaces and property rights. However, subletting a trading space with neither association membership nor cadre support can be risky: for long-term tenure security of trading space, and for a sense of physical security (i.e., protection from possible attack for resisting political force), traders find it both convenient and necessary to 'cooperate' with the cadres. While party cadres have a long history of allocating market spaces, research participants noted that the situation is increasingly out of control, and currently verges on localized gangsterism. This situation is leaving food dealers with very little space to negotiate and protect their rights to freely trade in the market.

Some traders do not register with the LCC, political parties, or a produce association. Nonetheless, they still are forced to comply with and pay levies to the political cadres. Lack of compliance with cadres can lead to loss of trading space and physical attacks. By contrast, other traders and food dealers pay multiple levies to multiple centres of control and regulation (e.g., the LCC, produce associations, and cadres) in order to access services such as trading space and physical protection from various market players. Nearly all traders lamented the rising cost of doing business in the Market, attributing the high costs to multiple and unexplained levies that have not translated into an improved business environment or protection of rights.

Overlapping interests and responsibilities

While the produce associations and the LCC together have reasonable control over the movement of food products, they have limited control over other aspects – both formal and informal – of the Market, which most traders and LCC staff say is dominated by the party cadres. For example, despite the regulation requiring the market to open at 06:00 and close at 18:00, some traders indicated they can enter the market any time. Traders also say they trade in a very dirty environment, largely due to indiscriminate dumping of solid waste by themselves, and the local authority's failure to implement water and sanitation programmes to keep the market clean.

Thus, our study observed contradictions and overlapping interests and responsibilities between market actors. This observation challenges the normative notion of democracy, largely espoused in the global North, where public spaces in general, and urban markets in particular, are/should be publicly owned and managed, and market interest groups are well-organized and seen as working to promote the public good and guarding against manipulation and unproductive practices (Robins et al., 2008).

By contrast, in Soweto Market we found multiple mechanisms controlled by various actors to facilitate food businesses, regulate and control traders, protect consumers, provide opportunities for raising financial capital, and grant access to trading spaces including shops. These actors, both formal and informal, in some cases were promoting public good, and in others, very much protecting personal/ group interest. For example, most traders access capital largely via informal lending by produce associations, supplemented by financing from formal micro-enterprises. This again demonstrates the loose integration of both the formal and informal systems. Other mechanisms of control and regulation that include collaboration between (formal) state and (informal) non-state institutions are the police and cadres, which collectively ensure law and order, a state that also draws on LCC and cadre collaboration to jointly allocate and manage trading spaces. Finally, the study also established the existence of 'fronts' in the administration and management of shops and other trading spaces in the Market, where people used political agents to acquire spaces that supposedly were only available for those with LCC and/or association membership.

Clientelism

The nature of the relationship between the state and other actors in Soweto Market has created fertile grounds for clientelism. Having established that in Soweto Market, anything goes and no one escapes the overwhelming and dominating presence of political cadres, the study also demonstrated that party cadres have near total control of the Soweto Market, to the extent that they even can overrule the LCC. In many instances, decisions made by the Council are overturned by the cadres, which have gone so far as to assume most Council responsibilities in the Market. Thus, actions and decisions such as allocating trading space, collecting levies, providing security, and enforcing the regulations and norms for food dealers are largely the purview of party cadres, with the local authority reduced to a subordinate position.

While many state agents with an interest in the Market lament this frustrating situation, they have limited decision-making power, or power to change the course and occurrence of the Market's function. The party cadres wield sizable power due to their linkages to the ruling party. Challenging the cadres may leave traders or state agents vulnerable to intimidation and violence. Personal interviews further revealed that LCC hesitates to enforce the established market regulations and rules uniformly in Soweto because of fears of interference and possible punishment.

While this dynamic may be hard to understand if viewed from a northern perspective, in Soweto Market, as in other spaces in African cities, urban governance 'encompasses multiple sites where practices of governance are exercised and contested' and 'a variety of players, various layers of relations, and a broad range of practices of governance that may involve various modes of power, as well as different geographical scale of occurrence' are found (Lindell, 2008, p. 1880). Robins et al. (2008, p. 1079) posit that: 'urban populations in the South tend to adopt plural strategies; they occupy multiple spaces and draw on multiple political identities, materialistic identities, and social relationships, often simultaneously'. This has certainly been the case in Soweto, where the study observed food traders taking on materialistic identities, or various assumed identities that ensure access to the Market and protect their interests in the food sector.

Goodfellow (2010) argues that clientelism and patronage are very much part of political cultures, as citizens straddle 'civil society' and 'state' spaces in Soweto Market, which reality is vividly displayed in the ways that party cadres carry out their activities. The success of strategies for survival and well-being in the Market depend on one's ability to establish multiple strategic relationships and become visible to several powerful players. The relationship between 'the citizen' and 'the state' in many urban African settings seldom resembles the kinds of deliberative, democratic models of citizen participation promoted by normative discourses on state-society relations in the mainstream urban governance literature. We see this in Soweto Market, where unproductive practices in the formal systems are countered by clientelistic relations that simultaneously consolidate the resilience of the Market's informal systems.

We observed that the ability to effectively trade in Soweto depends largely on networks and clientelistic relations, and that the workings of the state and society are clearly not monolithic, but rather divided and fractured. Finally, all of these relationships are weakened by infighting, poor organization, manipulation, and corruption across the spectrum of Market actors. Relations in the market are constantly modifying and never take on one permanent feature. What happens in the market is under the bedrock of messy and wickedly complex relations between the top-down state and bottom-up urban populations seeking to survive the harsh conditions of urban poverty. Both the state and society use multiple tactics involving loyalty, identity, solidarity, and clientelism to exert influence on each other and extract benefits form the marketplace.

Analysis: conceptual implications

A lucrative space for both formal and informal food dealers in the Lusaka City region, Soweto Market markedly manifests the politics of livelihood systems. Here we see various actors deploying a range of tactics and tools to participate, and ensure their continued operation and access to Soweto, as traders or otherwise. This fight for access is seen most clearly in the way political party cadres force other actors (traders, wholesalers, and farmers) to pay multiple 'unexplained levies' in order to participate in the Market. Using the traders' fear of eviction, party cadres extract taxes and enforce other localized regulations. Meanwhile, the state systems and organizations (LCC and associations) intended to promote accountability and participation in the Market are weak, failing to regulate food trading or, perhaps more significantly, to resist the very strong informal sector power of the party cadres. The combination of these characteristics of market management systems in Soweto Market have resulted in persistent low-level conflicts and persistent clashes of interests.

The following section analyses the social and economic implications of the formal-informal relations and interactions in Soweto on food traders. Identifying and analysing the conceptual significance of relations in Soweto Market on urban studies and urban interventions in the African context, our findings also speak to a gap in that body of literature and research. As such, it is our hope that these findings will contribute to conceptual innovations and generate new learnings on urban food markets and governance in African cities.

Significance of findings to questions of formal-informal interface

The study shows how intertwined the formal and informal systems are in Soweto Market, and that the market's formal and informal systems are contradictory, complementary, and interdependent. The allocation of space and enforcement of physical security and health and hygiene standards are undertaken by both city officials and political party cadres. The produce associations are also major players in enforcing both formal and informal norms, regulations, and laws governing operations in Soweto Market. Next to those realities is the fact that political cadres ultimately have final say about what happens in the Market. As such, delineating formal from informal systems and practices in the Market is a fool's errand. The market space is a continuum that is neither formal nor informal, but rather a zone of constant change and evolution, the character of which is shaped by both formal and informal rules concerning market operations. Ideas around belonging and becoming in Soweto Market are subject to various multiple factors that are both contradictory and complementary.

Arbitrary 'urban things' and a clash of governmentalities in Soweto Food Market

The study established that use of force for manipulative purposes is rampant in Soweto Market, and has given birth to a rampant case of what Pieterse (2011a) calls arbitrary 'urban things' – or how the arbitrary exercise of power gives rise to manipulative urban politics in African city contexts. As discussed earlier, the political cadres constantly and arbitrarily exert force over other actors, imposing serious sanctions (from intimidation to forfeiture of trading spaces) if those actors refuse or report such 'illegal' behaviour to the LCC, which in any case is largely impotent to act against the cadres. Further, the difficulty of delineating genuine from non-genuine party cadres in Soweto has created a behavioural free-for-all where anyone can claim to be part of the ruling political party, thus throwing the idea of spatial and social order, rule of law, and protection of urban rights in deep jeopardy, while also rendering traders 'space-less', as they are deprived of any form of proper recourse.

This study has shown that the ability to engage in food trading in Soweto Market is a direct outcome of one's ability to successfully connect with agents who control the Market. Market efficiency has been undermined by fractured relationships within civil society (associations and groupings), as well as the relationships between the state and civil society, which are characterized by corruption and manipulative acts (Lindell, 2008; Robins et al., 2008). Unsurprisingly, trust among Market-space players has eroded, causing rampant manipulative acts from both state and non-state actors to flourish. The reality of this state of affairs has served to increase costs for food traders, reduce the Market into a site for manipulation and criminality, and exclude weaker members of society (e.g., members of opposition political parties, women, and disabled food dealers), despite state practices that claim to offer physical and social security at Soweto Market. That said, the state is also constantly evolving. This speaks to how the governance of Soweto Market 'encompasses multiple sites', meaning the state authority engages with a variety of players, various layers of relations, and a 'broad range of practices of governance that involve various modes of state power at different scales' (Lindell, 2008, p. 1880). In other words, while the state in many instances is not sovereign over Soweto Market's networks and trading spaces, operations, activities, and outcomes, it retains the potential to steer all of these (Rhodes, 1997).

The existence of governance from above – that is, the state presence as embodied by the LCC as well as the political party cadres – provides a sense of legitimacy and power to market relations, and allows certain actors to claim due and undue privilege (e.g., levies paid to party cadres, allocation of trading rights in the Market, etc.). In Soweto, one cannot trade if not recognized by the 'right' people; specifically, ruling party cadres, the LCC, and/or other structures recognized by the ruling party. This system where political recognition (through the local state and ruling party agents) is tied to the allocation of responsibilities and privileges allows the state to control traders in Soweto Market, as the latter require registration and recognition to do business. Thus, the state and party cadres give or take traders' rights and freedoms in Soweto Market, and, most importantly, bend the rules to their advantage.

At the same time, conflict and deviance from the norm also exist in Soweto Market. Manifesting 'governmentality from below' (Roy, 2009), non-state actors such as produce associations and political party cadres have formed rules and

norms of operating in Soweto Market and sub-locations within the food section. Thus, while party cadres on one hand assume the role of state actors, on the
other hand they camouflage themselves, taking on multiple roles in order to make
claims from various positionalities of privilege in Soweto Market. Meanwhile,
although our research concluded that there is space and a need for the development of SSE in the Market, currently there is no group that has shown an inclina-
tion to take this on.

In sum, players in Soweto Market management exhibit various traits (Roy,
2009): collude with the state and act against weaker Market groups; become
exclusionary in their practices; collaborate with the state to deliver services such
as security, sanitation, etc.; and behave unilaterally and arbitrarily to protect their
interests. This array of practices serves to either increase or undermine the legitimacy of a wide spectrum of the Market's actors, with questions of legitimacy
creating grounds for conflicts. Such fluidity in turn creates fertile ground for state
rules (through LCC) to clash with community rules (as established and implemented by party cadres and interest groups), as evidenced by food traders opting
to register with and obtain trading rights from party cadres only, thus snubbing
LCC and produce associations.

As decentralization efforts in Zambia coincide with Lusaka's rapid growth,
Lusaka's urban food security issues appear to suffer from a lack of horizontal
cooperation across sectors, as well as vertical coordination across tiers of government (Resnick, 2017). We argue for a conceptualization of the state, society,
and relations between them that views the whole as a contested sociopolitical
mosaic. Further, this view acknowledges that governmentalities from both above
and below are constantly clashing, thus shifting the power and political dynamics
that structure that mosaic.

Conclusion

Critically analysing the dynamics shaping relations in the Soweto Food Market,
this chapter has shown how the formal-informal duality is in fact nonexistent. We
argue that Soweto Market is a contested political commodity, and that relations
between food traders and centres of control are largely based on political rational-
ity. Further, we observed that food systems in the Market are under a political grip
that uses food trading to manipulate the publics in Soweto. These findings point
to the reality that while designated as a 'formal' space, the urban marketplace is
largely an informal site, where the state is weak, and much governance happens
beyond it. Governance, then, must be understood as 'a broad range of practices
that may involve "various modes of power and contestations"' (Lindell, 2008,
p. 1880), where the complex relations between formal and informal actors are a
form of 'provisional governance' (Simone, 2004; Pieterse, 2010; Schindler, 2017;
Foucault, 1980; Foucault & Hurley, 1990; Allen, 2004), and where the idealized
figure of the 'stakeholder' – who is theoretically free, and encouraged to participate in governance, and by extension, governance of public space – does not have
much sway (Swyngedouw, 2005).

That is, in urban public spaces like Soweto Market, state promises of empowerment are paralleled by often undemocratic and authoritarian state processes and actions that lead to a substantial democratic deficit (Swyngedouw, 2005), uneven access to resources and livelihood opportunities (Pieterse, 2010), and skewed influence on governance institutions that collectively can result in outright exclusions, but also to partial and problematic inclusions that must be examined critically. The Soweto Market's hybridized governance framework, with its contradictory tendencies and manipulative acts (Swyngedouw, 2005), complicate citizens' relationships to and influence on the formal and informal systems and structures operating therein, thus keeping those relationships insufficiently codified to support the emergence of a strong social solidarity economy and/or good governance. Indeed, the lack of effective counterhegemonies, as could be manifested by food trader groupings, exacerbates the existing political hegemony. While SSE theoretically could serve as a counterhegemony to normative urban market management and operationalization, the reality remains that SSE would only work in circumstances where civil society and social mobilization are well thought out and organized. Currently, social mobilization for public good remains a challenge in many African cities and urban markets, including Soweto.

In sum, the Soweto Market case supports our conclusion that urban governance in African cities is undergoing informalizations; that is, it is highly fragmented and fluid, and contests the assumptions that underlie northern debates on urban governance and, by extension, the nature of the urban in Africa. Based on our findings, we argue that the interwoven formal-informal relations in Soweto Market are structured by 'multiple sites' of power and control, and that this conceptual finding is extremely relevant to the debates over the politics of urban livelihoods in African settings, and the political economy of urban informality and urban markets (Van Gent et al., 2014; MacLeod, 2011). Conceptual and policy innovations designed to transform African urban spaces must be driven by this concept of power and control located in 'multiple sites' power, which demands more nuanced understandings of the richly layered nature of urban settings like that found in Soweto Market.

The work presented in this chapter was only possible thanks to the use of co-production methods, which forced us to challenge traditional disciplinary approaches to urban space governance, and brought all relevant teams together in one room to critically dissect a complex and wicked issue. Collaboratively exploring policy options for better-managed urban markets in Lusaka, we came to appreciate the significant and emotive challenge facing public servants who deal with the daily politics of urban markets while striving to remain professional. Thus the co-production approach enabled us to explore the real feasibility of policy options, such as phased and partial integration of various informal food actors (e.g., food brokers) into the Market's formal management systems.

We argue that further comparative studies of such sites could offer robust and concrete possibilities for radically contributing to a new body of urban theory, urban studies, and critical urban theory, as well as advancing ideas of state-society relations and understanding of collective production of the urban in Africa. Such a progressive intellectual positioning could serve as a bedrock to radically transform the current deeply entrenched hegemonic policy caricatures of African urbanism, and thus begin shifting the balance of power in favour of diversity, inclusivity, and a globally transformative urban agenda.

Recommendations

This chapter has argued that urban governance and, by extension, governance of urban public spaces is in a post-political or post-democratic governance era, and that a new fusion of formal-informal systems and practices of governance must be acknowledged and reckoned with if transformative interventions are to meet with success in African cities. We have shown that urban market governance as seen in Soweto Market is based on the realities of the formal-informal continuum, where dynamic and subjective semi-formal protocols are grounded in ideas of loyalty and power and the survivalist nature of urban livelihoods. As such, any policy hoping to transform African cities must understand and speak to these realities. Based on these findings, we submit the following recommendations:

Firstly, interventions in urban markets need to be framed within the political reality of those market spaces. Soweto is a political and economic space that is governed by highly intertwined formal and informal systems and institutions. Thus, policy and practical measures to improve food trading needs to recognize and engage with the actual political forces at work in the Market.

Secondly, having established that governance in Soweto Market does not conform to western democratic norms, interventions to promote and protect urban rights must acknowledge and incorporate the 'arbitrary urban things', and how they play out in real life.

Thirdly, authorities' efforts must move beyond the formal-informal binary, and rather seek to engage with the formal-informal continuum as the site for transformative Market policy in particular, and urban policy in general. This could involve actions like revising capital sourcing to formalize the informal sources of capital (e.g., strengthening the lending capacity of produce associations) and establishing a formally recognized hybrid governance structure, such as a Market Board composed of both state agencies and informal actors (e.g., party cadres, interest groups such as loaders, among others).

Finally, the co-produced research presented here reinforces the need for studies of urban spaces, particularly in the global South, to methodologically extend beyond traditional disciplinary silos if they are to advance either policy or intellectual agendas.

Notes

1 Zambia's Markets and Bus Stations Act of 2007, which covers governance around marketplaces, divides markets into 'formal' and 'informal', rendering traders and vendors who do not comply with statutory requirements illegal and thus subject to sanction. Based on this framing, the activities taking place in the Soweto Market can be defined

as extra-legal in terms of the Act, though in practice the trading taking place reflects new norms and evolving realities.

2 Pieterse (2010) describes 'tough material conditions' as a context in which exploitative systems of daily rule govern every facet of life in African informal spaces (markets and settlements), and where the overwhelming majority of the urban population is left largely to its own devices for daily survival.

3 Political party cadres grant access to the markets usually through rent seeking; traders who oppose or refuse to comply are vulnerable to physical violence and/or being barred from trade.

4 Political parties that have governed Zambia since political independence in 1964 have included UNIP, MMD, and PF.

5 www.africancentreforcities.net/programme/mistra-urban-futures/citylab/

6 Market leadership management structures include the chairpersons and secretaries of produce associations, political parties, and LCC as well as various stakeholders and interest groups that do not belong to associations, including the loaders.

References

Allen, J. (2004). The whereabouts of power: politics, government and space. Geografiska Annaler. *Series B, Human Geography*, 86(1), pp. 19–32. DOI: https://doi.org/10.1111/j.0435-3684.2004.00151.x

Battersby, J. (2013). Hungry cities: a critical review of urban food security research in sub-Saharan African cities. *Geography Compass*, 7(7), pp. 452–463. DOI: https://doi.org/10.1111/gec3.12053

Battersby, J., Marshak, M. & Mngqibisa, N. (2016). *Mapping the invisible: the informal food economy of Cape Town, South Africa*. Urban Food Security Series No. 24. Cape Town and Waterloo: AFSUN and Balsillie School of International Affairs.

Battersby, J. & Watson, V. (2018). Addressing food security in African cities. *Nature Sustainability*, 1(4), pp. 153–155. DOI: https://doi.org/10.1038/s41893-018-0051-y

Biehl, J. & McKay, R. (2012). Ethnography as political critique. *Anthropological Quarterly*, 85(4), pp. 1209–1227. DOI: https://doi.org/10.1353/anq.2012.0057

Blekking, J., Tuholske, C. & Evans, T. (2017). Adaptive governance and market heterogeneity: an institutional analysis of an urban food system in sub-Saharan Africa. *Sustainability*, 9(12), p. 2191. DOI: https://doi.org/10.3390/su9122191

Chikulo, B.C. (1993). Democracy and development in Africa: problems and prospects. *Mphatlalatsane*, 3(1), pp. 41–54.

Crush, J. & Frayne, B.G. (2011). Urban food insecurity and the new international food security agenda. *Development Southern Africa*, 28(4), pp. 527–544. DOI: https://doi.org/10.1080/0376835X.2011.605571

Crush, J. & Riley, L. (2017). *No. 11: urban food security, rural bias and the global development agenda*. Hungry Cities Partnership Discussion Paper 11. Waterloo, ON: Hungry Cities Partnership.

Culwick, C., Washbourne, C.L., Anderson, P.M.L., Cartwright, A., Patel, Z. & Smit, W. (2019). CityLab reflections and evolutions: nurturing knowledge and learning for urban sustainability through co-production experimentation. *Current Opinion in Environmental Sustainability*, 39(9), pp. 9–16. DOI: https://doi.org/10.1016/j.cosust.2019.05.008

De Boeck, F. & Plissart, M.F. (2014). *Kinshasa: tales of the invisible city*. Leuven: Leuven University Press.

Diouf, M. (2003). Engaging postcolonial cultures: African youth and public space. *African studies review*, 46(2), pp. 1–12. DOI: https://doi.org/10.2307/1514823

Dixon, J. (1999). A cultural economy model for studying food systems. *Agriculture and Human Values*, 16(2), pp. 151–160. DOI: https://doi.org/10.1023/A:1007531129846

Duminy, J., Andreasen, J., Lerise, F., Ondendaal, N. & Watson, V. (2014). *Planning and the case study method in Africa: the planner in dirty shoes*. London: Palgrave Macmillan.

Flyvbjerg, B. (2004). Phronetic planning research: theoretical and methodological reflections. *Planning Theory & Practice*, 5(3), pp. 283–306. DOI: https://doi.org/10.1080/1464935042000250195

Flyvbjerg, B. (2011). Case study. In: Denzin, N. & Lincoln, Y. (Eds.), *The Sage handbook of qualitative research*, 4th edition. Thousand Oaks, CA: Sage, pp. 301–316.

Foucault, M. (1980). *Power/knowledge: selected interviews and other writings, 1972–1977*. New York: Vintage.

Foucault, M. & Hurley, M. (1990). *An introduction: vol. 1 of the history of sexuality* [Hurley, R. (Trans.)]. New York: Vintage.

Goodfellow, T. (2010). *'The bastard child of nobody'?: anti-planning and the institutional crisis in contemporary Kampala*. Crisis States Research Centre Working Papers Series No. 2 (67). London: London School of Economics and Political Science, Department of International Development. Retrieved: http://eprints.lse.ac.uk/id/eprint/39768

Hampwaye, G., Mataa, M., Siame, G. & Lungu, O. (2016). *City region food systems situational analysis – Lusaka Zambia*. Working Document FAO and RUAD Foundation. Retrieved: www.fao.org/3/a-bl822e.pdf

Horelli, L., Jarenko, K., Kuoppa, J., Saad-Sulonen, J. & Wallin, S. (2013). *New approaches to urban planning-insights from participatory communities*. Espoo, Finland: Aalto University. Retrieved: http://urn.fi/URN:ISBN:978-952-60-5191-8

ILO. (n.d.). *Social and solidarity economy* [online]. Retrieved: www.ilo.org/global/topics/cooperatives/projects/WCMS_546299/lang-en/index.htm [Accessed on 4 February 2019]

Jolly, S. & Raven, R.P.J.M. (2015). Collective institutional entrepreneurship and contestations in wind energy in India. *Renewable and Sustainable Energy Reviews*, 42, pp. 999–1011. DOI: https://doi.org/10.1016/j.rser.2014.10.039

Jones, P. (2017). Formalizing the informal: understanding the position of informal settlements and slums in sustainable urbanization policies and strategies in Bandung, Indonesia. *Sustainability*, 9(8), p. 1436. DOI: https://doi.org/10.3390/su9081436

Knorr, D., Khoo, C.S.H. & Augustin, M.A. (2018). Food for an urban planet: challenges and research opportunities. *Frontiers in Nutrition*, 4, p. 73. DOI: https://doi.org/10.3389/fnut.2017.00073

Lang, D.J., Wiek, A., Bergmann, M., Stauffacher, M., Martens, P., Moll, P. & Thomas, C.J. (2012). Transdisciplinary research in sustainability science: practice, principles, and challenges. *Sustainability Science*, 7(1), pp. 25–43. DOI: https://doi.org/10.1007/s11625-011-0149-x

LCC. (2019). *Lusaka city council* [online]. Retrieved: www.lcc.gov.zm/about-city-council/ [Accessed on 25 July 2019]

Lindell, I. (2008). The multiple sites of urban governance: insights from an African city. *Urban Studies*, 45(9), pp. 1879–1901. DOI: https://doi.org/10.1177/0042098008093382

Lyon, F. (2003). Trader associations and urban food systems in Ghana: institutionalist approaches to understanding urban collective action. *International Journal of Urban and Regional Research*, 27(1), pp. 11–23. DOI: https://doi.org/10.1111/1468-2427.00428

MacLeod, G. (2011). Urban politics reconsidered: growth machine to post-democratic city? *Urban Studies*, 48(12), pp. 2629–2660. DOI: https://doi.org/10.1177/0042098011415715

Mbembé, J.A. & Nuttall, S. (2004). Writing the world from an African metropolis. *Public Culture*, 16(3), pp. 347–372. Retrieved: https://muse.jhu.edu/article/173737/summary

Mukwena, R.M. & Lolojih, P.K. (2002). Governance and local government reforms in Zambia's third republic. In: Olowu, D. & Sako, S. (Eds.), *Better governance and public policy: capacity building for democratic renewal in Africa*. Bloomfield, CT: Kumarian Press Inc, pp. 215–231.

Nchito, W.S. (2007). Local governance and urban economies: what role for urban markets in Zambia? In: Momba, J.C. & Kalabula, D.M. (Eds.), *Governance and public services delivery in Zambia*. Addis Ababa: OSSREA, pp. 53–61.

Parnell, S. & Robinson, J. (2012). (Re)theorizing cities from the global South: looking beyond neoliberalism. *Urban Geography*, 33(4), pp. 593–617. DOI: https://doi.org/10.2747/0272-3638.33.4.593

Pieterse, E. (2010). Cityness and African urban development. *Urban Forum*, 21, pp. 205–219. DOI: https://doi.org/10.1007/s12132-010-9092-7

Pieterse, E. (2011a). Grasping the unknowable: coming to grips with African urbanisms. *Social Dynamics*, 37(1), pp. 5–23. DOI: https://doi.org/10.1080/02533952.2011.569994

Pieterse, E. (2011b). Rethinking African urbanism from the slum. *Power*, 26(14.1), pp. 40–48.

Porter, G., Lyon, F. & Potts, D. (2007). Market institutions and urban food supply in West and Southern Africa: a review. *Progress in Development Studies*, 7(2), pp. 115–134. DOI: https://doi.org/10.1177/146499340600700203

Resnick, D. (2014). *Urban poverty and party populism in African democracies*. New York: Cambridge University Press.

Resnick, D. (2017). Governance: informal food markets in Africa's cities. In: *2017 global food policy report*. Washington, DC: International Food Policy Research Institute (IFPRI), pp. 50–57.

Rhodes, R.A. (1997). From marketisation to diplomacy: it's the mix that matters. *Australian Journal of Public Administration*, 56(2), pp. 40–53. DOI: https://doi.org/10.1111/j.1467-8500.1997.tb01545.x

Robins, S., Cornwall, A. & von Lieres, B. (2008). *Rethinking 'citizenship' in the postcolony*. Rome: Pantheon.

Roy, A. (2005). Urban informality: toward and epistemology of planning. *Journal of the American Planning Association*, 71(2), pp. 147–158. DOI: https://doi.org/10.1080/01944360508976689

Roy, A. (2009). Civic governmentality: the politics of inclusion in Beirut and Mumbai. *Antipode*, 41(1), pp. 159–179. DOI: https://doi.org/10.1111/j.1467-8330.2008.00660.x

Satterthwaite, D. (2016). Successful, safe and sustainable cities: towards a new urban agenda. *Commonwealth Journal of Local Governance*, 19, pp. 3–18.

Schindler, S. (2017). Towards a paradigm of Southern urbanism. *City*, 21(1), pp. 47–64.

SERI. (2015). *The end of the street? Informal traders' experience of rights and regulations in inner city Johannesburg*. Johannesburg: Socio-Economic Rights Institute. Retrieved: www.seri-sa.org/images/Seri_informal_traders_report_FINAL_FOR_SIGN_OFF_2.pdf

Simone, A.M. (2004). People as infrastructure: intersecting fragments in Johannesburg. *Public Culture*, 16(3), pp. 407–429.

Simone, A.M. & Simone, T.A. (1994). *In whose image?: political Islam and urban practices in Sudan*. Chicago: University of Chicago Press.

Skinner, C. (2016). *Informal food retail in Africa: a review of evidence*. Consuming Urban Poverty Project Working Paper No. 2. Cape Town: African Centre for Cities, University of Cape Town.

Smit, W. (2016). Urban governance and urban food systems in Africa: examining the linkages. *Cities*, 58, pp. 80–86. DOI: https://doi.org/10.1016/j.cities.2016.05.001

Steynor, A., Padgham, J., Jack, C., Hewitson, B. & Lennard, C. (2016). Co-exploratory climate risk workshops: experiences from urban Africa. *Climate Risk Management*, 13, pp. 95–102. DOI: https://doi.org/10.1016/j.crm.2016.03.001

Swyngedouw, E. (2005). Governance innovation and the citizen: the Janus face of governance-beyond-the-state. *Urban Studies*, 42(11), pp. 1991–2006. DOI: https://doi.org/10.1080/00420980500279869

Van Gent, W.P., Jansen, E.F. & Smits, J.H. (2014). Right-wing radical populism in city and suburbs: an electoral geography of the Partij Voor de Vrijheid in the Netherlands. *Urban Studies*, 51(9), pp. 1775–1794. DOI: https://doi.org/10.1177/0042098013505889

Wragg, E. & Lim, R. (2015). Urban visions from Lusaka, Zambia. In: *Habitat international vol. 46*. New York: Columbia University Press, pp. 260–270.

3 Formal-informal interface

Comparative analysis between three Egyptian cities

Omar Nagati and Beth Stryker[1]

Introduction

Research on informality tends to treat informal and formal zones as discrete, and often homogenous entities, thus reproducing the segregation, marginalization, and exclusion of informal neighbourhoods. Seeking to challenge the perception of the dualistic city, we examine the formal-informal interface as a place with links to both spaces, and from which we can ultimately formulate appropriate integrated policies.

Current policy in Egypt around urban informality is based on a characterization of informality as an abnormal and inherently negative phenomenon that can only be solved by its removal from the city, or, at best, through upgrade and reform. This characterization, bolstered by the lack of economic profit extracted from informal settlements in the form of property taxes, continues to influence the two current policy approaches to engaging with urban informality: preventative and interventionist. The former, which includes 'belting' measures that build formal districts around informal areas, seeks to limit expansion of the informal. Meanwhile, interventionist approaches endeavour to remove, displace, or upgrade informal areas through measures like the resettlement process, whereby unsafe areas are cleared and residents are relocated to newly built areas in the outskirts of the city (Hasan, 1989).

Despite the general trend towards the integration of informality in the urban fabric, urban policies continue to uphold a formal-informal dichotomy. This dualistic view of the city continues to engender challenges, controversies, and contradictions around how informality is perceived and handled.

Problem statement: current policy

In the Greater Cairo Region (GCR), current policy dictates that district boundaries are delineated based on the informal or formal nature of the built environment. This key policy contradiction – effectively institutionalizing the separation of formal and informal neighbourhoods – may be said to represent Egyptian government policies for urban areas more generally. Such urban policies further perpetuate existing imbalances between formal and informal areas through budget allocations.

Comparing the local development budget allocation per capita in the GCR districts with a map of Cairo's formal and informal areas, we see that informal areas receive far less funding for development than do formal districts (Tadamun, 2015). For example, the informal areas of Bulaq al-Dakrur and Shubra, which have the highest concentrations of urban poor and thus require more services, receive a comparatively lower percentage of the local development budget per capita than formal areas such as Madinat Nasr, Ma'adi, and Misr al-Jadida, which already enjoy many services and established infrastructure. Such examples show a clear funding discrepancy, resulting in continued unequal access to basic services, including education and health care (Tadamun, 2015). Meanwhile, the GCR's policies around upgrading informal areas continue to be grounded in the assumption that informal areas do not fit the norm, and as such must be demolished and reconstructed according to national norms, rather than adapting infrastructures and services to the needs of informal areas.

Given these challenges in the ways in which formality and informality are understood and treated, this research has three aims:

- Challenge the status quo bifurcation of the city into formal and informal areas.
- Deliver a series of policy recommendations based on the aim of integrating informal practices into the city.
- Provide a comparative framework that facilitates knowledge-sharing between African cities, allowing further insight into the nature of the formal-informal interface across the continent, while also promoting a nuanced understanding of their local contexts.

Context: introduction to informality

Over the last few decades, urban informality has emerged as a critical issue impacting large metropolises today (Soliman, 2004; Simone, 2002; AlSayyad, 2004). A literature review reveals that research on informal areas tends to examine their historic, socioeconomic, and geographic aspects independently from those of the formal sector.[2] While both informal and formal areas are marked by spatial and social segregation, previous literature has at times deepened the divide between informal and formal areas, enhancing existing social and physical boundaries with theoretical constructs that reinforce a story of two separate cities (Viquez Abarca & Hernandez Garcia, 2017; UN-Habitat, 2010).

What is informality?

Our research hinges on an analysis of urban informality as a spatially produced urban condition that takes place outside formal regulations in response to the withdrawal of the state. In Egypt, informality emerged in the early 1960s, and proliferated in response to state deregulation in the 1970s (Sims, 2010). Thus, informality is understood to refer to actions undertaken by individuals and communities to meet their own needs, outside of legal means recognized by the state.

Formal-informal interface in Egypt

In Egypt, as elsewhere, informality is influenced by responses to governmental policies, but also triggers new governmental responses. Egyptian central authorities' response to informality has evolved over the decades in relation to perceptions and definitions of informal areas. By examining the evolution of urban informality in Egypt, we see how cities' morphologies have changed alongside gradual policy shifts.

Evolution of urban informality in Egypt: 1950–2018

Informal housing development has existed in Egypt since the 1950s, when new rent control laws reduced rental market profitability, prompting the mainstream real estate market to become predominantly owner-occupied. A housing shortage resulted, as demand for housing outweighed supply (Khadr & Bulbul, 2011). The earliest manifestations of informality in Egypt responded to this housing demand, with informal construction developed on agricultural lands at urban fringes. The

Figure 3.1 Izbat Awlad al-'Alamin Duqqi: Informal Enclave within the Formal City
Source: Authors

government presented no official resistance to these first informal settlements, and while officials granted permission to some dwellers to remain in their locations, they also abdicated responsibility to provide basic amenities for informal settlers (Center for Sustainable Development, 2013). During the 1960s, informal settlements expanded due to rural-urban migration, spurred by employment opportunities in industrial zones adjacent to large cities.

During the Arab-Israeli conflict (1967 to 1973), financial resources mobilized for military needs led to decreases in public housing project investment. Meanwhile, 1.5 million people evacuated from the Suez Canal zone fled to other cities. With formal housing development stalled due to war efforts, informal development grew considerably (Soliman, 2007). Again, authorities overlooked this growth, partly because it largely took the form of village expansions in the rural peripheries, where building permits were not required (Hassan, 2012).

Post-war, the government intensified efforts to rebuild the country's economy, directing resources to modernize formal area infrastructure and to develop new cities (e.g., Sadat, Sixth of October, and Tenth of Ramadan), as dictated by new town policies, which aimed to redistribute the urban population and build alternatives to informal development (Sims, 2010). New town development was undertaken in the context of Sadat's Open Door Economic Policy (*Infitah*), which marked the first wave of the liberalization of Egypt's economy (Mkandawire & Soludo, 1999). Significant capital investments in housing increased land values to unprecedented levels, leading to high inflation, a real estate bubble, and a lack of affordable housing (Evin, 1985). As a result, low-income and middle-class residents, and Egyptian workers returning from the Gulf countries, turned to the informal sector and peri-urban suburbs to address their housing needs (Sims, 2010).

By the 1980s, the prominence of urban informal areas prompted measures limiting 'illegal' urbanization, such as Egyptian Military Decrees 1 and 7, which forbid encroachment on agricultural land (Séjourné, 2009). However, informal settlements continued to grow. With the state declining to provide basic services for these settlements, civil society networks funded by religious charitable groups stepped in to provide services, infrastructure, hospitals, education, security, and more. During this time, political discourse began demonizing informal areas as breeding grounds for Islamic fundamentalism. By the close of the 1980s, the growth rate of informal settlements had surpassed that of formal areas in Egypt. Between 1986 and 1996, the growth of informal construction in Egypt was estimated at 3.2% per year, compared to 1.1% in formal districts, while the population growth rate in informal settlements reached 3.4% per year, compared to 0.3% in legal areas (Payne, 2005).

In the early 1990s, another policy shift occurred. Attempting to capitalize on existing housing stock in informal areas, the government undertook to upgrade informal settlements. The 1992 National Program of Urban Upgrading classified informal areas based on their potential for upgrade (1,201 areas) or for eviction (20 areas). It also began to provide basic infrastructure and municipal services in almost all informal settlements in the GCR. Meanwhile, the presidential decree for the 'Citizen's Right to Appropriate Infrastructure' focused on providing a combination of infrastructural improvements, social services, and physical restructuring in 'safely built' settlements (Hassan, 2012).

In 1996, the al-Shura Council (the upper house of representatives) produced a report arguing for an integrated approach to the problem of informal settlements (Khalifa, 2011). Governmental policies consequently shifted from a singular focus on physical upgrading, to plans that integrated informal neighbourhoods within the formal city. During the early 2000s, this notion of 'integration' came to replace the concept of 'upgrading'. Integration included three basic aspects. Firstly, physical integration involved opening roads, connecting infrastructure networks and public services, and integrating informal areas in the city's official maps. Secondly, social integration sought to promote social development. Thirdly, juridical integration involved property regularization, land titling, and the resolution of land tenure issues, as a means to complement citywide cadastral needs to enable property tax collection (Hassan, 2012).

In the mid-2000s, policy shifted again. With the Ministry of Local Development counting 1,171 informal areas with a total population of 15 million in 2007 (Payne, 2005), a new approach was undertaken to control informal growth by planning the fringes of the city before they could be occupied by informal construction. From 2004 to 2008 the government implemented an informal settlement belting programme (*Tahzim al-'Ashwa'iyat*) intended to restrict the growth of informal settlements through the construction of formal housing in strategic regions (Tadamun, 2016).

In 2008, the Informal Settlement Development Facility (ISDF) was established to coordinate efforts and finance the development of informal areas. The ISDF initiated a significant ideological shift in the government's approach to informal urbanization, notably by modifying the vocabulary used to describe informality. Common terms such as 'Slums', 'Informal Settlements', or *''Ashwa'iyat'* were replaced by two distinctive terms: 'Unsafe Areas' and 'Unplanned areas'. Unsafe areas are characterized as subjecting people to life-threatening conditions, such as inappropriate housing, exposure to health threats, or tenure risks, while unplanned areas are usually noncompliant with planning and building laws and regulations (Nassar & Elsayed, 2018). Thus, informality could be defined on the basis of either legal status and/or physical conditions (Piffero, 2009). The ISDF's approach to unsafe areas was either to remove and rebuild in situ, or to relocate residents (Hassan, 2012). In high land-value areas, informal settlements were removed and people relocated, in many cases to unsuitable areas.

The current period (since the 25 January 2011 revolution), is marked by large-scale national construction of new housing projects using public funds, and alternative approaches to informality undertaken by new urban practices. While international organizations (e.g., Deutsche Gesellschaft für Internationale Zusammenarbeit GIZ, Agence Française de Développement [AFD], and United Nations Women) are funding research and implementation of projects promoting in situ upgrading grounded in participatory engagement of neighbourhood residents, new urban practices (e.g., CLUSTER, Takween, Madd, and 10Tooba) are attempting to address informality as part of the solution, rather than the essential problem, facing large metropolises today. Collectively, this research on the inter-action between formal and informal zones is contributing to a redefinition of informality.

Methodology and framework

The core of this project took the form of fieldwork conducted in three cities, which were selected based on their relative size, location, and specific socioeco-nomic characteristics: Cairo, the capital; Alexandria, Egypt's second largest city; and Minya, a regional centre.

Informing our fieldwork process was a literature review on informality in Egypt and globally, utilizing academic sources, and government and international reports to extract statistical information, data, district boundaries, and more. In each city, the team identified and collaborated with local individuals and groups to compile literature, maps, and additional background material. The team identi-fied practitioners, academics, community leaders, and experts in relevant fields of study in each city, utilizing local contacts to facilitate analyses on the ground, and to review findings.

CLUSTER utilized Cairo as a pilot for further field encounters, building on our experience undertaking urban research and design interventions in the city since 2011. CLUSTER's urban research methodologies aim to engage stakeholders in all stages of research. Such an approach seeks to promote an alternative mode of participatory planning and urban governance, which is particularly pertinent in Egypt, where elected city or district councils do not exist. Since 2011, CLUSTER has been documenting rapid political and urban change in Cairo, raising questions concerning informal economies and the right to the city, while focusing on the spatial manifestation of these practices.

CLUSTER's research team conducted its first fieldwork stage in Cairo in August and September of 2017; Alexandria in October; and Minya in November of the same year.

The team's proximity to and familiarity with Cairo enabled it to use the city as a pilot for the development of a set of four variables, which were used to exam-ine the specificities of the formal-informal interface within each case study, and developed as an analytic framework for the comparative analysis. These four vari-ables are:

- **Borders**: elements that separate the formal from the informal urban fabric. Borders can refer to infrastructural elements such as walls, railway lines, or artificial waterways (canals), or can result from topographical features. In the context of this research, borders are critical elements that impact the flow, or lack thereof, between formal and informal areas.
- **Crossings**: physical means to overcome borders, including features like rail-way crossings, bridges, and tunnels. Whether built formally by the state, or informally by the community, crossings address a need for accessibility or flow, and often act as magnets for both informal and formal activities.

- **Activities**: develop along the borders separating the informal and formal sectors of the city. Some activities mainly serve the needs of residents in the informal sector – such as tuktuk networks connecting residents to planned components of the traffic network. Other activities serve both the formal and informal sectors, such as markets (formal or informal), often found around transportation hubs.
- **Flows**: the movement of goods, labour, or capital between or across both formal and informal sectors.

In each city, we examined earlier four variables at three different scales, from the macro to the micro-level. Each scale focused on different aspects of the formal-informal interface.

- **City scale:** providing a macro overview of the relationship between the formal and informal, this scale generally looks at urban corridors, transportation axes, infrastructural lines, topographical changes, urban fabrics, patterns of expansion, and overall density.
- **District scale:** focusing on select neighbourhoods where the symbiotic relationship between the informal and formal is relevant, this scale casts an eye to border lines, linkages, patterns, and footprints in terms of density, services, and flows across areas.
- **Node scale:** utilized to study the intersection between multiple axes where the informal and formal connect, this micro-scale examines the people traversing the formal-informal interface, and the activities arising around crossings and transfer points.

Based on a preliminary cycle of fieldwork in Cairo, and using the four variables and three scales of analysis as a coherent framework, the team was then deployed to Alexandria and Minya to examine the formal-informal interface in both cities.

In undertaking a comparative analysis of the three cities across the four variables (borders, crossings, activities, and flows), we sought to investigate two key questions:

- Despite existing physical borders, do the experiential flows and nodes at crossings challenge the formal-informal separation?
- What alternative planning policies could be adopted to foster integration and build on the complementarity between formal-informal modes of development?

Pictograms representing interface typologies were utilized throughout the research as a means to abstract a complex web of relations and facilitate a comparative analysis, such as the ones used in Figures 3.4 and 3.8.

Following fieldwork, we processed research materials, maps, images, and interviews, and employed visualization strategies to give shape to the patterns

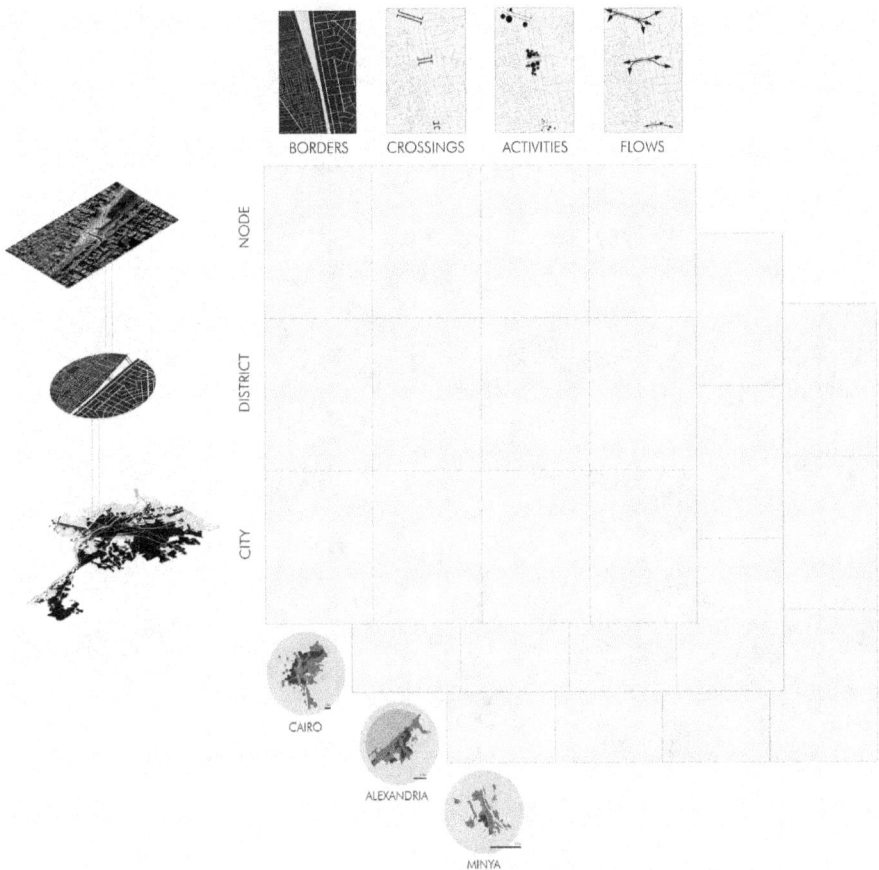

Figure 3.2 Comparative Framework
Source: CLUSTER, 2018

analysed in the three cities. In this final stage, we also examined the opportunities interfaces provide to challenge formal-informal divisions.

Case studies: findings

Cairo

Located along the Nile Valley, Egypt's capital city is the country's cultural, political, and economic centre. The GCR is comprised of three Governorates: Cairo, Giza, and Qalyubiya (which includes the district of Shubra al-Khayma). The GCR is the 16th largest metropolitan area in the world, with a 2017 population

Figure 3.3 Map of Cairo

Source: CLUSTER, 2018

of over 19,846,000, and an annual growth rate of around 2.2% since 2000 (World Population Review, 2018). The presence of industrial zones in the cities of Sixth of October and Tenth of Ramadan (both part of the GCR), have contributed to the capital's role as a key manufacturing centre (Euromonitor, 2017; UCL, 2003). In 2016, Cairo accounted for 33% of Egypt's total gross domestic product (Euromonitor, 2017).

For centuries Cairo has expanded through successive waves of development and ever-increasing urbanization. Today, informality is one of Cairo's defining features, and its dominant mode of urbanization. With the informal economy estimated to incorporate over half of Cairo's labour force, and informal neighbourhoods constituting 52.7% of Greater Cairo's residential areas (World Population Review, 2018), distinctions between formal systems and informal practices have blurred.

Formal-informal interface: three scales

Our analysis of Cairo, based on case studies conducted at three scales (city, district, node), identifies ways in which informality has contributed to the capital's urbanization process, and how informality manifests within Cairo's multilayered fabric.

City scale

Despite Cairo's size and complexity, broad trends in the organization of the formal and informal sectors emerge at the city scale:

- Cairo is characterized by an historic core, around which a ring of informality has progressively developed since the 1960s. Through expansion, formerly rural enclaves became part of its formal urban agglomeration (e.g., Mit 'Uqba within Muhandisin). Informal construction also occurred along urban corridors (e.g., along Hilwan Road to the south, and Pyramids Road to the southwest).
- Cairo is a mega-city, with infrastructural systems such as highways, railways, and major roads forming its dominant borders (e.g., al-Isma'iliya Canal in the north and al-Autostrad to the east). In some cases, these infrastructural lines produce a sharp divide between formal and informal areas (e.g., between Ard al-Liwa and al-Muhandisin in the west, and Nasr City and 'Izbat al-Hajjana in the east). In other cases, the formal-informal border is blurred, such as at the intersection of infrastructural lines, as is the case at Ghamra Station (a complex transport hub examined in this study; see Figure 3.4).
- Formal road infrastructures at the periphery of informal neighbourhoods are largely not connected to the road networks within informal areas, limiting access for residents of informal neighbourhoods to main transportation services, and by extension, access to education, employment opportunities, and health services.

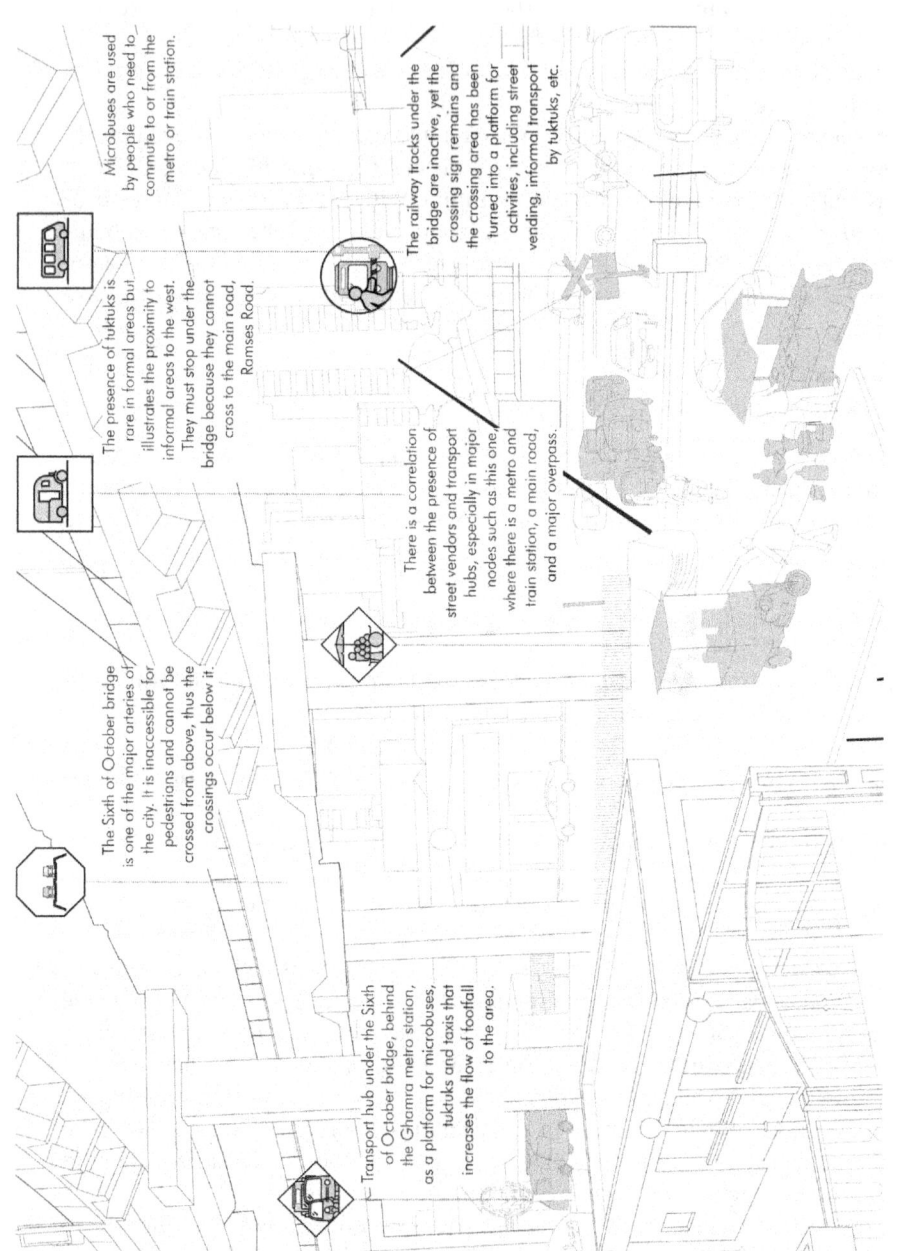

Microbuses are used by people who need to commute to or from the metro or train station.

The presence of tuktuks is rare in formal areas but illustrates the proximity to informal areas to the west. They must stop under the bridge because they cannot cross to the main road, Ramses Road.

The railway tracks under the bridge are inactive, yet the crossing sign remains and the crossing area has been turned into a platform for activities, including street vending, informal transport by tuktuks, etc.

The Sixth of October bridge is one of the major arteries of the city. It is inaccessible for pedestrians and cannot be crossed from above, thus the crossings occur below it.

There is a correlation between the presence of street vendors and transport hubs, especially in major nodes such as this one, where there is a metro and train station, a main road, and a major overpass.

Transport hub under the Sixth of October bridge, behind the Ghamra metro station, as a platform for microbuses, tuktuks and taxis that increases the flow of footfall to the area.

Figure 3.4 Ghamra Station Activities and Flows Around a Major Transportation Hub

Source: CLUSTER, 2018

District scale

Through fieldwork, four district-scale areas were analysed: Ard al-Liwa, Hilwan, Ghamra Station, and 'Izbat al-Hajjana. In Ard al-Liwa, the strict division of formal and informal areas that can occur along infrastructural borders is evident where the railway line separates this informal area from the formal area of al-Muhandisin (Figure 3.5). Crossings, including pedestrian stairs and vehicle bridges, are distributed along this boundary to enhance the connection between the areas. Multiple public services, transportation hubs, commercial and entertainment activities can be found in the spaces adjacent to these crossings.

Node scale

At the node scale, the critical relationship between people's needs and government response can be seen through the evolution of physical infrastructure, as in the case of the railway crossing in Ard al-Liwa. Isolated from adjacent areas due to the presence of the railway tracks, Ard al-Liwa was linked to al-Muhandisin via an informal crossing. However, due to frequent train accidents, the government closed this crossing, replacing it with formal bridges for cars and pedestrians. This evolution from informal to formal exemplifies how local demand and community-built solutions can be capitalized on by the government to improve mobility and accessibility across the network.

Analytical tools

BORDERS AND CROSSINGS

In Cairo, infrastructural lines form some of the main borders. In some cases, these boundaries mark a deliberate state effort to delineate formal and informal zones, as with the construction of the Ring Road in the late-twentieth century. However, over time, informal development around these 'borders' transformed them into mixed formal-informal urban corridors.

Isma'iliya Canal in northern Cairo constitutes an important fixed border, as it separates not only the formal and informal areas, but also demarcates the Cairo and al-Qalyubiya Governorates. Other canals in Cairo have either been infilled and developed or are in the process of being urbanized. As such, peri-urban irrigation canals are often rendered irrelevant once agricultural land is lost through urbanization, thereby increasing the likelihood these canals will be incorporated into the urban fabric, as in the case of al-Zumur Canal.

Topographical borders define some informal areas in Cairo. In such cases, local, incremental community efforts, such as the building of staircases, serve to mount otherwise impassable geographical barriers. Government upgrading efforts of informal areas often involve the reconstruction of such informal stairways, using more durable materials, and adding handrails. As excluded communities reclaim their rights to the city through makeshift solutions, the interfaces between

Figure 3.5 Railway Border between Ard al-Liwa and al-Muhandisin
Source: Authors

formal and informal areas develop beyond spatial barriers symbolic of structural division, to present opportunities for connection and reclaimed agency.

Cairo's complex traffic and transit network has given rise to compound crossings that include pedestrian, overpass, and flyover crossings, and in some cases informal street-level crossings. Frequently, these formal and informal crossings act as hyper-junctures, where layers of public transit, including metro and regional train lines, intersect with informal transit networks, such as microbuses and tuktuks.

ACTIVITIES AND FLOWS

Cairo's dynamic transport hubs and crossings function as nodes concentrating activities and flows of capital, labour, and goods between the informal and formal sectors. Formal and informal modes of transport generate significant pedestrian traffic in these areas, accounting for the correlation between street vendors and transport hubs.

Alexandria

Alexandria is Egypt's second largest city, with a population of about 4.9 million, increasing at an average annual rate of 2.3% since 1999 (Population of Alexandria, 2017). Alexandria accounts for 40% of Egypt's industry, and approximately 80% of the country's imports and exports move through its large seaport (Shoup, 2017). Situated on the Mediterranean Sea, and in close proximity to numerous lakes, Alexandria attracts over 3 million visitors per year (Al Masalla, 2010).

Urban informality in Alexandria mainly emerged in the 1960s, when formal construction declined nationally, while migration to major cities like Alexandria increased. The majority of informal urban construction took place on agricultural land, without adequate urban infrastructure, as can be observed in Burj al-'Arab al-Jadida and around Lake Maryut.

Today, 50% of Alexandria's residential areas are informal. Occupying a net surface area of 34.2 km² (Soliman, 2002) and housing an estimated 1.5 million people, informal areas are high-density with poor road conditions, and lack community services and utilities (e.g., paved streets, adequate access to healthcare, education, and community facilities [Barthel et al., n.d.]). As such, informal areas in Alexandria are largely dependent on services from the formal areas, with residents in informal areas often relying on neighbouring areas to access services like secondary education. Urban sprawl and the densification of informal areas have exacerbated the inequality in access to services. Meanwhile, the continued influx of migrants from neighbouring areas to Alexandria has also increased land speculation, leading to the demolition of numerous historical buildings to make way for new developments.

Formal-informal interface: three scales

CITY SCALE

Successive periods of development over the twentieth century have reshaped Alexandria's urban development, expanding urban areas from the old central districts (Wasat, Jumruk, and Gharb) towards the northeastern (al-Muntazah, Sharq) and southwestern (al-Amiriya) districts that today comprise modern Alexandria. Several patterns delineating the formal-informal interface in Alexandria are evident:

- The city's linear urban development has resulted in the creation of multiple urban layers: from older to newer housing, higher- to lower-income neighbourhoods, and formal to informal modes of development.
- Socioeconomic inequalities are spatially inscribed in the city: upper-class residential areas have developed along the coast, south of which are the middle-class districts, with low-income areas typically constructed informally, behind the railway track and south of al-Mahmudiya Canal.
- Urban informality expanded the city mainly to the south of the Mahmudiya Canal and the railroad, and is characterized by the construction of urban blocks following the pattern of agricultural subdivisions.

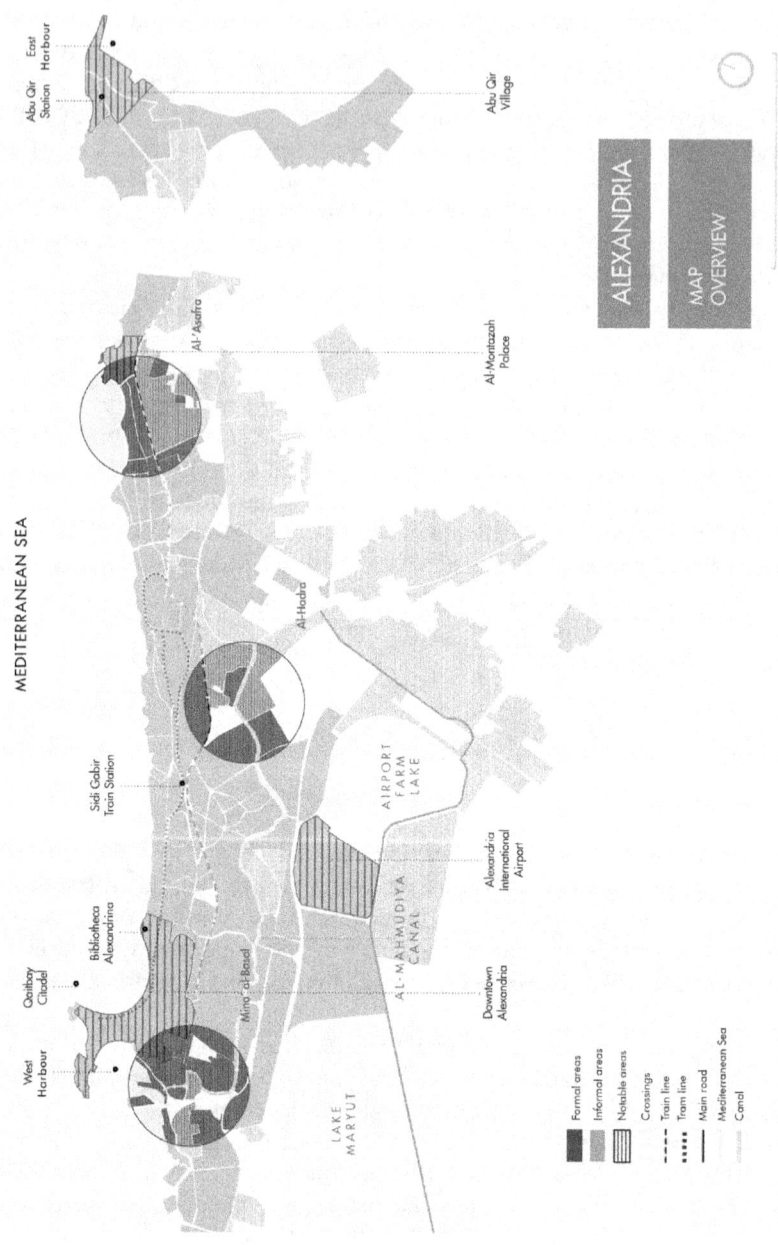

Figure 3.6 Map of Alexandria

Source: CLUSTER, 2018

DISTRICT SCALE

Case studies were conducted on three districts: al-'Asafra, al-Hadra, and Mina al-Basal.

The district of al-Hadra exemplifies the postindustrial transition that is changing the face of Alexandria through the conversion of old factories and warehouses, thus altering the area's development from industrial to mixed-use.

Meanwhile, the Mahmudiya Canal is set to be filled and turned into a road in the context of the 'Artery of Hope' national project. Despite this transformation, the canal remains both a separator and a connector of the formal and informal. It connects by linking the formal industrial areas north of the canal with the more informal, mixed-used development, craftsman shops, and small workshops in the south, through symbiotic flows in terms of production lines and distribution.

NODE SCALE

Alexandria's linear development has created a sequence of nodes at crossings along the railway tracks and canal. In al-'Asafra, a sequence of railway crossings along the tracks are formed by staircases and pedestrian bridges. In addition to these formal crossings, several informal crossings over the railway illustrate the permeability of this border. Near these crossings, activities such as commercial kiosks and tuktuk and microbus stops have been established.

Analytical tools

BORDERS AND CROSSINGS

In Alexandria, infrastructural borders between the formal and informal include roads, tramway lines, and the railway parallel to the coast. Other borders are created by waterways, such as al-Mahmudiya Canal in the southwest. These borders are crossed by bridges, overpasses, and a few tunnels, which together form a complex of nodes.

Informal crossings, such as the informal railway crossings in al-'Asafra, have evolved in response to local demand. In some cases, the government has formalized such crossings to address safety concerns, in response to accidents that have occurred. For example, in Mina al-Basal, a pedestrian bridge was constructed in 2016 by the Alexandria Governorate, to link Kafr 'Ashri to the main road, following several accidents involving students seeking passage by informal ferry to schools on the other side.[3]

ACTIVITIES AND FLOWS

In Alexandria, crossings are the dominant exchange points of activities and flows between the formal and informal sectors. Street vendors, often located at crossings, serve those waiting for tuktuks, buses, and taxis. Further, the location of industrial zones to the south and west of the formal districts of Alexandria marks them as areas in transition. This transition can be seen both in geographical terms, as the formal districts transition to informal sprawl to the south, as well as temporal terms, as many of the old factories and warehouses are being demolished or converted, giving way to new mixed-use developments, contributing to a further blurring of the formal-informal interface.

Minya

The City of Minya is located in Upper Egypt, on the western bank of the Nile, 241 km south of Cairo. It is the capital of the Minya Governorate, a rural governorate which represents approximately 6.5% of Egypt's total agricultural land. According to the 2012 residential census, 256,732 people reside in the city's total area of about 11km² (Populationcity.com, n.d.).

Throughout the nineteenth century, investment in large urban infrastructures (e.g., al-Ibrahimiya Canal and the railway line) contributed to the city's urban expansion towards the Nile, as well as to the south and west. In the twentieth century, the city expanded largely to the north, where administrative offices and economic activities were located.

In 1960, Minya became the capital of the governorate, and some neighbouring regions were included within the formal city borders. Areas adjacent to the historic city centre were upgraded, and residents relocated. During the period from 1977 to 1995, urban expansion continued towards the western region, where both formal and informal buildings were developed on the numerous agricultural plots available.

A population increase followed Minya's physical urban expansion, particularly after the founding of the Minya University, which prompted the relocation of many services to the northern part of the city, and led to an increase in immigration from surrounding villages.

Formal-informal interface: three scales

CITY SCALE

The interface between formal and informal urban development in Minya is delineated by the Ibrahimiya Canal, which divides the old planned district from recent informal development on agricultural land, marking a sharp distinction between the two conditions. Other characteristics of the formal-informal interface in Minya include:

- Northern expansion from the city centre has been driven by new district and investment plans, while southern expansion has been driven by private and informal development.
- Except for a few industrial installations and associated public housing, development west of the canal is mostly informal, with persistent links to agricultural land and a rural economy.

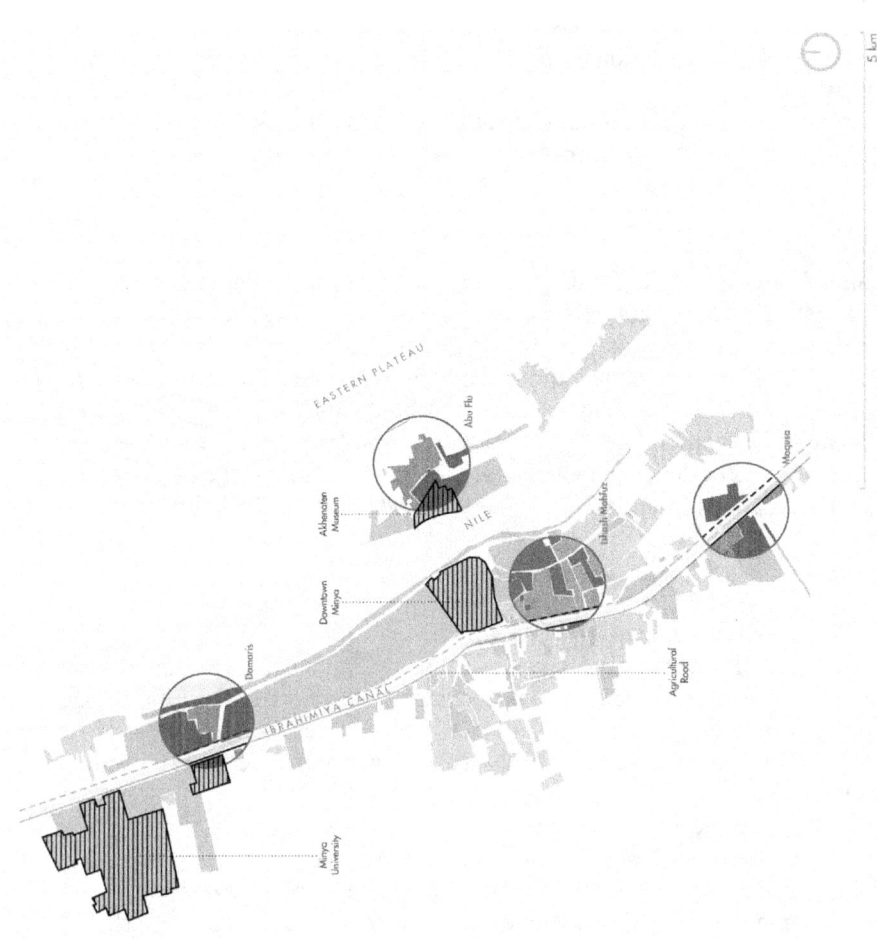

Figure 3.7 Map of Minya

Source: CLUSTER, 2018

- The area between the old core in the city centre and informal development to the south includes public housing projects encroached upon by informal areas, making it impossible to delineate clear boundaries between the formal and informal urban conditions, even on the block scale. Informal areas continue to expand to the southwest of the city, immediately adjacent to formal areas.
- Formal housing has been built surrounding rural villages, creating a belt of formal infrastructure that converts rural villages into informal enclaves.

DISTRICT SCALE

Formal and informal urbanization patterns were explored at the district scale in four informal districts: Abu Flu, Damaris, Maqusa, and 'Ishash Mahfuz.

At this scale, the stark juxtaposition of formal-informal areas is evident. The district of Abu Flu features institutional and civic development (museum, parks, etc.) and private high-end housing along planned roads, as well as informal developments built around the former hamlet of Abu Flu. The close proximity of the different types of development creates stark juxtapositions: the tourist attraction of Akhenaten Museum sits less than 100 metres from the informal village of Abu Flu.

NODE SCALE

Minya has different types of crossings over the al-Ibrahimiya Canal and railway (Figure 3.8), some for vehicles and pedestrians, and others in the form of fuel infrastructure and pipes. The crossings not only connect the two banks of the waterway barrier, but also serve as conduits for flows of people, goods, services, and capital.

A wide range of activities is concentrated around each crossing, ranging from transportation hubs to informal markets and local services.

This study illustrates how all of these nodes tend to specialize according to context; for example, the Minya University pedestrian bridge was established to connect the Faculty of Dentistry on the western side with the areas of al-Akhsas, Ard al-Sultan, and Damaris. On both sides of the bridge there are Minya Youth Houses for students, as well as services such as print shops and stationary stores targeting university students.

Analytical tools

BORDERS AND CROSSINGS

Minya expanded linearly along the Nile and is bordered by the Eastern Desert Road and the Western Desert Road. The city has three compound urban separators: the Agricultural Road, which cuts through the city from north to south, the railway, and Ibrahimiya Canal, all of which run parallel to one another. The canal

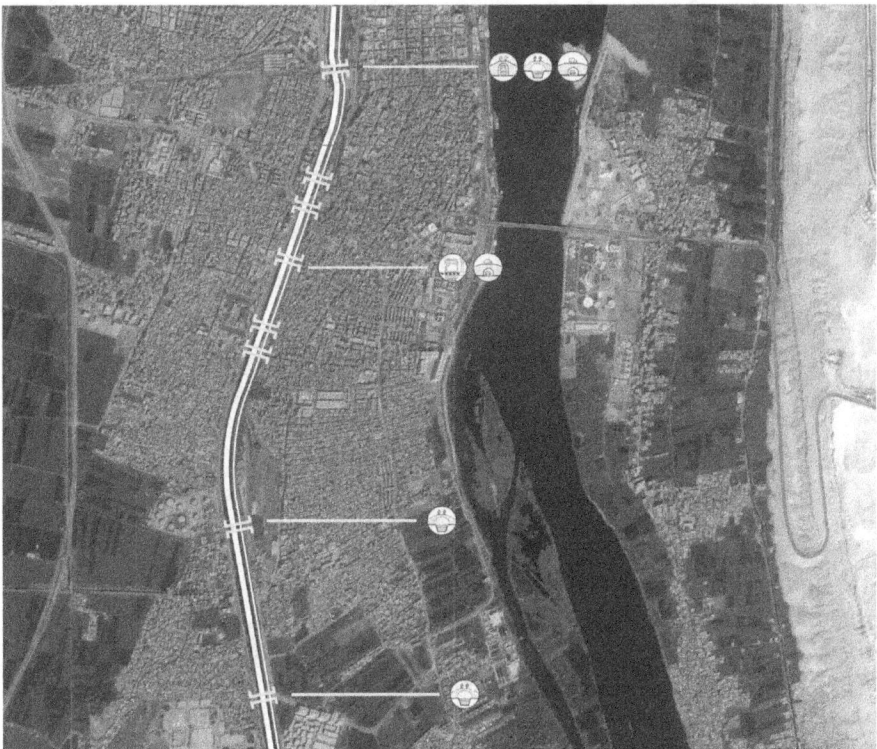

Figure 3.8 Crossings Along the al-Ibrahimiya Canal in Minya
Source: CLUSTER, 2018

circumscribes the expanding city, demarcating the formally built city on one side from the largely informal development on the other.

ACTIVITIES AND FLOWS

Like Alexandria, Minya's formal-informal interface is most visible at crossings throughout the city, where flows of goods, people, and capital contribute to flourishing markets. The flow of people to formal areas is driven by the presence of job opportunities and services, and is facilitated by the availability of public and private transportation. The flow of people to informal areas is driven by the low prices of goods and raw materials.

The complex layering of crossings can, in cases, limit the diversity of activities and flows. For example, staircases leading to pedestrian bridges are inconvenient for the elderly and people with disabilities. Street vendors posted along and underneath the staircases sometimes impede the dense flow of people.

Table 3.1 General profile comparing the three cities under study

	Cairo, capital city	Alexandria, second largest city	Minya, city in upper Egypt
Population	19,846,000[4]	4,930,000[5]	287,723[6]
Density (inhabitants/km²)	45,000[7]	30,000[8]	26,157[9]
Informal residential areas	52.7%[10]	50%[11]	32%[12]
Dwellers of informal areas	60%[13]	40%[14]	56%[15]

Source: Multiple (see endnotes)

Comparative analysis

City overview

Conducting a comparative analysis of the formal-informal interfaces in Cairo, Alexandria, and Minya, our methodology sought to arrive at a comprehensive understanding of the relationships between informal and formal areas in different urban contexts. To do this we analysed four variables (borders, crossings, activities, and flows) at three scales (city, district, node).

Adjusting the lens of analysis from macro to micro, we surfaced various dynamics that are essential to understanding the interaction between informal and formal areas, and which challenge a dualistic vision of the city. While the macro view presents what appears to be a fragmented urban fabric that is starkly divided between formally organized neighbourhoods and ostensibly spontaneously and haphazardly constructed areas, a closer micro-examination reveals a range of urban orders with different organizing principles and levels of 'planning'.

At the micro-scale, we see how 'crossings' facilitate a wide array of activities and flows (of people, labour, and capital) between the informal and formal, and how these crossings help to overcome formal urban borders and resultant spatial segregation.

We now return to the two key questions driving this comparative analysis of three cities across the four variables of borders, crossings, activities, and flows:

- Despite existing physical borders, do the experiential flows and nodes at crossings challenge the formal-informal separation?
- What alternative planning policies could be adopted to foster integration and build on the complementarity between formal-informal modes of development?

On borders

Borders are defining boundaries that demarcate one area from another. Borders can also be compounded by additional barriers: for example, a railway may run parallel to a highway or a waterway. These compound borders often create less permeable interfaces, as people must bypass multiple obstacles to cross them. We divide border conditions into the following three types: infrastructure, topography, and waterways.

Infrastructure

These include physically constructed borders such as a railway, or highway, some of which were constructed with the intent of marking the edge of the city limits. Unlike topography, these borders are dynamic, marked by temporal traffic and intermittent crossings. Infrastructure like railways and highways usually have a buffer zone, resulting in a wider barrier, while also accommodating informal activities along those edges. Borders such as these usually pose safety issues and risks to cross, unless formally bridged by over- or underpasses.

Comparing the three cities, we found that railways and highways consistently acted as critical separators between formal and informal areas. In Cairo and Alexandria, the railways were constructed at the cities' outer limits in the late nineteenth and early twentieth centuries. As the cities expanded, these former borders became urban corridors traversing and reinforcing the formal-informal divide. In Cairo, infrastructure borders are generally compounded, combining layers of railways, highways, and in some cases, metro lines. In Minya, these infrastructure borders are distinct, and continue to clearly separate the formal city from the largely agricultural hinterland. In the industrial port of Alexandria, multiple infrastructural lines (tram and train) have been built parallel to the sea, thus reinforcing the segregation between the northern and southern strips of the city.

Topography

Natural borders created by changes in elevation, topographical borders may be dangerous, as informal development along hilltops can lead to hazards and risks of rockslides.[16] Topographical borders bar the movement of people, since crossings require vertical circulation systems, such as stairs, ramps, escalators, or elevators. As such, they often pose exclusionary barriers to elderly citizens or those with special needs.

In both Cairo and Minya, we found topographical borders located in the eastern parts of the city. In Cairo, the Muqattam Hills act as a powerful urban separator, while in Minya, the hilly topography of the Eastern Plateau creates a natural edge to incremental expansion eastwards. Minya's topographical border is not considered as restrictive a barrier as the Muqattam Hills, in the sense that informal development leapfrogs the Eastern Plateau, extending further east to New Minya. There is no topographical change in Alexandria that affects the border condition of the city.

Waterways

Borders created by waterways (e.g., rivers, canals) cannot be traversed without an artificial crossing, which requires both capital and technical resources to build. The banks of waterways, which are in the public domain, are often occupied by informal activities, including small ferries, storage areas, and leisure activities.

In Cairo, Alexandria, and Minya, rural to urban transformation is linked to the presence of canals originally built for irrigation purposes. In Minya, where rural activities remain dominant, waterways continue to be functional and well-maintained. By contrast, in Cairo and Alexandria, canals are being filled or tunnelled (e.g., al-Zumur Canal in western Cairo, and the potential redevelopment of al-Mahmudiya Canal in Alexandria). These border transformations influence the relationship between formal and informal areas, changing the nature of crossings and the activities taking place around them.

POLICY-ORIENTED LESSONS LEARNED CONCERNING BORDERS

Opportunities   Infrastructural lines such as railways and roadways tend to be more stable as borders than waterways, which can be filled or tunnelled and rendered obsolete. In many cases, waterways are converted into infrastructural lines, thus transforming from one type of border to another, rather than being utilized for service or green corridors. Topography has proven to be the most uncompromising type of border, only bypassed by the construction of stairways and ramps. Topographic edges can nonetheless offer rare opportunities for city views and potential recreational sites above the city smog.

Risks and challenges   Some borders pose a security risk when crossing (e.g., accidents have been caused by the train passing through the border to Ard al-Liwa in Cairo, or at crossings on the al-Mahmudiya Canal in Alexandria). Topographic borders often pose the biggest risks; for example, in the case of a rock collapse in al-Duwayqa in 2008, the result of informal development built along the cliff's edge without a proper drainage network or infrastructure.

Towards a successful policy   Policies need to take into consideration the physical aspects and environment of each border, and identify the best and safest ways to create crossings. Successful strategies may entail turning borders into zones of exchange and interface, by either increasing crossing points (and thus rendering borders more permeable), and/or turning urban corridors along these borders into development zones, including parks and greenways in highly dense districts, which would be accessible to both sides of the (former) borders.

On crossings

Crossings connect informal and formal zones, and themselves may have formal or informal origins. Informally built crossings may sometimes be upgraded by the government, utilizing more durable materials. Conversely, formal crossings are often followed by informal adaptations. Formally built pedestrian overpasses bridging railways, for example, are generally encroached upon by informal marketplaces on both ends, and sometimes along the crossings themselves.

The sheer size and complexity of infrastructures in Cairo and Alexandria contribute to the presence in both places of multi-junction crossings, which in turn structure the relationship between formal and informal areas. Comparatively, Minya's connections are simpler, due to the city's relative size and infrastructure network.

Infrastructure

Unlike the multi-nodal urban pattern of Cairo, Alexandria and Minya are characterized by linear urban developments, parallel to the sea and the Nile respectively. Crossings in both Alexandria and Minya tend to follow established traffic corridors built perpendicular to the waterfront, extending into the narrow street networks of informal areas. This is visible in Minya's infrastructure detailed in Figure 3.8.

Topography

Cairo and Minya share the eastern hills as borders and limits to urban expansion. In the Muqattam Hills and their extended plateaus in Cairo, a number of stairways connect the planned districts below to informal housing on top. In Minya, a planned suburb has been developed beyond the eastern hills, connecting to the city core (which is both formal and informal) through a main artery. Alexandria has no significant topographical borders dividing informal and formal areas.

Waterways

Comparisons of waterway crossings in the three cities of Cairo, Alexandria, and Minya highlight the differences between Minya's largely rural economy on agricultural land, and Cairo and Alexandria's industrial complexes. Crossing al-Ibrahimiya Canal in Minya are flows of rural products, as well as individuals seeking access to services lacking in the informal peri-urban area. Alexandria has a wide variety of crossings, including bridges for pedestrians and vehicles, as well as informal ferry crossings. In Cairo, most waterway canals within the urban agglomeration have been filled and transformed into traffic arteries.

POLICY-ORIENTED LESSONS LEARNED CONCERNING CROSSINGS

Opportunities
- Adapted to the flow of goods and people: a crossing that acts as a major node is one that accommodates dense flows and welcomes a wide array of activities and services. An example is Ghamra Station in Cairo, which accommodates kiosks, informal commercial activities, seating areas, and flows of people.

- Adapted to needs: crossings must be adapted to the needs of residents, with ramps, escalators, and facilities for the elderly and people with disabilities. Crossings are more inclusive if they provide seating spaces, such as al-'Asafra crossing in Alexandria.
- Adapted to the context: the environment surrounding a crossing can have a significant impact. For instance, crossings in Minya, a city of predominantly agricultural industry, must include space for the transportation of cattle and large carts of fresh produce.

Risks and challenges
- Some crossings are unsafe for pedestrians. For instance, street-level crossings of railway lines and highways, such as the Ring Road in Cairo, are very dangerous and have repeatedly witnessed accidents.
- Some formally built crossings are not adapted to the needs of the residents, in which cases there have been informal responses to adapt them. This was the case in the renovation of the pedestrian crossing from Ard al-Liwa to al-Sudan Street, where authorities built a three-metre wide pedestrian bridge to replace the preexisting 30-metre wide street-level crossing. Ten times narrower than the previous crossing, the new bridge was subject to many stresses, and heavy traffic was a factor in the breakdown of the sole escalator leading to the pedestrian bridge.
- Old and deteriorating infrastructures are safety hazards.

Towards a successful policy   To ensure connectivity across borders, a comprehensive policy plan must ensure that multiple crossings are placed along the borders. Key connection nodes should be identified as a way to alleviate pressure on traffic. Furthermore, crossings should be adapted to the needs of residents and to the context in which they are built. Studies of flows should be undertaken to determine the appropriate size and structure of crossings. In sum, crossings should act as nodes for development opportunities, connecting both sides, rather than operating as bottlenecks hindering flows and limiting traffic.

On activities

Nodes are bustling with energetic social and economic activity due to their strategic locations at the intersection of formal and informal neighbourhoods (Figure 3.9). Our field research identified several categories of activities at these formal-informal intersections.

Informal markets

Informal markets are often located near crossings and transportation hubs, due to the flow of pedestrians. They may be semipermanent (booths, kiosks, or stands) or mobile and easily disassembled, and may be arranged in a linear fashion along the street, or in marketplace agglomerations. Markets vary in type, selling a range of products, including fresh produce, accessories, clothing, and more.

Transportation hubs

Transportation hubs at the intersection of formal and informal areas are typically organized informally, with rules set and enforced by individuals who mitigate disputes. These hubs act as transfer points between informal and formal areas, which include differing modes of transport. For example, as one moves from informal to formal areas, the number of tuktuks decreases, as they are illegal and not adapted to wide roads and highways.

Municipal services

Due to the absence of municipal services in informal areas, nodes act as the first point of service provision accessible to residents of informal areas, with official services such as police checkpoints, post offices, and ATMs located in these areas. The land surrounding public infrastructure lines such as highways, railways, canals, electrical lines, and oil and gas pipelines, is reserved for maintenance or possible expansion. Therefore, a legal buffer zone is created around these major infrastructure lines, which is used for public services, while it is simultaneously encroached upon by informal activities.

Entertainment services

As critical sites of interaction, crossings are prime locations for entertainment services such as Ferris wheels, amusement parks, and games for children. Entertainment services may be built on private land in a deliberate effort to prevent alternative uses by people, or as temporary installations on public land during seasonal festivities and celebrations.

Waste disposal

Municipal dumpster pickup points are often located in the interfaces between formal and informal areas. When dumpsters are absent or removed, these sites can accumulate waste.

POLICY-ORIENTED LESSONS LEARNED CONCERNING ACTIVITIES

Opportunities Nodes act as centres for the exchange of goods and services and are sites of formal and informal transport and entertainment facilities. The activities concentrated around nodes allow residents from underserved informal areas to access needed services and goods.

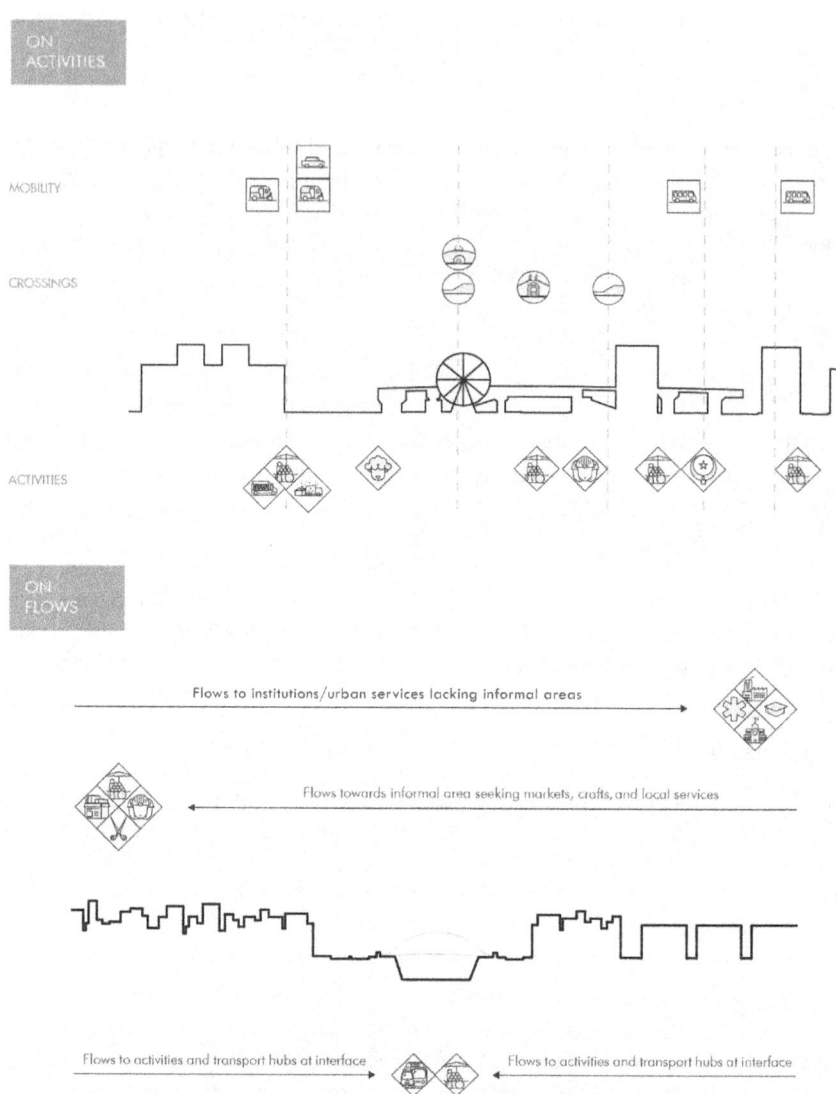

Figure 3.9 Activities and Flows
Source: CLUSTER, 2018

Risks and challenges   The interface along railways and similar borders risk being turned into waste disposal areas, contributing to pollution, and raising questions of security for children. Another challenge presented by these sites is increased traffic congestion, if activities are not properly managed.

Towards a successful policy   Considering each node as a planning and development package can foster linkages and flows around traffic hubs. Such urban interventions at the node scale can act as a form of urban acupuncture, transforming
sites of exclusion into opportunities for integration.

On flows

Flows trace the movement of residents between informal and formal areas, highlighting the social and economic interconnections between these areas (Figure 3.9). Our field research identified three types of flows: goods, labour, and
capital.

Goods

In the movement from informal to formal areas, the flow of raw materials and
fresh produce is typical, along with manufactured products such as wood, met-
alwork, and clothing. Raw materials may also be sent from formal areas to be
manufactured in informal areas, then sold to the formal sector, as exemplified in
the supply chain for small workshops in the furniture industry in Ard al-Liwa.
Conversely, manufactured industrial goods such as air conditioners, cars, and
pharmaceutical products move from formal to informal areas.

Labour

Most jobs in informal areas are held by neighbourhood residents. Some workers
in informal areas do not work in the informal sector, instead finding employment
in the formal service economy (such as in domestic services), while others work in
universities, government, schools, hospitals, and so on. Examining the reverse
flow, we find workers from health clinics, municipal services, or religious institutions moving from the formal to informal sector.

Capital

Informal to formal flows of capital occur through investment in formal educational and health institutions, or through capital used to purchase manufactured
goods. Formal to informal flows occurs through revenue of labour in the formal
market, capital to purchase goods and services in informal areas, capital invested
in the construction industry and real-estate economy, and capital invested in
infrastructure building and urban services. Investment from government (through
different ministries, such as the Ministry of Health and Education, Local Development, and Social Solidarity) and international agencies (e.g., German International Development Agency GIZ, AFD, UN-Habitat, and the World Bank)
provide services for low-income residents, and also contribute to flows of capital
entering the informal sector.

POLICY-ORIENTED LESSONS LEARNED CONCERNING FLOWS

Opportunities   Based on a comparison of flows, we can identify opportunities to facilitate movement between zones that are conducive to the integration of informal and formal areas. Flows from informal to formal areas are more frequent than the reverse, as there are essential services, such as administrative and educational services, as well as job opportunities, that can only be accessed in formal zones. Flows vary in relation to activities in surrounding areas. For instance, in Minya, flows of goods from peri-urban informal areas to formal areas contain a concentration of agricultural products, such as fresh produce. In Alexandria's industrial areas, flows include raw materials such as wood or metal. In informal areas where garbage is recycled, such as Manshiyat Nasir and Ard al-Liwa in Cairo, there is a flow of domestic waste from formal to informal areas. This material is then recycled and redistributed.

Risks and challenges   Overemphasizing the directionality of certain flows may perpetuate a division between labour and service zones. Further, while permeability may be posited as a desirable urban quality, the spillover of activities into areas for which these undertakings are not zoned may result in undesirable tensions and conflicts. Further, one-directional flow from informal to informal areas indicates a draining of resources that might otherwise be potentially invested in local development.

Towards a successful policy   An integrated policy not only entails improving physical connectivity across borders, but also improving the distribution of services within neighbourhoods. The two-way movement of flows between informal and formal areas should be leveraged to promote the interdependence of these city sectors. Borders should be made more porous and crossings more efficient to promote flows of goods as well as services. Services (e.g., municipal, health, and financial) should be distributed across all zones to promote equal opportunity and access.

Conclusion and reflections

This research seeks to challenge an understanding of the city as divided along informal and formal lines, and to provide policy recommendations that promote a vision of an integrated city. Attempting to recontextualize informality in relation to the formal, we seek to understand the interconnections between informal and formal urban areas (Figure 3.10).

We utilized the variables of borders, crossings, activities, and flows to compare and highlight similarities and differences between the three cities, and to illuminate larger questions around how to challenge the perception of a dualistic city; how to promote integrated urban policy; and how this comparative framework can be extended for use in other African cities.

The boundaries between the formal and informal are blurred around central crossing nodes.

The formal and informal are interconnected.

The urban experience from the formal and informal reflects continuity and complexity rather than division and contrast.

Figure 3.10 Reflections on the Formal-Informal Interface

Source: CLUSTER, 2018

Employing different levels of analysis to examine the formal-informal interface in the context of Cairo, Alexandria, and Minya, our major findings can be summarized as:

- Informal processes are both diverse and intrinsic to the expansion of urban centres in the global South.
- Borders shape and continue to segregate the urban fabric in many ways, but they are also shaped and mediated by crossings. That is, where crossings meet borders, the formal-informal interface itself becomes a central node, where generative activities and sites such as marketplaces, kiosks, transportation hubs, and meeting places are likely to be found, and where flows of capital, labour, and goods take place.
- Despite the non-dualistic nature of this interface, governments and municipalities continue to adopt policies that treat formal and informal spaces and activities as if they were distinct parts of different cities.

Towards challenging the dualistic city

Throughout this chapter we have attempted to highlight elements that constitute and define the formal-informal interface. In the following section we propose three key concepts to frame this interface as a way to understand the city and challenge a dualistic perception.

1 The boundaries between the formal and informal blur around central crossing nodes

The connection between formal and informal is amplified at key nodes, where major borders intersect with crossings. In all three cities, crossings that intersect compound layers of infrastructural and/or natural borders represent hyperjunctures, where informal activities thrive, and economic opportunities are created (e.g., the Ghamra Station in Cairo or downtown Minya Bridge).

Such crossings are often key nodes in the multimodal transportation system, including everything from tuktuk services to microbuses, public buses to metro lines. Within these spaces we see stands and kiosks established to sell fresh produce, manufactured goods, personal services, and much more. Also, emergent here is their relevance as social spaces, often providing entertainment for families and children.

2 The formal and informal are interconnected

As seen in Cairo, Alexandria, and Minya, formal and informal areas exist in contrast to each other, but also as intertwined patchworks, where borders can be hard to define. The formal and informal are interconnected as a result of different processes, including:

- The juxtaposition of contrasting layers of urbanization, such as industrial installations, high-end development projects, state-owned developments,

public housing, and informal development. Together these layers create a complex matrix of housing types that can coexist within a single area.
- The tendency of informal developments to encroach upon formal structures (such as public housing in Minya, industrial buildings in Alexandria, or historical areas in the south of Cairo), which in turn adapt to the informal.
- Formal urban development expanding to engulf rural settlements, in what used to be the outskirts of the city, rendering those settlements as informal enclaves, as is especially visible in Minya.
- The fragmented nature of formal planning encourages informal development in the interstices between formal developments, as seen in the unplanned spaces between state-owned lands and military barracks in northeast Cairo.

Finally, the formal-informal distinction is not only spatially blurred, but also economically and socially interconnected through flows of capital and labour. The informal economy's impact is felt throughout all three cities, and to varying degrees at all scales, particularly around crossings.

3 The urban experience from both the formal and informal reflects continuity and complexity rather than division and contrast

The journey between the formal and informal parts of these three cities can be characterized by continuity and complexity. We argue that residents' lived urban experience cuts across notions of separation produced by the spatial borders attempting to delineate formal and informal areas.

As depicted in CLUSTER's collage (Figure 3.11) and animated video 'Objects in the Mirror are Closer than They Appear',[17] which both depict the typical daily commute from the informal periphery to Cairo's formal city core, the transition from the informal to the formal is marked by common elements, such as the presence of street vendors, informal fruit and vegetable stands, and vendors in the metro. The video also highlights the existence of informal practices within the heart of the formal city, emphasizing the theme of continuity over contrast. Illustrating the interface connecting formal and informal areas, the animation seeks to challenge perceived distinctions between the two, highlighting instead their interconnected nature.

Towards an integrated urban policy

An integrated urban policy that enhances the permeability of borders, if well-implemented, could help overcome city fragmentation. It could also serve to improve equality and spatial inclusion (Mohamed et al., 2014) by countering the social segregation wrought by urban expansion that has cut off peripheral neighbourhoods from city networks (Nagati & Stryker, 2013).

To mend this fragmentation, we propose authorities adopt policies that enhance the permeability of borders at the formal-informal interface. By fostering connections instead of separations, we submit, a wider ripple effect may positively

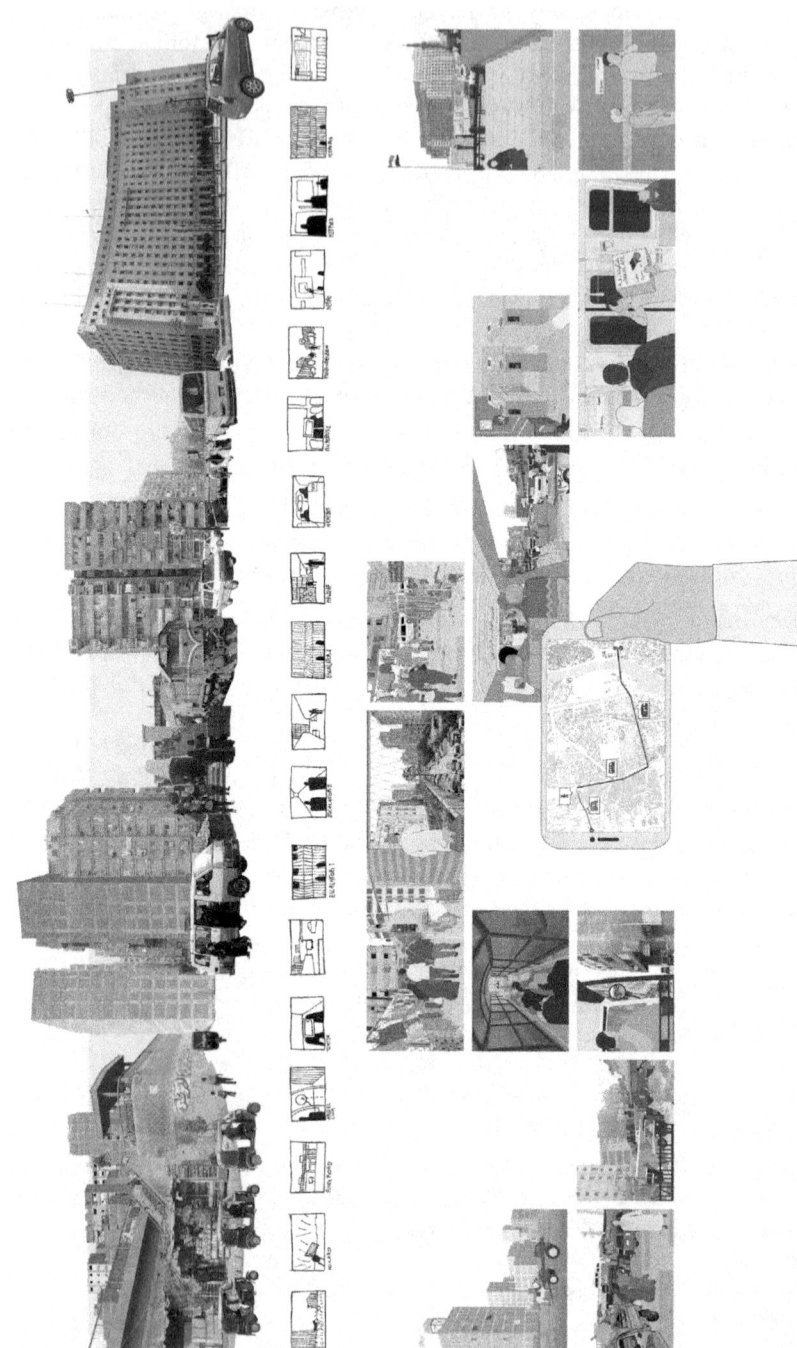

Figure 3.11 Urban Experience Across the Formal-Informal Interface

Source: CLUSTER, 2018

influence the urban fabric of adjacent neighbourhoods. We argue for an integrative policy that builds upon relationships between informal and formal neighbourhoods, and addresses the current territorial disparities.

Three main principles of proposed policy changes are as follows:

1 Revise district boundaries to include both formal and informal areas

Current development plans rarely consider informal areas in relation to surrounding neighbourhoods, thus reinforcing the divide between formal and informal areas. Instead, urban works should be surveyed and planned across a wider geographic area that intentionally includes both planned and unplanned areas, ensuring an equal distribution of services throughout. These new inclusive boundaries should be carefully accounted for when collecting census district data, to ensure that skewed data and misrepresentations do not occur.

2 Increase the porosity of borders between informal and formal areas

This study found that borders represent critical connection points that can foster movement of people and flows through the construction of crossings and development of infrastructure. As such, policy development should treat borders as areas of opportunity to link planned and unplanned areas.

3 Identify nodes as key points of urban interventions

The development of nodes as sites for urban acupuncture could positively impact both informal and formal areas. CLUSTER has piloted such development efforts, beginning in 2012 with our public-participatory proposal for a community park in the informal neighbourhood of Ard al-Liwa, located near a crossing, to the formal neighbourhood al-Muhandisin. This project is organized around lateral connections between the formal and informal sides, aiming to restructure the relationship from one of marginalization and dependency to one of integration and interdependence. Such pilot interventions at these nodes could be scaled-up to develop integrated urban planning visions (Nagati & Elgendy, 2013).

Over the years, a number of CLUSTER's design projects and pedagogical programmes have focused on the interface between formal apparatuses and informal practices, including the Urban Solid Waste workshop held in 2012, the Ard al-Liwa Community Park 2012–15, the Ard al-Liwa Youth Centre design proposal in 2018, and CLUSTER's ALFABRIKA Creative Lab, opened in 2019. ALFABRIKA brings students and young designers together with local craftsmen through an exchange between design ideas and new technologies, on the one hand, and grounded practice and apprenticeship, on the other. ALFABRIKA acts as an inclusive space that fosters sustainable solutions, while supporting young designers, students, local craftspeople, and creative industries, through workshops, exchange, production, and exhibitions.[18]

Further, CLUSTER has undertaken extended pedagogical engagements in informal areas, such as *Housing Cairo: The Informal Response*, a collaboration led by MAS Urban Design ETH Zurich, which set new precedents to engage informality on its own terms (Angélil et al., 2016). Acknowledging the value of creative informal solutions, CLUSTER's extended work on learning from informality has sought to decode the seemingly 'spontaneous' urbanism in Cairo, and develop tools to contribute to improving living standards in informal neighbourhoods without disrupting their ecosystems. This approach must be viewed against the state's approach of demonizing, demolition, relocation, and replanning.

Towards a comparative framework between African cities

This study further seeks to lay the groundwork towards a framework for comparative urban research across African cities. Such a framework could serve as an entry point to confront, compare, and bring forth the particular challenges that emerge in informal areas, while avoiding the traps of localism and cultural relativism.

The study and framework also offer a practical step towards changing perceptions of urban informality, calling for the inclusion of informal areas as a focus of urban policy. Most importantly, learning from the comparative experience of African metropolises, it seeks to inform alternative policies to better use the formal-informal interface as a key entry point to advance urban integration.

In the context of the African Urban Research Initiative (AURI), our proposed next step is to further develop the analytical tools and comparative methods set out here, through a joint research collaboration between the cities of Lusaka (Zambia), Ouagadougou (Burkina Faso), Cairo, Alexandria, and Minya (Egypt), and Dar es Salaam (Tanzania).

The proposed research has three main goals:

1   To study the specificities of the question of the formal-informal interface in different African cities and regions, in order to identify patterns and propose local solutions.
2   To challenge the global discourse of the New Urban Agenda, by offering local codes and performance-based standards in an attempt to localize Sustainable Development Goals and Millennium Development Goals.
3   To establish a framework for further comparative research by developing a clear methodology and procedure through joint workshops, an exchange of tools and experiences, and the co-production of knowledge.

To this end, a joint research endeavour has been initiated with researchers from the cities of Cairo, Dar es Salaam, Lusaka, and Ouagadougou, and a series of workshops undertaken. A preliminary workshop in Dar es Salaam in October 2018 aimed to exchange research methodologies and set the roadmap for a comparative framework to illustrate the formal-informal processes beyond their binary definitions. A second workshop in Lusaka in May 2019 included relevant stakeholders and policymakers, and sought to establish a common research framework.

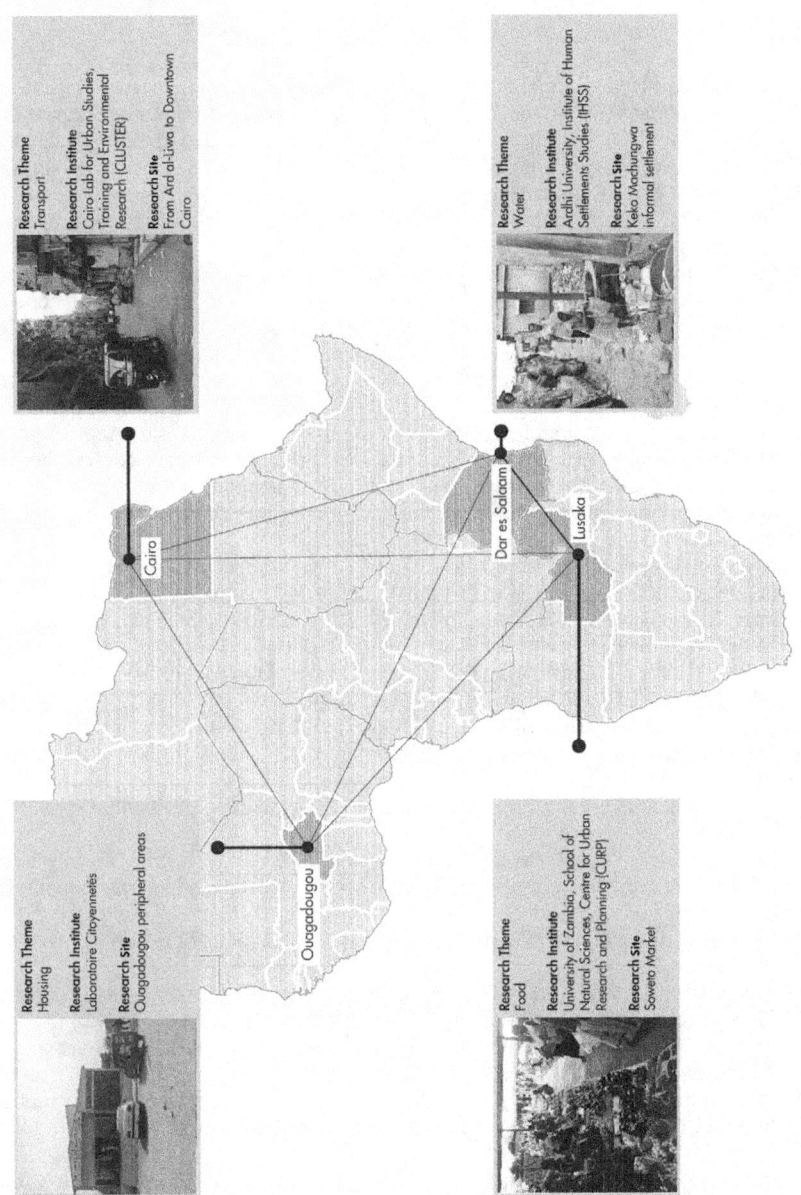

Figure 3.12 Formal-Informal Interface in Four African Cities

Source: CLUSTER, 2018

In December 2019, a third workshop in Cairo focused on the development of a joint research paper, consolidating the research teams' comparative findings on the formal-informal interface. (Figure 3.12).

Notes

1 CLUSTER Principals: Omar Nagati and Beth Stryker. Research team: Hanaa Gad Mahmoud, Tamer Aly, Marina El-Najjar, Mayar Salama, Martina AbuAlam, Mayar El-Sayed, Amin El-Didi, Martha Meijer, Laura Meynier, Katrine Mandrup Bach, Rana ElRashidy, Rana Gharib, Ahmad Salah, Reem Khorshid, Nour Tarek, Mariam Mahdally, Farah Wahby, Raghda Hatem, and Mary Sprague.
2 Examples include UN-Habitat. (2003). *The challenge of slums: global report on human settlements 2003*. London: Earthscan; UN-Habitat (2016). Urbanization and development: emerging futures. In *World cities report 2016*. New York: United Nations; Susan Eckstein (1990). Urbanization revisited: inner-city slum of hope and squatter settlement of despair. *World Development* 18(2), pp. 165–181; Lisa Peattie & Jose A. Aldrete-Haas (1981). 'Marginal' settlements in developing countries: research, advocacy of policy, and evolution of programs. *Annual Review of Sociology*, 7(1), pp. 157–175.
3 While Kafr 'Ashri is not an informal area, but rather a historic residential neighbourhood surrounded by large industrial and institutional hubs, the stark contrast between its urban fabric and street network and that of its surroundings marks its inclusion in this comparison relevant, despite the historical roots of its evolution and thus definition.
4 Total population of the Greater Cairo Region (World Population Review, 2018).
5 Total population of Alexandria in 2016 (Population2017.com).
6 Estimated population in 2017 based on the 2012 population census with 1.66% growth per year (Populationcity.com).
7 Density of Cairo, not considering the Greater Cairo Region (CAPMAS, 2017).
8 Population per sq. km. (Alexandria Fact Sheet, 2013).
9 Density based on our calculations: area (11km2)/total population.
10 Informal residential areas represent 52.7 percent of Greater Cairo's residential areas (Soliman, 2002).
11 Informal residential areas represent 50 percent of Alexandria's residential areas (Soliman, 2002).
12 In the absence of available data, the percentage of informal residential areas was estimated by calculating the area of informal neighbourhoods on the land use map, divided by the total area of Minya city.
13 In 2009, 60% of the Greater Cairo population were inhabitants of informal areas (Kipper & Fischer, 2009).
14 The population of the informal housing areas is estimated at over 1,584,000 people, which represents 40% of the total population of the city (Barthel et al., n.d.).
15 Percentage of population of Minya living in informal areas (Ministry of Housing, Utilities and Urban Communities, 2006).
16 As in the famous case of a rockslide in September 2008 in Duwayqa, an informal area to the east of Cairo, where the official number of casualties was estimated to be 119 dead and 55 injured.
17 The video is available on CLUSTER Cairo's YouTube channel. www.youtube.com/watch?v=iytq_pTCOe4
18 Urban Solid Waste workshop was a workshop in collaboration with Basurama, local architects, urban artists, and the *zabbalin* (traditional trash collecting community) exploring the structural forms available in garbage, and their potential reuse towards an engagement within local Cairo communities. Ard al-Liwa Youth Centre is a design

proposal for the local youth centre located at the edge Ard al-Liwa and one of its vehicular and pedestrian connections to al-Muhandessin. ALFABRIKA is a fabrication lab located in Ard al-Liwa, created for the purpose of bridging the gap between formal design practice and local craftsmanship through multiple programmes and workshops.

References

Alexandria Fact Sheet. (2013). *SUP Alex 2032*, vol. 1. Cited in: Barthel, P.A., Davidson, L. & Sudarskis, M. (n.d.). *Alexandria: regenerating the city: a contribution based on AFD experiences*. Paris: Agence Française de Développement (AFD). Retrieved: https://inta-aivn.org/images/cc/Transmed/AlexandriaContribution.pdf

Al Masalla. (2010). Alexandria attracts 3 million visitors annually. *Al Masalla-Official Tourism* [online]. Retrieved: http://almasalla.travel/alexandria-attracts-3-million-visitors-annually/ [Accessed on 1 April 2018]

AlSayyad, N. (2004). Urban informality as a 'new' way of life. In: Roy, A. & AlSayyad, N. (Eds.), *Urban informality: transnational perspectives from the Middle East, Latin America, and South Asia*. Lanham: Lexington Books, p. 8.

Angélil, M., Malterre-Barthes, C. & Cluster and Something Fantastic. (2016). *Housing Cairo: the informal response*. Berlin: Ruby Press.

Barthel, P.A., Davidson, L. & Sudarskis, M. (n.d.). *Alexandria: regenerating the city: a contribution based on AFD experiences*. Paris: Agence Française de Développement (AFD). Retrieved: https://inta-aivn.org/images/cc/Transmed/AlexandriaContribution.pdf

CAPMAS Central Agency for Public Mobilization and Statistics. (2017). *Statistical yearbook 2017*. Cairo: CAPMAS.

Center for Sustainable Development. (2013). *Input for Egypt's strategy for dealing with slums*. Cairo: American University in Cairo.

CLUSTER. (2018). *Formal-informal interface: Comparative analysis between three Egyptian cities*. Cairo: CLUSTER. Unpublished report.

Euromonitor. (2017). *Cairo city review* [online]. Retrieved: www.euromonitor.com/cairo-city-review/report [Accessed on 10 October 2018]

Evin, A. (Ed.). (1985). *The expanding metropolis: coping with the urban growth of Cairo*. Singapore: Concept Media, Aga Khan Award for Architecture.

Hasan, A. (1989). *Technical review 1989 of East Whadat upgrading program*. Aga Kahn Architectural Award, pp. 1–21. Retrieved: https://www.akdn.org/project/architecture-and-plurality

Hassan, G.F. (2012). Regeneration as an approach for the development of informal settlements in Cairo metropolitan. *Alexandria Engineering Journal*, 51(3), pp. 229–239.

Khadr, Z. & Bulbul, L. (2011). *Egyptian red crescent in Zeinhum: impact assessment of comprehensive community development model for slums upgrading*. Cairo: Social Research Center, The American University in Cairo.

Khalifa, M. (2011). Redefining slums in Egypt: unplanned versus unsafe areas. *Habitat International*, 35(1), pp. 40–49. DOI: https://doi.org/10.1016/j.habitatint.2010.03.004

Kipper, R. & Fischer, M. (Eds.). (2009). *Cairo's informal areas between urban challenges and hidden potentials*. Cairo: GTZ Egypt and Participatory Development Programme in Urban Areas.

Ministry of Housing, Utilities and Urban Communities. (2006). *Arab republic Egypt national report: third united nation conference on housing and sustainable urban development (HABITAT III)*. Cairo: Ministry of Housing. Retrieved: http://Habitat3.Org/Wp-Content/Uploads/Egypt-Final-In-English.Compressed-1.Pdf

Mkandawire, T. & Soludo, C. (1999). *Our continent, our future: African perspectives on structural adjustment*. Dakar, Senegal: Council for the Development of Social Science. Retrieved: www.idrc.ca/sites/default/files/openebooks/855-4/index.html

Mohamed, A.A., Van Nes, A., Salheen, M.A., Khalifa, M.A. & Hamhaber, J. (2014 December 14–16). Understanding urban segregation in Cairo: the social and spatial logic of a fragmented city. In: *Smart, sustainable and healthy cities: proceedings of the 1st international conference of the cib Middle East and North Africa research network*. Abu Dhabi: CIB Middle East and North Africa Research Network.

Nagati, O. & Elgendy, N. (2013). Ard al-Liwa park project: towards a new urban order and mode of professional practice. *Planum: The Journal of Urbanism*, 1(26), pp. 64–74. Retrieved: https://issuu.com/planumnet/docs/ctbt_planum_n.26-2013_section_4

Nagati, O. & Stryker, B. (2013). *Archiving the city in flux: Cairo's shifting landscape since the January 25th revolution*. Cairo: CLUSTER.

Nassar, D.M. & Elsayed, H.G. (2018). From informal settlements to sustainable communities. *Alexandria Engineering Journal*, 57(4), 2367–2376. DOI: https://doi.org/10.1016/j.aej.2017.09.004

Payne, G. (2005). Getting ahead of the game: a twin-track approach to improving existing slums and reducing the need for future slums. *Environment and Urbanization*, 17(1), pp. 135–46.

Piffero, E. (2009). Beyond rules and regulations: the growth of informal Cairo. In: Kipper, R. & Fischer, M. (Eds.), *Cairo's informal areas between urban challenges and hidden potentials*. Cairo: GTZ Egypt and Participatory Development Programme in Urban Areas, pp. 21–27.

Population of Alexandria. (2017 February 27). *Population of 2017.com* [online]. Retrieved: http://web.archive.org/web/20171008072720/http://populationof2017.com/population-of-alexandria-2017.html [Accessed on 10 October 2018]

Populationcity.com. (n.d.). Retrieved: https://web.archive.org/web/2019*/populationcity.com [Accessed on 10 October 2018]

Séjourné, M. (2009). The history of informal settlements. In: Kipper, R. & Fischer, M. (Eds.), *Cairo's informal areas between urban challenges and hidden potentials*. Cairo: GTZ Egypt and Participatory Development Programme in Urban Areas (PDP), pp. 17–19.

Shoup, J. (2017). *The Nile: an encyclopaedia of geography, history, and culture*. Santa Barbara, CA: ABC-CLIO, p. 101.

Simone, A. (2002). The dilemmas of informality. In: Parnell, S. & Pieterse, E. (Eds.), *Democratising local government: the South African experiment*. Landsdowne: University of Cape Town Press, p. 294.

Sims, D. (2010). *Understanding Cairo: the logic of a city out of control*. Cairo and New York: The American University in Cairo Press.

Soliman, A. (2002). Typology of informal housing in Egyptian cities: taking account of diversity. *International Development Planning Review*, 24(2), pp. 177–201.

Soliman, A. (2004). Tilting at sphinxes: locating urban informality in Egyptian cities. In: Roy, A. & AlSayyad, N. (Eds.), *Urban informality: transnational perspectives from the Middle East, Latin America, and South Asia*. Lanham: Lexington Books, pp. 171–208.

Soliman, A. (2007). *Urban informality in Egyptian cities: coping with diversity*. Fourth Urban Research Symposium. Retrieved: www.scribd.com/document/116736161/Soliman-Urban-Informality

Tadamun. (2015). *Adequate housing approach as a targeting tool for local development*. Retrieved: www.tadamun.co/adequate-housing-approach-targeting-tool-local-development/?lang=en [Accessed on 31 December 2015]

Tadamun. (2016). *Coming up short: Egyptian government approaches to informal areas.* Retrieved: www.tadamun.co/coming-short-government-approaches-informal-areas/? lang=en [Accessed on 10 October 2018]

University College London (UCL). (2003). *Understanding slums: case studies for the global report on human settlements.* London: University College London, Development Planning Unit.

UN-Habitat. (2010). *State of the world's cities: bridging the urban divide.* Nairobi: United Nations Human Settlements Programme.

Viquez Abarca, R. & Hernandez Garcia, J. (2017). Public space, between regulations and informality: a tale of two cities, San José (Costa Rica) and Bogotá (Colombia). *Revista Rupturas*, 7(1), pp. 75–87.

World Population Review. (2018). *Egypt population* [online]. Retrieved: http://worldpopu lationreview.com/countries/egypt-population/ [Accessed on 10 October 2018]

4 Dialogues on informality

Land sharing as a sustainable approach to tenure security in Kiandutu informal settlement in Thika town, Kenya

Peter Ngau and Philip Olale

Introduction

Lack of access to land and poorly defined tenure rights continue to characterize informality in urban areas in Africa. In most African countries, conventional land administration systems (land titling and individual ownership) that are inappropriate for their tenure context and unsustainable financially or in terms of available capacity remain dominant (Clarke, 2009). As a result, the overwhelming majority of African urban land transactions takes place in informal land markets (UN-Habitat, 2010).

In spite of a growing acknowledgement of the importance of secure land tenure, in practice, establishing land rights in informal settlements often is a protracted engagement that pits the government against landowner(s) and slum dwellers. In the ensuing contestations, the government (at either national or local level) must also contend with its responsibility to maintain order and safety by exercising policing power and control over planned developments. The result is that the government finds itself in a stalemated position where it is unable to fully support the claims of either landowners or slum dwellers. Consequently, landowners cannot evict slum dwellers and proceed with development plans, while slum dwellers – facing the omnipresent threat of eviction – remain limited in their ability to invest in housing improvement initiatives.

However, a growing emphasis on participatory and inclusive approaches targeting housing, infrastructure services, community assets, and social capital may offer new options in contemporary development discourse. The shift is captured both in theoretical works on urban planning (Friedmann, 1987; Healey, 2006; Watson, 2002) as well as more recently in the global development frameworks and conventions adopted since 2015. For instance, both the 17 Sustainable Development Goals (SDGs) of Agenda 2030 – which include stand-alone goals on inequality (SDG 10), justice (SDG 16), and inclusive, safe, resilient, and sustainable cities and human settlements (SDG 11) – and the subsequently adopted New Urban Agenda were formulated through extensive processes of consultation (Rudd et al., 2018).

These approaches move planning from a narrow, technical, and procedural focus, towards rights-based and collaborative models for achieving common purposes in the shared spaces of our fragmented societies. Moreover, while previous develop-ment agendas such as the Millennium Development Goals did not mention land directly, the SDGs include six goals with a significant land component, ranging from goals on poverty (SDG 1), hunger (SDG 2), gender equity (SDG 5), and life on land (SDG 15), in addition to SDGs 11 and 16 mentioned earlier. However, without good land governance and well-functioning land administration systems in place, these goals will remain only that (Enemark, 2016, pp. 3–4).

Focusing on Kiandutu informal settlement in the town of Thika, Kenya, this chapter presents the findings of a co-production approach to seeking solutions for improving tenure security and land governance. Building on a long-standing col-laboration with stakeholders in the Municipality of Thika, the Centre for Urban Research Innovations (CURI) at the University of Nairobi organized a 'CityLab' to explore the benefits and challenges to land sharing as a sustainable approach to tenure security for urban slum dwellers occupying public land.

Context

The urban land challenge in Africa

The majority of urban dwellers in Africa lack secure access to land. This absence does not just have an impact on housing conditions, but also on people's levels of poverty and access to services and health, all of which are compounded by the effects of rapid urbanization and climate change. Land challenges for informal dwellers manifest in many ways – including restricted access to land, inequalities in landownership, and insecurity of tenure – and have resulted in environmental, social, economic, and political problems, including deterioration of land qual-ity, squatting and landlessness, disinheritance of groups and individuals, urban squalor, and conflict (UN-Habitat, 2010).

Various scholars have argued for the need to improve tenure security for the urban poor so that they have sustainable access to land, and, in turn, incentives towards investment and improvement of their housing and living environment (Olale, 2015; Durand-Lasserve & Royston, 2002). Long considered an essential public good and basic foundation for development, land and shelter are widely seen as preconditions to securing basic living conditions and livelihood oppor-tunities, as well as a means of reducing poverty and gender inequality (Rakodi, 2014). Komjathy et al. (2001) define access to land as the right or opportunity to use, manage, or control land and its resources. 'Access' thus refers to the ability to use land and other natural resources, to control resources and transfer rights to the land, and to take advantage of other opportunities such as access to credit.

Scholars such as De Soto (2000) have argued that property rights play a key role in shaping economic decision-making and increasing productivity of those living in informal settlements. While some rights can be accessed without necessarily possessing formal landownership (e.g., the right to use, occupy, and develop/cultivate/produce, and the right to access basic services, including sanitation), key levers like formal credit can only be accessed with formal title as collateral.

Thus, enhancing tenure security for informal settlement residents is integral to a range of different policies and interventions, such as land titling programmes and urban upgrading, many of which are supported by extensive international funding (Buckley & Kalarickal, 2006).

However, practice shows that land tenure is a relative and contested concept. With different perceptions and understandings on the ground, and a range of actors and practices involved, policy interventions around land tenure have resulted in varied and unintended outcomes (Payne, 2002; Payne et al., 2009; Napier et al., 2013). Meanwhile, most African countries continue to adhere to conventional land administration systems, such as land titling and individual ownership, which are inappropriate to the African tenure context and unsustainable financially and in terms of capacity to administer (Clarke, 2009). Moreover, stagnancy in the management and administration of land remains a massive challenge facing African governments and cities today (Durand-Lasserve, 2004).

Resolving land rights in informal settlements is a protracted engagement that usually involves the government, landowner(s), and slum dwellers. In cases where informal settlements have arisen on private land, private landowners generally take the view that government must protect their legal rights, and assist in clearing slums so the landowners can use their land as they see fit. In many other cases, informal settlements have arisen on public or government-owned land. In both cases, slum dwellers variously argue that they have a claim to the land through prolonged habitation, that they have nowhere to go without losing their means of livelihood, that the law is unjust if so many must suffer so that a few may benefit, and that the government has both a social and constitutional responsibility to provide them with proper housing. Such claims illustrate the global shift towards rights-based approaches to development, which recognize de facto land access, occupation, and the use of urban space as matters of urban citizenship in the context of a 'right to the city' (Vogiazides, 2012).

While most African governments formally adhere to both legal and rights-based understandings of land tenure in their constitutional laws and urban policies, this often does not translate to practice. In best case scenarios, this leads to the continued growth of informal settlements. In the worst cases, governments opt for the eradication of slums, replacing them with planned housing developments (Huchzermeyer, 2011). In the ensuing contestations, governments often find themselves in the awkward position of being both the landowner and a supposedly neutral arbiter and protector of citizen's rights. Further, the government, at either national or local levels, also has a responsibility to maintain order and safety through planned development, where government exercises its police power/development control.

Arising from these conflicting rationalities, a dialogue-oriented approach is germane in offering pragmatic solutions to land governance, especially when it is clear that none of the parties is willing to surrender its claims or positions. This study provided such a dialogue-oriented approach to unlocking tenure security in Kiandutu informal settlement in Kenya, through an exploration of the concept of 'land sharing' in a local CityLab.

Tenure security in urban Kenya: the post-colonial challenge

Kenya has a population of 47.6 million persons based on 2019 population census data (KNBS, 2019). The previous census in 2009 showed the population at 38.6 million, an increase from 28.7 million in 1999, 21.4 million in 1989, and 15.3 million 1979 (GoK, 2009). The urban population was last estimated at 14.5 million, with an annual growth rate of 4.2% (KNBS, 2009).[1] Of Kenya's urban population, about 65% live in informal settlements (Olale & Opiyo, 2017). In Nairobi, the capital city, about 60% of the population lives in over 180 different informal settlements. This phenomenon of rapid urbanization facilitated by both natural factors (natural population growth within the urban areas) and exogenous factors (forced rural-urban migration or urban-urban migration due to a plethora of factors including poverty, joblessness, and conflict) has led to the contemporary growth of informal settlements in Kenya (Tacoli et al., 2015).

Increasing urban populations in Kenya continue to put pressure on infrastructure and other basic services such as housing, water, sanitation, and land. Unlike other basic services, however, land is a fixed asset, and therefore captive to its use (i.e., no longer available for any other use). This complexity particular to land increases the need for land management administration tools and policies whose creativity and sustainability can match the rapid rate of urbanization.

According to the Constitution of Kenya 2010, every person has the right to accessible and adequate housing, and a reasonable standard of sanitation. However, it has become increasingly difficult for the government to provide sufficient affordable housing units for the urban poor. Kenya Vision 2030[2] notes that the government is only able to meet 23% of the annual demand of 150,000 affordable housing units. The lack of appropriate and affordable housing has forced thousands into overcrowded and expanding informal settlements, and even left many homeless. Factors such as rapid population growth, stringent planning regulations, restrictive building standards, high costs of infrastructure, poverty, and perhaps most fundamentally, lack of affordable land, compound the problem.

Article 60 of Kenya's Constitution establishes equitable access to land as a principle in which land is held, used, and managed (GoK, 2010). Since the adoption of the 2010 Constitution, Kenya has further ratified several global development agreements, such as Agenda 2030 and the New Urban Agenda, and adopted a series of institutional and policy frameworks to implement these agendas in the field of housing and basic services, urban and human settlements infrastructure, land, urban and regional planning, urban economy, environmentally sustainable and resilient urban and human settlements, and urban governance (GoK, 2017).

Despite all this, lack of access to land and poorly defined tenure rights continue to characterize informality in Kenya's urban areas. While some 66% of the total urban population lives in informal settlements, conventional recognized systems like land titling and individual ownership only apply to just over a third of cases. This leaves the majority of Kenya's urban citizens to the uncertainties defining the informal land administration system. In fact, Kenya's National Land Policy[3] recognizes the absence of security of tenure and planning as the essence of 'informal', 'spontaneous', or 'squatter' settlements (GoK, 2009).

Kenya's current land question is rooted in its colonial history, and three distinct but interrelated processes that shaped land management provide important context (Sorrenson, 1967). The first process was the alienation and acquisition of land in preparation of the establishment of a colonial state. What followed was the imposition of English property law, with its support of title and private property rights in those alienated areas. Those processes gave rise to distinct but related sets of problems regarding access and control of land, thereby laying the basis for today's complex land matrix. In urban areas, this matrix is characterized by limited access to land, unsuitable tenure systems, and increasing illegal settlements in the form of slums. Meanwhile, those who can access titled land tenure use it as a store of wealth against which they leverage financial assistance such as loans, making tenure security a fundamental principle of housing rights advocacy in informal settlements, as well as legal protection against forced eviction, harassment, and other threats that symbolize rising urban inequalities (Syagga, 2011).

Defining land sharing

Land sharing is a negotiated agreement between landowners, developers, and land occupants, to partition and share a plot of land, even in the absence of legal tenure (Angel & Boonyabancha, 1988). The practice of land sharing first emerged in Bangkok in the context of a booming property market that led to intense conflicts between landowners and landholders (Rabé, 2010; Angel & Boonyabancha, 1988; Boonyabancha, 2005; D'Cruz et al., 2009).

Land sharing becomes a useful option between landlords and slum dwellers when the intentions of a landlord to repossess the land become clear to the resident, and the resident decides to resist or contest the imminent eviction or loss of the land they occupy (Angel & Boonyabancha, 1988). According to Parry (2015), land sharing is a compromise solution, whereby the owners of land that is encroached upon and the community that lives there collectively agree to split the land between them. Parry (2015) further elaborates that in this scenario, the community buys, leases, or receives one portion of the contested land for free, while the more commercially attractive part of the site is returned to the developer or owner. The notion of land sharing advanced by Parry (2015) is similar to that discussed by Rabé (2005), who notes that in Cambodia, land sharing also cedes the most commercially viable portion of the land to the landowner, with the remaining portions leased, sold, or given to land occupants for legal occupation.

Although the land-sharing option is not suitable for all cases of land-use conflict, it can be a flexible and successful strategy. Using this approach, the owner of land occupied by an informal settlement is encouraged to lease or sell part of the property to the occupants at a rate below market value, allowing the owner to recover and develop the remaining land. Parry (2015) also observes that the land-sharing approach catalyses occupants to take the initiative to considerably improve their settlements. In most cases of land sharing, the slum dwellers organize themselves into a viable organization, initiate negotiations with the landowner, and then share the land – allocating the prime parcels of land to the owner, and using the remaining land for their housing. The housing development that arises under this arrangement is generally more organized than in cases where land is occupied without engaging the residents or landowner (Srinivas, 2015).

Finally, land sharing offers part of a solution for a larger problem, in that land-sharing arrangements can serve as a step towards providing universal access to housing, while also creating an opportunity to remodel the city in a more participatory and inclusive way (Abott, 1996). However, to be successful, land sharing must be accompanied by reforms to regulate the land market, restrict land uses, allow higher building standards, and enable implementation of incremental development (Montressor, 2015).

The Kiandutu CityLab project

The Kiandutu CityLab is part of a larger research drive undertaken by the Centre for Urban Research Innovations (CURI), at the University of Nairobi in partnership with stakeholders in the Municipality of Thika, Kenya over the last eight years. The overall purpose of the larger project is to facilitate the consideration and adoption of policy strategies that can respond sustainably to the lack of affordable shelter and to land-access constraints faced by the urban poor. The collaboration, which goes back to 2011, has involved the community of the Kiandutu informal settlement, the NGO Muungano Support Trust (MuST), the Thika Municipality, and the University of Nairobi represented by CURI. The community living in Kiandutu are members of the Federation of Slum Dwellers in Kenya called *Muungano wa Wanavijiji*, while MuST is a member of Slum Dwellers International (SDI).

The collaboration emerged in 2011 with the Kiandutu community and MuST's mutual interest in the upgrading of the informal settlement through processes such as mobilization, enumeration, group savings, demonstration of housing improvement, and advocacy for tenure security. The Thika Municipality and County Government of Kiambu were also interested in improving urban public services such as water supply, sanitation, electricity, and solid waste management in Kiandutu. However, while the former Thika Municipality (pre-2013) and the first County Government of Kiambu (2013–2018) were positively engaged with the programme for slum upgrading and land tenure security in Kiandutu settlement, the current County Government of Kiambu (2018-present) has been hesitant to engage in the partnership for slum upgrading.

As a member of the Association of Africa Planning Schools (AAPS), CURI/DURP intends to transform urban planning education and practice in Africa by equipping upcoming urban planners with the relevant skills and methodology to address the challenges facing the African city. That is, using participatory community planning studios so that young planners (students) and community members can actively engage in problem solving and urban revitalization of informal settlements. The university team thus supports community mobilization and slum upgrading by deploying scientific and technical skills for mapping settlements and infrastructure services, conducting household surveys, and preparing layout plans for informal settlement upgrading.

From 2015–2016, with support from the Global Land Tools Network (GLTN) Urban CSO Cluster Project, CURI, working with partners SDI and AAPS, conducted a literature review and rapid survey on alternatives to land access in Kiandutu (Olale & Opiyo, 2017). Through rapid research, we gathered existing literature and secondary data from local SDI civil society partners. The survey report showed the status of the land and the available approaches towards land access in Kiandutu settlement. Using this data, we prepared a policy brief to advise the Kiandutu community on the various options it could leverage to access land and improve tenure security, which included land sharing. Prior to the report, the community had engaged in endless contestation over land tenure in an ad hoc manner with various stakeholders since 1969.

While the report represented the first structured basis for a discussion on sustainable tenure security, it also became clear that it was primarily based on existing policy and legal frameworks and discussions with Kiambu County (the custodians of the land). In other words, it lacked adequate input from the community members living in the informal settlement. As such, we saw the need for a dialogue-based participatory framework on land sharing, which would become the Kiandutu CityLab. The questions at the heart of the CityLab dialogue, and to which the bulk of this chapter is addressed, are:

- What are the prospects for land sharing in Kiandutu informal settlement?
- How do existing land-use systems and structures in Kiandutu informal settlement influence a land-sharing approach?
- What might an acceptable physical-planning model based on the principles of land sharing look like in terms of densification, mixed-use housing layout, housing reconstruction, infrastructure, and amenities provision?

Methodology

CityLabs have emerged as forums for practical learning that provide participants with hands-on understanding of urban challenges, especially from a spatial planning perspective. Scholl and Kemp (2016) argue that CityLabs may be used to generate ideas for city projects and to explore visions of sustainability, democracy, and devolution of public tasks and responsibilities. CityLabs can also be oriented towards actions such as idea-generation and evaluation, and/or to experiment with new forms of urban planning (Scholl & Kemp, 2016).

The Kiandutu CityLab commenced in November 2017 with a literature review, followed by community sensitization and stakeholder identification, which were complete by January 2018. While all partners attended the preparatory meetings at the CityLab's initial phase (through January 2018), the intensification of campaigns for the national, county, and local elections across the country caused county officials, politicians, and local administrators to withdraw from the joint stakeholder workshops, stating that 'the land question' was too emotive to engage in during a campaign period.

Nonetheless, a series of three CityLab workshops targeting Kiandutu informal settlement residents in Thika town were organized in March 2018 within Kiandutu settlement (at Muungano Hall). Workshop participants were chosen by gender and age, creating one workshop for women, one for youth, and one for men, each with 12 participants. The aim was to enable optimal engagement in a free atmosphere, and to better capture divergent and sometimes gender-specific tenure issues. Participants came from all the settlement's villages, and included individuals from the set criteria (i.e., structure owners/landlords, tenants, business operators, service providers, and community leaders).

The workshops all included two main sessions: a general discussion session and a planning session. During the general discussion session, participants were taken through various models of accessing tenure security, including resettlement, community land buying, adverse possession, and land sharing. The discussion was however centred on the land-sharing option, which was extensively explained to the participants, who were later solicited for their ideas and responses with regard to the land-sharing process and its applicability in Kiandutu settlement. The planning session mainly focused on the land-use planning aspects of the land-sharing process, including aspects of survey, densification, and housing layout/reconstruction. During this session, participants used a printed base map to show their preferred areas for settlement, to be issued back to the County Government.

The outputs from the workshops included an articulation of the stakeholders' ideas about land sharing, especially from a youth- and gender-based lens. The data were collected through note-taking and also recorded using a Dictaphone, and later transcribed and organized in themes based on the workshop discussion questions. The resultant data from the workshops were triangulated to arrive at common themes of argument from the three workshops.

The following sections provide background and historical context to the Kiandutu informal settlement, its land governance, and settlement characteristics, before turning to the outcomes of the CityLab workshops.

Background to Kiandutu informal settlement

With a total area of 110 acres, Kiandutu is the largest informal settlement in Thika town, from which it is located two kilometres to the southeast. It lies within Hospital ward, Thika Town Constituency, just off Garissa Road (A3). Administratively, Kiandutu falls under Kianjau Sub-Location of Thika Sub-County, Kiambu County (Figure 4.1).

Currently Kiandutu is made up of ten villages: Biashara, Centre Base, Kianjau, Mikinduri, Molo A, Molo B, Mosque, Mtatu A, Mtatu B, and Stage Wariah (Figure 4.2). Started as a milk depot in 1978, Biashara village later developed into a business hub for the settlement, and is the location of Kiandutu market. Kianjau

THIKA TOWN LOCATION CONTEXT

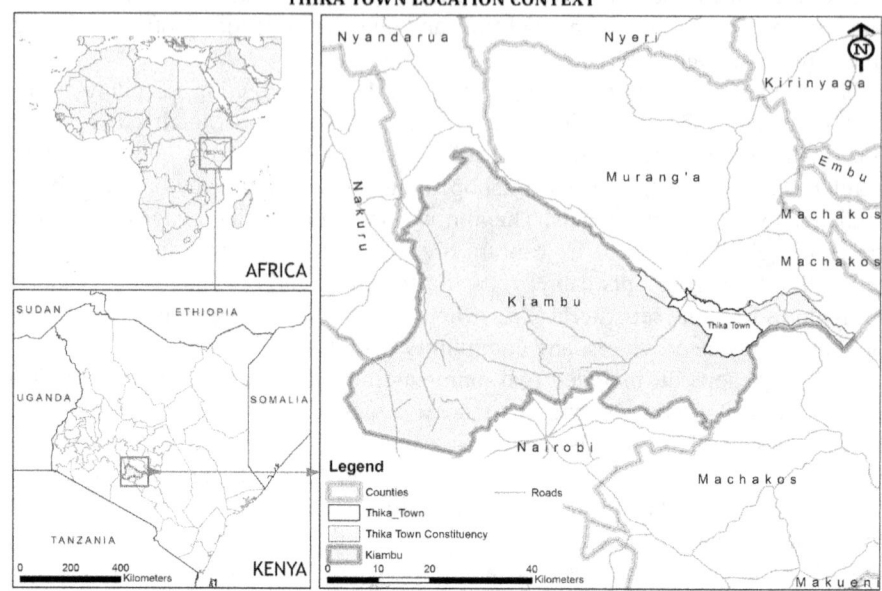

LOCATION CONTEXT OF KIANDUTU IN THIKA TOWN

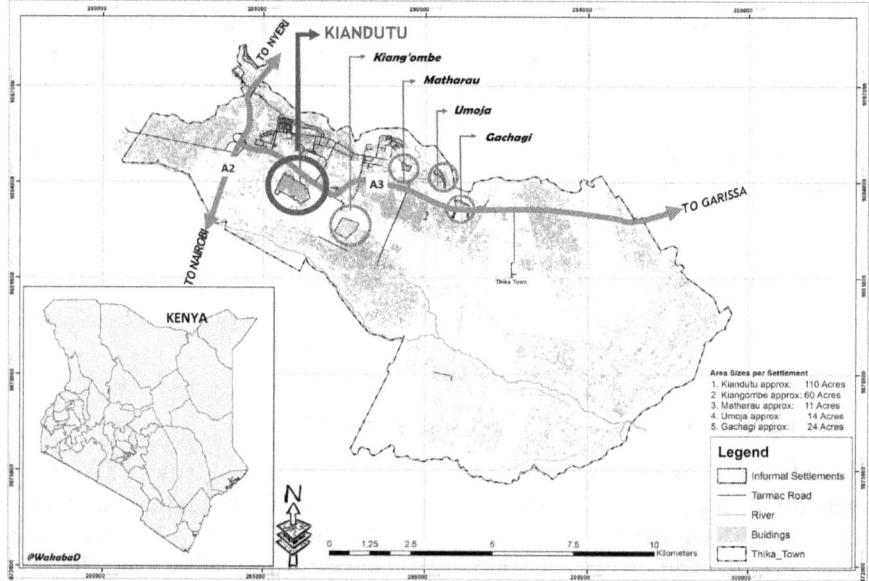

Figure 4.1 Location of Kiandutu

Source: CURI, 2013

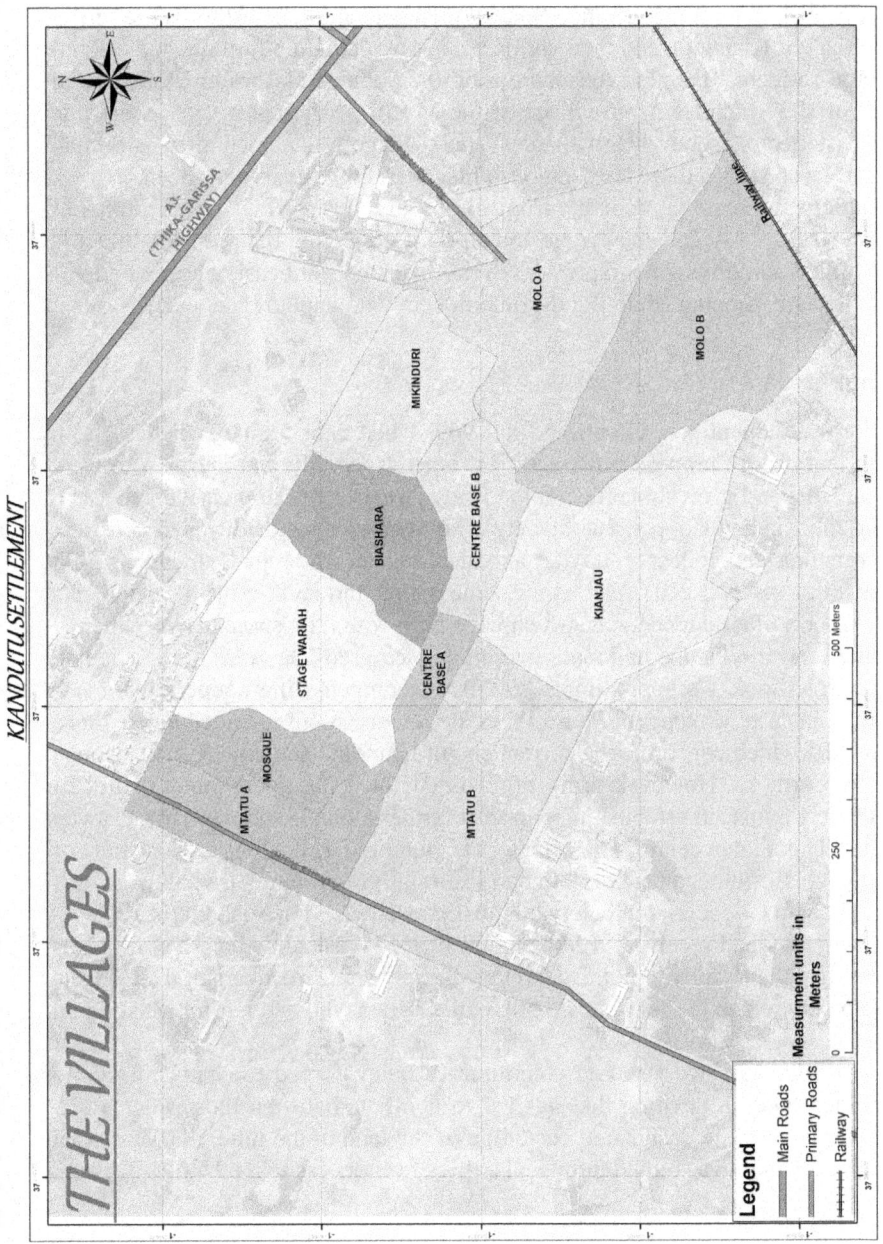

Figure 4.2 Kiandutu Villages

Source: CURI, 2013

village was previously known as Nyakinyua, named after a women's group that operated a community water point. Mikinduri village was named after a type of indigenous tree by the Kikuyu people, who in 1963 formed Kianjau Farmers' Cooperative Society. These Cooperative Society members are believed to be the 'original' settlers of Kiandutu, and their children and grandchildren form the majority of Kiandutu residents. People displaced during the political clashes in Molo area of Kenya in 1997 founded Molo village, while Muslims who constructed a mosque in 1978 started Mosque village. Stage Wariah village was named after its Somali residents, who settled there after establishing a market for goats and sheep.

Kiandutu's climate is moderate tropical, with typical average temperatures of 25°C during the day and an average annual rainfall ranging between 900 mm and 1,250 mm. Kiandutu's topography slopes northwest to southeast, where Molo village is located, making Molo flood-prone in heavy downpours.

History

Kiandutu settlement was established in 1969, when cooperative societies began buying land from European settlers after independence. The Europeans who were rearing cattle and growing coffee on the land surrendered it to their workers, who formed the Kianjau Cooperative Society. The Society's mandate was to construct new structures and collect rent. After a modest start in which many members built homes for themselves and began letting some rooms, further housing developments took the form of mud tenements, which were built with little space between them.

In the early 1970s, the national government acquired 100 acres of the Kianjau Cooperative Society's approximate 800 acres, compensating cooperative members with land in Makongeni Phase IV estate. Government intended to use those 100 acres – which constitute the current site of Kiandutu settlement – to establish an army barracks. However, army officials declined the government's offer of the 100 acres, instead establishing barracks farther along Garissa Highway, away from the Thika town centre. The Municipal Council of Thika thus took custody of the 100 acres, and began subdividing and selling it to private individuals. At this point, Kianjau Cooperative Society members raised grievances about the replacement land they had received in Makongeni Phase IV estate, which they said was smaller than the Kiandutu plot. Due to this dispute, some members of the Cooperative Society refused to leave Kiandutu, while others who had left for Makongeni Phase IV estate returned.

This resulted in two separate communities being forced to share informally subdivided land, a situation that has led to conflicts between the residents and the government. The designated custodian of the land at the time, the Municipal Council of Thika[4] was pulled into legal battles over access to the land.

Settlement population and demography

Establishing an accurate population size for any informal settlement is never a straightforward affair. This is due both to the dynamics of residency for the majority of slum dwellers, and the variations in methodology used for data collection. Unsurprisingly, Kiandutu settlement lacks a single consistent population count. The last national population census in 2009 reported a population of 13,240 residents and 5,086 households. The latest figures from a 2011 enumeration by Muungano Support Trust (MuST), a slum dwellers organization, indicated an estimated population of 17,337, with 8,307 households. A settlement enumeration carried out in 2015 by Slum Dwellers International Kenya reported a total population of 14,532 residents, with 5,693 households. The variation in population size is attributed to the dynamic changes in informal settlements, such as high turnover of tenants, who either move to other settlements or return to their villages, especially during official government census-taking. Demographically, Kiandutu's population mirrors the national pyramid, with the majority of the population below 15 years (CURI, 2013).

Using an annual informal settlement growth rate of 5%, and holding all factors constant, Kiandutu's total population is expected to reach 43,809 by the year 2030, resulting in a population density of 47,515 persons per km^2 on the current 0.922 km^2 (92.2 acres) area covered by the settlement (Figure 4.3). Such an increase will not only create overwhelming space contestation, but also strain existing infrastructure. With no currently recognized form of tenure security for residents, settlement improvement may prove unattainable, putting the sustainability and health of this community at great risk.

Land administration and management

Land administration and management in Kiandutu is based on existing formal and informal institutional dynamics. The formal institutions include a full spectrum of both the national and county government structures, with the Chief serving as the most local-level of representation.[5] Within the informal settlement, the Chief is usually assisted by village elders representing each village cluster. Meanwhile, the informal institutions are largely constituted by various interest groups, such as association of tenants, structure owners, Community Based Organizations (e.g., Muungano Wa wanavijiji), and service providers such as water vendors.

Today Kiandutu informal settlement occupies public land that falls under the custody of the County Government of Kiambu. Under its first (2012–2017) administration, the County Government demonstrated willingness to engage in a land-sharing approach with the community, offering to provide community facilities and utilities (as discussed earlier). However, a new County Government administration was elected in 2017, and this administration has not shown the same level of political will or appetite for enabling land-sharing arrangements.

Currently, Kiandutu lacks a structured, formal land-management and tenure system. Each cluster of residents in the different villages have laid claim to the land where they reside. Such claims are based on land as currently occupied, albeit with no official government-issued ownership documents. All land transactions, from subdivision to allocation, occur informally through a 'gentleman's agreement' in which payment is presented in exchange for possession or use of a

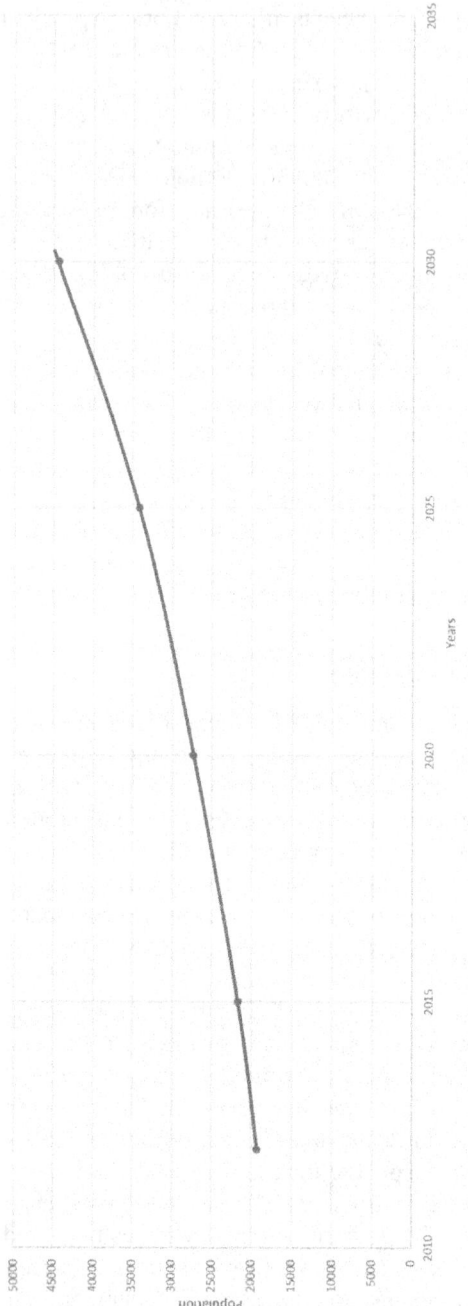

Figure 4.3 Kiandutu Projected Population Growth

Source: CURI, 2013

piece of land. Such 'ownership' can only be legitimized by the elders/chiefs in the village, who were the land's original settlers. With the settlement's growth over time, inhabited areas have extended into private land adjacent to the settlement.

Because Kiandutu lacks any structured or centralized system of land management, landownership record systems are also a challenge. By law, details of ownership and use must be recorded in a title deed registration system that is linked to cadastre information (GoK, 2012).[6] However, the reality in Kiandutu is that this is not happening, and the established 'owners' ultimately determine the use and boundaries of a piece of land, with no legally recorded proof of these details. This has led to haphazard subdivisions, the development of informal structures without accompanying infrastructure provision, and frequent and deep conflict between occupants and owners.

Settlement morphology, density, and typology

Having grown organically, Kiandutu settlement lacks a structured pattern, though development mostly aligns with existing roads and footpaths (e.g., Athena Road, which is the main access road along Kiandutu's northwest edge, and directly links to Garissa Road). These and other primary roads and footpaths act as the main corridors for activities such as business, recreation, and transportation. Commercial activities are mostly found along the main arterial routes that lead to the main road and Mtatu village. Mtatu A&B, Stage Wariah, and Mosque are Kiandutu's busiest villages, harbouring its major commercial activities, which decrease as one moves from west to east (i.e., from Mtatu to Molo), or as distance increases from Thika town.

The settlement has been built on irregular blocks of land, whose delineation corresponds with the road grid structure. The blocks generally measure about 385 square meters. Building structures form organic clusters with an average of eight units per block measuring between eight and 36 square metres each. Building orientation is predominantly northeast-southwest and northwest-southeast in terms of the longer axis of structures.

Building densities are higher in the northern and western parts of Kiandutu (e.g., Mtatu, Mosque, and Stage Warrior villages), and lower on the southern and eastern parts (e.g., Molo and parts of Mikinduri villages) (Figure 4.4). The unit densities at village level range from a low of 54 to a high of 136 units per acre. The most congested villages are found closer to the main road, and are characterized by closely built, iron-sheet structures that each contain at least eight households.

Kiandutu's predominant house typology is terrace (row) housing, consisting of 3–12 single rooms in a line, with the rows of rooms arranged back-to-back. With an average structure containing eight rooms (units), the average unit density for Kiandutu informal settlement is 84 units per acre. The housing units are laid out in a parallel or interlocking formation, sometimes producing residual clusters with micro-courtyards (popularly referred to as the 'plot' type). There are also smaller and relatively newer house in-fills, with a randomized orientation. The average

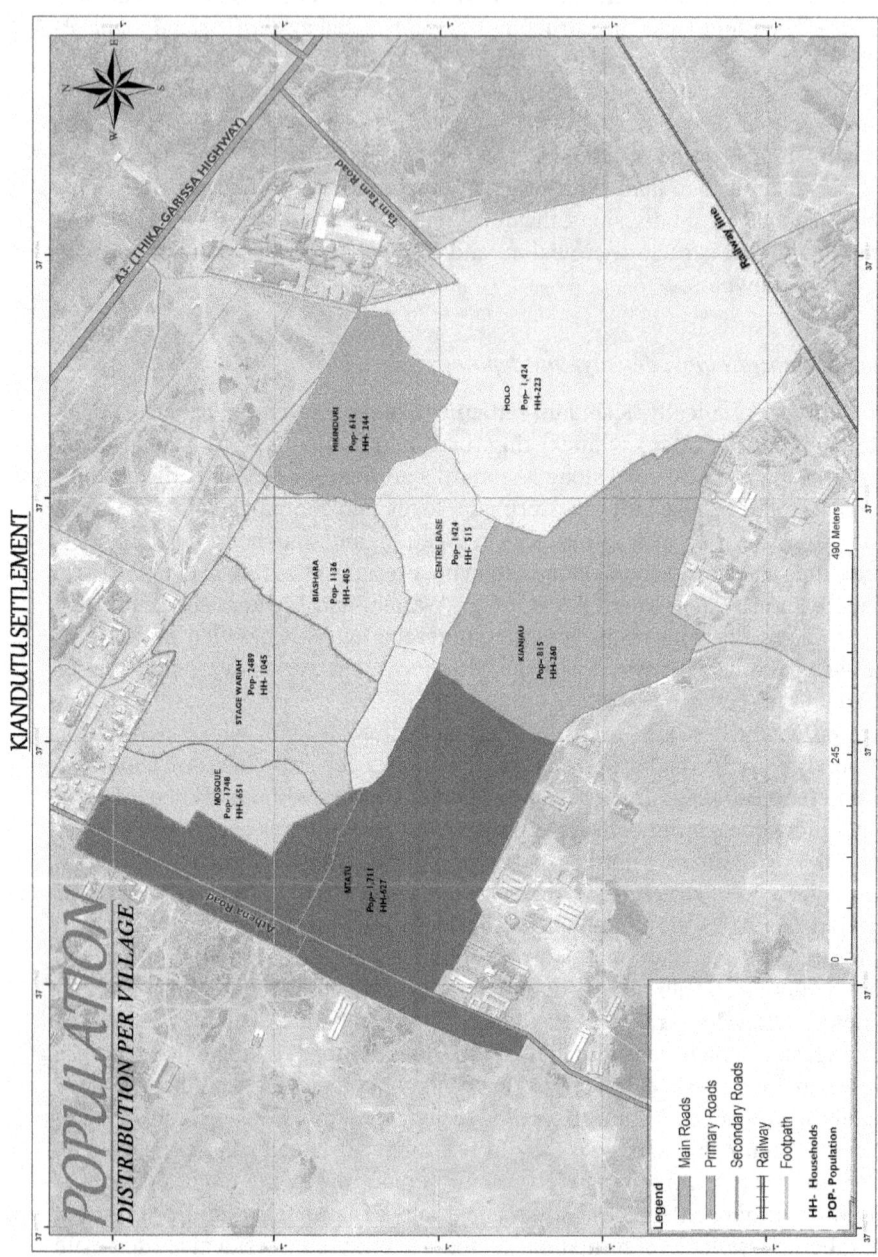

Figure 4.4 Density Distribution Map in Kiandutu

Source: CURI, 2013

size of a room in the settlement measures 3m x 3m, with those used for businesses tending to be smaller.

The average occupancy per room is four persons. There are also special types of buildings serving as community facilities (churches, classrooms, eateries, etc.), whose sizes exceed that of a single room. The housing structures are predominantly temporary: single floor of either unfinished earth (94%) or cement floor finish; walls of mud (52.7%) or wood (30.4%), and roofs of galvanized iron sheets (98%).

The majority of the residents (53%) are tenants paying rent (from Ksh500–2,500). The majority (53%) pay between Ksh500–1000, while 37% pay rent of Ksh500. Rent values are determined by the house condition and the unit location, with structures that have services like electricity and those close to the roads attracting higher rent value.

Infrastructure and utilities

Access to infrastructure and other basic amenities is a challenge in Kiandutu. Although piped water is provided by Thika Water and Sewerage Company (THIWASCO), access is not provided at household level, and over 90% of the households rely on communal water points. The settlement's main water access challenges are high costs and an underdeveloped water reticulation network.

Figure 4.5 Temporary Housing in Kiandutu

Source: Authors

In terms of energy access, 75% of residents access electricity for lighting (the majority being informal access), and 25% have no electricity at all. For cooking, 20% use paraffin and 60% charcoal as fuel.

There is a lack of storm water drainage and solid waste management facilities. Residents heavily rely on pit latrines for sanitation, with over 60% sharing. Informal methods are used in solid waste disposal, such as indiscriminate dumping/burning of waste.

Findings

On land sharing

The CityLab was held with the Kiandutu community and other stakeholders to discuss various models and options for tenure security, including resettlement, community land buying, adverse possession, and land sharing. That said, the City-Lab centred on the land-sharing option, which was extensively discussed with regard to its applicability and potential process in Kiandutu settlement. During the discourse, participants noted that they would be willing to support the land-sharing option and process, provided the proper channels for community engagement and negotiations were put in place, and gentrification could be avoided. Key issues raised by stakeholders in the CityLab are discussed in more detail next.

Perceived legitimate versus legal ownership

Kiandutu presents a classic case of perceived legitimate ownership versus legal ownership. Some residents perceive themselves as legitimate landowners, as they were the original settlers after the purchase from colonial settlers in 1969. However, the law only recognizes title deeds as proof of individual ownership of land. In Kenya, a title deed also serves as a precondition for building development approval and all forms of land transactions. The fact that none of Kiandutu's residents possesses a registered title deed has ultimately led to the settlement's informal status, despite many residents having lived there for generations with a sense of perceived ownership. This issue of perceived ownership came up in the women's forum, where a participant stated: 'Kiandutu is the only home we know, most of us were born and found ourselves here, we have nowhere else to go and our families are here as well'.

Impact of land tenure on investment

Lack of secure tenure is known to discourage residents from investing either in improvements to their household environment, or in home-based activities that could alleviate poverty. The study saw this dynamic playing out in Kiandutu, where residents have made no attempts to improve their shelter conditions. Kiandutu residents live in semi-permanent, structurally unsound buildings constructed from mud or rusty galvanized iron. Economic investments in the settlement are

Table 4.1 Summary of infrastructure-services conditions in Kiandutu

Infrastructure/ service	Coverage/ Quality	Key actors/ Providers	Challenges
Water	Piped water available; over 90% rely on Communal Water Points	Thika Water and Sewerage Company	▪ High Cost ▪ Reticulation Network
Transport	70% Reliance on non-motorized/para-transit facilities	Private/Informal Undertakers; Self Initiatives	▪ Poor Road Network ▪ Lack of Space for Reticulation
Sanitation	Reliance on pit latrines, with over 60% sharing; lack of storm drainage and solid waste management facilities	Community/ Self; County Government of Thika (Sewer Development)	▪ High Cost ▪ Lack of Space for Reticulation ▪ Accessibility/ Servicing
Health	Informal within settlement; formal health centre outside the settlement; up to 75% rely on informal provision within settlement for primary health care	Private Undertakers in Settlement; Public & Private Outside Settlement	▪ High Cost ▪ Traditional/ Uncertified Interventions ▪ Retrogressive Community Attitudes ▪ Accessibility
Education	93% of school goers attend formal education; only 5% attend formal secondary school; one public primary school within Kiandutu Settlement	Public and Private Undertakers	▪ Poor Infrastructure Conditions ▪ Substandard Quality of education ▪ High Cost
Solid Waste	Informal methods; indiscriminate dumping/ burning of waste	Community/Self	▪ Lack of Infrastructure ▪ Retrogressive Community Attitudes
Energy	75% access electricity (majority being informal access); 20% use paraffin and 60% charcoal as fuel	Public Undertakers; Illegal Middlemen/ Brokers/ Connectors	▪ High Cost ▪ Lack of Space for Reticulation ▪ Accessibility/ Servicing ▪ Environmental Concerns
Security	12 lighting masts at strategic positions; only one street furnished with lighting	Public (Police) and Community-led	▪ Fear of Victimization ▪ Poor Accessibility/ Navigation ▪ Lack of Infrastructure

Source: CURI, 2013

limited to small shanties used as retail shops and groceries, or water vending shops that are similarly structurally unsound. Participants highlighted this scenario in the workshops, expressing fear of investing in the settlement due to their insecure tenure status. One participant from the men's forum argued:

> This is not my place, it belongs to the government, so I cannot say it is my home because this land does not belong to anyone. If I am told to move away, I will move because it is not our home, as we do not have the title deed for us to settle here.

Similarly, a youth workshop participant noted:

> We cannot build storey or high-rise houses because we are uncertain if we will be here tomorrow. But if we are assured and everyone is given a title deed, we can build such storey buildings

Fears around land sharing

Generally, residents' lack of secure tenure had a negative impact on their initial acceptance of the land-sharing approach, due to long-standing fears about losing the limited rights they do have to the land. Participants in all three workshops expressed concern over the likelihood of rich individuals infiltrating and then excluding them from the process. They also noted the possibility that the list of land-sharing beneficiaries could be changed, and other persons not residing in the settlement could be introduced to benefit. The fears raised by Kiandutu community have also been witnessed in other informal settlement upgrading programs. These fears and perceptions impeded the community's acceptance of the land-sharing concept, initially causing people to state a preference for the more conventional securing of tenure through titling, despite the difficulties inherent to that process.

Morphology, density, and land sharing

Differing village structures and varying population densities impacted participants' attitudes towards the land-sharing approach. For example, some workshop participants felt that should they adopt land sharing, the less densely inhabited village clusters should be taken by the County Government, as the process of relocation would then cost less. There was general agreement that the County Government should consider taking areas that are inhabitable due to steep slopes, susceptibility to flooding, and proximity to the railway line (e.g., parts of Molo Village).

On planning considerations

In the workshops, the CURI team explained that as a policy option, land sharing offers slum settlement dwellers faced with imminent eviction and tenure insecurity a strategy by which they can organize, lobby, and bargain for a share of the land they already occupy. Such bargaining would occur with the landowner (either a private entity or the state). Following negotiations, the landowner can agree to sell or lease all or part of the land in question to the slum dwellers.

Because Kiandutu is located on public land, any such negotiations would need to comply with Section 12 of the Land Act 2012, which provides that the National Land Commission may, on behalf of the national or county governments, allocate public land by way of, among others, applications confined to a targeted group or groups of persons, in order to ameliorate their disadvantaged position. This provision provides sufficient legal grounds for the Kiandutu community and the County Government of Kiambu to negotiate a land-sharing deal.

For a land-sharing option between Kiandutu residents and the County Government to be viable, the workshops identified five further principles as fundamental:

The informal settlement community must be well-organized

Organization will enable the community's ability to bargain effectively in the negotiations for land sharing. Land sharing is not successful where communities are weak, as once implemented, a plethora of challenges can arise around numerous issues, including resale of some houses (which then command a higher market value); conflict over beneficiaries; and noncompliance to the land-sharing agreement.

A 2013 CURI study found that only 15% of all adults in Kiandutu are members of formal community organizations. The study attributed these numbers to the fact that Kiandutu, like many informal settlements in Kenya, is a community with high levels of apathy and low levels of trust and unity – suspicion is common and exacerbated by poor leadership and various forms of corruption. It is our conclusion that this attitude together with different priorities at both individual and collective levels can compromise collective action as a possible strategy to enhance collective initiatives.

A clearly documented land-sharing agreement must be in place

The land-sharing agreement must be negotiated, clearly documenting aspects such as the portion of land allocated to the landlord and community, the preferred tenure, how the land will be managed and administered by the parties, and how conflict will be resolved, among other issues. Negotiating a land-sharing agreement is usually a protracted process requiring the commitment of an informed and well-organized community leadership.

Residents must accept that densification will occur

Land-sharing agreements will rehouse the community over a smaller total area, and therefore require higher/increased residential densities. The community has to accept the likelihood of vertical densification, and the fact that they will not all occupy an individual and independent piece of land. This vertical densification argument was discussed and supported across the three CityLab workshops.

Residents must accept that reconstruction will be required

The increase in density and the need to clear part of the site usually necessitates the reconstruction of houses (Figure 4.6). This was discussed in the men's workshop, with a participant noting that if land sharing is to be adopted, the most suitable model would be multistorey housing developments. The need for both densification and reconstruction necessitates the preparation of a Special Area Physical Development Plan that clearly illustrates details such as the level of densification, plot ratios and setbacks, preferred housing typologies, etc.[7]

Based on our analysis of the preferred scenarios expressed by the CityLab participants, Figure 4.6 illustrates a possible outcome of a negotiated land-sharing planning process. In this outcome, the County could potentially recover 49 acres, while the remaining 51 acres would go to the community. Such a planning process would take time and require support from the County Government, which is also responsible for development control. Additionally, support would be needed to facilitate the adoption of planning and building standards that are appropriate to an informal settlement, but would not adversely compromise public health.

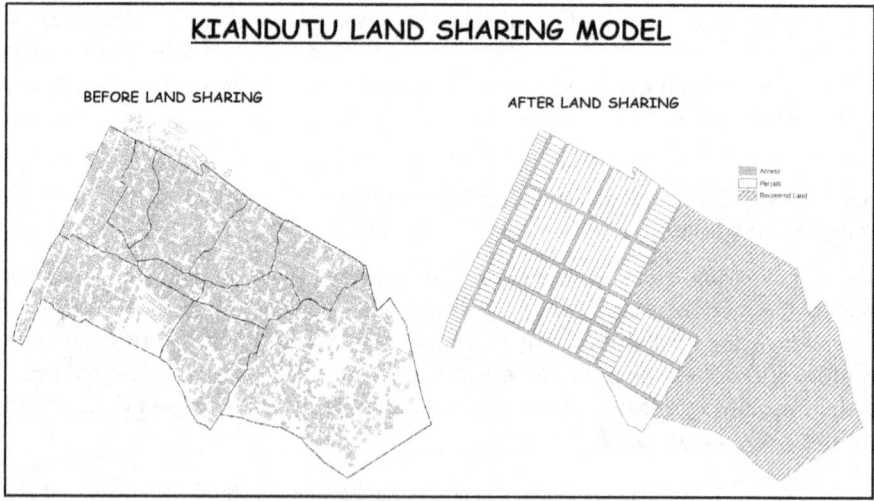

Figure 4.6 Land Sharing Scenario
Source: Authors

Capital is needed

The land-sharing processes discussed earlier all require capital – either from the community's domestic savings or in the form of loans from outside sources – and the ability to access capital will be tied to the community's organizing and mobilizing capacity. Resource mobilization in Kiandutu is currently focused on income-generating activities, savings, and establishing a revolving fund. Mobilizing networks such as Kiandutu Residents Association and Muungano wa Wanavijiji (the federation of slum dwellers) already exist, but membership remains low and needs to grow to a settlement-wide scale. For a land-sharing agreement to work, there is a need for increased sensitization and a fairly good level of coordination, cooperation, and buy-in for community-based initiatives.

Analysis, recommendations, and lessons

Implications of a land-sharing solution for Kiandutu

Land sharing is as simple as it is complex. Its simplicity stems from the existence of two (or more, in certain situations) contesting parties, who want to reach an amicable solution to the challenge of ownership and tenure security. Complexity arises in the process, which requires a united community voice, lengthy negotiations, and subsequent land surveying and settlement planning. All of these processes demand resources, both in time and finances. The Kiandutu CityLab found that land sharing as a way to attain sustainable security of tenure will likely be more complex than simple, due to the following key issues:

Lack of understanding of land-sharing concept

Although land sharing is not an entirely new concept, it has not been widely applied in Africa and specifically Kenya. Although the land-sharing approach offers the prospect of a 'win-win-win' solution for all main parties involved, informal settlement residents occupying government land often continue to prefer individual tenure through titling over land sharing. That said, the process of titling requires formal surveys and a rigorous land management and regulatory framework – an expensive prerequisite that many informal settlement dwellers cannot afford. In addition, it should be noted that titling may be detrimental to some households living in informal settlements, especially those with vulnerable legal and social status; for example, tenants/subtenants on squatter land, newly established occupants who are not considered eligible, single young men and women, and female heads of households.

While the experience of case studies, such as those in India and Thailand, may prove a useful starting point, it is worth noting that tenure issues in informal settlements in Kenya specifically, and sub-Saharan Africa generally, tend to be more contentious. In the case of Kiandutu settlement, the lack of understanding of the land-sharing concept was distinctly revealed. For example, the community wondered why they should share the land, despite a common understanding that it is public land. In addition, while typical land-sharing agreements return the more commercially attractive part of the site to the registered landowner (in this case, Kiambu County Government), community members in Kiandutu preferred to give the County the least attractive or economically viable land in the settlement.

Concerns and fears of externalities from the land sharing process

Slum dwellers live in perpetual fear of eviction and therefore understandably approach any external intervention with a sceptical eye. The Kiandutu community viewed land sharing as a lengthy process, during which they feared the settlement might be opened to land grabs by affluent members of the wider society, and subsequently lead to gentrification. They also feared the possibility that approaching the government with the idea of land sharing would reignite the government's interest in repossessing the land. Finally, the community also raised concerns over the possibility that its poor and marginalized members ultimately would be excluded from the land-sharing process, should it be adopted.

Lack of trust in public processes

Trust in governance, public processes, and public actors and institutions is fundamental to legitimize state action, and the lack of trust presents a massive obstacle to public policy and development. Studies have shown that citizens' mistrust of public process emanates from widespread corruption in public institutions in Africa (Armah-Attoh et al., 2007). The land-sharing process entails the government acting as a third-party beneficiary between the community and the landowner. However, in the case of Kiandutu, the County Government of Kiambu is also the landowner.

The land-sharing process also requires surveying, planning, densification, and/or resettlement, which all necessarily involve public institutions. According to the Kiandutu community, government involvement in tenure negotiations and housing initiatives would make these processes susceptible to corrupt deals made in 'top offices'. As such, the community fears that such deals could condemn them to losing the land or getting locked out of any benefits accruing from the process.

Lack of a strong community organization

Land sharing relies on strong community organization and the community's ability to negotiate effectively with the landowners to create a 'win-win' situation for both parties (Parry, 2015; Srinivas, 2015). In the CityLab workshop, Kiandutu community members said that they lacked a strong community organization, which will likely be required to champion negotiations. Currently the only visible organization is Muungano wa Wanavijiji, which only has a few members, and cannot effectively represent the whole community's issues when called upon. In the women's workshop, it was noted that there is a need to develop a shared vision, given that other organizations exist within the community (besides Muungano), and they all have different goals pertaining to land matters. The lack of strong community organization also impedes the community's ability to raise the necessary funds for a land-sharing process.

Structure owners/landlords-tenants dichotomy

In Kiandutu, a landlord-tenants dichotomy exists, and we found that landlords (or more accurately 'structure owners', who in Kiandutu can own a structure without having title to the land) felt entitled to a bigger share of the potential land-share plots than the tenants. The landlords' sense of entitlement stems from having settled earlier, being in-born (seeing their claim as a birth right), or having invested in the settlement. By the same token, tenants felt entitled to the land they reside on in Kiandutu, with some having rented for a lengthy period of time.

Recommendations

These recommendations were mainly derived from the Kiandutu CityLab community engagements. They represent the knowledge, expertise, thoughts, sentiments, and feelings shared by the community concerning land sharing as a sustainable approach to tenure security in Kiandutu. These sentiments were then supplemented by existing literature and case studies on successful land-sharing approaches in settings similar to Kiandutu.

Promote broad-based community involvement/participation

The participation of the Kiandutu community in improving the quality of its settlement is an important resource that must be tapped for this settlement's long-term sustainability. This will be in line with global agreements such as the New Urban Agenda, which have been locally adopted to promote equity and inclusion in human settlement development and urban poverty mitigation measures. Ideally, community participation cuts down the high cost associated with traditional community development approaches, monetary and human-power constraints, and supports the realization that local solutions can be effective. In addition, community participation provides an opportunity for developing solidarity in the struggle against oppression and resultant marginalization in the community. In light of this, special emphasis must be made to develop ways to ensure that the needs of marginalized groups in Kiandutu are taken into consideration throughout the entire land-sharing process so that no one is excluded from the benefits.

Redefine the role of third parties in fostering a strong community organization

Strong community organization is an important ingredient in the negotiations that are integral to the land-sharing process. This is because community organizations present a unified front to the landowner during negotiations, discouraging the latter from exploiting differences among residents, and/or attempting to buy off certain community members (Rabé, 2010). More often than not, community strength increases through alliances with local organizations, NGOs, human rights groups, political parties, and other groups that may give the community cause more visibility (Rabé, 2010).

Given the current situation in Kiandutu and its existing intra-community dichotomies, the role of nongovernmental and voluntary organizations must be emphasized in mobilizing the people into an organization, training and educating them, forming a link with the authorities, and in various other catalytic ways (Srinivas, 2015).

Develop an effective community financing strategy

The land-sharing process requires finances for surveying, planning, and redeveloping the settlement. In Kiandutu, options for financing may be two-fold: the residents may opt to let the government finance the housing redevelopment, and pay that back through rent; or the community may join to pool resources and finance the process. Whichever financing model the Kiandutu community opts for, it is imperative to centre it on a firm foundation of community-based savings and/or loan systems along with County Government commitments.

Community organization

As mentioned, for land sharing to succeed, strong community organization with a clearly defined vision and leadership structure that the community trusts to negotiate on its behalf is vital. However, like many informal settlements, Kiandutu currently lacks such organization. Because the existing community groups have different interests, dialogue initiatives must be carefully crafted to ensure that they do not become a source of conflict in these small and disaggregated groups.

Create checks and balances in the existing institutional structures

The institutions involved in the process (including the national and county government departments) must commit to transparency and ensure public participation and involvement. These efforts must also be coupled with strong commitments to accountability and public information sharing. This helps to ensure the sustainability of the land-sharing effort, and reduces the possibility that laudable goals are subverted by other interests.

Ensure and implement a holistic approach to land sharing as an option to tenure security improvement

During the planning phase of the process, intensive and efficient land-use planning that promotes economic growth and empowerment of the Kiandutu community is a necessity. As noted by Montressor (2015), there should also be comprehensive reforms geared towards regulating the urban land market, restricting land uses, and enabling incremental upgrading of the settlement.

Lessons from CURI CityLab

As a method of co-production, the CityLab approach requires effective participation from both the government agencies and the informal settlement dwellers. Key factors – political, institutional, as well as social and community-organization based – that affected the success of Kiandutu Settlement CityLab are listed here, in the hopes that they might inform future similar efforts.

Strong community collaboration

Since 2007, CURI, which started as a project called Urban Innovations Project (UIP), has worked with various informal settlements including Kiandutu through collaborations with local community organizations, NGOs, international partners, and government agencies. Through continuous engagement with the Kiandutu community and these other stakeholders, CURI succeeded in building trust and being seen as a neutral partner. The success of the Kiandutu Settlement City-Lab co-production process hinged on this acceptance and trust on the part of the community.

Timing

Given Kenya's historical injustices, land is a very emotive issue, and the Kiandutu settlement presents a typical case of perceived land injustice. The CityLab dialogues informing this study were held against the backdrop of a national electioneering period – a period when any discussions centred on land issues were liable to solicit suspicion or volatile reactions. Planning for future similar CityLab work should therefore factor in the political environment, and devise methodologies that can mitigate against political influence. One way to do this would be to ensure that such projects do not coincide with election years.

Changes to political leadership

While Kenyan national elections are held every five years – often bringing a shift of power(s) and resultant personnel changes in key government institutions – land sharing is a lengthy process that may extend beyond the five-year term of any given administration. It is important to note that when personnel change, the new team may not necessarily be amenable to the previous government's interests and priorities. Such shifts may unnecessarily frustrate the land-sharing process, potentially leading to an impasse.

Conclusion

There is an urgent need to address and resolve the formal-informal sector division and resultant poor relations that collectively constrain efforts to advance informal settlement upgrading in Kenya today. This shift will require practical, negotiated approaches to tenure security, access to land rights, and tenure regularization, which also understand and respond to local conditions and factors. The aim of this CityLab was to co-produce an innovative approach to securing land tenure through land sharing. Even though land sharing has the potential to unlock the current tenure situation in Kiandutu, its adoption as a policy strategy still faces challenges. These challenges emanate from the majority of the slum dwellers being unaware of the actual mechanisms of land sharing; the enormity of the resources needed for successful implementation of a land-sharing agreement; and the degree of mistrust from the community towards government. There are also challenges that relate to the County Government of Kiambu as the legal custodian of the land. It was noted that support of tenure regularization in Kiandutu depended on the goodwill of specific officers, and not through a deliberate county programme. The issue here is that when such officers leave either due to transfer or regime change (following the five-year cycle of elections), supportof the community process would also dissipate.

Despite these significant obstacles, a major takeaway from this CityLab was that Kiandutu slum dwellers are willing to engage in land sharing as an innovative way of securing their tenure. Providing a framework that can be leveraged by both the national and county governments in Kenya, this CityLab thus presented an option for tackling land access constraints faced by the urban poor in securing respectable, sustainable shelter. Key to this success was the presence of a trusted third party that is seen as neutral in the land contestation question, and thus could create an atmosphere conducive to participatory and inclusive dialogue. However, this CityLab also demonstrated that the community always prefers to own the land in its entirety, and that any other approach to securing tenure such as land sharing would only succeed after the community is convinced that it is the only viable option.

The CityLab provided the Kiandutu community and the technical experts involved with platforms for knowledge and information exchange. Able to engage in deeper discussions with the community about their daily challenges and how they felt these could be addressed, the technical experts were able to rationalize their expert opinions with those of the community, especially concerning scenarios for a potential land-sharing outcome. The Kiandutu community similarly benefited from receiving technical input about land sharing directly from professionals engaged in such processes. Through the workshops, the community members were trained in the tenets of the land-sharing approach, their roles in the process, and potential benefits. This enabled the community to gain vital skills germane to the implementation and monitoring of progress and change within their settings, should the land sharing approach be adopted. The CityLab underscored that communities living and experiencing tenure security challenges are the actors best suited to inform and document changes taking place in the settlements before and after any interventions. The CityLab methodology also offers government (national and county), partner organizations, and technical experts a platform to gauge the effectiveness of a proposal and intervention for tenure regularization, helping to ensure that policy intervention for slum dwellers are negotiated and co-produced.

Finally, the Kiandutu CityLab demonstrated the urgent need to add new methodologies to the university planning curriculum and training framework for urban studies. Such a new framework should target a better appreciation of urban informality through continuous discourse and engagement with key stakeholders. In sum, the research presented in this chapter demonstrates the value of and need for a more practical and effective type of university training for urban planners in Africa; this necessarily involves the academy opening to communities to facilitate direct contact and experiential learning to enrich the relevance of the curriculum and the overall contribution of the university to societal development, which in turn will further the agenda of inclusive and sustainable urban development on the continent.

Notes

1 The Government is yet to release disaggregated 2019 data based on urban rural population.
2 Kenya Vision 2030 is the government's development blueprint. Covering the years 2008–2030, its aim is to transform Kenya into a newly industrializing, middle-income country, providing all citizens a high quality of life in a clean and secure environment by 2030.
3 Sessional Paper No. 3 of 2009.
4 This land is now public land under the custody of County Government of Kiambu, based on the devolved system of government under the Constitution of Kenya 2010.
5 The Chief is considered a representative of national government.
6 An official register showing details of ownership, boundaries, and value of real property in a district, made for taxation purposes.
7 Special Area Physical Development Plans are affected by the Physical Planning Act, Section 23, which mandates the declaration of areas with unique development potential or problems as Special Planning Areas.

References

Abott, J. (1996). *Sharing the city: community participation in urban management*. London: Routledge. DOI: https://doi.org/10.4324/9781315070759
Angel, S. & Boonyabancha, S. (1988). Land sharing as an alternative to eviction: the Bangkok experience. *Third World Planning Review*, 10(2), pp. 107–127. DOI: https://doi.org/10.3828/twpr.10.2.v54j0130h27j4r32

Armah-Attoh, D., Gyimah-Boadi, E. & Chikwanha, A. (2007). *Corruption and institutional trust in Africa: implications for democratic development.* Working Papers No. 81. Afrobarometer. Retrieved: https://afrobarometer.org/sites/default/files/publications/Working%20paper/AfropaperNo81.pdf

Boonyabancha, S. (2005). Baan Mankong: going to scale with 'slum' and squatter upgrading in Thailand. *Environment and Urbanization,* 17(1), pp. 21–46. DOI: http://dx.doi.org/10.1177/095624780501700104

Buckely, R.M. & Kalarickal, J. (2006). *Thirty years of world bank shelter lending: what have we learned?* Washington: World Bank. DOI: https://doi.org/10.1596/978-0-8213-6577-9

Clarke, R.A. (2009). Securing communal land rights to achieve sustainable development in sub-Saharan Africa: critical analysis and policy implications. *Law, Environment and Development Journal,* 5(2), pp. 130–151. Retrieved: www.lead-journal.org/content/09130.pdf.

CURI. (2013). *Kiandutu settlement profile.* Nairobi: Centre for Urban Research and Innovations (CURI).

D'Cruz, C., Mcgranahan, G. & Sumithre, U. (2009). The efforts of a federation of slum and shanty dwellers to secure land and improve housing in Moratuwa: from savings groups to citywide strategies. *Environment & Urbanization,* 21(2), pp. 367–388. DOI: https://doi.org/10.1177%2F0956247809342360.

De Soto, H. (2000). *The mystery of capital: why capitalism triumphs in the west and fails everywhere else.* New York: Basic Books.

Durand-Lasserve, A. (2004). Land for housing the poor in African cities: are neo-customary processes an effective alternative to formal systems? In: Hamdi, N. (Ed.), *Urban futures: economic growth and poverty reduction.* Rugby: ITDG Publishing, pp. 160–174.

Durand-Lasserve, A. & Royston, L. (Eds.). (2002). *Holding their ground: secure land tenure for the urban poor in developing countries.* London: Earthscan. DOI: https://doi.org/10.1016/S0197-3975(03)00033-X

Enemark, S. (2016). *Sustainable land governance in support of the global agenda.* ILMI Working Paper No. 3, Windhoek. Namibia: Integrated Land Management Institute, Namibia University of Science and Technology, pp. 1–10.

Friedmann, J. (1987). *Planning in the public domain: from knowledge to action.* Princeton: Princeton Univeristy Press.

Government of Kenya (GoK). (2009). *Sessional paper no. 3 of 2009 on national land policy.* Nairobi: Government Printer.

Government of Kenya (GoK). (2010). *Constitution of Kenya.* Nairobi: Government Printer.

Government of Kenya (GoK). (2012). *Land act.* Nairobi: Government Printer.

Government of Kenya (GoK). (2017). *Kenya's popular version of the new urban agenda: towards inclusive, safe, resilient and sustainable cities and human settlements.* Ministry of Transport, Infrastructure, Housing and Urban Development. Retrieved: www.kara.or.ke/Kenya%27s%20Popular%20Version%20on%20New%20Urban%20Agenda.pdf

Healey, P. (2006). *Collaborative planning: shaping places in fragmented societies.* New York: Palgrave Macmillan.

Huchzermeyer, M. (2011). *Cities with slums: from informal settlements eradication to a right to the city in Africa.* Cape Town: University of Cape Town Press.

KNBS. (2009). *Kenya population and housing census 2009: volume I.* Nairobi: Kenya National Bureau of Statistics (KNBS).

KNBS. (2019). *Kenya population and housing census 2019: volume I.* Nairobi: Kenya National Bureau of Statistics (KNBS).

Komjathy, K., Nichols, S.E. & Ericsson, A. (2001). *Principles for equitable gender inclusion in land administration: fig guidelines on women's access to land (Fig Publication No. 24)*. Frederiksberg, Denmark: International Federation of Surveyors. Retrieved: www.fig.net/resources/proceedings/fig_proceedings/korea/full-papers/pdf/session6/komjathy-nichols-ericsson.pdf

Montressor, F. (2015). *Preconditions of land sharing and development of the principle*. Retrieved: www.hdm.lth.se/fileadmin/hdm/Education/Undergrad/ABAN06_2013/Montresor_Francesco.pdf

Napier, M., Berrisford, S., Kihato, C.W., McGaffin, R. & Royston, L. (2013). *Trading places: accessing land in African cities*. Somerset West: Urban LandMark and African Minds.

Olale, P.O. (2015). *Implications of land tenure security on sustainable land use in informal settlements in Nairobi*. Nairobi: University of Nairobi.

Olale, P.O. & Opiyo, R.O. (2017). *Policy brief: alternatives to eviction, scenarios for access to land by the urban poor in Kiandutu informal settlement Thika, Kenya*. Nairobi: Centre for Urban Research and Innovations, University of Nairobi.

Parry, J. (2015). *From slums to sustainable communities: the transformative power of secure tenure*. Issue Paper on Secure Tenure for Urban Slums. Habitat for Humanity. Retrieved: https://www.habitat.org/sites/default/files/issue-paper.pdf

Payne, G. (Ed.). (2002). *Land, rights and innovation: improving tenure security for the urban poor*. London: ITDG Publishing.

Payne, G., Durand-Lasserve, A. & Rakodi, C. (2009). The limits of land titling and home ownership. *Environment and Urbanization*, 21(2), pp. 443–462. DOI: https://doi.org/10.1177/0956247809344364

Rabé, P.E. (2005 December 8–9). *Land sharing in phnom penh: an innovative but insufficient instrument of secure tenure for the poor*. Paper presented at Expert Group Meeting on Secure Land Tenure: New Legal Frameworks and Tools UN-ESCAP, Bangkok, Thailand.

Rabé, P.E. (2010). *Land sharing in Phnom Penh and Bangkok: lessons from four decades of innovative slum redevelopment projects in two Southeast Asian boom towns*. Washington, DC: World Bank.

Rakodi, C. (2014). Expanding women's access to land and housing in urban areas. *Gender Equality and Development, Women's Voice and Agency Research Series*, 8, pp. 1–56.

Rudd, A., Simon, D., Cardama, M., Birch, E.L. & Revi, A. (2018). The UN, the urban sustainable development goal, and the new urban agenda. In: Elmqvist, T. (Ed.), *The urban planet: knowledge towards sustainable cities*. Cambridge: Cambridge Univeristy Press, pp. 180–196.

Scholl, C. & Kemp, R. (2016). City labs as vehicles for innovation in urban planning processes. *Urban Planning*, 1(4), pp. 89–102. DOI: https://doi.org/10.17645/up.v1i4

Sorrenson, M.P. (1967). *Land reform in the Kikutu County: a study in government policy*. Nairobi: Oxford University Press.

Srinivas, H. (2015). *Urban squatters and slums: defining squatter settlement*. Kobe, Japan: Global Development Research Center. Retrieved: www.gdrc.org/uem/squatters/define-squatter.html

Syagga, P.M. (2011). Land tenure in slum upgrading projects. In: *Les cahiers d'Afrique del'Est*. Nairobi: French Institute for Research in Africa (IFRA), pp. 103–113.

Tacoli, C., McGranahan, G. & Satterthwaite, D. (2015). *World migration report 2015: urbanization, rural-urban migration and urban poverty*. London: International Organization for Migration.

UN-Habitat. (2010). *The state of African cities 2010: governance, inequality and urban land markets*. Nairobi, Kenya: United Nations Human Settlements Programme (UN-Habitat).

Vogiazides, L. (2012). *'Legal empowerment of the poor' versus 'right to the city'*. Uppsala: The Nordic Africa Institute. Retrieved: http://urn.kb.se/resolve?urn=urn%3Anbn%3Ase%3Anai%3Adiva-1560

Watson, V. (2002). The usefulness of normative planning theories in the context of sub-Saharan Africa. *Planning Theory*, 1(1), pp. 27–52. DOI: https://doi.org/10.1177/147309520200100103

5 Urban infrastructure and inequality

Lessons from Cairo and Johannesburg

Deena Khalil and Margot Rubin

Introduction

Africa has been making significant strides in regards to many development and economic indicators, but the continent continues to face gaps in its infrastructure and service provision. According to the latest African Economic Outlook report, Africa's infrastructure needs face a financing gap of between US$68–108 billion (AfDB, 2019). Many African cities continue to face challenges in keeping up with the pressures of growing population sizes and the concomitant growing demand on water, sanitation, and electricity provision. As stated by the World Bank, 'In many African countries, only the upper 5 to 10 percent of the population can afford the cheapest form of formal housing' – a reality that results in 60–70% of Africans residing in housing provided by the informal sector (World Bank, 2015). While many institutional reports focus on national level infrastructure, service, and housing provision, or rural-urban disparities, less attention has been devoted to intra-city inequalities.

This chapter seeks to examine spatial inequality in African cities in research and practice, looking at Cairo and Johannesburg. Specifically, the chapter explores the primary factors contributing to inequality, how spatial configurations and inequality correlate, the connection between informality and inequality, and how governance affects the spatial distribution of services and inequality.

The motivation for the chapter arises from intersecting research, theorizations, and contemporary debates, all of which recognize inequality as a central feature of cities in regions both north and south of the Sahara. As Obeng-Odoom (2015, p. 551) notes, 'inequality everywhere is on the rise, but in African cities, the rise is meteoric'. Though the body of literature on inequality in African cities is large, its focus has been primarily on economic measures of inequality (e.g., Gini coefficients and GDP growth) rather than inequality's complex spatiality, and the different ways it manifests across various spaces in the same city. However, these gaps are beginning to be addressed: a 2017 World Bank report on 64 African cities noted the large discrepancies in service provision within African cities, and how these inconsistencies signal the relationships that exist between poverty, spatial and political marginalization, and service provision (Lall et al., 2017). Graham and Marvin (2001) speak of a 'splintered urbanism' in which those who can afford to, 'bundle' themselves into settlements with good (often private) services and infrastructure, leaving poorer urban residents to spatially marginalized islands of deprivation with limited provision.

Adopted in 2015 as part of Agenda 2030, the United Nations Sustainable Development Goals (SDG) recognize the importance of addressing inequality through the inclusion of a special goal to 'reduce inequality within and among countries' (SDG 10), and incorporate indicators that distinguish between gender, age, disability, and geographic location when assessing infrastructure and service provision. However, the main focus of inequality as understood in the SDG is on social inclusion and inclusive growth (Fukuda-Parr, 2019). Moreover, while there are stand-alone goals on infrastructure (SDG 9) and cities (SDG 11), SDG reporting usually takes place at the national level, meaning intra-city inequalities and the ways in which they affect the vulnerability of certain population groups to the impact of, for instance, climate change, are often not taken into account (Reckien et al., 2017).

Similarly, the academic literature still largely ignores the recursive relationship between service provision and inequality: that is, how a lack of public services not only is indicative of inequality within cities, but, we would argue, also is key to embedding inequality (see McFarlane & Rutherford, 2008; Graham, 2010). In other words, the lack of service provision is not only a manifestation or measure of inequality, but also a producer of social inequality, embedding and entrenching inequality within cities through a set of provision practices.

As McFarlane and Rutherford (2008) highlight, infrastructure decision-making is embedded in political ideologies and agendas. Decisions made for or against a specific infrastructural intervention further solidify positions of power. This process highlights how material infrastructure can simultaneously connect and disconnect, and also showcases the embedded sociopolitical nature of material infrastructures. Therefore, the role of infrastructure cannot be seen as politically neutral, given that an active decision is made to provide in some areas, and not in others.

This chapter seeks to engage with the spatiality of service provision and its relation and contribution to urban inequality, examining case studies in Johannesburg and Cairo. By mapping and understanding the spatiality of services, we aim to clearly see both where inequality is most pronounced, and by extension, where interventions are most needed to combat the multigenerational and long-term impacts of service deficits.

From a methodological perspective, we endeavour to respond to the challenge of new comparative urbanism, which calls for comparisons between contexts and cities that have traditionally not been found in conversation with each other (Ward, 2010; McFarlane, 2014; Brenner & Schmid, 2015; Robinson, 2011). Ward (2008) argues that by looking at one context through the lens of another, new questions or ways of seeing processes, paradigms, and practices emerge, forcing us to rethink our analytical frames. In addition, we wish to contribute to the construction of new 'South-South' knowledges, outside of the traditional paradigms of thought, responding to an emerging call to move away from dominant North-South comparisons (Robinson, 2005, 2011; Watson, 2009).

This chapter thus reexamines questions of urban inequality, using infrastructure and service provision as both indicators of inequality, as well as contributors to inequality. More specifically, we look at infrastructure/services and inequality in Cairo, Egypt and Johannesburg, South Africa, using a comparative lens to deepen our thinking around these questions. Exploring water, sanitation, and electricity provision, as well as tenure and housing provision at the urban scale – and particularly within informal settlements and areas of high deprivation – this chapter uses the spatial distribution of different services and forms of infrastructure as a way of examining the spatiality of urban inequality.

Conceptualizing poverty and inequality

The following section explores some of the conceptual underpinnings in the relationship between infrastructure provision, inequality, and governance. It engages with three main thematic areas: the centrality of infrastructure and embedded poverty; the question of power and politics, and how decisions are made regarding infrastructure provision and distribution; and lastly, the spatialized nature of infrastructure, which is a manifestation of urban governance relations, as well as an indication of the location of poverty and privilege in cities of the South.

Currently, infrastructure provision and access are seen as a measure of inequality, and not as a contributing factor to deepening inequality. In line with McFarlane and Rutherford's (2008) argument that infrastructure can simultaneously connect and disconnect, this chapter argues that access to infrastructure is both a measure of and contributor to inequality, as seen through the examples of Johannesburg and Cairo.

The centrality of infrastructure

Infrastructure in the global South is often viewed through the unequal struggles to access reliable forms of various services, with very few cities achieving the reliability of infrastructure that renders services invisible or taken for granted (Graham, 2010). This struggle for equal access to infrastructure and its subsequent services, forms a central part of this chapter's focus.

Access (or lack thereof) to infrastructure – and thus services, such as water, sanitation, and power – makes a material difference in the quality of people's lives, their daily existence, as well as their aspirations and potential for addressing intergenerational poverty. Poor access to water, sanitation, and power have natural and clear impacts on the health and well-being of residents who have to make do without these services (Satterthwaite, 2001). These impacts are also felt differentially: women and children – usually responsible for water collection, disposal of waste, and other domestic chores that increase physical vulnerability and extend the working day – often bear the brunt of the lack of infrastructure provision.

That said, linear relationships between poverty, inequality, and the impacts of lack of infrastructure cannot be drawn. As Graham and Marvin (2001, p. 11) explain, 'such large technological systems (Summerton, 1994) or technical networks (Offner, 1993) are closely bound up within wider socio-technical, political, and cultural complexes, which have contingent effects in different places and different times' (see Tarr & Dupuy, 1988; Joerges, 1999). Thus, when it comes to the relationship between infrastructure and inequality, the quality and material existence (or lack thereof) of infrastructure is just one aspect of the question. The larger issue is how lack of infrastructure not only reflects existing inequality in daily life, but also contributes to continued inequalities, causing the institutional, political, and social structures that entrench these issues to surface.

The centrality of governance in determining inequality

Infrastructure decisions can serve as a way of understanding aspects of urban governance. That is, if governance is seen as the process through which multiple actors from various sectors – in collaboration and contestation – shape and manage a city (Pierre, 2014) and urban politics, decisions made around infrastructure can provide insight into the structure and nature of power and power relations in cities. McFarlane and Rutherford (2008) posit that where infrastructural decisions are made in any urban context, there is an immediate and inherent mobilization of political ideals and political ideologies. This relationship to power shows that infrastructure is not neutral, but rather an additional form of political expression (McFarlane & Rutherford, 2008). Where infrastructure is placed, and for whom, is a highly politicized choice that reflects the power, status, and social standing of various groups, illustrating respective abilities to leverage support from the state and other institutions or not. The location, siting, and provision of infrastructure should also be located within an understanding of other material contestations. According to Graham and Marvin (2001, p. 18), 'social biases have always been designed into urban infrastructure systems, whether intentionally or unintentionally. In Ancient Rome, the City's sophisticated water network was organized to deliver first to public fountains, then to public baths, and finally to individual dwellings, in case of insufficient flow' (Offner, 1999, p. 219).

Questions around infrastructure and related socioeconomic rights are further complicated within the context of informal settlements or potentially illegal locations, which can lack legal claim to service provision. Harris (2011) and Chatterjee (2004) further note that differentiation in legal status means not just differential ability to access service provision, but, in fact, differential ability to have one's rights to access basic services and amenities recognized at all. In contrast, middle income and higher income residents are seen as rights-bearing legitimate citizens, and are able to access and utilize the formal institutions of the state to represent their needs, access resources, and influence decisions that affect them (Rubin, 2014). Such differential exclusion perpetuates the poverty and inequitable treatment that poorer and informal communities face, and so deepens their reduced status within these urban environments.

The spatial nature of inequality

Spatial inequality is in many ways one dimension of overall inequality. Despite this, as Kanbur and Venables (2005) note, spatial inequality becomes increasingly significant when it aligns with political tensions, which undermine social and political stability. Through a historical lens, it is clear that there are many factors which have resulted in almost all cities having sites of wealthier and poorer households. How this geography manifests, and what it means to the lives of its residents, is key to understanding the causes and implications of inequality within a given city. History has played a key role in the location of communities and their access to services. In cities with colonial origins or strong colonial influences, formal urban areas designed for 'Europeans' or imperial residents saw lower densities and better provision of services than those earmarked for indigenous populations (Andersen et al., 2015; Buire, 2014). South African cities (like Johannesburg), which remain in many ways stubbornly spatially segregated, are a clear example (Turok & Parnell, 2009).

Separated by *cordon sanitaires*, or buffer strips and transport routes, colonial rulers created spatial divisions in municipalities, and with them, distinct hierarchies of infrastructure provision. Additionally, unlike the 'bundled' or generalized service provision offered by public entities or monopolies in northern cities, cities in lower-income countries generally have had diverse suppliers and forms of supply, the result of which is that most have never achieved universal access to service provision (Zérah, 2008).

Today we are seeing new forms of infrastructural segregation and separation, some of which is related to the privatization and corporatization of infrastructure (Coutard, 2008). Graham and Marvin (2001) discuss a 'splintering urbanism', stating: 'a parallel set of processes are underway within which infrastructure networks are being 'unbundled' in ways that help sustain the fragmentation of the social and material fabric of cities' (2001, p. 33). This conceptualization argues that the elite can access premium services, often provided by international service providers, which 'bypass' those who cannot afford their services. Located on the periphery of existing cities, such privately developed new towns or suburbs are thus built, complete with superior infrastructures that often bypass the older and often failing public service provisions. All of this serves to construct patchwork landscapes of access and denial, further layered by other spatial processes, such as the peripheral or marginalized location of 'auto-constructed' communities, informal settlements, and poorer households (Caldeira, 2017). The result of these multiple processes is a historically rooted spatialization of unequal access, which continues to be driven by contemporary commercial motivations located in privatization and new formulations of access.

Research methodology

This chapter is the product of a larger research project conducted jointly by Takween Integrated Community Development in Cairo and Wits University CUBES/SA&CP in Johannesburg between July 2017 and June 2018.

To produce this research, we conducted a literature survey and combined secondary data on the spatial distribution of services across Cairo and Johannesburg – creating a 'bird's-eye view' of the spatial distribution of services: housing, water, sanitation, and electricity. The research conducted in Cairo builds on the Planning [in] Justice: Spatial Analysis for Urban Cairo study, published in 2018 by Tadamun: The Cairo Urban Solidarity Initiative (a joint initiative by Takween Integrated Community Development and the American University in Washington, D.C.) (Tadamun, 2018). We also conducted a closer examination of inequality in the case-study areas of East Madinat Nasr (EMN), Cairo, and Soweto, Johannesburg, by deepening the use of the available secondary sources. EMN is a relatively large district with a wide range of income levels, including relatively upscale neighbourhoods alongside one of Cairo's largest informal areas. Soweto, equally, is home to a diverse range of income groups, and has received vast amounts of government funding to upgrade its services and infrastructure, but these remain unevenly distributed.

Data on Cairo's distribution of housing and utilities was drawn from the 2006 national census, produced by the Central Agency for Public Mobilization and Statistics (CAPMAS). Johannesburg data was drawn from the Quantec service, which offers comparable data between the 1996, 2001, and 2011 national censuses.[1]

The Johannesburg team also utilized maps and data from the City of Johannesburg's nodal review exercise, which was carried out in response to a legislative requirement that mixed-use, mixed-intensity nodes are identified for planning and investment purposes (CoJ, 2018a). We created the maps in this chapter using the data noted earlier and GIS software.

Aside from the data retrieval mentioned earlier, the teams sought to consider and engage with new comparative urbanism; i.e., the systematic study of similarities and differences between cities and urban processes, particularly looking at cities whose very different histories and economic and political systems do not invite comparison (Nijman, 2007). Attempting to develop 'knowledge, understanding, and generalization at a level between what is true of all cities and what is true of one city at a given point in time' (Nijman, 2007, p. 1), the two teams worked closely to codevelop research questions, research instruments, and a common language for understanding inequality. The teams met via Skype and used online platforms to develop questionnaires, research frameworks, and sets of indicators that were appropriate in both contexts. Through the research process, we also came to appreciate the relational comparative approach that Ward (2010) advocates for, where we 'use different cities to pose questions of one another' (2010, p. 480), and get 'away from searching for similarities and difference between two mutually exclusive contexts' (2010, p. 480). In this manner, specific outcomes or phenomena in one city provoked us to ask related questions in the other.

Findings: context and background to service provision

Johannesburg

Population and informality

Growing at 3.24% per annum between 2010–2015 (UN-Habitat, 2014), South Africa's largest and most populous city is home to between 4.43 to 9.4 million people (the difference being that between the official city border [StatsSA, 2011] and the entire urban agglomeration [UN-Habitat, 2014]). The City government is divided into seven administrative regions (see Figure 5.1), each of which is operationally responsible for the delivery of services to its constituencies. Policy and strategic decisions are taken centrally within the Johannesburg Metropolitan Municipal council. The City's poverty and livelihood data demonstrate high levels of need, with over 40% of the employed population earning below R3,200 a month (US$235) and one quarter of the City's population unemployed (StatsSA, 2011). However, poverty throughout the city is not homogenous, and regions that host economic nodes record higher individual and household incomes than do those areas on the city's periphery, which are home to large townships and informal settlements (Karuaihe, 2015). In addition, economic diversity exists within different regions, where poverty and wealth coexist in relatively close proximity (see Figure 5.2). Johannesburg further offers a highly attractive environment for national and cross-border migrants, most of whom cannot find or afford accommodation in the formal sector. As a consequence, there have historically been a number of informal settlements around the City (estimated at 189 in 2013) accommodating about 9% of the City population.

Interestingly, the number of dwellings in Johannesburg's informal settlements has dropped considerably in the ten-year period between 2001–2011, declining

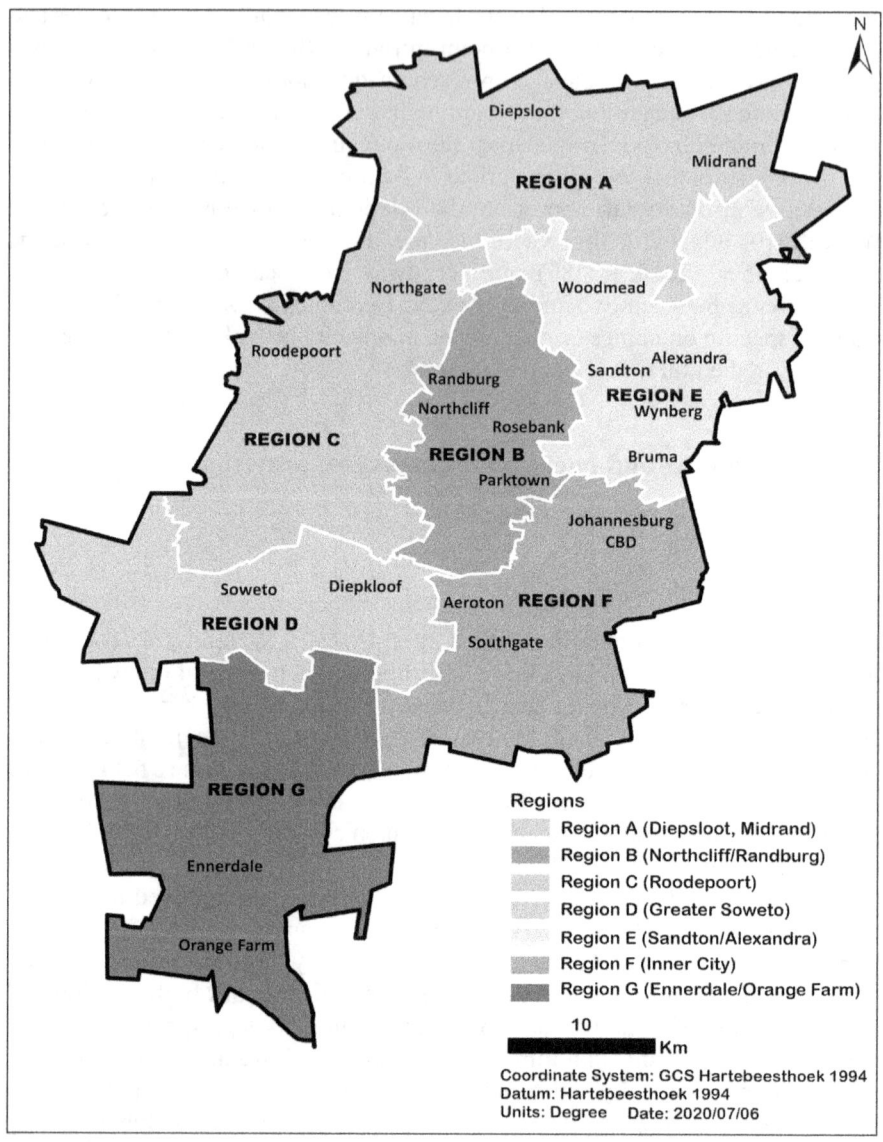

Figure 5.1 Structure of Johannesburg's Regions
Source: CoJ, 2012

by over 8,000 households, and contributing 4% less to the city's household composition. That said, informal units in backyards or on the premises of other houses increased by almost 58% over the same period (CoJ, 2016; Gardner & Rubin, 2016).

Institutional structure and responsibility

As designated by the Constitution, a local government like the City of Johannesburg (CoJ) is an autonomous sphere of government, separate but equal to national and provincial spheres. While each sphere of government has its specific set of responsibilities, they also share certain joint responsibilities (e.g., human settlements). This division of responsibilities can and historically has caused some tensions between the spheres, as seen in the realms of planning, land-use management, and housing provision. Of particular relevance to this chapter are the tight constraints South African legislation puts on public expenditure, with the state prohibited from investing in services on land that it does not own (or with which it does not have an agreement with the landowner), or on land that has not been formally designated as residential. Because informal settlements often do not meet these criteria, until recently, many have not been able to receive state-provided infrastructure.

The sharp turn in the South African bureaucracy to New Public Management (Cameron, 2015) in the 2000s, under which many services were corporatized, has further complicated service provision. Following its financial crisis in the late 1990s, the CoJ established separate municipal owned entities (MOEs) responsible for service delivery on a citywide basis. These city-owned entities include Joburg Water, City Power, and the refuse removal company, Pikitup, among others. Managed by local government, these entities are all intended to function as commercial companies: billing for services, collecting revenues, assuming debt for capital projects, and making capital expenditures with board approval to improve and extend services. Although such corporatized entities were expected to more efficiently ensure quality delivery and recover costs, this has not been the case for all of the MoEs, and in 2016 the Democratic Alliance and Economic Freedom Fighter coalition leading the council chose to bring many of these functions back in-house. With the late 2018 dissolution of that coalition and return to an African National Congress mayor (Geoff Makhubo), the future of these entities remains uncertain.

That said, structured basic services are a key income source for the CoJ. Within this structure, local government must ensure access and provision of basic services to all urban residents, which means finding a budget to pay for or subsidize costs. Generally, the city has accomplished this through cross-subsidization mechanisms, which allow for taxes and rates generated in wealthier wards and suburbs to pay for infrastructure costs and services in the city's poorer areas. Although cross-subsidization has been a vital part of paying for services across the CoJ, it remains insufficient to meet the demand.

The seeming paradox at play – on one hand, the need for cost recovery, and on the other, a constitutional pledge guaranteeing citizens the right to these services – has led to a number of court cases. Since 2009, the Constitutional Court determined that the CoJ and all South African municipalities must provide residents with minimum quantities of free water, sanitation, and power (SERI, 2018). Exact amounts and details around how these services are provided and administered have been a matter of contention, leading to further litigation, social movements, and protests.

In sum, Johannesburg's current service delivery situation presents a promising but complicated narrative in which older, 'previously white suburbs' continue to enjoy high levels of service provision and a very good quality of life, while older 'black townships' indicate generally good but uneven service provision thanks to massive state investment. However, despite Constitutional Court rulings, the city's highly contested informal settlements still experience uneven service provision, and many lack satisfactory levels of water, sanitation, and/ or power.

Cairo

Population and informality

Cairo is home to 10% of Egypt's total population (CAPMAS, 2017), or more than 9.7 million inhabitants residing on an area of 188,982 km². One of the world's more densely populated cities, its chaotic landscape has been the focus of many studies throughout the last few decades. According to Sims (2012), 'Two-thirds of the city's population now live in neighbourhoods that have sprung up since 1950, devoid of any planning or control, and which are considered by officialdom as both illegal and undesirable' (2012, p. 3). Such uncontained growth has led to encroachments onto state and private lands and the rise of a parallel system of informal services, some of which employ illegal connections to public services and facilities. Unsurprisingly, the spatial distribution of access to services is highly uneven, with some areas enjoying very good access to high quality services, and others struggling to access services that are of generally poor quality. In regards to poverty, according to Cairo's 2013 national poverty map, 18.3% of the population lives below the national poverty line (set at a mean annual expenditure of EGP 7,240). This seems a relatively low percentage compared to other governorates in Egypt (e.g., Qena Governorate, where the poverty rate is 60%), but the distribution of poverty within Cairo is highly unequal, especially when expanding the focus to look at the Greater Cairo Region (GCR), which encompasses Cairo, Giza, and Qalyoubeya Governorates (with poverty rates of 18.3%, 32.3%, and 22.3%, respectively).

Institutional structure and responsibilities

Egypt's National Constitution (Arab Republic of Egypt, 2014) guarantees the right of all citizens to basic services, including infrastructure and social services such as healthcare and education. As in South Africa, Egypt's institutional structure for urban administration includes both national and local levels of governance.

Central institutions include ministries, each of which is responsible for a different aspect of high-level governance for service provision. For example, the Ministry of Housing, Utilities and Urban Development (MHUUD) is responsible for setting policies related to housing, potable water, and urban planning, while the Ministry of Planning (MoP) is responsible for developing Egypt's annual national socioeconomic plan.

At the local governance level, the highest spatial and administrative unit is the governorate, which is responsible for service provision governance, and implements policies and plans that are set at higher levels of government (Figure 5.2). Within the governorate office, line ministries are represented by directorates (e.g., the Cairo Governorate Directorate of Housing represents the Ministry of Housing within Cairo), and the directorates are responsible for much of the local management of services and budgeting.

Egypt is divided into 27 governorates. Fully urban governorates like Cairo are divided into spatial units of municipalities, each of which is further divided into subdistricts.[2] Cairo is divided into four geographical areas (eastern, western, northern, and southern), each of which contain a number of municipalities.

Local governance becomes complicated when looking at the chain of command. Although the governorates are responsible for the day-to-day management of local services and local budgeting (through the municipalities and the directorates, which represent line ministries within the governorate), the directorates do not actually report to the governor (who is the appointed head

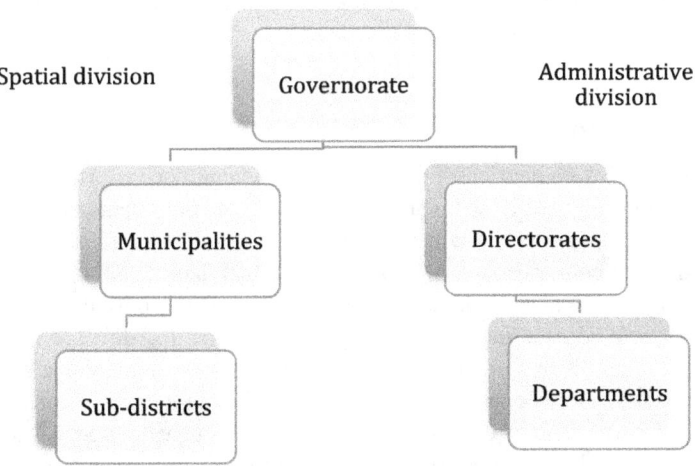

Figure 5.2 Cairo's Administrative and Spatial Structure

Source: Authors

of the governorate), but rather to their respective ministries, from which they also receive their budgets. Thus, the institution directly responsible for local service management does not answer to its own administrative head (i.e., the governor), but rather to the relevant national level ministry. This fragmentation within the urban governance system – as well as the number of institutions involved in urban management – has created an infamously messy institutional system, where responsibilities of the various institutions sometimes overlap (Khalil et al., 2018). The consequence of this fragmented and overlapping system is a service-provision scheme that is incredibly inefficient and often ineffective in providing residents with sufficient, good quality, and reliable services.

Further complicating matters is the fact that utility services such as water, sanitation, electricity, and natural gas are provided through publicly-owned national holding companies. These entities operate largely autonomously, without interference from the governorate/directorate, and are accountable only to their respective national ministries. Although fully owned by the Egyptian state, these companies operate as commercial entities, meaning they are mandated to cover their costs and generate a profit.[3]

Analysis

In this section we present the outcomes of the secondary data analysis that we conducted, in the form of maps showing access to different services across the cities of Cairo and Johannesburg. The maps shed light on service distribution throughout the two cities, revealing how certain services are more equally distributed than others. All the findings and analysis provided in this section are based on secondary sources.

Income and poverty

The collection and comparison of poverty and income data is problematic. First, there is a strong tendency for respondents' to keep income data private, meaning people may not provide entirely accurate information. Second, comparing data between the two countries is complicated by the fact that the data sets come from different dates and scales. In Johannesburg, a full census is only undertaken every 10 years, which, considering the rate of growth, means that data are quickly outdated. Cairo's data is in some cases more up to date, but not available at the same (finer) geographical scale as Johannesburg's. Finally, although we converted both data sets for income into the same currency, comparisons were complicated by the fact that these numbers do not provide insight into the differences of cost of living and expenditures that poorer people have to endure in each context. Thus, poverty and income are difficult to use as measures of inequality, and especially hard to compare.

Johannesburg

Earlier work from the National Income Dynamics Study provides some context about poverty in the CoJ: in 2011, 50% of households in the city were earning less than R3,543 a month (citywide median), 40% less than R2,487, 33% less than R2,224, and 25% less than R1,751 (CoJ, 2018b). Meanwhile, Figure 5.3 spatializes more recent data on income, taken from the Gauteng City Region's 2017/2018 survey. Beginning with the CoJ municipality at the centre, one can discern the higher income patterns in the north, and poorer communities located to the south and far north.

Cairo

Figure 5.4 shows how poverty rates compare across Greater Cairo's different municipalities; the numerical data is even more striking when we compare the highest and lowest poverty rates: 70.6% in Al-Ayyaat municipality and .7% in Al-Nozha municipality. The mean expenditures are equally striking, with the lowest expenditure level of EGP 3,511 in Al-Ayyaat, compared with the highest expenditure level of EGP 19,323 in Al-Nozha. There is also a strong relationship between the distribution of poverty and informality, as the darkest areas on the map fall within Giza's peri-urban periphery, which has been informally transitioning from agricultural land into urbanized housing.

Housing market: tenure and informality

In this section we examine certain dimensions of access to housing in the two cities, such as different forms of tenure, housing conditions, and informality. In doing this, we are setting the context for discussing the relationship between inequality and basic services, since inequality in service access manifests most clearly in informal areas. However, we are also looking at housing itself as a basic service, and thus are curious to see how its distribution and equality of access manifests in both cities.

Johannesburg

Statistics are difficult to come by, but according the CoJ's Spatial Development Framework, in 2012 there were an estimated 164,939 informal structures, and about 320,652 families living in backyard dwellings (CoJ, 2016). In the CoJ, informal dwellings are located in two types of areas. Firstly, low-income areas (either old townships or newer 'RDP' settlements), where informal stock is situated in the 'backyard' of the main 'formal' dwelling (Gardner & Rubin, 2016).[4] Secondly, informal settlements, which are areas consisting almost exclusively of shacks or informal dwellings made of temporary materials, and are mostly located on the city's peripheries.

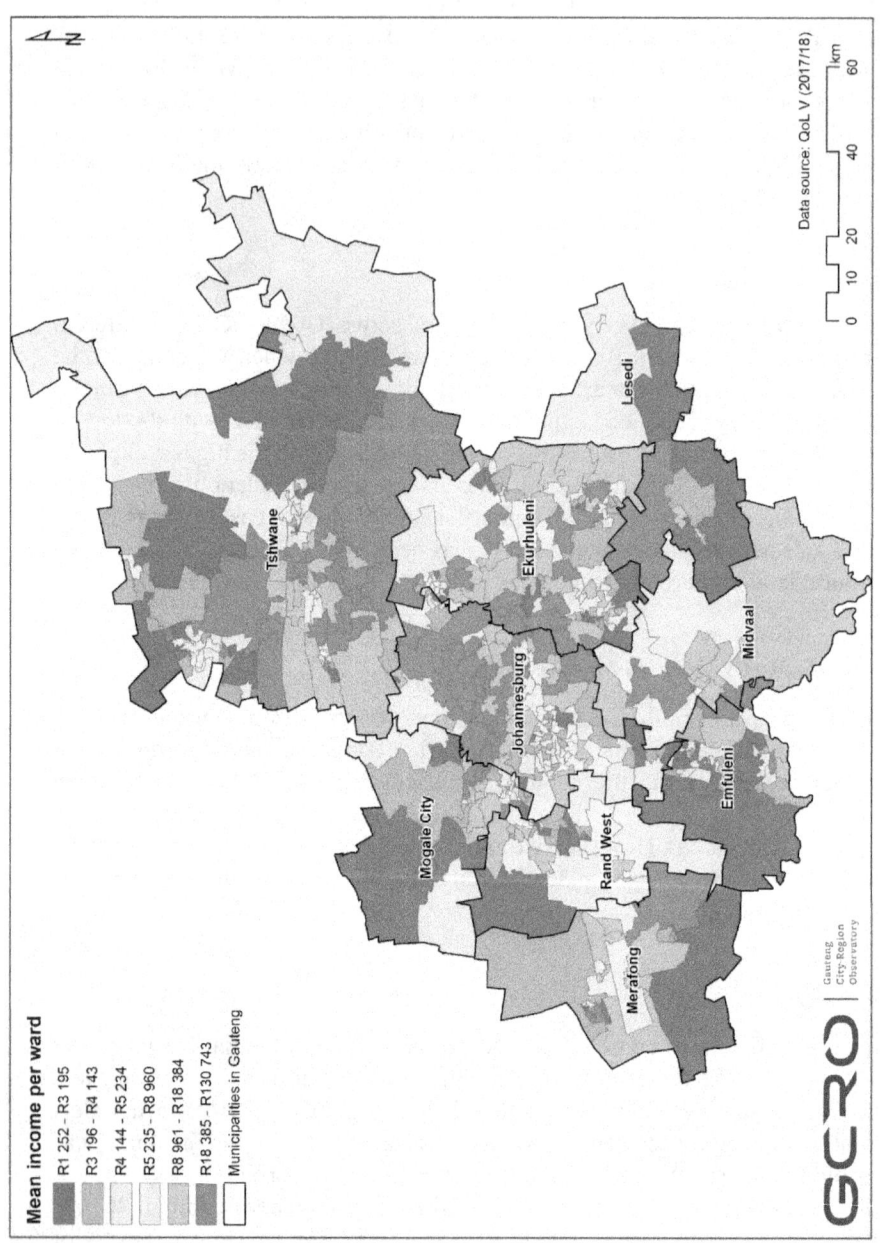

Figure 5.3 Gauteng City Region Mean Incomes

Source: GCRO, 2018

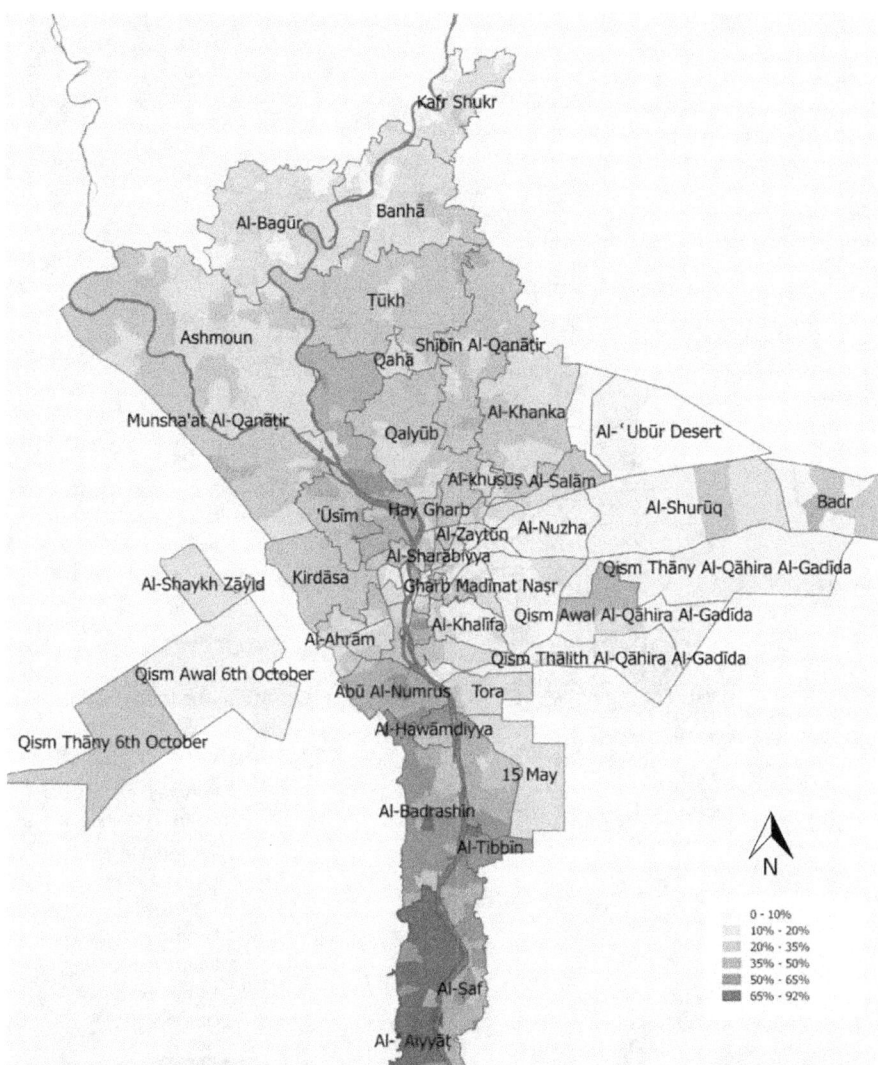

Figure 5.4 Poverty Rates in Greater Cairo

Source: Tadamun, 2016

Correlating Figure 5.3 with Figure 5.5 and Figure 5.6, we see that informal settlements are primarily inhabited by the poor majority. Taken together, these figures also indicate the high population densities and low incomes common to informal settlements, old townships, and the inner city alike (and in contrast to formal, higher-income areas) (Hamann et al., 2018).

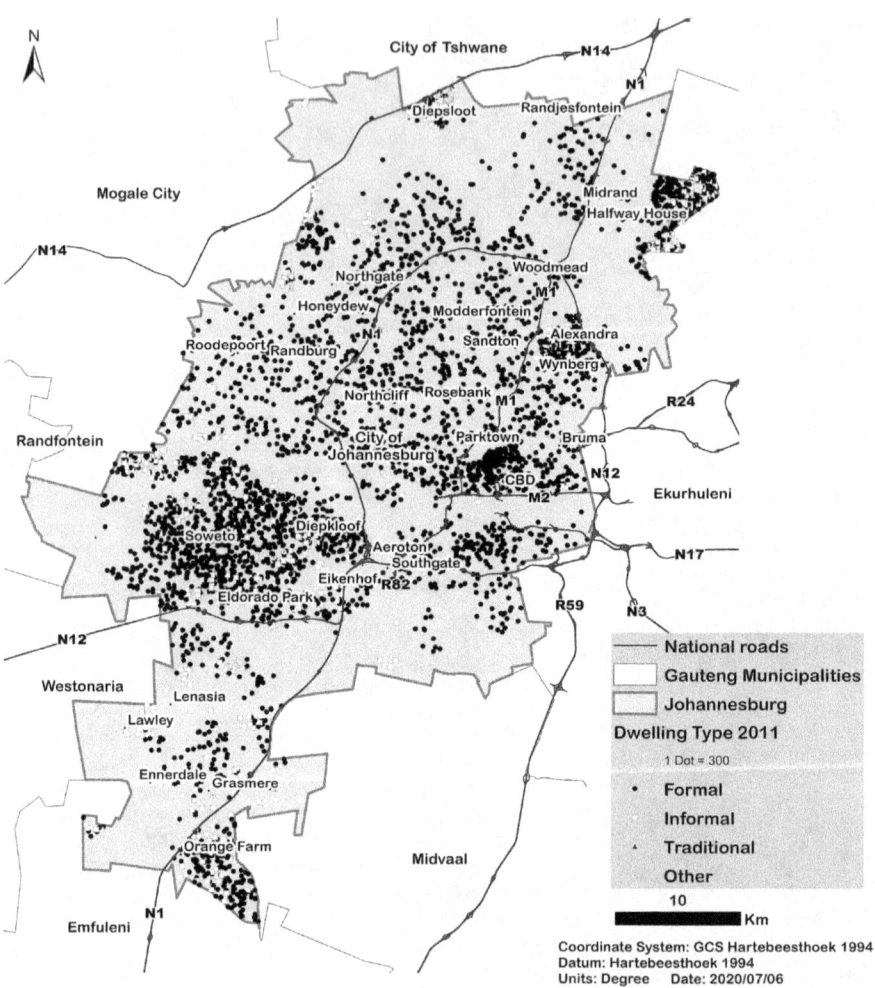

Figure 5.5 Formal, Informal, and Traditional Tenure in Johannesburg, 2011

Source: Authors

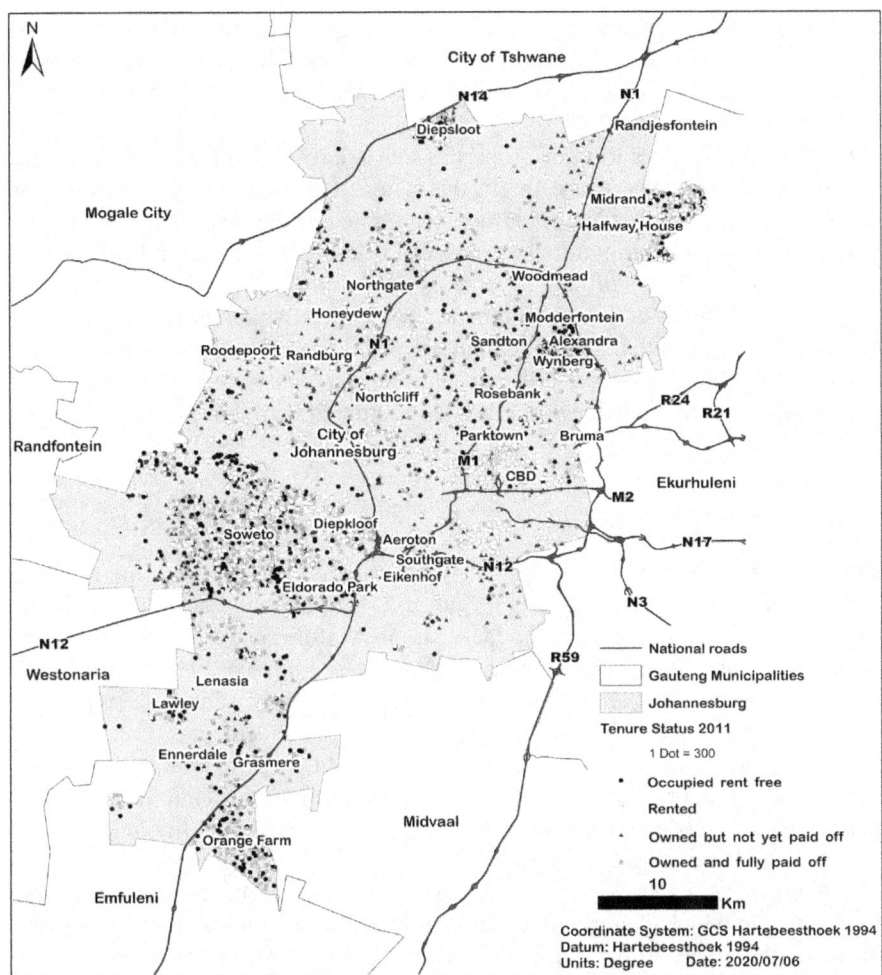

Figure 5.6 Tenure in the City of Johannesburg

Source: Authors

Figure 5.6 shows clusters of tenure types within the CoJ. One of the highest concentrations of rentals is found in the area around Johannesburg's original Central Business District (CBD). Known as a reception area for the highly mobile cross-border and national migrant demographic, the CBD and inner city mostly offer rental opportunities in the form of multistorey buildings, where apartment sharing and subletting are prevalent. Other rental concentrations are found in Soweto, Diepsloot, and other townships, where rentals generally take the form of backyard dwellings. The distribution of rentals across Johannesburg (in the inner city and backyards across the city) reflects the spatial location of poorer households that are renting properties.

The highest concentration of properties that are owned and fully paid off are located in the townships. Interestingly, this is not an indicator of wealth, but rather of the apartheid and post-apartheid housing strategies that supplied low-income households with sub-economic units and full title deeds. Although these properties are owned, they are difficult to leverage, and thus few households are willing or able to use them as collateral (Finmark, 2004). Meanwhile, the highest concentrations of properties that are owned but not paid off are found in the older white suburbs, reflecting the mortgages that these households were able to secure for their relatively more valuable properties (as compared with those in the townships or inner city).

Cairo

Cairo's housing market is dominated by apartments, followed by one or more rooms within shared housing units (Figure 5.7). Shacks and backyard dwellings are rare in Cairo, underscoring the fact that most informal areas in Cairo consist of apartment buildings quite similar to those in formal areas. The main factors distinguishing informal areas from formal ones are the lack of state-led planning, and in most cases, the lack of formally registered tenure documents. Furthermore, many buildings in informal areas are in violation of building codes, and illegally located on agricultural land. Finally, services in informal areas tend to be of lesser quality and quantity, and housing often tends to be of poorer quality in regards to materials used and adherence to safety standards and building codes.

Looking at tenure in Cairo (Figure 5.8), two things become clear: firstly, the great extent to which Cairenes depend on the rental market to access housing; and secondly, that spatial distribution of ownership versus rental corresponds with income. That is, ownership is more predominant in Cairo's better-off districts (located in the middle, east, and south of the city) as compared with the city's poorer districts in the west, where rental is more common.

Figure 5.9, which depicts rates of overcrowding in Cairo, almost mirrors the distribution of rental and ownership in Figure 5.8. The rate of overcrowding in Cairo's poorer western districts can be easily contrasted with the much lower rates seen in Cairo's middle, and especially eastern, districts – once again mirroring poverty levels seen in Figure 5.4.

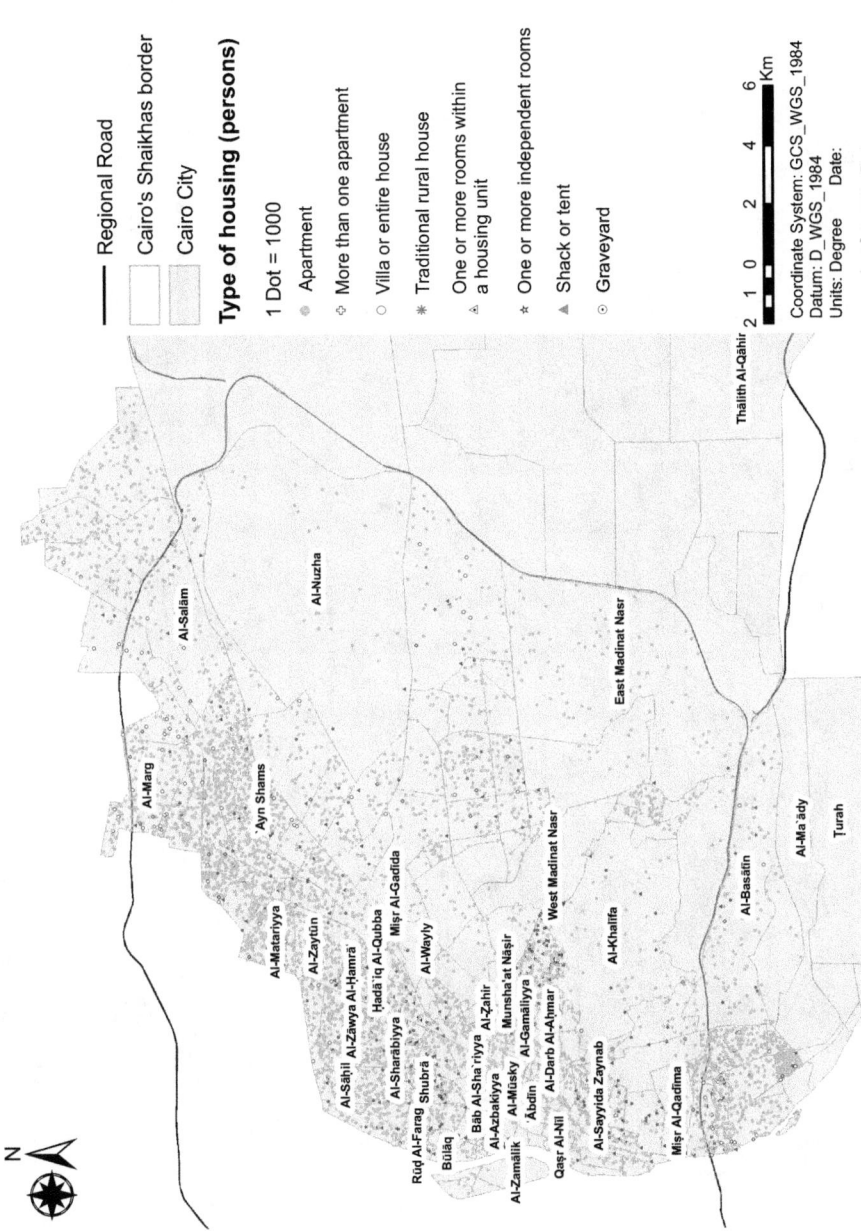

Regional Road

Cairo's Shaikhas border

Cairo City

Type of housing (persons)

1 Dot = 1000

⊕ Apartment

✛ More than one apartment

○ Villa or entire house

✳ Traditional rural house

△ One or more rooms within a housing unit

✩ One or more independent rooms

▲ Shack or tent

⊙ Graveyard

Coordinate System: GCS_WGS_1984
Datum: D_WGS_1984
Units: Degree_ Date:

Figure 5.7 Type of Housing Unit, Cairo, 2006
Source: Authors, based on CAPMAS (2006) data

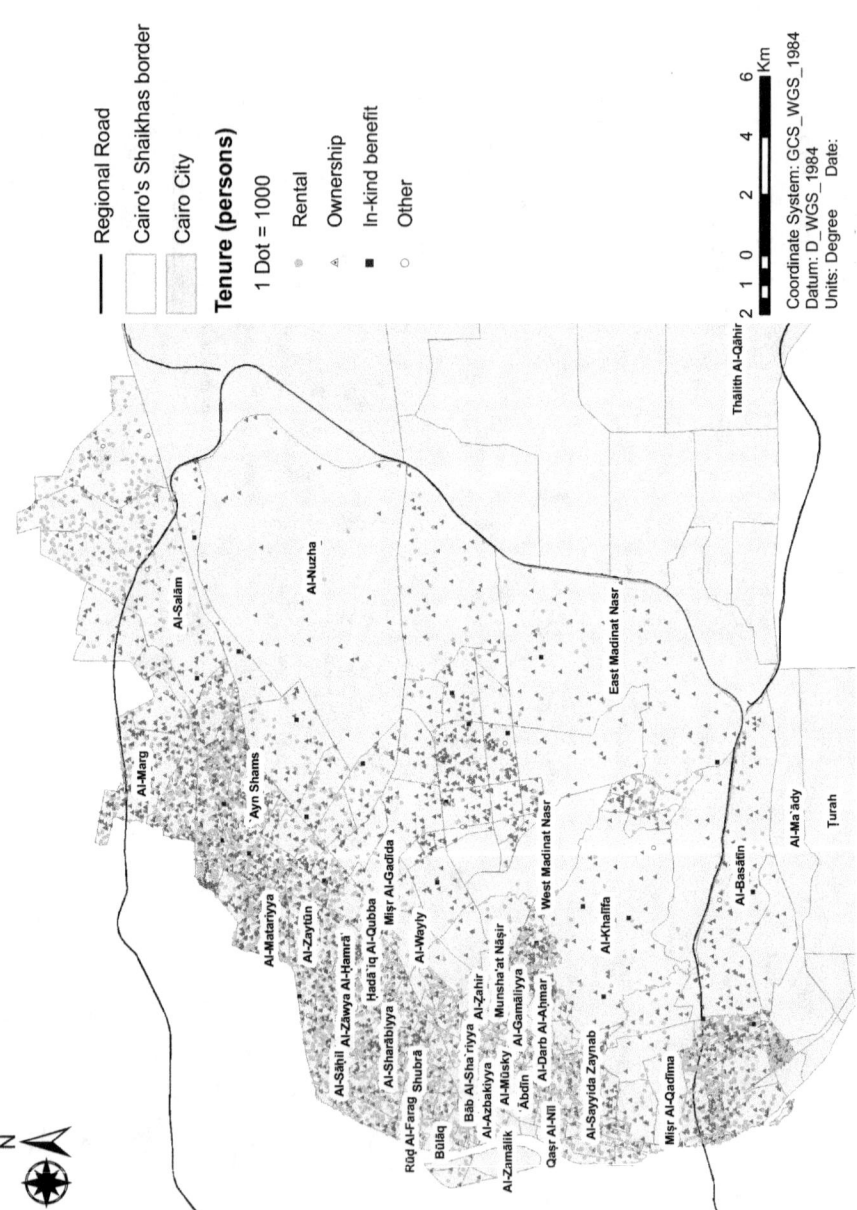

Figure 5.8 Type of Tenure, Cairo, 2006[5]

Source: Authors, based on CAPMAS (2006) data

Figure 5.9 Overcrowding Rate, Cairo, 2006

Source: Authors, based on CAPMAS (2006) data

Access to basic services

In terms of levels of access, Table 5.1 shows both cities' population's access to main infrastructure facilities (water supply facilities, sources of electricity, and sewage facilities), according to their most recent respective national censuses (2016 for Egypt, and 2011 for South Africa). Access to these fundamental services is useful in providing an idea of the average levels of access in the two cities, which can easily be contrasted with the local levels of access demonstrated later in the chapter.

Cairo and Johannesburg generally indicate similar patterns of electricity and water access, with both at first glance appearing to enjoy significant coverage. However, informal areas show the largest number of residents using off-grid means, demonstrating a clear lack of access in informal settlements. The remainder of this section demonstrates the extent and limits of these services.

Unlike many cities in Africa, Johannesburg residents and Cairenes generally enjoy relatively good access to piped water and sanitation. This is largely due to the fact that access to both is guaranteed by the Constitutions in both countries (as well as Prime Ministerial Decree 886/2016 in Egypt, which outlines provisions for informal buildings to apply for water and electricity meters). However, closer examination once again reveals stark differences at the local level, with informal settlements being the least well-served in both cities. In Figure 5.10 and Figure 5.11, we see the same patterns persisting in both cities: most formal households have access to piped water, either to the home or the stand, while areas where water is communal (shared taps) coincide largely with areas of informality.

Table 5.1 Provision of services in Cairo and Johannesburg

Service	Type of access/provision	Cairo (2016)	Johannesburg (2011)
Water	Access to in-house tap water	98.5%	91%
	Access to inside building tap water	0.9%	n/a
	Access to outside building tap/ Communal water on private stand	0.2%	7%
	Other: households using water pumps, wells, rain water, bottled water	0.4%	n/a
	No access to water	n/a	1.4%
Energy	Access to the public electricity network	99.87%	87%
	Electric generator	0.06%	n/a
	Gas/Kerosene/Paraffin or other	0.03%	11.5%
	Wood/coal	n/a	0.3%
	Renewable (e.g., Solar)	0.019%	n/a
	Other (e.g., animal dung)	0.01%	0.7%

Source: Authors

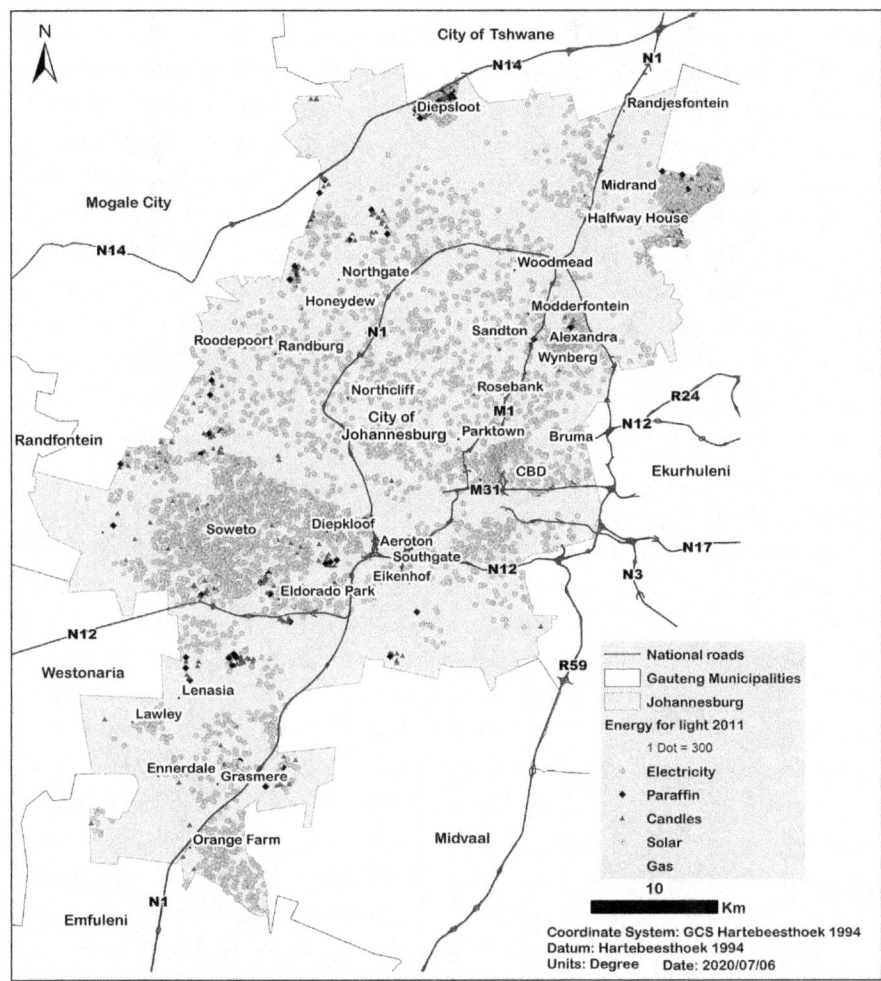

Figure 5.10 Access to Piped Water in Johannesburg, 2011

Source: Authors

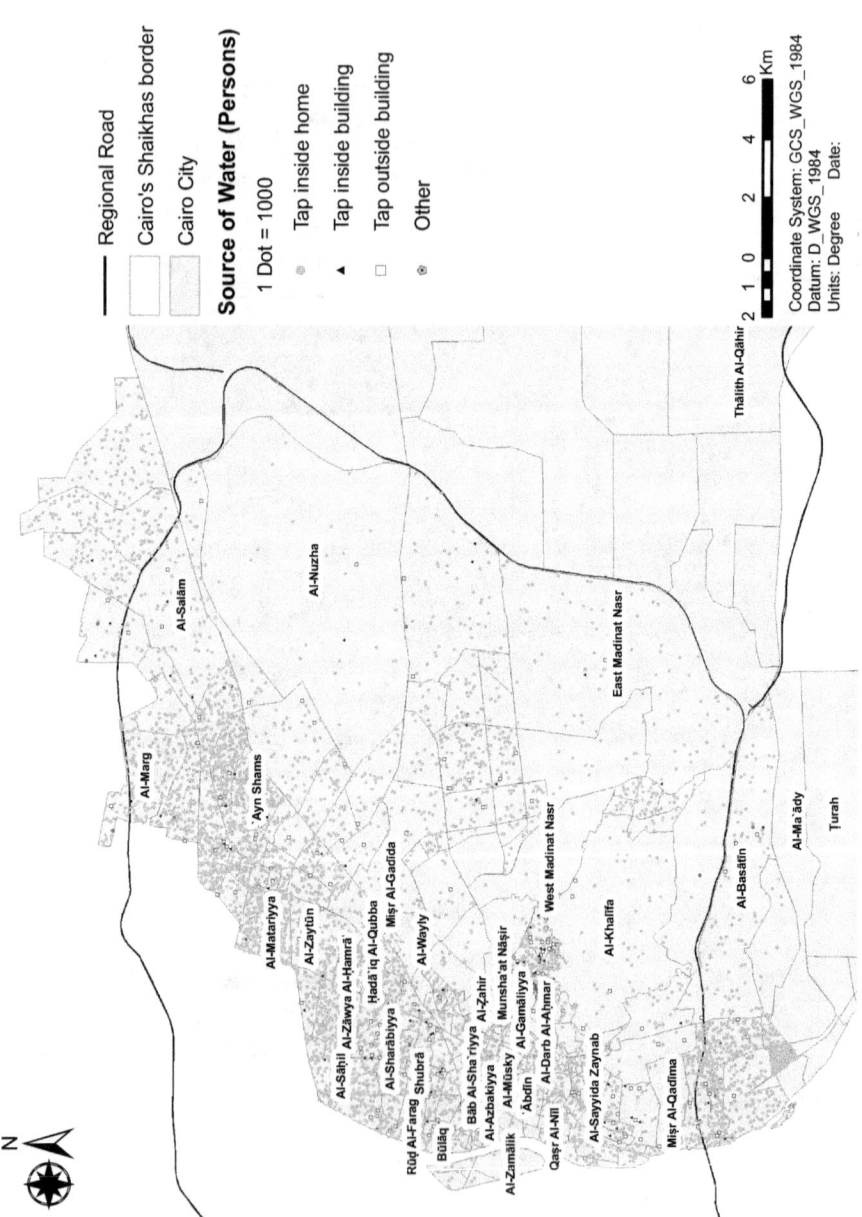

Figure 5.11 Source of Water, Cairo, 2006

Source: Authors

In Cairo, this relationship is made even more explicit, as the most concentrated cluster of shared taps lies in Munsha'at Nasir, Cairo's largest informal area.

As for electricity access, using the energy source for lighting as a general proxy for access to energy, a general trend emerges clearly (Figure 5.12): Johannesburg's older areas and townships have access to and utilize on-grid power sources, while in informal settlements, candles are the chief source of lighting, thus indicating a different level of access. Although there is significant informality within Johannesburg's older areas and townships (i.e., backyard accommodation and inner-city shared rooms in 'bad' buildings), many of these units and households are still hooked into the formal power grid, either legally or illegally. In this regard, the map demonstrating electricity provision is slightly misleading, as it indicates broad state provision, when the reality is that near-to-universal coverage has been achieved through other modes, such as illegal connections and self-provisioning.

Turning to Cairo, Figure 5.13 confirms government officials' (within Cairo's electricity companies) claims that virtually all of Cairo is connected to the electricity network, including informal areas (which find ways to informally connect). Even in neighbourhoods such as Ayn Shams, Al-Marg, East Madinat Nasr, and Al-Basatin, where the map shows some red dots indicating off-grid methods of energy access (e.g., kerosene, butane gas, etc.), the number of residents employing these off-grid methods is very low. As with the map of electricity access in Johannesburg, Cairo's data on electricity access does not distinguish between formal and informal access (i.e., illegally tapping into the public network without going through the electricity company), thus presenting a misleading picture of universal public access, which in reality is achieved by people accessing electricity through illegal means.

Case studies: a finer-scale spatial analysis

The earlier sections have offered a sense of access to infrastructure, service provision, and distribution in the aggregate, offering a picture of the distribution and limitations at the city scale, and indicating inequalities at the intra-urban scale. However, when narrowing the focus to a more fine-grained set of case studies, a set of further dynamics and complexities emerge.

Looking at Soweto (Johannesburg) and East Madinat Nasr (Cairo), we see that even municipal data (like that showcased by the maps shown earlier) has yet another more-localized level that can expose further hidden inequalities. Additionally, the following case studies, which examine access within certain municipalities/neighbourhoods, reveal how patterns of service delivery can provide more insight into the complex relationship between services, inequality, and informality, and also potentially illuminate why inequality is so entrenched in some areas, and thus how it can be addressed.

Case-study: Soweto

Located 16 kilometres from Johannesburg's city centre, Soweto traditionally housed the cheap black labour pool that serviced the city's white population. It

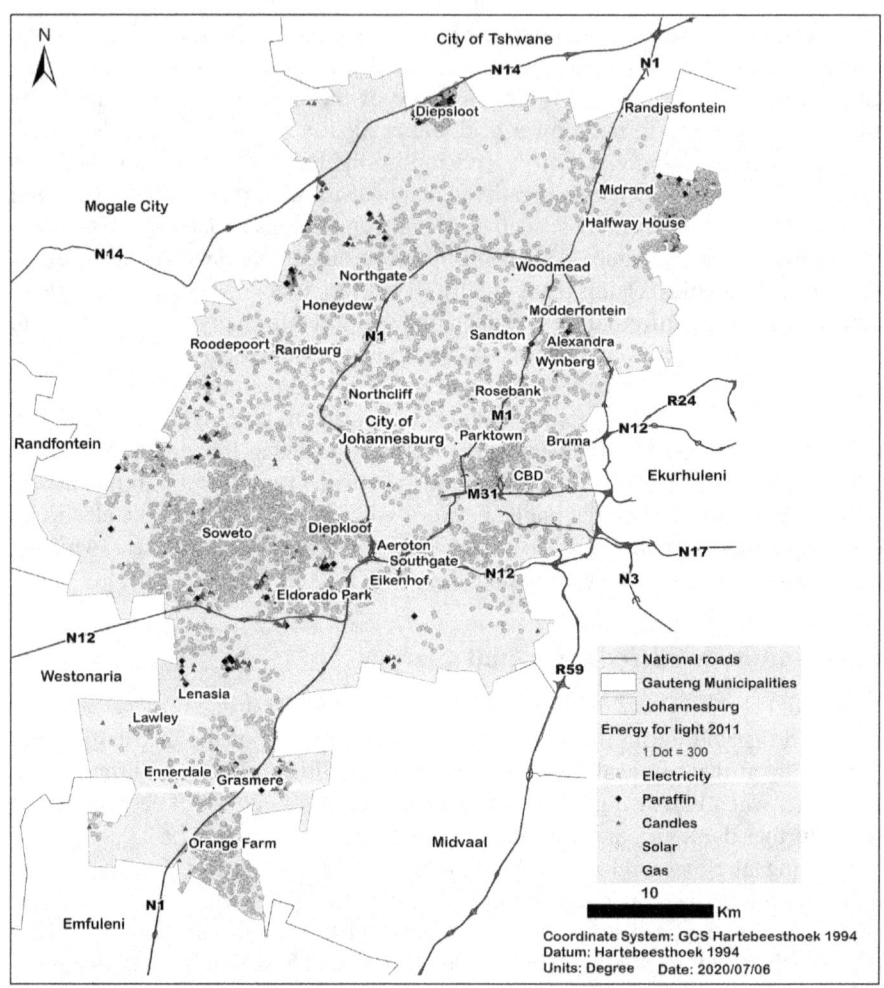

Figure 5.12 Source of Lighting Johannesburg, 2011
Source: Authors

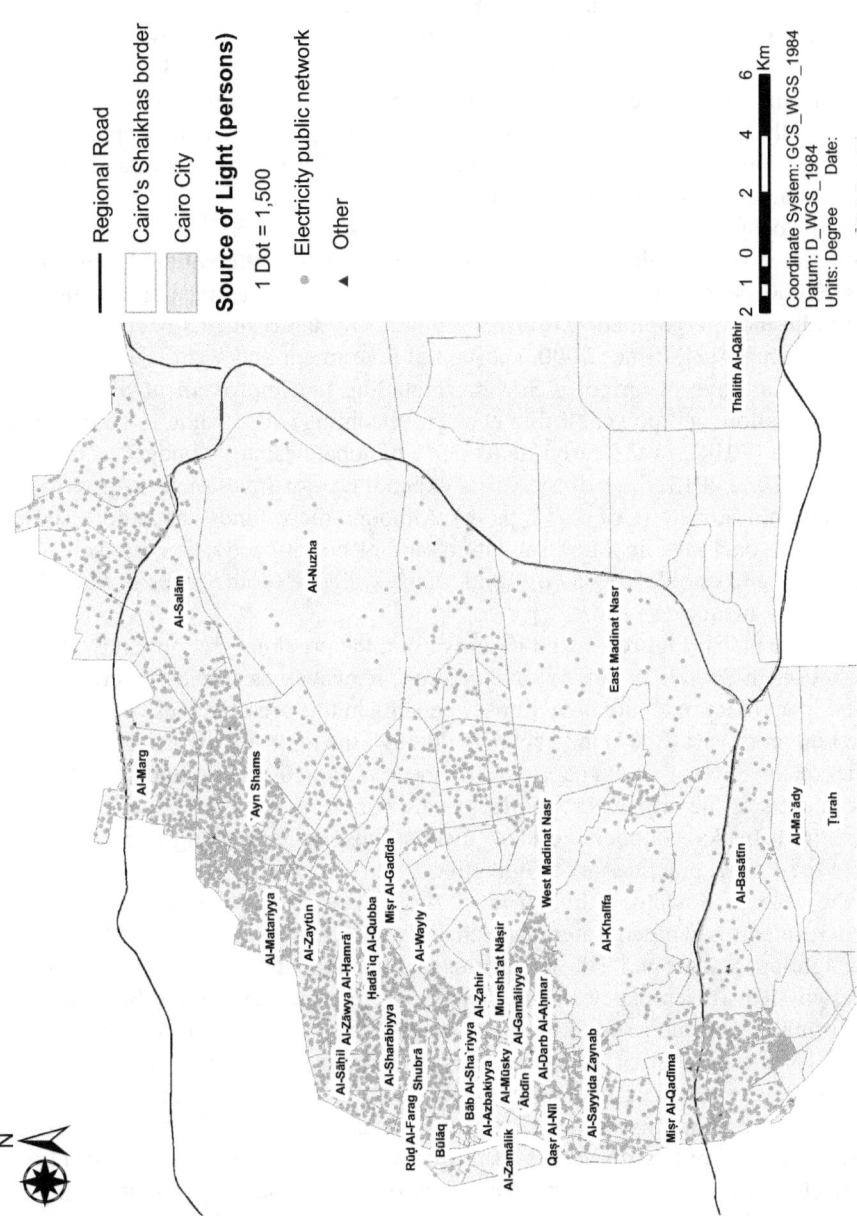

Figure 5.13 Source of Lighting Cairo, 2006

Source: Authors

was only in 1963 that its 29 separate precincts came to be called SOWETO, an acronym drawn from the descriptor, 'South Western Townships' (Harrison & Harrison, 2014). The state provided housing as well as basic services and amenities to Soweto residents from its inception. However, the quality of the infrastructure was always inferior to that found in residential areas intended for white South Africans or those classified as Indian and 'coloured'. Very few roads connected Soweto to the rest of the city, an intentional choice that ensured the township could literally be closed off in times of political turmoil. By the end of apartheid in the mid-1990s, Soweto's population of approximately three quarter of a million people remained underserviced in almost every way.

Soweto today is home to about 1.3 million people (StatsSA, 2011), or over 40% of the CoJ's population. That population is highly differentiated, with at least 600,000 people (nearly half) in poverty (CoJ, 2011), alongside a significant middle-income population (most wealthier Sowetan residents have left the area [Chipkin, 2012]). Since 2000, substantial investment and significant spatial transformation have occurred in Soweto, including the improvement of roads, clinics, sanitation, and power (Rubin et al., forthcoming). According to Harrison and Harrison (2014), in the early 2000s, 35% of Johannesburg's budget went to Soweto. In 2012/2013, 52% of the CoJ's expenditure for investment in priority areas went into Soweto (CoJ, 2012, p. 94). Although these funds have addressed infrastructure backlogs in water, sanitation, and electricity provision, as well as tarring roads and establishing a bus rapid transit system (Rubin, Todes & Mabin, forthcoming), inequities persist.

The tenure maps (Figure 5.5 and Figure 5.6) in the previous sections show that many houses in Soweto are owned and paid off. However, as already mentioned, ownership and secure tenure have limited benefits in this area. Studies conducted by the Finmark Trust (2004) indicate that although the units are owned, the housing market in Soweto is stagnant. Unlike the traditionally white and wealthier northern parts of the city, where mortgages are common, we see here an unwillingness from banks to undertake loans against these units, making one suspect that old red-lining[6] practices are still in effect.

In the case of Soweto, although the 2011 Census shows that only 55% of Soweto residents had piped water inside their dwellings, around 93% had electricity for lighting, and around 91% had access to a flush toilet connected to a sewerage system. This discrepancy seems to support the notion that while Soweto is being formalized, some issues remain disguised (StatsSA, 2011). To wit, between 2001–2015, the number of backyard units in Soweto increased by as much as 4,000 dwellings per square kilometre (GCRO, 2018); considering that most backyard units share ablutions, water access, and power with the main dwelling, the number of households with access to power, water, and sanitation is probably not reflected in the general statistics, as many backyard households share utility connections. Thus the higher densities could mean that there is overcrowding, overuse of insufficient services for the population in question, and resultant health issues and social concerns that remain hidden in the seemingly positive numbers concerning access to services.

Case-study: East Madinat Nasr (EMN)

East Madinat Nasr (EMN) is a district in Cairo's eastern region, and became a municipality in 1999 when the Madinat Nasr district was split into East Madinat Nasr and West Madinat Nasr. Covering 227,350 km², its built area is only 6,907 km², and in 2017 its population stood at 634,818 (Cairo Governorate, 2017a). Originally a vacant piece of desert, Madinat Nasr ('City of Victory') was established by President Gamal Abdul Nasser as part of a broader plan to create a new modern city adjacent to Cairo. Official statements promised that the new city would provide improved housing and services, host modern facilities such as a football stadium and convention centre, and that many ministries would relocate there. Although the new housing for Madinat Nasr primarily targeted upper- and middle-class Egyptians, several 'masakin', or social housing blocks, were also built in certain parts of Madinat Nasr as part of Nasser's efforts to establish himself as head of a revolutionary regime for the people (El-Shahed, 2015). Today EMN is split into 18 subdistricts (Cairo Governorate, 2017b). Two thousand six census data paint a picture of a relatively well-off neighbourhood with relatively low rates of illiteracy (6.7%) and unemployment (4.5%) (CAPMAS, 2006).[7]

According to Egypt's urban governance system, the governorate distributes to each municipality a local development budget earmarked for built environment maintenance, and EMN enjoys relatively good access to its share of that budget. Comparing EMN's budget to two other municipalities with similar populations, it is clear that EMN is relatively fortunate (Table 5.2).

Furthermore, 2006 census data show 74% of residents in EMN own their homes, which corresponds with EMN's reputation as a middle-class area. Census data also show good access to services across the whole of EMN (electricity, water, and sanitation access rates are very high at 99%, 95%, and 98%, respectively), which is reflected in the maps throughout this chapter.

However, despite its relatively large per capita share of the local development budget, as well as the high level of access to services, EMN is home to intra-district inequalities that are obscured in the municipality-level data. Many of these inequalities are concentrated within one of EMN's most significant pockets of poverty: the Ezbet El-Haggana subdistrict, which is also one of Egypt's largest informal areas. Data on Ezbet El-Haggana's population varies widely:

Table 5.2 Budget comparison of EMN, Helwan, and Ein Shams districts

District	Population size	Local budget 2017/2018	Per capita budget
Helwan	521,239	EGP 2,028,966 (USD 113,286)	EGP 3.89
Ein Shams	614,391	EGP 3,676,000 (USD 205,248)	EGP 5.98
EMN	634,818	EGP 6,965,000 (USD 388, 888)	EGP 10.97

Source: Authors, based on Cairo Governorate (2017a) data

from 67,165 (the 2006 census) to 400,000 (Soliman, 2002) to 1 million (data collected by local NGO, Al-Shihab Foundation for Comprehensive Development). However, an examination of satellite imagery, or even a simple visit to this area spanning approximately 3km² (Bremer & Bhuiyan, 2014), reveal the 2006 census figure to likely be a severe underestimation.

Looking at some comparisons between Ezbet El-Haggana subdistrict and the whole of EMN (see Table 5.3), we gain some insight into what the maps provided throughout this chapter disguise.

According to CAPMAS (2013), across all of EMN's subdistricts, a total of 14,135 residents live below the poverty line. From this total, 6,817 live in Ezbet El-Haggana, meaning that almost half of the municipality's poor live in one subdistrict, while the other half is spread out over the other 17 subdistricts. A comparison of Ezbet El-Haggana to the four subdistricts adjacent to it is even more striking, as its neighbours record poverty rates of 0.2%, 1.9%, 2.2%, and 1.9% respectively, compared to Ezbet El-Haggana's poverty rate of 10% (CAPMAS, 2013).

Looking at the data on housing, as shown in Table 5.3, Ezbet El-Haggana's overcrowding rate is much higher than that of the average in EMN (1.24 and 1, respectively), and in fact constitutes the highest of all of EMN's subdistricts.

Figure 5.14 The Borders of Ezbet El-Haggana

Source: Google Earth

Table 5.3 Living conditions in EMN compared to Ezbet El-Haggana

	Overcrowding (CAPMAS, 2006)	Poverty rate (CAPMAS, 2013)	Tap outside of housing unit (CAPMAS, 2006)	Number of schools (CAPMAS, 2006)	Illiteracy (CAPMAS, 2006)
Ezbet El-Haggana subdistrict	1.24	10%	9%	2	29.6%
East Madinat Nasr (EMN) municipality	1	2.5%	5%	62	6.7%

Source: Authors

Furthermore, while the percentage of EMN families living in accommodation other than an independent housing unit (i.e., a room, shack, tent, or graveyard)[8] is 4.7%, in Ezbet El-Haggana that percentage is markedly higher at 11.2% (CAPMAS, 2006). Regarding access to basic services, the percentage of people who do not have a tap inside their homes is somewhat higher in Ezbet El-Haggana than the average percentage in EMN (9% and 5%, respectively). Meanwhile, the percentage of those who have access to the public electricity network is quite high within Ezbet El-Haggana at 98% (the average in EMN is 99%).

The data comparing the EMN average percentages to those within the Ezbet El-Haggana subdistrict show that intra-municipal inequalities reflect the inter-municipal inequalities showcased in the maps displayed throughout this chapter. In other words, while access to basic services (water and electricity) appears to be relatively evenly distributed, access to adequate housing conditions displays far higher levels of inequality in certain areas like Ezbet El-Haggana, which is classified as both informal and 'unsafe'.

Indeed, one of the crucial considerations this case study raises is around informality. Although there is a lack of government data on formality/informality of tenure at the municipal level, different state institutions produce various lists concerning informal areas. These lists classify Ezbet El-Haggana as an informal area, with the Informal Settlement Development Facility (ISDF) further classifying part of it as an 'unsafe' area. The 'unsafe area' label is an official classification encoded in Egypt's 2008 Universal Building Law, to identify places with physically unsafe characteristics, such as locations in the path of potential rockslides or significant numbers of buildings prone to collapse. Within EMN, the only unsafe areas are two clusters of homes within Ezbet El-Haggana, which are located under high-voltage electricity cables, with severe health repercussions for residents. This again points to the fact that despite Ezbet El-Haggana's high level of access to water and electricity, the neighbourhood still suffers from significant challenges in regards to housing conditions.

What does this case study data tell us about the relationship between services/infrastructure, inequality, and informality? Firstly, that access to basic infrastructure/services – namely water and electricity – cannot be considered an indication of good housing conditions, as the two do not necessarily go hand in hand. Secondly, that the relationship between informality and poor housing is much stronger than the relationship between informality and lack of services. Services were shown to be distributed quite evenly throughout Cairo and throughout EMN, while housing was found to be much poorer within EMN's informal area. Finally, we conclude that the relationship between informality and inequality is strong but not at all straightforward, as particular forms of inequality are tied to informality, but many of these are only revealed when looking at extremely localized data. That is, when looking for evidence of inequality in data from any spatial level, we must always be mindful that there is often a more local level of data that can expose inequalities hidden at the broader scale. We see this in the EMN case, where maps presenting municipal-level data hide the inequalities found between subdistricts.

Conclusions

Looking at the cities of Cairo and Johannesburg, this chapter has examined aspects of spatial inequality in African cities, namely, the primary factors contributing to inequality, how spatial configurations and inequality correlate, and the connection between informality and inequality. Our study reveals two cities where inequalities in terms of income, poverty, and access to many services – especially housing – are still very prevalent, and take a decidedly spatial form. In Johannesburg we found access to infrastructure better in the city's historical centre (CBD) and areas designated as 'white' under apartheid, while peripheral locations – which also house some of the largest informal settlements as well as state-provided housing – have fewer amenities and often worse access to services. In Cairo, although access to the basic utilities infrastructures (water and electricity) seems to be equally distributed throughout the city, deep spatial inequalities exist when it comes to housing conditions, with denser and poorer conditions tending to coincide with informal-area locations.

What the built form can tell us about inequality also differs significantly between the two cities. Comprised largely of apartment buildings, Cairo has higher built-form densities, in which we observed that the spatial difference between ownership and rental can be taken as a proxy for wealth or lack thereof. In Johannesburg, the picture is slightly more complex, with both rental and full ownership being likely indicators of poverty. State intervention in the housing market (i.e., subsidized houses in peripheral areas) and the scarcity of formal rental accommodation have resulted in a concentration of informal rentals (in backyards of formal townships and informal areas alike, as well as in inner-city apartment shares), where hidden types of inequality persist. In addition, areas characterized by full ownership by means of bank loans are located in better-off and mostly white areas, demonstrating where banking institutions are willing to invest and place risk, and thus underscoring where poorer people are less able to gain access to formal loans (Haferburg & Huchzermeyer, 2017).

In both cities, we found high densities, informality, and low incomes to be closely correlated. However, we found that this reality is not as clearly expressed in terms of infrastructure and housing provision as we would have first assumed, and that different realities are revealed at finer spatial levels of analysis. It must also be noted that through simply mapping location and access to infrastructure and amenities, what remains hidden is the private or public nature of those services as well as their quality. Even within a single district, spatial inequalities can be seen in the distribution of infrastructure – especially related to housing – and poverty rates. For example, in Soweto some residents enjoy good access to services, whilst those living in backyards of formal units and in informal settlements have highly variable access, and may experience overcrowded and under-resourced conditions. Similarly, in East Madinat Nasr, the low average poverty rate and good average access to infrastructure obscure the actual elevated levels of poverty, overcrowding, and generally poor conditions dominant in Ezbet El-Haggana subdistrict.

What is clear from the analysis is that in both contexts, historically poorer sections of both cities maintain that status, and there is no question that despite massive intervention, spatial, social, and economic transformation have yet to occur. The relationship between poverty, informality, and lack of services endures, with the poorest areas receiving the fewest services, and the poorest in terms of quality of provision. Thus, the recursive relationship between poverty and service provision means that poor provision continues to lock people into poverty due to lack of access to the very services that would facilitate their upward mobility. In other words, poorer people have less access to quality facilities, and so seem to be less able to change their economic status.

Our study further shows the importance of taking intra-urban inequality into account when monitoring and reporting on global as well as local urban development policy agendas, and the importance of using city-level and localized data and indicators that reflect local realities and can better support more equitable allocations of infrastructure and services (see also Klopp & Petretta, 2017; Cole et al., 2018). Furthermore, the research underscores the importance of moving beyond the purely financial and economic measures of development, poverty, and inequality that continue to dominate the literature.

Additionally, the findings also point to some of the challenges that African cities continue to face around multilevel governance and coordination around urban planning and service delivery in large city regions. Although not a focus of this chapter, we would speculate that the conditions outlined earlier also hinder the poor from advocating for their rights or for the implementation of their rights. Informality tends to exist in tandem with myriad legal issues that make the governance of services and infrastructure complex, and this often creates legal obstacles blocking upgrading projects. Furthermore, for residents in both Cairo and Johannesburg, mechanisms and modes of participation and engagement with the state are largely dysfunctional. That said, in Johannesburg, wealthier residents have been better able to gain the ear of the state, often through threatening litigation or the rates base (Clarno, 2013). When that has failed, self-provisioning through privatized, off-grid solutions allows wealthier residents to 'splinter' from the state, ensuring access to services that poorer residents simply cannot afford. Thus, the dynamics of provision in Johannesburg are mediated by the politics of who has power to demand from the state or self-provide, and who does not. In Cairo, mechanisms for poor and marginalized citizens to claim their rights have historically been quite limited, and are arguably becoming even more scarce, as the space for civil society and freedom of assembly becomes ever more restricted. However, Egypt is also currently undergoing a moment in its history when informal areas are incredibly high on the public agenda, and addressing their issues has become part of the public narrative. Making use of data such as that presented in this chapter can aid such efforts and ensure that state efforts and resources are targeted where they are most needed.

The value of comparison

Responding in many ways to the growing call for a more comparative approach to understanding the urban, the comparative work undertaken in this chapter has proven useful in unmasking general trends and demonstrating how they persist in different contexts (Robinson, 2011; Brenner & Schmid, 2015). Comparing these cities helped us consider the idea of what is disguised as well as what is revealed in the two contexts: when we saw specific outcomes or phenomena in one city, it provoked the need to ask questions of the other. Asking questions of clarity that may have been obvious to researchers about their own context caused us to dig deeper into the data, and the discussion and debate that followed gave greater depth to our interpretations of the various phenomena. For example, it was useful to consider issues of property and tenure, and how they are expressed in both contexts. However, what is not always apparent in the relatively high-level literature is the need for depth in the empirical data in order to make useful comparisons. Whilst looking at outcomes has merit, there is a need for taking 'deep dives' into other contexts in order to make better sense of what can be seen.

This comparative approach was not without its challenges – especially where definitions, expectations, data sources, and reliability differed. Expressions of poverty look very different when examined in the two contexts, which rendered terms like formal and informal less useful, as they mean very different things in the two cities. For example, poor housing conditions manifest differently: in Johannesburg, poor households live in backyards, informal settlements, and inner-city 'bad buildings', while in Cairo, informal areas take the form of multistorey buildings constructed from reinforced concrete, but with much higher densities and overcrowding, and poorer facilities and services.

This study highlighted some of the benefits of conducting comparative analysis, especially South-South comparison, and particularly comparisons across African cities. In particular, it shed light on the utility of somewhat nascent concepts such as 'African urbanism', which encourage the extraction of insights and lessons from African cities for African cities, rather than those imported from the global

North. As McFarlane (2010) argues, the comparative method is more than a methodological comparison, but also an 'implicit mode of thought' (2010, p. 726), which informs how knowledge and theory are constructed in the urban.

Overall the research presented here should be seen as a first step in mobilizing the practicalities of comparative urbanism, and as an exercise to generate better bilateral relationships and generative questions of context. The lens of inequality and infrastructure was a useful one, but given the constraints of time and budget, it too should be seen as a first step in moving towards a deeper and richer analysis. Such an analysis would stem from acquiring a better sense of the historical and political contexts in which infrastructural decisions have been made, and in doing so, reveal more about the politics of decision-making and offer greater insight into the many actors and modes of governance at play.

Notes

1 Despite numerous concerns about the reliability of the data, these are the only national datasets that exist.
2 Urban-rural governorates differ from fully urban governorates in terms of how they are divided spatially; because Cairo is fully urban, this chapter will only cover the spatial dynamics of fully urban governorates.
3 There is some involvement of the private sector in the water, sanitation, and electricity sectors, but it is still in its early stages and not very significant.
4 RDP settlements are publicly provided houses (with titles deeds and state-provided services) for households earning less than R3,500/month. The acronym comes from the 'Reconstruction and Development Programme', under which this form of housing delivery was first initiated.
5 In-kind benefit refers to people who receive housing in exchange for work. It includes domestic workers who live with their employers, but also persons who work in a factory that provides housing for workers, or, for example, a CEO of a multinational who is providing housing as part of their contract. Any work benefit that is given in-kind in the form of housing is included in this category. The category 'Other' includes those who are living somewhere under any arrangement that is not via renting, owning, or provided through employment (e.g., those who were given homes as a gift).
6 The practice of banks not loaning money to people based on where they live.
7 Although the most recent census was conducted in 2016, the results that have been publicly released are only at the level of the governorate and do not go down to the level of the municipality and subdistrict. The most recent census available at such a local level is the 2006 one.
8 In Cairo there are a number of impoverished people who, rather than remain homeless, have taken up shelter in Cairo's graveyards and tombs.

References

AfDB. (2019). *African economic outlook 2019*. African Development Bank Group. Retrieved: www.afdb.org/fileadmin/uploads/afdb/Documents/Publications/2019AEO/AEO_2019-EN.pdf

Andersen, J.E., Jenkins, P. & Nielsen, M. (2015). Who plans the African city? A case study of Maputo: part 1 – the structural context. *International Development Planning Review*, 37(3), pp. 329–350. DOI: https://doi.org/10.3828/idpr.2015.20

Arab Republic of Egypt. (2014 January 18). *Constitution [Egypt]*, Retrieved: https://www.refworld.org/docid/3ae6b5368.html [Accessed on 23 September 2020]

Bremer, J. & Bhuiyan, S.H. (2014). Community-led infrastructure development in informal areas in urban Egypt: a case study. *Habitat International*, 44, pp. 258–267. DOI: https://doi.org/10.1016/j.habitatint.2014.07.004

Brenner, N. & Schmid, C. (2015). Towards a new epistemology of the urban? *City*, 19(2–3), pp. 151–182. DOI: https://doi.org/10.1080/13604813.2015.1014712

Buire, C. (2014). The dream and the ordinary: an ethnographic investigation of suburbanisation in Luanda. *African Studies*, 73(2), pp. 290–312. DOI: https://doi.org/10.1080/00020184.2014.925229

Cairo Governorate. (2017a). *The portal of Cairo governorate, district local development budgets 2017*. Retrieved: http://www.cairo.gov.eg/en/Pages/default.aspx

Cairo Governorate. (2017b). *The portal of Cairo governorate, the executive plans for developing East Madinat Nasr district, 2017*. Retrieved: http://www.cairo.gov.eg/en/Pages/default.aspx

Caldeira, T.P. (2017). Peripheral urbanization: autoconstruction, transversal logics, and politics in cities of the global South. *Environment and Planning D: Society and Space*, 35(1), pp. 3–20. DOI: https://doi.org/10.1177/0263775816658479

Cameron, R. (2015). Public service reform in South Africa: from apartheid to new public management. In: Massey, A. & Johnston, K. (Eds.), *The international handbook of public administration and governance*. Cheltenham and Northampton: Edward Elgar Publishers, pp. 135–157.

CAPMAS. (2006). *Central agency for population mobilization and statistics*. Population Estimates, Egypt in Figures 2006. Retrieved: https://egypt.unfpa.org/sites/default/files/pub-pdf/PSA%20Final.pdf

CAPMAS. (2013). *Central agency for population mobilization and statistics*. Population Estimates, Egypt in Figures 2013. Retrieved: https://reliefweb.int/sites/reliefweb.int/files/resources/EgyptFactsheetweb.pdf

CAPMAS. (2017 December). *Central agency for population mobilization and statistics*. Population Estimates, Egypt in Figures 2017. Retrieved: https://knoema.com/atlas/sources/CAPMAS

Chatterjee, P. (2004). *The politics of the governed: reflections on popular politics in most of the world*. New York: Columbia University Press.

Chipkin, I. (2012). *Middle classing in Roodepoort: capitalism and social change in South Africa*. Public Affairs Research Institute, PARI Long Essay No. 2. Retrieved: https://www.gtac.gov.za/Whatsupeditions/Edition_3_2014_files_/PARI-L.E.-2-middle-classing-in-roodepoort-final-edited-version-5June20121.pdf

City of Johannesburg (CoJ). (2011). *Remaking of Soweto, end of term report, 2006–2011*. Retrieved: https://www.jstor.org/stable/10.18772/22014107656.19?seq=1#metadata_info_tab_contents

City of Johannesburg (CoJ). (2012). *Integrated development plan, 2012–2016: committing to a promising future*. Retrieved: http://www.klipsa.org.za/Data/Sites/1/media/policies/joburgidp201216.pdf

City of Johannesburg (CoJ). (2016). *Spatial development framework 2040*. Retrieved: www.parkview.org.za/docs/townplanning/Johannesburg%20Spatial%20Development%20Framework%202040.pdf

City of Johannesburg (CoJ). (2018a February). *Draft nodal review*. Retrieved: www.joburg.org.za/documents_/Documents/POLICIES/Draft%20nodal%20review%20policy/Draft%20Nodal%20Review%20For%20Public%20Comment%2028%20Feb%202018.pdf

City of Johannesburg (CoJ). (2018b). *Bringing about transformational change.* Retrieved: https://issuu.com/glen.t/docs/city_of_joburg_2018

Clarno, A. (2013). Rescaling white space in post-apartheid Johannesburg. *Antipode*, 45(5), pp. 1190–1212. DOI: https://doi.org/10.1111/anti.12015

Cole, M.J., Bailey, R.M., Cullis, J.D.S. & New, M.G. (2018). Spatial inequality in water access and water use in South Africa. *Water Policy*, 20, pp. 37–52. DOI: https://doi.org/10.2166/wp.2017.111

Coutard, O. (2008). Placing splintering urbanism: introduction. *Geoforum*, 39(6), pp. 1815–1820. DOI: https://doi.org/10.1016/j.geoforum.2008.10.008

El-Shahed, M. (2015). *Revolutionary modernism? Architecture and the politics of transition in Egypt 1936–1967* (Doctoral dissertation, New York University, New York).

FinMark Trust. (2004 June). *Township residential property market, final report, findings, conclusions and implications.* Prepared by Shisaka Development Management Services. Johannesburg: Finmark Trust. Retrieved: www.finmarktrust.org.za/documents/2004/JUNE/TRPMPhase3_Report.pdf [Accessed on 18 January 2020]

Fukuda-Parr, S. (2019). Keeping out extreme inequality from the SDG agenda: the politics of indicators. *Global Policy*, 10(1), pp. 61–69. DOI: https://doi.org/10.1111/1758-5899.12602

Gardner, D. & Rubin, M. (2016). The 'other half' of the backlog: (re)considering the role of backyarding in South Africa. In: Cirolia, L., Görgens, T., van Donk, M., Smit, W. & Drimie, S. (Eds.), *Pursuing a partnership based approach to incremental informal settlement upgrading in South Africa.* Cape Town: University of Cape Town Press, pp. 77–94.

Gauteng City-Region Observatory (GCRO). (2018). *Quality of life survey V (2017/2018).* Retrieved: www.gcro.ac.za/research/project/detail/quality-of-life-survey-v-2017/

Graham, S. (2010). *Disrupted cities: when infrastructure fails.* New York: Routledge.

Graham, S. & Marvin, S. (2001). *Splintering urbanism: networked infrastructures, technological mobilities and the urban condition.* New York: Routledge.

Haferburg, C. & Huchzermeyer, M. (2017). Redlining or renewal? The space-based construction of decay and its contestation through local agency in Brixton, Johannesburg. In: Kirkness, P. & Tijé-Dra, A. (Eds.), *Negative neighbourhood reputation and place attachment.* London: Routledge, pp. 74–94.

Hamann, C., Mkhize, T. & Götz, G. (2018 February 28). *GCRO map of the months: backyard and informal dwellings (2001–2016).* Retrieved: http://gcro.ac.za/outputs/map-of-the-month/detail/backyard-and-informal-dwellings-2001-2016/

Harris, J. (2011). Compromised democracy: observations on popular democratic representation from urban India. In: Tornquist, O., Webster, N. & Stokke, K. (Eds.), *Re-thinking popular representation.* New York: Palgrave Macmillan, pp. 161–177.

Harrison, P. & Harrison, K. (2014). Soweto: a study in socio-spatial differentiation. In: Harrison, P., Gotz, G., Todes, A. & Wray, C. (Eds.), *Changing space, changing city: Johannesburg after apartheid.* Johannesburg: Wits University Press, pp. 293–318.

Joerges, B. (1999). Do politics have artefacts? *Social Studies of Science*, 29(3), pp. 411–431. DOI: https://doi.org/10.1177/030631299029003004

Kanbur, R. & Venables, A.J. (2005). *Spatial inequality and development.* Oxford: Oxford University Press.

Karuaihe, S. (2015). The state of the economy: city of Johannesburg. *HSRC Review*, 12(6), pp. 9–11. Retrieved: http://hdl.handle.net/20.500.11910/1965

Khalil, D., Abdelaal, A., Khalafallah, Y. & Barakat, M. (2018). *Inclusive services for youth in Cairo's informal areas.* Economic Research Forum Working Papers No. 1204. Retrieved: https://erf.org.eg/app/uploads/2018/06/1204_Final.pdf1_.pdf

Klopp, J.M. & Petretta, D.L. (2017). The urban sustainable development goal: indicators, complexity and the politics of measuring cities. *Cities*, 63, pp. 92–97. DOI: https://doi.org/10.1016/j.cities.2016.12.019

Lall, S.V., Henderson, J.V. & Venables, A.J. (2017). *Africa's cities: opening doors to the world*. Washington, DC: World Bank. Retrieved: https://openknowledge.worldbank.org/handle/10986/25896

McFarlane, C. (2010). The comparative city: knowledge, learning, urbanism. *International Journal of Urban and Regional Research*, 34(4), pp. 725–742.

McFarlane, C. (2014). Studies in comparative urbanism. In: Desai, V. & Potterp, R. (Eds.), *The companion to development studies*. London and New York: Routledge, pp. 296–298.

McFarlane, C. & Rutherford, J. (2008). Political infrastructures: governing and experiencing the fabric of the city. *International Journal of Urban and Regional Research*, 32(2), pp. 363–74.

Nijman, J. (2007). Introduction – comparative urbanism. *Urban Geography*, 28(1), pp. 1–6. DOI: https://doi.org/10.2747/0272-3638.28.1.1

Obeng-Odoom, F. (2015). The social, spatial, and economic roots of urban inequality in Africa: contextualizing Jane Jacobs and Henry George. *American Journal of Economics and Sociology*, 74(3), pp. 550–586. DOI: https://doi.org/10.1111/ajes.12101

Offner, J.M. (1993 July–December). Le développement des réseaux techniques: un modèle générique. *Flux*, pp. 11–18. DOI: https://doi.org/10.3406/flux.1993.960

Offner, J.M. (1999). Are there such things as small networks? In: Coutard, O. (Ed.), *The governance of large technical systems*. London: Routledge, pp. 217–238.

Pierre, J. (2014). Can urban regimes travel in time and space? Urban regime theory, urban governance theory, and comparative urban politics. *Urban Affairs Review*, 50(6), pp. 864–889. DOI: https://doi.org/10.1177/1078087413518175

Reckien, D., Creutzig, F., Fernandez, B., Lwasa, S., Tovar-Restrepo, M., Mcevoy, D. & Satterthwaite, D. (2017). Climate change, equity and the sustainable development goals: an urban perspective. *Environment and Urbanization*, 29(1), pp. 159–182. DOI: https://doi.org/10.1177/0956247816677778

Robinson, J. (2005). Urban geography: world cities, or a world of cities. *Progress in Human Geography*, 29(6), pp. 757–765.

Robinson, J. (2011). Cities in a world of cities: the comparative gesture. *International Journal of Urban and Regional Research*, 35(1), pp. 1–23. DOI: https://doi.org/10.1111/j.1468-2427.2010.00982.x

Rubin, M.W. (2014). *Courting change: the role of apex courts and court cases in urban governance: a Delhi-Johannesburg comparison* (Doctoral dissertation, University of the Witwatersrand, Johannesburg).

Rubin, M.W., Todes, A. & Mabin, A. (forthcoming). What a difference a metro makes! Or did it? Suburbanization and local government consolidation in Johannesburg. In: Hamel, P. (Ed.), *Governing suburbia: comparing collective action on eight urban peripheries around the world*. Toronto: University of Toronto Press.

Satterthwaite, D. (2001). Environmental governance: a comparative analysis of nine city case studies. *Journal of International Development*, 13(7), pp. 1009–1014.

Sims, D. (2012). *Understanding Cairo: the logic of a city out of control*. Oxford: Oxford University Press.

Socio-Economic Rights Institute (SERI). (2018 May). *Informal settlements and human rights in South Africa*. Submission to the United Nations Special Rapporteur on adequate housing as a component of the right to an adequate standard of living. Retrieved: www.ohchr.org/Documents/Issues/Housing/InformalSettlements/SERI.pdf

Soliman, A. (2002). Typology of informal housing in Egyptian cities: taking account of diversity. *International Development Planning Review*, 24(2), pp. 177–201. DOI: https://doi.org/10.3828/idpr.24.2.5

StatsSA. (2011). *National census of South Africa*. Retrieved: www.statssa.gov.za/census/census_2011/census_products/Census_2011_Census_in_brief.pdf

Summerton, J. (Ed.). (1994). *Changing large technical systems*. Boulder, CO: Westview Press.

Tadamun. (2016). *Mapping spatial justice in the greater Cairo region*. Cairo: Tadamun the Cairo Urban Solidarity Initiative. Retrieved: https://issuu.com/87709/docs/mapping-spatial-injustice

Tadamun. (2018). *Planning [in] justice: spatial analysis for urban Cairo*. Cairo: Tadamun the Cairo Urban Solidarity Initiative. Retrieved: www.tadamun.co/planning-justice-report/?lang=en#.Xi2GfFMzaqA

Tarr, J.A. & Dupuy, G. (Eds.). (1988). *Technology and the rise of the networked city in Europe and America*. Philadelphia: Temple University Press.

Turok, I. & Parnell, S. (2009). Reshaping cities, rebuilding nations: the role of urban national policies. *Urban Forum*, 20, pp. 157–174. DOI: https://doi.org/10.1007/s12132-009-9060-2

Un-Habitat. (2014). *The state of African cities 2014: re-imagining sustainable urban transitions*. Nairobi: United Nations Human Settlements Programme (UN-Habitat).

Ward, K. (2008). Toward a comparative (re)turn in urban studies? Some reflections. *Urban Geography*, 29(5), pp. 405–410. DOI: https://doi.org/10.2747/0272-3638.29.5.405

Ward, K. (2010). Towards a relational comparative approach to the study of cities. *Progress in Human Geography*, 34(4), pp. 471–487. DOI: https://doi.org/10.1177/0309132509350239

Watson, V. (2009). Seeing from the South: refocusing urban planning on the globe's central urban issues. *Urban Studies*, 46(11), pp. 2259–2275. DOI: https://doi.org/10.1177/0042098009342598

World Bank. (2015). *Growing African cities face housing challenge and opportunity*. Washington, DC: World Bank. Retrieved: www.worldbank.org/en/news/press-release/2015/12/01/growing-african-cities-face-housing-challenge-and-opportunity

Zérah, M.H. (2008). Splintering urbanism in Mumbai: contrasting trends in a multi-layered society. *Geoforum*, 39(6), pp. 1922–1932.

6 Weathering the storm

Reflections on a community-based approach to flood-risk management in Kumasi, Ghana

Divine Ahadzie, Irene-Nora Dinye, and Rudith Sylvana King

Introduction

The Intergovernmental Panel on Climate Change has identified sub-Saharan Africa (SSA) as one of the world's regions most vulnerable to the effects of climate change (IPCC, 2007; Serdeczny et al., 2015; Chirisa et al., 2016; Mail&Guardian, 2018; IPCC, 2018). Although climate vulnerability translates into altered environmental conditions that increase weather-related risks to human settlements and infrastructure (IPCC, 2013), there has been limited research on climate adaptation in African cities (Magadza, 2000; Filho et al., 2018). Moreover, the policy directives and discussions that do exist to help vulnerable urban communities in SSA-countries continue to focus largely on mitigation rather than adaptation (Muller, 2007; Jagers & Duus-Otterström, 2008; van Vuuren et al., 2011). While mitigation efforts focusing on the drivers of climate change are critical, the conversation on adaptation requires further attention (Muller, 2007). Adaptation models that deal with perceptions, social responsibilities, and appropriate community-based public relations interventions can be decisive in helping vulnerable communities improve their responses to flooding (Mullins & Soetanto, 2011; Kellens et al., 2013; Kruse et al., 2017).

In many African countries, there is limited state capacity to address infrastructure deficits and socioeconomic challenges. In such cases, innovative and collaborative approaches to urban risk management response are vital. An example is the flood-risk management paradigm integrating social cohesion and community preparedness methodologies (cf. Kellens et al., 2013; Kruse et al., 2017). While such methods recognize the importance of the human dimension in creating resilient communities in a flood-risk management context, there is a need to better understand the specific interventions or actions that help communities integrate and utilize the existing knowledge, perceptions, and values that are key to a community-based flood-risk management approach (Wood et al., 2012; Chong et al., 2018). This work aligns with the Africa Climate Resilient Infrastructure Summit (ACRIS II), held in Addis Ababa from 20–21 April 2015, which emphasized the development of resilient communities as a priority in African urban disaster-management work (see also Sylla et al., 2016).

Global development frameworks such as the Sustainable Development Goals (SDGs) also stress the importance of community resilience with a specific target, as part of the stand-alone urban SDG 11 (cf. Parnell, 2016). This focuses on the need to 'increase the number of cities and human settlements adopting and implementing integrated policies and plans towards inclusion, resource efficiency, mitigation and adaptation to climate change, resilience to disasters, and develop and implement, in line with the Sendai Agreement for Disaster Risk Reduction, holistic disaster risk management at all levels' (SDG target 11.b; see also Rodriguez et al., 2018).

This chapter aims to add to this conversation by understanding how communities at high risk of flooding perceive their own adaptive preparedness within a sub-Saharan West African context. The purpose therefore was to analyse the level of awareness of communities to current flood-risk management issues, and also understand the state of citizens' participation in seeking to proactively and collectively build a resilience spirit towards flood hazards. Through a co-production process to develop engagement strategies, the community showed keen interest and participated expressly in the series of engagements. It was further observed that being part of the data gathering process made it more acceptable to community members to appreciate and associate with the project.

The chapter begins with an overview of flood risk in Ghana and various frameworks for risk management, after which we introduce the research site of Sepe-Buokrom, and our CityLab approach to understanding community responses to the flooding risk in that community. After presenting our key findings, the chapter concludes with reflections on the enabling factors and challenges for knowledge co-production in this area.

Managing flood risks

In Ghana, as in many other SSA countries, flooding ranks highly among disasters in terms of casualties and property destruction. While the government is already overwhelmed in its attempts to tackle the hazard, the frequency and impacts of flooding have increased. Records from 1990 to 2015 indicate that flooding in Ghana killed over 500 people, affecting more than 4 million, and causing economic losses of roughly US$800 million (Asumadu-Sarkodie et al., 2015).

Most of the existing measures employed to control flooding are structural in nature and have achieved little in terms of mitigation (e.g., river dredging, desilting, and the construction and rehabilitation of primary drains). Severe loss and damage continue, with property in the Accra metropolis worth US$43 million lost due to flooding in 2009, an amount that increased to US$150 million in 2011 (Frimpong, 2014). In June 2015, the International Federation of the Red Cross and Red Crescent Societies reported that flooding in Accra affected over 46,000 people, displaced 9,200 people, and resulted in over 200 deaths (IFRC, 2015). These numbers are unprecedented in Ghana's annals of flood disaster (ibid.). The trend in the ensuing years is indeed worrying. In March-June 2016, about 13 people died and 4,000 were displaced as a result of flooding (Nkrumah, 2016). In 2017, Ghana experienced widespread flooding, with five regions severely affected, devastating impacts to health, safety, property, and livelihoods, and about 1,500 people displaced to seek refuge in schools and churches (IFRC, 2017). In 2018, after just a few hours of rain, another devastating flood hit capital city Accra particularly hard, with images on social media showing streets submerged under one metre of water (Floodlist, 2018). In 2019, another flood hit seven of the country's traditional ten[1] regions, resulting in the drowning of 12 children in the middle of the country, 29 deaths in the Upper East region, and over 1,000 buildings destroyed (Floodlist, 2019).

These increasing and severe impacts of flooding across urban Ghana call for a new integrated approach to tackling the risk, emphasizing considerations that assist communities in 'living with the risk' rather than solely focusing on prevention (Proverbs & Lamond, 2017). This new resilience paradigm for reducing flood risk has not been given due consideration in many SSA countries, either theoretically or practically, in terms of developing integrated community flood-risk management frameworks.

Mitigation versus adaptation

Adaptation requires that communities consciously leverage social responsibility to identify their exposure to flood hazards, and to proactively undertake actions that engender a response to those threats, including how to recover from an event, and perhaps more importantly, how to build resilience for sustainable development (Mullins & Soetanto, 2011; Kruse et al., 2017; Chong et al., 2018). Drawing on grey and academic literature on adaptation at the city-scale level in developing countries, it is clear that changing environmental conditions are increasing the weather-related risks facing human settlements, including increasing flood hazards (Douglas et al., 2008; Proverbs, 2011; Huong & Pathirana, 2013; Serdeczny et al., 2015).

As a strategy to handle weather-related risk, adaptation is achieving greater prominence, particularly as societies recognize the gravity of their vulnerability to the impact of flooding (cf. van Vuuren et al., 2011). Given the documented trend of increasing flooding and the challenges posed by this reality, the need for supporting, facilitating, and enhancing communities' adaptive capacities for sustainable development is clear (cf. Lwasa, 2010; Jones & Boyd, 2011; Jha et al., 2012). In addition, developing country contexts of extreme vulnerability and weak structural and economic foundations require bespoke adaptation solutions (Mertz et al., 2009; Serdeczny et al., 2015; Chirisa et al., 2016).

Mitigation is about reducing the short-term impact of flooding, while adaptation focuses on learning to cope over the long-term with flooding (van Vuuren et al., 2011). While mitigation is critical, adaptation is also vital to help vulnerable communities better respond to the flooding that is happening and will continue to happen. Adaptation work concerns influencing perceptions and social responsibilities, and instigating appropriate public relation models for effective community engagement (cf. Mullins & Soetanto, 2011; Kellens et al., 2013). As implied by Niehm et al. (2008), shifting values through influencing perceptions and social responsibilities engenders citizenry involvement and greater community ties (see also Shafer et al., 2007). Moreover, the literature suggests that the theoretical and practical basis of how communities adapt are both context-specific and functional within social limits (Adger et al., 2007, as cited in Wilby & Keenan, 2012). That is, while mitigation may often lead to global and/or international prescriptions, adaptation is localized and often culturally sensitive, suggesting the need to understand the social context of the community engaged (van Vuuren et al., 2011; cf. Bender, 2008; Pohl et al., 2010).

To contribute to such an understanding, the Centre for Settlements Studies (CSS) at Kwame Nkrumah University of Science and Technology (KNUST) undertook a community engagement study in a flood-prone community in Kumasi, Ghana's second largest city. The research wing of the College of Art and Built Environment at KNUST, the CSS researches urban and rural interventions that address the socioeconomic and housing needs of disadvantaged communities and settlements. The CSS also provides outreach programmes and training in settlement development and management. Over the last decade, the Centre's research has been guided by the Millennium Development Goals (MDGs) and, more recently, the SDGs approach to human settlements. The aim of this community engagement study was to assess a community's appetite to participate in the development of a community resilience framework (CRF) for flood-risk management.

CRFs intend to help vulnerable communities identify ways to prepare for and also cope with the occurrence of present and future flood-hazard events. Cutter et al. (2008) propose the Disaster Resilience of Place (DROP) model, which factors in localized information around the vulnerability of communities, and is specific to natural hazards such as flooding. Renschler et al. (2011) espoused what they call the PEOPLES model: Population and Demographics, Environmental/Ecosystem, Organized Governmental Services, Physical Infrastructure, Lifestyle and Community Competence, Economic Development, and Social-Cultural Capital. The PEOPLES Resilience Framework provides the foundation to integrate quantitative and qualitative models that measure systems' resilience against disasters. emBRACE is another CRF recently developed by a consortium of five European countries. The core domains of the emBRACE focus on conceptualizing community resilience of resources, capacities, actions, and learning. Chong et al. (2018) espouse a framework seeking to engender a spirit of community resilience towards flooding, and identify four conditions for communities to focus on as deliverables: securing basic needs, being able to adapt to change, minimizing vulnerabilities, and emerging from poverty. Further to this these four conditions, the authors emphasize the important contribution of institutions in assisting communities to execute well-prepared disaster-resilient frameworks, particularly relating to planning systems, and resilience initiatives in rural communities (Chong et al., 2018).

While these frameworks are all useful in their own right, it is agreed that any CRF will require further adjustments for different cultural backgrounds, hazard types, and sociopolitical contexts (cf. Renschler et al., 2011; Kruse et al., 2017; Chong et al., 2018). Developed mostly for advanced economies like those in Europe and Asia, these CRFs are thus not likely to be well-suited to the political and socioeconomic conditions of SSA. This suggests the importance of understanding the requirements of a suitable approach to engendering community resilience initiatives in the local context of SSA countries such as Ghana.

Given the looming threat that flooding poses to cities and conurbations in Ghana and the subregion, the CSS focused this study on understanding urban communities' perceptions of flood risk. The study also engaged communities on the need for adaptation to flooding based on social responsibility models and community-based initiatives. Our approach to this engagement centred around the use of a 'CityLab' approach, which sees stakeholders not only as subjects for data collection, but partners in knowledge production and critical in driving the research focus (Brown-Luthango, 2013; AURI, 2014; Patel et al., 2015). So far, the notion of co-production in Ghana has mainly been applied to research collaborations between the state and communities in the area of land and water management (McCusker & Carr, 2006; Akaateba et al., 2018; Mangai & de Vries, 2018). To our knowledge, this study represents the first effort to focus on the co-production of knowledge to develop a framework for implementing community-led resilience and flood-risk management initiatives in SSA.

Sepe-Buokrom

The research site of Sepe-Buokrom is a flood-prone community in Kumasi, Ghana's second largest city. For the last decade, Kumasi has been at high risk from flooding, with over half the city currently flood-prone, including the selected study area. Located in West Africa's forest zone, Kumasi has a wet, semi-equatorial climate, with two distinct rainy seasons (June and September), which produce an annual average rainfall of 1,400 mm. The mean annual temperature is 25.7°C and humidity ranges from 53% to 93%.

According to the 2010 National Census, Kumasi's population was 2,035,064, with an annual population growth rate of 5.7% (Ghana Statistical Service, 2012). Interpreting the trend in population increase, Owusu-Ansah (2016) observed that human activities relating to land use have intensified in Ghana's inner cities, spilling over into public parks and natural open spaces, including riparian areas and wetlands. This trend has led to increasing numbers of settlements on flood-prone terrain, large areas of land covered by impervious surfaces without sufficient drainage, and correspondingly increased volumes of runoff from precipitation (Afriyie et al., 2018).

Figure 6.2 illustrates the main flood-prone locations within Kumasi Metropolis, as well as the study area of Sepe-Buokrom, one of Kumasi's most vulnerable communities. Houses in Sepe-Buokrom settlement are largely constructed from cement and sand-block walls, and roofed with corrugated iron sheets. The structures are clustered together with little space between, and choked gutters and drains are also common. The major economic activities in Sepe-Buokrom are

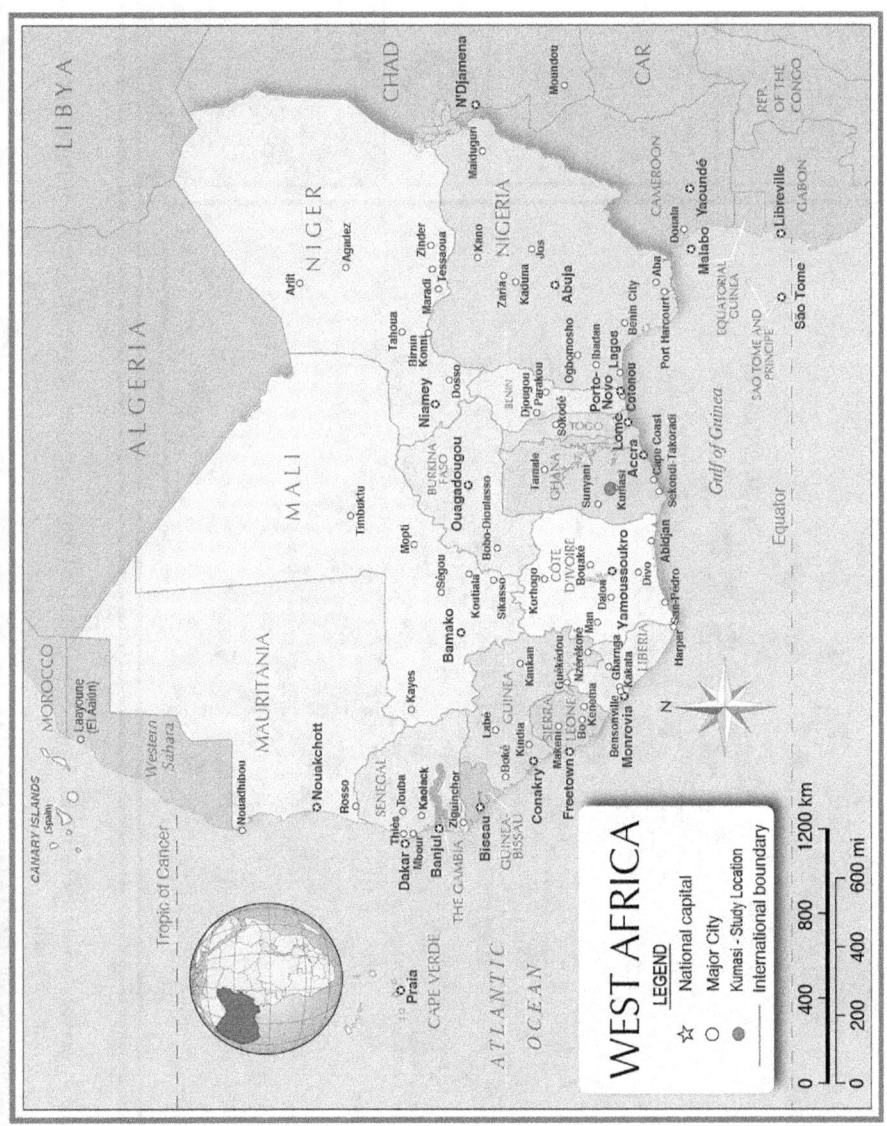

Figure 6.1 Map Showing Kumasi in the Context of West Africa

Source: Adapted from Nations online, 2018

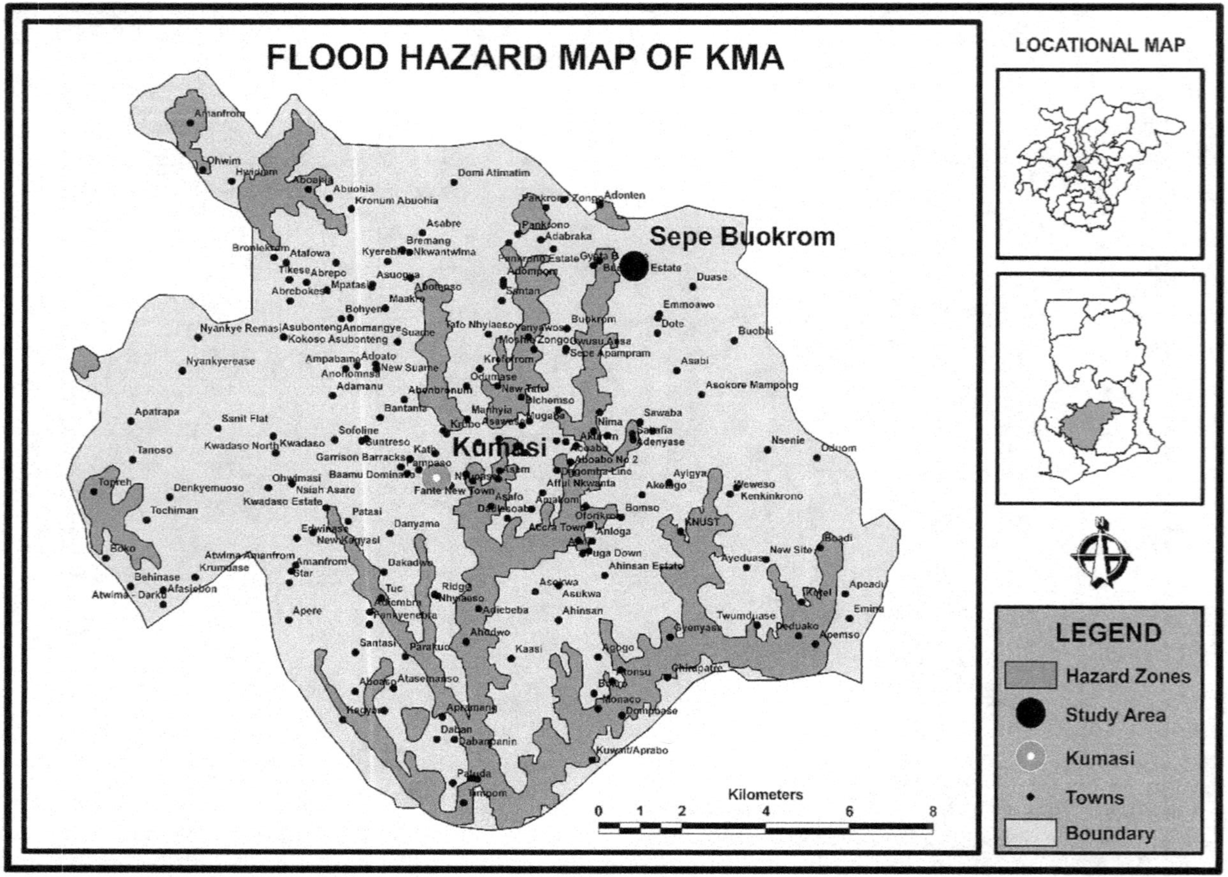

Figure 6.2 Map of Kumasi, Detailing the Flood-Prone Areas Within the Kumasi Metropolis. The Study Area Sepe-Buokrom Is Clearly Shown

Source: Adapted and edited from Ahadzie et al., 2016

small-scale microenterprises such as petty trading, mechanical workshops, and carpentry workshops (Asamoah et al., 2016).

Governance structure

Located in the Ashanti region (one of Ghana's traditional ten administrative regions), Kumasi is governed by the Kumasi Metropolitan Assembly (KMA). The KMA is one of 260 Metropolitan/Municipal/District Assemblies (MMDAs), the highest unit of local government in Ghana. The KMA is headed by a Metropolitan Chief Executive (MCE), who acts in the same capacity as an executive mayor (GoG, 2016). Thus the MCE is a political leader from the ruling government, appointed by the President to oversee and act in his capacity to champion development at the local government level, as enshrined in the 1992 Constitution of Ghana and backed by Local Government Act 462, 1993.

Below the level of KMA, there are various sub-metros in Kumasi,[2] including the Manhyia sub-metropolitan District Council, which includes the Buokrom Town Council, the body that oversees the community of Sepe-Buokrom (Figure 6.3). Like all the sub-metropolitan District Councils, the roles and functions of the Buokrom Town Council are stipulated under the Second Schedule of Legislative Instrument 2223 of 2015 (GoG, 2015). These functions include maintaining public spaces, waste management, and the administration of self-help projects (GoG, 2016), all of which are crucial in flood mitigation and adaptation efforts.

Sepe-Buokrom is an electoral area with its own elected assemblymen. Assemblymen (also known as assembly members) are elected local government officials within a community in the Metropolis/District, who represent their community at the District Assembly. Unlike members of parliament, assemblymen are apolitical.

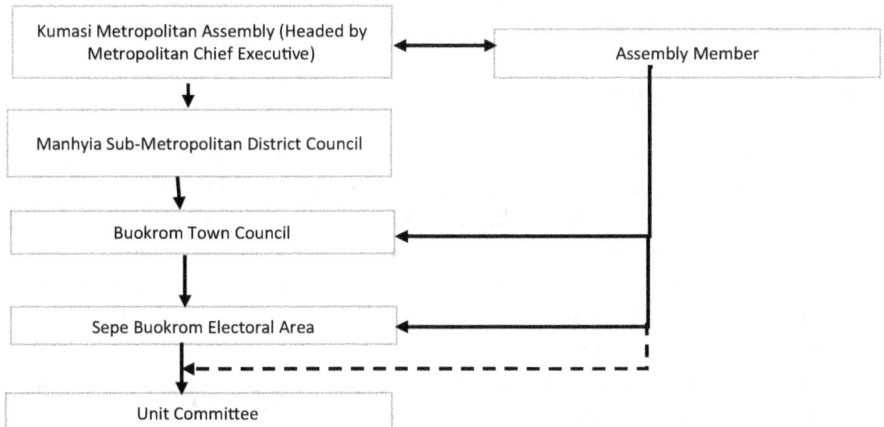

Figure 6.3 Local Governance Structure of the Kumasi Metropolitan Assembly Showing the Study Area, Sepe-Buokrom Electoral Area

Source: Authors

Assemblymen are responsible for the articulation and realization of their constituents' aspirations. Most decisions in MMDA are subject to the approval of the assemblymen.

The Unit Committee is the smallest component of local government in Ghana. Unit committee members are also elected representatives who work with assembly members to enforce bylaws within their electoral/community level, as dictated by the MMDA. As the local government entity closest to the community, the Unit Committee (UC) plays important roles in enforcing bylaws and mobilizing resources. The UC also provides a structured mechanism of representation, participation, and accountability from the lowest community levels upwards. Together with the assembly members, UC members are responsible to the MMDA through the concerned Urban, Zonal, or Town Councils. However, UC members are not necessarily accountable to the assemblymen, as shown in the governance structure in Figure 6.3.

Given the complex and multi-layered nature of local governance, the project's data collection required not only identification of key informants, but also careful negotiation between all of these different actors. In the section that follows we present our research approach and methods.

Research approach and methods

In September 2017 the project commenced with a literature review to better understand the study's theoretical background and research area. An earlier study, *Flood Risk Perception, Coping and Management in Two Vulnerable Communities in Kumasi, Ghana*, which included a review of books, journals, newspapers, and grey literature conducted by the authors, greatly facilitated this process (Ahadzie et al., 2016). Evidence from this earlier study suggests that while flood-prone communities may be aware of the risk they are exposed to, there is no commitment to the community, community support, and/or sense of social responsibility towards engendering citizens' participation in flood-risk management.

We executed the project in three main phases as follows:

Phase One: A month of inception meetings to set the project goals, identify key stakeholders, and define the communication plan. The identification of key stakeholders from Sepe-Buokrom was an important element of this phase. Key stakeholders included the assemblyman, unit committee members, and opinion leaders.[3] Once the stakeholders were identified, the research team began to build networks to assess stakeholder willingness and ability to participate in the project.

Phase Two: Data collection. The methodology was entirely qualitative, and included a mixture of segmented Focus Group Discussions (FGDs) and Stakeholder Meetings (SMs). In line with the CityLab approach, relationships were cultivated across institutions and interest groups to ensure broad participation. Five FGDs were held in total, followed by one SM. In all of these forums, we discussed participants' understandings of the causes of and potential solutions to flooding, and the potential role of community-based initiatives to improve flood-risk management.

Phase Three: This final closure phase focused on completion of all research activities and validation of project data. This involved a second 'End of Project' SM, which attracted locally elected representatives (e.g., assemblymen), politically appointed government representatives (e.g., the MCE), and representatives from the National Disaster Management Organization (NADMO), the Environmental Protection Agency (EPA), as well as the media.

Focus Group Discussions (FGD)

The success of the FGDs was largely due to the involvement of the Sepe-Buokrom assemblyman and UC members, who mobilized and organized the community to participate. Enjoying a close relationship with the communities, the assemblyman and UC members have a strong grasp of local challenges. For brevity's sake, henceforth, 'assemblyman' will be used to refer to both the assemblyman and his UC members.

The FGD research team was comprised of a moderator, camera operator, recorder, and two secretaries (the secretaries took notes and observed the participants' general mood and body language). The venue for all the FGDs was the Sepe-Buokrom Town Council Building. For maximum participant involvement and understanding, the local language (Twi) was used as the medium of communication during all FGDs, which were held during the week of the 19–23 September 2017, and lasted approximately one hour per session.

The FGDs were organized with Men, Women, Children, the Youth, and Opinion Leaders, with all participants from the Sepe-Buokrom community. The first FGD was with Women (average age 47), who were mostly self-employed and engaged in livelihoods such as hair dressing and petty trading. The second FGD of Men mostly included traders and artisans (average age 59). The third FGD of Opinion Leaders included two women and five men, including teachers, traders, and pensioners. The fourth FGD of Youth included three females and three males (average age 25). The final FGD of Children included six girls and four boys (average age 13).

Each FGD session began with carefully selected videos of major flood disasters from across the world, including Ghana. Depicting the devastating and destructive nature of floods, they captured participants' attention, and in some cases, elicited strong emotions. The videos clearly made quite an impression on all participants, paving the way for what appeared animated and genuine engagements from participants.

Although community members were divided into groups based on gender and power in the community, hierarchies within these groupings still existed. For example, among the women were 'queen mothers' (female leaders in the communities), and among the men, representatives of the chief/chief linguist and the assemblyman (who have more power than other men in the communities) were present. However, the participants in all the FGDs appeared relaxed both before and during the discussions, and there were no signs of intimidation in any of the FGDs, with participants expressing themselves freely.

Stakeholder Meetings (SM)

Following the conclusion of the segmented FGDs, the research team conducted its analysis and facilitated two SMs, which included key urban stakeholders comprised of select residents, assemblymen, NADMO officials, and the media. Held five months apart, these SMs were used to discuss the study's preliminary findings, and also represented the first meetings specifically arranged (not only in Kumasi, but in all of Ghana) to discuss CRFs and how communities can respond to flood-related issues.

The first SM, which took place at the town council meeting in the Sepe-Buokrom community, attracted educators, religious leaders, unions, market/trader associations, opinion leaders, and representatives from traditional leadership (chiefs) (Figure 6.4). Despite asking the assemblyman to ensure a gender balance, the stakeholder groups composition was overwhelmingly male – females constituting just over one third of the participants – reflecting the male-dominated nature of Ghanaian culture, particularly in areas of decision-making.

The second SM was planned for April 2018. However, local elections held in the same period required the research team to delay the meeting until August 2018. The second SM included heavy representation from assemblymen, along with officials from the Kumasi Metropolitan Assembly (KMA), the National Disaster Management Organization (NADMO), and the media. Held at the KMA (the seat of the local government in Kumasi), the second SM was opened by the MCE,

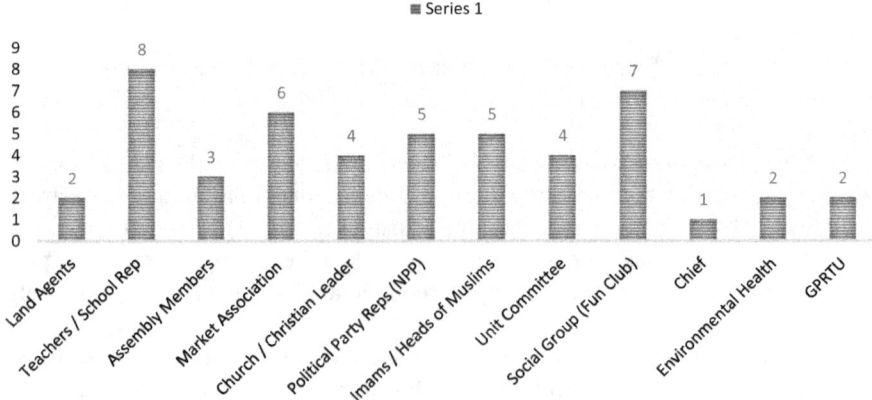

Figure 6.4 Participants' Affiliations in Second Stakeholder Meeting

Source: Authors

whose participation spoke to the event's significance and government's interest in the discourse.

During his opening remarks, the MCE highlighted the increasing threat of flooding to the city in recent times, and assured government support for any flood-risk management initiative in the metropolis. Towards the end of the meeting, the MCE requested that the CSS research team join the KMA in preparing a proposal that will extend this type of stakeholder engagement to all MMDAs in the Greater Kumasi area, intimating that the KMA was ready to offer all the necessary support in facilitating these meetings.

Data analysis

Data analysis was undertaken in two stages. First, FGD data (in the form of notes, audio, and video) were transcribed from the local dialect, Asante-Twi, to English, with research assistants verifying the translations for validity. Thereafter, our senior researchers held a group meeting to go through the transcribed data again, using the audio and video versions to verify and validate that data.

We chose the qualitative data analysis (QDA) computer software package NVivo desktop, version 10.0 for its ability to accommodate numerous data formats in a single analysis (Dollah et al., 2017; Zamawe, 2015). Data was coded paragraph by paragraph, at multiple nodes, and analysed data were presented in the form of graphs, pictures, and the 'Word Cloud'. The Word Cloud was generated by running Word Frequency queries that identify key phrases within the data. Figure 6.5 depicts findings from Focus Group Discussions, using Word Cloud after the Nvivo analysis. The results visually depict the degree to which prominent personalities (assemblyman, chief, and MP) are expected to drive the common vision of the community towards achieving flood resilience.

Visually highlighting the relative frequency of words in a text, the Word Cloud offers a way to capture text responses from qualitative data using visual means to reflect insights drawn from peoples' social setting, background, and experience of socioeconomic issues (cf. Lohmann et al., 2015). As a form of analysis, Word Clouds have the marked advantages of being very fast and simple to conduct once the difficult work of transcribing has been done. The results of the analyses are also easy to comprehend and visually appealing, reveal only the essential variables, and provide a form of emotional connection that sets the tone for further discussions (McNaught & Lam, 2010).

Key findings

This section provides the key findings from the FGDs and the SMs.

To evaluate our findings we used Norris et al.'s (2008) four primary 'community adaptive capacities': economic development, social capital, information and communication, and community competence. We also draw on Chong et al.'s (2018) position that the values and roles that institutions/agencies involved in disaster management bring on board are key in helping to build resilient communities. In

Figure 6.5 Word Cloud on Achieving Flood Resilience

Source: Authors

terms of economic development, the study revealed that, like many deprived communities in SSA countries, Sepe-Buokrom lacked the capacity or readiness to leverage economic resources to engender community resilience. Also, while social capital is deep-seated and used for individual mutual support (e.g., funerals), the community is yet to leverage this quality and apply it collectively in the interest of building a resilient communal spirit towards flood hazards. Regarding information and communication, within the community, access to and sharing of flood information is nonexistent, and there is no engagement on how to handle communication collectively during a flood disaster. Most flood victims we encountered at the FGDs intimated that the assemblyman would be the first point of contact in a crisis situation (via mobile phone), though this was based on individual intuition rather than being an official policy. Finally, while the community was aware of its extreme vulnerability to flooding, no attempts to build a community competence towards engendering adaptive capacities to flood hazards have been made.

Through analysing the FGD and SM data, three main factors identified by participants as necessary to developing an urban CRF for flood-risk management emerged. These are: 1) the importance of local leadership; 2) residents' initiative; and 3) community commitment, loyalty, and togetherness. The importance of local leadership aligns with the CRF developed by Chong et al. (2018) for Malaysia, suggesting the value of institutions and the need to integrate their role. This is particularly the case for places like Sepe-Buokrom, where, as in many Ghanaian communities, sociopolitical circumstances have led to a lack of social responsibility, meaning communities will continue to rely on institutions while they work on developing community resilience initiatives towards flood hazards. However, Cutter et al. (2008) observe that financial considerations often make institutions reluctant to focus energy on communities' hazard vulnerability – a concern that also arose and is discussed further in the next sections. That said, we argue that the way forward involves building a common vision of leadership requirements, which are detailed next.

Leadership is key

The FGD data established that participants viewed strong collaboration between residents and the 'leadership trio' (i.e., assemblyman,[4] chief, and MPs) as important to improving the community's ability to mitigate, prepare for, respond to, and recover more quickly from flood disasters. This echoes findings from a similar study conducted in the capital of the country, Accra, which found that while community leaders participated in the implementation of flood-risk management strategies, they were often not involved in the formulation of these strategies (Atanga, 2020). Considering the assemblyman's role and responsibility to consult and maintain close contact with his electoral area while also liaising between his people and the District Assembly on development issues, the study identified him as the best person to mobilize the community and initiate the community resilience approach. Per the Local Government Act, the assemblyman is to 'maintain close contact with his electoral area, consult his people on issues to be discussed in the District Assembly and obtain their views, opinions, and proposals; present the views, opinions, and proposals to the District Assembly; and meet with the electorate before each meeting of the Assembly' (Act 462, 1993).

It must be noted here that the role of the assemblyman at the local level in Ghana is similar to that of an MP at the national level. That is, he is expected to represent his peoples' views at the District Assembly, and to share Assembly decisions with his constituents.[5] The District Assembly meanwhile exercises deliberative, legislative, and executive functions at the local government level, complementing the central government. Thus, District Assemblies are responsible for the overall development of local communities, and should promote and support relevant socioeconomic programmes. For example, the District Assemblies are expected to 'be responsible for the development, improvement, and management of human settlements and the environment in the district' (Act 462, 1993).[6] This includes managing flood risks and other disasters to ensure properties and people are protected. The assemblyman is thus the community's elected representative tasked with carrying out such activities at the community level. However, unlike MPs, who are remunerated and can draw from the District Assembly Common Fund (DACF)[7] for developmental projects in their constituencies, assemblymen are neither remunerated for their services, nor can they directly access the DACF. The assemblymen receive some allowances for attending assembly meetings, and ex gratia after their tenure expires (a four-yearly cycle). In other words, assemblymen rarely have the resources at their disposal to execute their mandate of ensuring that services are delivered at the local level efficiently and effectively (Abdallah, 2011).

According to our study, despite having the mandate and commanding the respect, the assemblyman felt incapable of mobilizing the community for meetings to discuss issues related to flood-risk management, or to undertake communal work to manage flood risk. Thus, our study revealed that although the zeal to work may exist, the assemblyman's inability to harness the resources to do that work disempowers the role. This is particularly undermining given that, according to the FGD data, the electorate's expectations of assemblymen are very high, in spite of the assemblymen's frequent inability to deliver. Adequately resourcing assemblymen therefore could empower and enable them to carry out their mandate.

Unlike the assemblymen, the MP was seen by FGD participants as able to access the resources needed to promote community resilience. That is, the MP can ensure that communities in flood-prone areas receive a share of the DACF to promote CRF activities. The FGD participants also identified traditional leadership (the chief) as key to the promotion of a CRF. As a respected and influential person who occupies the role of community custodian, the chief's participation in resilience efforts was deemed critical.

Thus, the importance of these three key stakeholders working together to promote community resilience to flood risk through a common vision came through strongly from the FGDs. Table 6.1 shows some of the striking comments emerging from the FGDs around the 'Leadership is Key' sub-themes (e.g., role of the key personalities and residents).

Residents initiative

The second major finding from the FGD data analysis was the need for individual households to participate in community-based initiatives to help promote a CRF. FGD participants identified two ways for households to do this. First, ensuring proper disposal of refuse, and second, fully committing to any flood-management initiatives undertaken in the community.

Commitment, loyalty, and togetherness

The third and final element needed to facilitate community flood-risk resilience was articulated as a combination of 'commitment, loyalty, and togetherness'. The

Table 6.1 Emergent themes and supporting notable comments from FGDs

Themes and sub-themes	Example of survey response
Leadership is key	*As my colleagues have already mentioned, the core members of the leadership are the assemblyman, the MP, and the chief. If these three come together and mobilize and educate the youth and the elders of the community, there is no way the community would not get involved.*
a Role of the assemblyman	*I believe all responsibilities lie on the assemblyman. He is in the best position to identify the problems facing the community. Hence, he should be the one to mobilize the youth to take steps in fixing those problems.*
b The role of the chiefs	*The chief is the owner of the community. Without him the assemblyman cannot work effectively. So, the chief must be involved, together with his team.*
c The role of MPs	*Looking at our community now, the MP has played very little role in the community's development. If the assemblyman is to work and work effectively, it will be upon the shoulders of the MP.*
d Role of residents	*It is therefore important for us the residents to maintain and clean our homes and this will help prevent flooding*

Source: Authors

shared commitment was expressed as a prerequisite for the community's successful undertaking of its own initiatives to reduce flood risk. This shared commitment and unified vision would need to be negotiated with an understanding of the community's history, conflicts, and shared future.

In contrast to the FGDs, the Stakeholder Meetings were focused on data validation and consensus building. The data from these meetings were analysed manually from written and summary reports and notes taken at the meetings (versus using Nvivo qualitative data analysis software, as was the case with the FGDs). The two SMs were also used to ascertain how well various stakeholders would take up the challenge to mobilize their respective communities to achieve the common vision relating to building a CRF for flood-risk management.

At the first SM, we presented themes that arose from the FGDs, asking participants the following questions:

- Were the FGDs adequately representative of the community?
- Did stakeholders agree that Sepe-Buokrom is a flood-prone area? How did they reach their conclusion?
- Have there been any other gatherings to discuss flooding issues within the community?
- What can communities do to lessen the immediate impact of flooding?
- Is there a safe haven in the community where people can assemble when flooding occurs?

- Who would be the appropriate person/s to lead community-based resilience?
- What can the community do to help the area leadership in controlling floods?

The participants affirmed that the demographic groupings used for the FGDs were exhaustive and adequately represented the community. Based on their experiences, they expressed overwhelming support for the notion that Sepe-Buokrom (the study area) is flood-prone. However, while participants accepted that their area is highly flood-prone, it emerged that this understanding has never caused them to engage with the risk factors in terms of how they as a community can engender their own resilience. Regarding the question of a safe haven, participants identified a school block, which they believe is located at the community's highest point. However, the idea that this school is 'safe' is based not on proven fact, but rather on an incident that occurred about a decade ago, when a message claiming that a meteorite was aimed to hit a location in Ghana went viral. The instinctive response of many residents in Sepe-Buokrom was to congregate at this particular school – which may or may not actually be located at the highest point. As a result, this location continues to register in peoples' minds as a rallying point in the event of flood emergency.

Results from the first SM also strongly confirmed support for the 'leadership trio' of the assemblyman, the chief, and MP. Indeed, a participant specifically used the words 'Common Vision' (which originally came out of the FGD findings), which phrase has since been adopted by the research team, and could be used as a catchphrase to whip up public interest for the research findings. Participants further expressed their full support in rallying behind this leadership trio for any flood-risk management initiative. Based on this, we anticipate that stakeholders in any typical Ghanaian community would equally express similar willingness to collaborate.

It should be noted that the first SM in Sepe-Buokrom represented the first community platform where communities interrogated the idea that they can take responsibility for themselves to achieve flood-risk resilience. Going beyond the usual conversation that focuses only on the causes of flooding and government relief and support, this novel platform attracted publicity from electronic and print media in both the Kumasi Metropolis and across Ghana.

At the second SM, which was largely attended by assemblymen (Figure 6.6), the discussion focused on issues around how the assemblymen as elected community leaders regarded the community's expectation that the leadership trio (i.e., themselves, the MP, and chief) should initiate flood-risk management initiatives.

Manually analysing the data from this meeting, we divided the results into three thematic categories: 1) leadership for the common vision; 2) community role; and 3) the role of government institutions.

Leadership for common vision

Results highlighted issues around the expectation that the assemblyman should take the lead role in mobilizing and addressing community development, as such initiatives are often seen as threatening both to the MP's political career and to

Participants' Affiliations

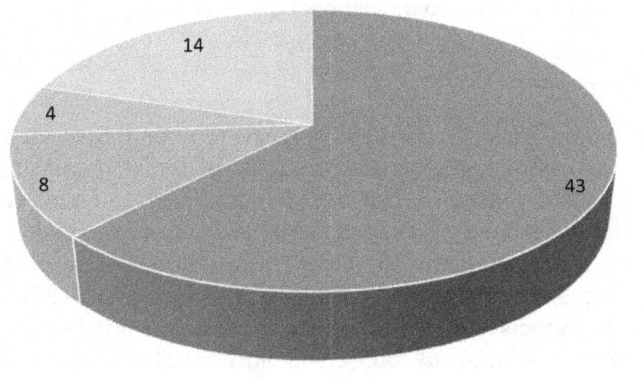

■ Assembly members   ■ KMA officials   ■ Nadmo officials   ■ The press (radio, print, and TV media)

Figure 6.6 Participant Affiliations in the Second Stakeholder Meeting
Source: Authors

traditional authority. As a result, it is unlikely those latter two stakeholders will cooperate, for fear of being unseated. Similarly, the assemblymen also believed that the level of recognition they receive in the community can be perceived as undermining the chief's role, resulting in traditional leaders ignoring assembly-men's advice on land-use issues in particular.[8] In other words, one of the key 'leadership trio' actors expected to drive the common vision expressed scepticism concerning their ability to play that role. It was therefore suggested that joint meetings of the leadership trio would be fundamental to driving any 'Common Vision'. Recommendations were also made for the Manhyia[9] palace directorate to host similar forums and discussions. This could leverage support from the King of the Ashanti Kingdom (Ashanti Region of Ghana), and therefore from numer-ous chiefs, to delve deeper into these issues, particularly addressing the lack of collaboration between key role players.

While we expected the leadership trio to operate from a common vision on all aspects of community development, including flood-risk management, the feedback we received – at least from the perspective of the assemblymen – contradicted this assumption. As previously noted, assemblymen lack direct access to funds that would allow them to take bold initiatives specific to their electoral areas. As such, it was suggested that an appeal be made to Parliament to review the allocation and use of the District Assembly Common Fund, to legally accommodate assemblymen. An alternative proposal was the establishment of an 'Assemblymen's Common Fund', to enable assemblymen to access resources for community development projects.

Following the SMs, these issues continued to be discussed in the media, including suggestions that government should consider implementing a 5% fund for assemblymen (Graphic Online, 2018). All of this shows the contribution co-produced research can make to the national discourse.

The community role

The role of communities was another key theme to emerge from the second SM. Participants expressed the belief that the spirit of social responsibility, which previously existed in Ghana's urban communities, needs to be reawakened. For instance, communal labour, which used to happen in most communities, no longer occurs. Most urban communities in Ghana today do not see communal labour or community and developmental challenges as their responsibilities, but rather those of the state and its agencies. Linked to community participation, stakeholders advocated for a scheme to train community-based volunteers in flood-risk management skills. These include but are not limited to pre-flood planning and flood clean-up. Participants also suggested training in the construction of simple flood defences; swimming and rescue measures; and preparation of flood-risk maps. Participants also discussed assemblymen's limited regulatory and enforcement authority when it comes to ensuring that communities adopt and adhere to resilience initiatives for flood management.

Currently Ghana lacks any Flood Control Act that could guide either Development Control Officers operations, or the specific roles and jurisdiction of assemblymen, including how they might enforce or regulate community-based flood-resilience activities. Participants indicated that if such a framework existed and informed community members of their rights and responsibilities when it came to flood resilience initiatives and actions, the people would play their part.

The role of government institutions

The last theme that emerged from the second SM was the role of government institutions in aggravating the flood problem. Specifically, respondents noted that development engineers and planners in local government departments contribute to the problem by approving permits for construction in low-lying areas susceptible to flooding. Respondents further indicated that the District Assembly itself refuses to act, even when such cases are reported by assemblymen or community members. These factors coupled with rent-seeking by government officials can result in permits being wrongfully allocated. The performance and ethics of local government officials were also discussed, followed by calls for appropriate penalties for officials found guilty of collusion with developers seeking to build in low-lying areas.

Data from the second SM also concluded that assemblymen needed to advocate harder for better collaboration between the various institutions (e.g., the NADMO, the Lands Commission of Ghana, the Engineers Unit of the Metro-works

Department) at assembly meetings, in the interest of promoting community resilience. It appears that local government officials fail to fully recognize the importance of risk communication, which continues to be played down (cf. Ahadzie & Proverbs, 2011), all of which reflects local government's relative weak appreciation for the importance of engaging communities in disaster risk management (cf. Terumoto, 2006; Chong et al., 2018).

Reflections of the Kumasi CityLab

This section highlights the reflexive discourse, examining the enablers of success for the community engagements, including the FGDs and SMs, as well as the challenges and prospects of promoting a CRF for flood-risk management.

Enabling factors

Previous CityLab experiences advocate for a good relationship and rapport between CityLab stakeholders (Patel et al., 2015). This is to engender trust and reciprocity, which are required for successful co-production of knowledge (ibid.). Fundamental to the success of the Kumasi CityLab project was our ability to identify key stakeholders, which was possible due to our prior engagements (e.g., with Sepe-Buokrom's assemblyman) and our development of new networks (e.g., with NADMO officials and the presiding member of the KMA). From the very onset, the project identified key actors (the assembly member and NADMO officials) with whom future partnerships were developed. The core principles underpinning these relationships were trust, transparency, embrace and respect for diversity, enhanced inclusivity, flexibility, and accessible communication.

The importance of taking the time to foster good relationships was seen in our research coordinator's engagement with the Sepe-Buokrom assemblyman. A continuation of the relationship we had developed with him due to a previous study in 2016 (see Ahadzie et al., 2016), this relationship played out over the course of preliminary meetings (in which we explained the purpose of the project, its benefits to the community, and the role he was expected to play in making the project a success), right through to the second SM in August 2018. The assemblyman's interest in the project came from a desire to find solutions to the serious problem of flooding confronting his constituency, the success of which also could win him more credibility and political visibility. This long-term process not only enabled support from the assemblyman and his unit committee (UC) members from the onset, but also helped put the community at ease, which translated into people willingly making themselves available to listen to our aims and objectives, and then participate in the study.

Although serving the same electoral area, the assemblymen and UC members generally operate independently of each other (Figure 6.3). If not carefully managed, this separation could create problems for community engagement project like ours. However, bringing both parties on board from the project's beginning led to one of the Kumasi CityLab's biggest findings, which is that to influence the level of community participation in flood-risk management and community-based resilience initiatives, early identification of and engagement with the assembly-man and his office as a key stakeholder are vital.

Due to the assemblyman's active participation, the research team was able to identify and mobilize participants for the Focus Group Discussions (FGDs) and the first Stakeholder Meeting (SM) at Sepe-Buokrom. Similarly, the researchers relied on the presiding member[10] of the General Assembly to attract assembly-men to participate in the second SM in August. Our engagements with the presiding member took place in early July 2018, and were made possible during prior relationship-building with the NADMO officials of the KMA.

Regarding NADMO, we found that recognition of NADMO's expertise was all the incentive needed to acquire their full participation in the project, which opened the way for frank discussions about the support and expertise they can offer towards developing a CRF. NADMO further helped to organize the second SM (where the NADMO Director of the KMA also made a presentation support-ing the project). It is clear that NADMO now appreciates the need for bringing on board communities confronted with flood issues, and they have recently par-ticipated in radio discussions to whip up citizen participation for developing flood resilience. This recent sensitization effort is new, and could be attributed to the CityLab engagements discussed in this chapter.

In sum, our research team's outreach efforts with the community's assembly members and opinion leaders played a critical role in successfully securing par-ticipants for all sessions, and making the best use of those sessions. When plan-ning the FGDs, the research team successfully identified participants' livelihood, sociodemographic, and economic situations within the various groupings so that our subsequent discussions on the impact of floods were relevant to participants' actual livelihoods, activities (in small-scale businesses or school), and gender issues. With this information in hand, the research team was better able to provide the most appropriate presentation to best engage with participants based on their individual situations, which was key to the success of the FGDs. For instance, based on what we knew about participants, we chose to show videos of flooding in Ghana and other parts of the world as part of the FGDs, which helped meet the needs of the varied stakeholders, including the schoolchildren (cf. Pasquali, 2007)

The primary aim of the Kumasi CityLab was to create a space for knowledge-exchange and experience-sharing between different stakeholders, with the further goal to produce knowledge that could serve to ignite continued collabora-tion between the different entities involved. Based on feedback from both the research team and CityLab participants, this objective was largely met. The research process provided a rich source of information about Sepe-Buokrom, uncovering important nuances, like the community's diversified nature based on ethnic lines, apparent tensions between two chiefs, and various perspectives on the potential for and challenges to successfully implementing a CRF for flood-risk management.

Our research also proved the value of using an Audio-Visual presentation during all FGDs and SMs, given the extent to which it engaged participants' attention and sparked interest in the discussions that followed. In particular, participants at the first SM deeply appreciated the visuals showing how devastating the impact of flooding can be, and requested copies for further engagements in their respective constituencies. All of these engagements gave the research team much deeper insight both into how individuals cope with flooding, and how there is a lack of collective engagement in terms of addressing flooding issues at the community level.

Participants of both SMs also commended the CSS and its research team for hosting this series of community engagements to tackle the problem of flooding in Ghana. The presiding member commented that the CityLab approach diverts attention from the 'populist approach' favoured by government functionaries (e.g., ministers of state). Mainly focusing on (admittedly much-needed) relief items and structural demolition, that approach is viewed by many Ghanaians as motivated more by the desire to win political favour than it is to address the root causes of and problems resulting from flooding. Moreover, demolition work is rarely carried through to completion, often ceasing with the end of the rainy season. By contrast, the CityLab approach offers a more socially, environmentally, and politically sustainable way of mobilizing the community to change mindsets and take initiative independently of government action. Participants therefore encouraged the CSS to continue educating the various stakeholders involved in promoting this sustainable community-based approach to flood-risk management.

Challenges

The nature of CityLabs as spaces where people from different backgrounds come together inherently makes them difficult to navigate. Other researchers have pointed to challenges ranging from micro-politics to time and budget constraints (Brown-Luthango, 2013; Anderson et al., 2013). The cannot be underestimated and should be factored in when doing this kind of research. The Kumasi CityLab process took place over one year, during which time we were able to build fruitful collaborations with the Sepe-Buokrom assemblyman and other key stakeholders. However, dynamics not uncommon to working in informal settlements (e.g., ad-hoc and impulsive decisions, and a general lack of adherence to time management principles) greatly affected meeting schedules (e.g., the commencement of the FGDs, as originally planned with the assemblyman). On four separate occasions (both before and then once during the FGDs), the assemblyman had to cancel attendance because of suddenly being called to emergency meetings at the District Assembly. Social gatherings in the community such as funerals also interfered with scheduling, as the assemblyman's position in the community obliges him to attend such functions.

When planning the second SM, we invited the MPs from the Kumasi metropolis who oversee communities deemed flood-prone. Mindful of their busy schedules, our invitations and interview questions were sent well ahead of the August meeting, but not a single RSVP was returned. Although we made several efforts to retrieve interview data from the MPs offices in the metropolis, we did not receive a single response.

As per feedback from the first SM documented here, it was suggested that the leadership trio (assemblyman, chief, and MPs), among others, should collaborate to support the Common Vision to help build the community's interest in social responsibility for a CRF for flood-risk management. After the first SM, efforts by the research team to bring these three personages together with other major stakeholders to deliberate on how best to advance a vision of community-based flood-risk management were made. Unfortunately, the inability to schedule a joint meeting with the chiefs and MPs meant that none of them attended the second (and final) SM in August. Finally, lack of time and the need to meet reporting deadlines prevented the research team from effectively monitoring and evaluating the project, and conducting follow-up initiatives for the project's third 'Closure' phase.

Prospects

Our reflections as documented in the enablers and challenges earlier conclude that it is indeed possible to achieve a shift in the way we conduct research with communities, such that community members go from being research subjects to equal partners in knowledge production. While there is increasing interest and experiences of such approaches, this remains a novel approach to research in Ghana. However, such a shift requires that the communities and other relevant stakeholders are involved in every stage of the research process.

While the Kumasi CityLab project achieved its goal of creating a space for different stakeholders to engage with community-based responses to flood-risk management and also set the stage for future community-engaged collaborations, it was unsuccessful in bringing the MPs and chiefs together to these engagements. Also, much of our success was based on the cultivation of a long-standing relationship, which may not be possible in every instance.

Other studies have shown the potential of co-production in the field of climate adaptation as a way to influence decision-makers and bridge the gap between research and policy in Africa (Steynor et al., 2016; Ziervogel et al., 2016). This is imperative for meeting both global and local development goals on community resilience for climate adaptation in more structural and sustainable ways.

As part of the project's Closure Phase, our intention was to capture the knowledge shared during the FGDs and SMs in a document to be shared with a wider audience. Although we have not yet been able to complete that document, we have prepared a proposal to expand the CityLab, as per the request from the Kumasi MCE (political leader and head of local government). Meanwhile, a September 2018 exhibition of KNUST College Activities caught the attention of the Ashanti Regional Minister, who then invited the CSS to discuss with him the expansion of the work. Additionally, the assemblymen who participated in the second SM have strongly advocated for multi-stakeholder/joint stakeholder engagements with the MPs and chiefs, which would significantly advance the agenda of CRFs for flood-risk management.

As noted, the presiding member commended the CSS research team's proposed approach to tackling flooding problems in Kumasi. He observed that the community-mobilization approach redirects public attention from a focus on demolishing structures to finding risk-management methods that are more socially, environmentally, and politically sustainable. Praising this approach, he suggested that stakeholders start thinking about which measures could be put in place to help manage flooding without focusing solely on demolition. Similarly, the Kumasi MCE and the Metropolitan Director of the National Disaster Management Organization called for this type of engagement to be extended to the rest of Ghana.

The KMA is in the process of executing an MOU with the College of Art and Built Environment/KNUST, which the CSS project discussed here was fundamental in engendering. One major area of interest for this MOU is the creation of a multi-stakeholder platform for the discussion of flood-risk management in Kumasi. Engagements are also ongoing with other local governments, and it is envisaged that the successful uptake of this CityLab's methodology and results will provide the necessary leverage for extending the flood-risk management agenda at the regional and national level.

Conclusion

Flooding has become a major threat in cities around the world, including in Ghana. While structural measures are critical, nonstructural measures that focus on mitigation and especially adaptation are also essential. This CityLab research engaged a flood-prone community to contribute to the development of a framework for implementing community-led resilience and flood-risk management initiatives.

FGDs and consultative SMs with the community and opinion leaders brought together a wide array of community interest groups, including religious leaders, teachers, civil society groups, community leaders, and representatives from traditional leadership and political parties. The project's objective – to empower and create awareness within the community concerning its own responsibility to develop and act on a common vision for mitigation and coping strategies that can minimize the impacts of flood hazards – was met.

Three key themes emerged from our community engagements: 1) leadership is key, 2) the community/residents must embrace initiatives, and 3) loyalty, commitment, and togetherness are prerequisites for successful community resilience frameworks (CRFs).

The project affirmed the key roles played by the leadership trio (assemblyman, chief, and MP) in mobilizing the community to manage and increase its own resilience to flood risk. It also affirmed that collaboration between this trio is key to developing and implementing a common vision and programme of community-based flood-risk management. Additionally, the project found that residents are ready to work towards achieving flood resilience if the leadership trio plays its role.

Through the project, it also emerged that:

To influence the level of community participation in flood-risk management and community-based resilience initiatives, there needs to be an in-depth understanding of the workings of local governance structures, including traditional authorities. Hence, early identification of and engagement with the assemblyman and his office as a key stakeholder is vital. Further:

- Joint meetings of the leadership trio will be fundamental to driving any 'Common Vision', and assemblymen need to advocate harder for better collaboration between the various institutions.
- More public forums and engagement with other stakeholders and chiefs are needed to help drive a change in mindsets about how to adapt to flood-risk through CRFs. Recommendations were made for the Manhyia palace directorate to host such forums and discussions, which, it is expected, would leverage support from the King of the Ashanti Kingdom.
- Political rivalry among the leadership trio (assemblymen, MP, and chief) is a barrier to success, as strong collaboration between that trio is fundamental to mobilizing community support for community adaptation to flood risks. Additionally, nuances in community dynamics (such as diversity along ethnic lines) and apparent tensions between two rival chiefs are also worth noting.
- Given the strategic and close role of the assemblymen to the community, the assemblymen's lack of access to resources to help facilitate engagements is highly problematic, but could be addressed through measures such as the establishment of an 'Assemblymen's Common Fund' for community development projects. It was also suggested that an appeal be made to Parliament to review the allocation and use of the District Assembly Common Fund.
- The CityLab approach diverts attention from the 'populist approach' used by government functionaries, and offers a more socially, environmentally, and politically sustainable way of mobilizing the community to change mindsets and take initiative independently of government action.
- Public interest in the project's stakeholder engagements was remarkable, with the project attracting a great deal of publicity in radio, television, and print media.

Future research and practical actions

The Kumasi CityLab project has demonstrated both the importance of adopting a community resilience approach for flood-risk management in Ghana, and the readiness of stakeholders to assume their respective roles. It also has demonstrated the benefits of knowledge co-production among various stakeholders in flood-risk management in Ghana, and has led to CRF development assuming a national dimension, with a number of other local government areas requesting the CSS to engage communities within their jurisdictions by holding similar forums.

Reflecting on our findings, the research team suggested that the House of Parliament play a lead role in making community-based flood-risk management part of the national agenda, by proposing a bill for a Flood Control Act in Ghana. Flood risk in Ghana by all accounts is a grave national threat, and in June 2019, the House of Parliament requested the Minister of Works and Housing to provide a national plan for addressing floods in the country (Citifm Online, 2018). Such legislation not only would help make this issue a national priority, but also would assist in the implementation and enforcement of an integrated flood-risk management framework, including aspects relating to community resilience. All of this would support community members in learning what they can do for themselves regarding flood-resilient construction and adaptation, without flouting the law. Meanwhile the CSS continues to work to create a broader platform for this national conversation on engendering a community-based flood-risk management agenda. For example, on 22 May 2019, we were invited by a local FM station to share lessons on the Kumasi CityLab project, with the resulting sound bite aired the following day on Ghana's most popular radio station, Joy 99.7 FM/Luv 99.5 of the Multimedia Group Ltd.

Notes

1 As of June 2019, new regions have been created out of the original ten, meaning Ghana now has 16 administrative regions.
2 The KMA was formerly comprised of nine sub-metros, but due to reforms in the governance structure within the last couple of years, it now comprises five sub-metros, including Manhyia sub-metro.
3 Opinion leaders are leaders of interest groups in the community who command respect and are influential in decision-making within the community.
4 The assemblyman and unit committee members will be referred to collectively as assemblyman/assemblymen. Assemblymen can be either men or women, but in the case of Sepe-Buokrom, the assemblyman is male.
5 The assemblyman is required to regularly brief his electorate on the general decisions of the Assembly and its Executive Committees, including the actions taken to solve problems raised by residents in his electoral area.
6 Under Function 3(e) of the District Assemblies in the Local Government Act 462.
7 DACF is a Development Facility allocated to MMDAs to supplement their revenue base to enable them implement planned projects and programmes in their respective communities (Ankamah, 2012). It is backed by Act 455, 2003 of the 1992 Constitution of Ghana, and Parliament annually makes a provision for its allocation. Members of Parliament are given a share of the fund to undertake development projects in their respective constituencies.
8 In the Ashanti region of Ghana in particular, chiefs are custodians of the land, a resource that is at the centre of infrastructure development and its associated floods in many parts of Kumasi.
9 Manhyia as used here refers to the overlord Chief Palace for the Ashanti Kingdom in Ghana. All chiefs in the Ashanti region (including Kumasi and the study area) owe allegiance to the occupant of Manhyia, who is the King of the Ashantis. There is a

suggestion that if the overlord's support is brought into the picture, it would provide much-needed attention for chiefs (in the metropolis in particular) to embrace this flood-risk management initiative.

10 The presiding member is an assemblyman elected by the house to lead the District Assembly, and also acts as the Chairman of the general assembly.

References

Abdallah, K. (2011 September 13). Assembly members deserve monthly salary. *Rumnet* [online]. Retrieved: https://rumnetwordpress.com/2011/09/13/assembly-members-deserve-monthly-salary/

Adger, W.N., Agrawala, S. & Mirza, M.M.Q. (2007). Assessment of adaptation practices, options, constraints, and capacity. In: Parry, M.L., Canziani, O.F. & Palutikof, J.P. (Eds.), *Climate change 2007: impacts, adaptation and vulnerability. Contribution of working group ii to the fourth assessment report of the intergovernmental panel on climate change*. Cambridge: Cambridge University Press, pp. 717–743.

Afriyie, K., Ganle, J.K. & Santos, E. (2018). The floods came and we lost everything: weather extremes and households' asset vulnerability and adaptation in rural Ghana. *Climate and Development*, 10(3), pp. 259–274. DOI: https://doi.org/10.1080/17565529.2017.1291403

Ahadzie, D.K., Dinye, I., Dinye, R.D. & Proverbs, D.G. (2016). Flood risk perception, coping and management in two vulnerable communities in Kumasi, Ghana. *International Journal of Safety and Security Engineering*, 6(3), pp. 538–549. DOI: https://doi.org/10.2495/SAFE-V6-N3-538-549/009

Ahadzie, D.K. & Proverbs, D.G. (2011). Emerging issues in the management of floods in Ghana. *International Journal of Safety and Security Engineering*, 1(2), pp. 182–192. DOI: https://doi.org/10.2495/SAFE-V1-N2-182-192

Akaateba, M.A., Huang, H. & Adumpo, E.A. (2018). Between co-production and institutional hybridity in land delivery: insights from local planning practice in peri-urban Tamale, Ghana. *Land Use Policy*, 72, pp. 215–226.

Anderson, P.M.L., Brown-Luthango, M., Cartwright, A., Farouk, I. & Smit, W. (2013). Brokering communities of knowledge and practice: reflections on the African centre for cities, citylab programme. *Cities*, 32, pp. 1–10. DOI: https://doi.org/10.1016/j.cities.2013.02.002

Ankamah, S.S. (2012). The politics of fiscal decentralization in Ghana: an overview of the fundamentals. *Public Administration Research*, 1(1), p. 33.

Asamoah, R.O., Nelson, I.D., Twumasi-Ampofo, K., Ayeh, B.S., Offei-Nyako, K. & Ankrah, J.S. (2016). Invasion of wetlands in Kumasi by informal economic activities and consequences for urban management. *Planning*, 1(1), pp. 11–16. DOI: https://doi.org/10.11648/j.urp.20160101.13

Asumadu-Sarkodie, S., Owusu, P.A. & Rufangura, P. (2015). Impact analysis of flood in Accra, Ghana. *Advances in Applied Science Research*, 6(9), pp. 53–78. DOI: https://doi.org/10.6084/M9.FIGSHARE.3381460

Atanga, R.A. (2020). The role of local community leaders in flood disaster risk management strategy making in Accra. *International Journal of Disaster Risk Reduction*, 43. DOI: https://doi.org/10.1016/j.ijdrr.2019.101358

AURI. (2014 February 18–19). *Institutional models of co-production in the African city*. Proceedings of the 2nd African Urban Research Initiative (AURI) conference. Nairobi, Kenya.

Bender, G. (2008 March). Exploring conceptual models for community engagement at higher education institutions in South Africa. *Perspectives in Education*, 26, pp. 81–95.

Brown-Luthango, M. (2013). Community-university engagement: the Philippi citylab in Cape Town and the challenge of collaboration across boundaries. *Higher Education*, 65(3), pp. 309–324.

Chong, N.O., Kamarudin, K.H. & Abd Wahid, S.N. (2018). Framework considerations for community resilient towards disaster in Malaysia. *Procedia Engineering*, 212, pp. 165–172. DOI: https://doi.org/10.1016/j.proeng.2018.01.022

Chirisa, I., Bandauko, E., Mazhindu, E., Kwangwama, N.A. & Chikowore, G. (2016). Building resilient infrastructure in the face of climate change in African cities: scope, potentiality and challenges. *Development Southern Africa*, 33(1), pp. 113–127. DOI: https://doi.org/10.1080/0376835X.2015.1113122

Citifm Online. (2018). *Minority summons Atta-Akyea over flooding fears* [online]. Retrieved: http://citifmonline.com/2018/02/minority-summons-atta-akyea-flooding-fears/ [Accessed on 24 January 2020]

Cutter, S.L., Barnes, L., Berry, M., Burton, C., Evans, E., Tate, E. & Webb, J. (2008). A place-based model for understanding community resilience to natural disasters. *Global Environmental Change*, 18, pp. 598–606. DOI: https://doi.org/10.1016/j.gloenvcha.2008.07.013

Dollah, S., Abduh, A. & Rosmaladewi, R. (2017). Benefits and drawbacks of NVivo QSR application. In: *Advances in social science, education and humanities research (ASSEHR)*. Proceedings of the 2nd International Conference on Education, Science, and Technology (ICEST), vol. 149, pp. 61–63. Retrieved: https://www.researchgate.net/publication/320893973_Benefits_and_Drawbacks_of_NVivo_QSR_Application

Douglas, I., Alam, K., Maghenda, M., Mcdonnell, Y., McLean, L. & Campbell, J. (2008). Unjust waters: climate change, flooding and the urban poor in Africa. *Environment and Urbanization*, 20(1), pp. 187–205.

Filho, W.L., Balogun, A., Ayal, D.Y., Bethurem, E.M., Murambadoro, M., Mambo, J., Taddese, H., Tefera, G.W., Nagy, G.J., Fudjumdjum, H. & Mugabe, P. (2018). Strengthening climate change adaptation capacity in Africa – case studies from six major African cities and policy implications. *Environmental Science & Policy*, 86, pp. 29–37. DOI: https://doi.org/10.1016/j.envsci.2018.05.004

Floodlist. (2018). Ghana – devastation floods hit Accra again. *Floodlist* [online]. Retrieved: http://floodlist.com/africa/ghana-floods-accra-june-2018 [Accessed on 24 January 2020]

Floodlist. (2019). Ghana – floods cause devastation in upper East region. *Floodlist* [online]. Retrieved: http://floodlist.com/africa/ghana-floods-upper-east-region-october-2019 [Accessed on 24 January 2020]

Frimpong, A. (2014). Perennial floods in the Accra Metropolis: Dissecting the causes and possible solutions. *African Social Science Review*, 6(1), pp. 1–14.

Ghana Statistical Service. (2012). *Ghana population and housing census 2010 report*. Accra: Ghana Statistical Service.

Government of Ghana (GoG). (2015). *Local government legislative instrument 2223*. Accra: Ministry of Local Government and Rural Development.

Government of Ghana (GoG). (2016). *Local governance act of 2016, Act 936*. Accra: Ministry of Local Government and Rural Development.

Graphic Online. (2018). Give Assembly members 5% of common fund. *Graphic Online* [online]. Retrieved: www.graphic.com.gh/news/politics/give-assembly-men [Accessed on 12 November 2018]

Huong, H.T.L. & Pathirana, A. (2013). Urbanization and climate change impacts on future urban flooding in Can Tho city, Vietnam. *Hydrology and Earth System Sciences*, 17(1), pp. 379–394.

International Federation of Red Cross and Crescent Societies (IFRC). (2015). *Emergency plan of action (EPoA) – Ghana: floods*. Retrieved: https://reliefweb.int/report/ghana/ghana-floods-emergency-plan-action-epoa-mdrgh011

International Federation of Red Cross and Crescent Societies (IFRC). (2017). *Emergency plan of action final report – Ghana: floods*. Retrieved: https://reliefweb.int/sites/reliefweb.int/files/resources/MDRGH014dfr.pdf

IPCC. (2007). *Climate change 2007: the physical science basis. Contribution of working group I to the fourth assessment report of the intergovernmental panel on climate change* [Solomon, S., Qin, D., Manning, M., Chen, Z., Marquis, M., Averyt, K.B., Tignor, M. & Miller, H.L. (Eds.).]. Cambridge and New York: Cambridge University Press.

IPCC. (2013). Summary for policymakers. In: Stocker, T.F., Qin, D., Plattner, G.K., Tignor, M., Allen, S.K., Boschung, J., Nauels, A., Xia, Y., Bex, V. & Midgley, P.M. (Eds.), *Climate change 2013: the physical science basis. Contribution of working group I to the fifth assessment report of the intergovernmental panel on climate change*. Cambridge and New York: Cambridge University Press.

IPCC. (2018). *Climate report* [Masson-Delmotte, V., Zhai, P., Pörtner, H.O., Roberts, D., Skea, J., Shukla, P.R., Pirani, A., Moufouma-Okia, W., Péan, C., Pidcock, R., Connors, S., Matthews, J.B.R., Chen, Y., Zhou, X., Gomis, M.I., Lonnoy, E., Maycock, T., Tignor, M. & Waterfield, T. (Eds.).]. Geneva: World Meteorological Organization.

Jagers, S.C. & Duus-Otterström, G. (2008). Dual climate change responsibility: on moral divergences between mitigation and adaptation. *Environmental Politics*, 17(4), pp. 576–591.

Jha, A.K., Bloch, R. & Lamond, J. (2012). *Cities and flooding: a guide to integrated urban flood risk management for the 21st century*. Washington, DC: World Bank.

Jones, L. & Boyd, E. (2011). Exploring social barriers to adaptation: insights from Western Nepal. *Global Environmental Change*, 21(4), pp. 1262–1274.

Kellens, W., Terpstra, T. & De Maeyer, P. (2013). Perception and communication of flood risks: a systematic review of empirical research. *Risk Analysis*, 33(1), pp. 24–49.

Kruse, S., Abeling, T., Deeming, H., Fordham, M., Forrester, J., Jülich, S., Karanci, A.N., Kuhlicke, C., Pelling, M., Pedoth, L. & Schneiderbauer, S. (2017). Conceptualizing community resilience to natural hazards – the emBRACE framework. *Natural Hazards Earth System Sciences*, 17, pp. 2321–2333. DOI: https://doi.org/10.5194/nhess-17-2321-2017

Local Government Act 462. (1993). *Local government service – Ghana*. Retrieved: https://lgs.gov.gh/index.php/laws-acts-and-legislative-instruments/

Lohmann, S., Heimerl, F., Bopp, F., Burch, M. & Ertl, T. (2015 July). *Concentri cloud: word cloud visualization for multiple text documents*. Information visualisation (iV), 19th International Conference on Information Visualisation, Barcelona, Spain, pp. 114–120. DOI: https://doi.org/10.1109/iV.2015.30

Lwasa, S. (2010). Adapting urban areas in Africa to climate change: the case of Kampala. *Current Opinion in Environmental Sustainability*, 2(3), pp. 166–171. DOI: https://doi.org/10.1016/j.cosust.2010.06.009

Magadza, C.H.D. (2000). Climate change impacts and human settlements in Africa: prospects for adaptation. *Environmental Monitoring and Assessment*, 61(1), pp. 193–205.

Mail&Guardian. (2018 October 11). The IPCC's latest climate report on 1.5 holds implications for African Countries. *Mail&Guardian* [online]. Retrieved: https://mg.co.za/article/2018-10-11-the-UN Climate Reports-latest-climate-report-on-15c-holds-implications-for-african-countries/

Mangai, M. & De Vries, M. (2018). Co-production as deep engagement: improving and sustaining access to clean water in Ghana and Nigeria. *International Journal of Public Sector Management*, 31(1), pp. 81–96.

McCusker, B. & Carr, E.R. (2006). The co-production of livelihoods and land use change: case studies from South Africa and Ghana. *Geoforum*, 37(5), pp. 790–804.

McNaught, C. & Lam, P. (2010). Using Wordle as a supplementary research tool. *The Qualitative Report*, 15(3), pp. 630–643.

Mertz, O., Halsnæs, K., Olesen, J.E. & Rasmussen, K. (2009). Adaptation to climate change in developing countries. *Environmental Management*, 43(5), pp. 743–752.

Muller, M. (2007). Adapting to climate change: water management for urban resilience. *Environment and Urbanization*, 19(1), pp. 99–113.

Mullins, A. & Soetanto, R. (2011). Enhancing community resilience to flooding through social responsibility. *International Journal of Safety and Security Engineering*, 1(2), pp. 115–125.

Nations Online. (2018). Political map of West Africa. *Nations Online Project* [online]. Retrieved: www.nationsonline.org/oneworld/map/west-africa-map.htm [Accessed on 17 December 2018]

Niehm, L.S., Swinney, J. & Miller, N.J. (2008). Community social responsibility and its consequences for family business performance. *Journal of Small Business Management*, 46(3), pp. 331–350.

Nkrumah, A.A. (2016). Ghana flood league table. *Ahaspora* [online]. Retrieved: www.ahaspora.com/ghana-floods-league-table-2016-guest-blog-the-green-ghanaian/

Norris, F.H., Stevens, S.P., Pfefferbaum, B., Wyche, K.F. & Pfefferbaum, R.L. (2008). Community resilience as a metaphor, theory, set of capacities, and strategy for disaster readiness. *American Journal of Community Psychology*, 41(1–2), pp. 127–150. DOI: https://doi.org/10.1007/s10464-007-9156-6

Owusu-Ansah, J.K. (2016). The influences of land use and sanitation infrastructure on flooding in Kumasi, Ghana. *Geojournal of Spatially Integrated Social Science and Humanities*, 81(4), pp. 555–570.

Parnell, S. (2016). Defining a global urban development agenda. *World Development*, 78, pp. 529–540. DOI: https://doi.org/10.1016/j.worlddev.2015.10.028

Pasquali, M. (2007). Video in science: protocol videos: the implications for research and society. *EMBO Reports*, 8(8), pp. 712–716. DOI: https://dx.doi.org/10.1038%2Fsj.embor.7401037

Patel, Z., Greyling, S., Parnell, S. & Price, G. (2015). Co-producing urban knowledge: experimenting with alternatives to best practice for Cape Town, South Africa. *International Development Planning Review*, 37(2), pp. 187–203.

Pohl, C., Rist, S., Zimmermann, A., Fry, P., Gurung, G.S., Schneider, F., Speranza, C.I., Kiteme, B., Boillat, S., Serrano, E. & Hadorn, G.H. (2010). Researchers' roles in knowledge co-production: experience from sustainability research in Kenya, Switzerland, Bolivia and Nepal. *Science and Public Policy*, 37(4), pp. 267–281.

Proverbs, D. (2011). Editorial. *International Journal of Safety and Security Engineering*, 1(2), pp. iii–iv.

Proverbs, D. & Lamond, J. (2017). Flood resilient construction and adaptation of buildings. *Natural Hazards Science*, 10(2), pp. 1–3.

Renschler, C., Reinhorn, A., Arendt, L. & Cimellaro, G. (2011 May 25–28). *The P.E.O.P.L.E.S. resilience framework: a conceptual approach to quantify community resilience* [Papadrakakis, M., Fragiadakis, M. & Plevris, V. (Eds.)]. 3rd ECCOMAS Thematic Conference on Computational Methods in Structural Dynamics and Earthquake Engineering, Corfu, Greece. DOI: https://doi.org/10.13140/RG.2.1.3355.1767

Rodriguez, R.S., Ürge-Vorsatz, D. & Barau, A.S. (2018). Sustainable development goals and climate change adaptation in cities. *Nature Climate Change*, 8, pp. 181–183.

Serdeczny, O., Adams, S., Baarsch, F., Coumou, D., Robinson, A., Hare, B., Schaeffer, M., Perrette, M. & Reinhardt, J. (2015). Climate change impacts in sub-Saharan Africa: from physical changes to their social repercussions. *Regional Environmental Change*, 15(8). DOI: https://doi.org/10.1007/s10113-015-0910-2

Shafer, W.E., Fukukawa, K. & Lee, G.M. (2007). Values and the perceived importance of ethics and social responsibility: the US versus China. *Journal of Business Ethics*, 70(3), pp. 265–284.

Steynor, A., Padgham, J., Jack, C., Hewitson, B. & Lennard, C. (2016). Co-exploratory climate risk workshops: experiences from urban Africa. *Climate Risk Management,*13, pp. 95–102.

Sylla, M., Nikiema, M., Gibba, P., Kebe, I., Klutse, N. & Browne, A. (2016). Climate change over West Africa: recent trends and future projections. In: Yaro, J.A. & Hesselberg, J. (Eds.), *Adaptation to climate change and variability in rural West Africa*, pp. 25–40. DOI: https://doi.org/10.1038/s41598-018-32736-0

Terumoto, K. (2006). Issues and attitudes of local government officials for flood risk management. In: Ikeda, S., Fukuzono, T. & Sato, T. (Eds.), *A better integrated management of disaster risks: toward resilient society to emerging disaster risks in mega-cities*. Tokyo: TERRAPUB and NIED, pp. 165–176.

van Vuuren, D.P., Isaac, M., Kundzewicz, Z.W., Arnell, N., Barker, T., Criqui, P., Berkhout, F., Hilderink, H., Hinkel, J., Hof, A. & Kitous, A. (2011). The use of scenarios as the basis for combined assessment of climate change mitigation and adaptation. *Global Environmental Change*, 21(2), pp. 575–591.

Wilby, R.L. & Keenan, R. (2012). Adapting to flood risk under climate change. *Progress Physical Geography*, 36(3), pp. 348–378.

Wood, M., Kovacs, D., Bostrom, A., Bridges, T. & Linkov, I. (2012). Flood risk management: US army corps of engineers and layperson perceptions. *Risk Analysis: An International Journal*, 32(8), pp. 1349–1368.

Zamawe, F.C. (2015). The implication of using NVivo software in qualitative data analysis: evidence based reflections. *Malawi Medical Journal*, 27(1), pp. 13–15.

Ziervogel, G., van Garderen, E.A. & Price, P. (2016). Strengthening the knowledge – policy interface through co-production of a climate adaptation plan: leveraging opportunities in Bergrivier municipality, South Africa. *Environment and Urbanization*, 28(2), pp. 455–474.

7 Housing for whom?

Rebuilding Angola's cities after conflict and who gets left behind

Allan Cain

Introduction

Following a civil war of nearly three decades, the period after the 2002 peace accords saw oil-producing Angola become Africa's fifth-biggest and fastest-growing economy. Between 2004 and 2008, Angola's GDP surged by an average of 17% a year, topping 22% in 2007. With foreign investment rising at a rate of more than US$10 billion a year, and GDP per person tripling by 2012, Angola has been heralded as one of Africa's economic successes, at least until the global slump in oil prices in 2014 (The Economist, 2012). At the same time, decades of rural-urban migration have turned Angola into one of Africa's most urbanized countries, with 62% of its population living in cities (UN-Habitat, 2014). As a result, public demand for housing and services in Angola's cities is enormous. This is especially the case in the capital of Luanda, which counts an estimated 8,000,000 inhabitants – about a third of the country's total population. With an average annual growth rate of 5.77%, Luanda's population is set to continue to increase over the next decade, making it a 'megacity in waiting' (UN-Habitat, 2014, p. 192; see also GoA, 2016b).

While the country's exploding post-war economy impacted the Luanda real estate market's higher end through the construction of new suburbs and gated communities, it bypassed informal settlements. Over two-thirds of Luanda's residents continue to live in shelters that are self-built with people's own resources and savings, often with a lack of adequate and affordable basic public services, and on land for which they do not have formal titles. In an effort to address the country's housing shortfall, in 2009 the Angolan government launched the country's first Urbanization and Housing Programme (PNUH) with the goal of building 1,000,000 housing units through construction by the state, private sector, and cooperatives, as well as by supporting self-help building through the provision of titled land, infrastructure, services, construction material, and technical support. In doing so, the PNUH represents not only an important pillar of Angola's post-war reconstruction efforts, but also an important instrument in implementing a range of global agreements ratified by the Angolan government. These include the UN Millennium Development Goals (MDGs), replaced in 2015 by the Sustainable Development Goals (SDGs), as well as the New Urban Agenda (NUA), adopted at the third UN Human Settlements Conference in 2016.

Since its inception, significant public resources involving a range of different actors have been invested into the PNUH. However, the government's implementation of the PNUH generally, and the extent to which it has effectively provided housing for the urban poor or met the principles and objectives of global urban development agendas, have not been well monitored. This chapter presents research conducted by the NGO Development Workshop (DW) on Angola's PNUH. The research builds on decades of action research conducted by DW among peri-urban communities and informal settlements, as well as its monitoring of the implementation of global agendas at the Angolan government's request.

The chapter starts with a review of housing policy, practice, and research in post-war Angola, before moving to the work of the DW, its approach to co-production, and its role in monitoring Angola's implementation of global policy agendas. Based on the lessons learned from these experiences, and using a variety of participatory tools and methods developed therein, the study presented here assesses the outcomes and beneficiaries of the PNUH's different sub-programmes, comparing their outcomes to those from the 'social production of housing' (i.e., built without state support) as well as slum upgrading. The chapter concludes by proposing principles to inform more sustainable and inclusive approaches to Angola's monitoring and implementation of the NUA and other related policy agendas.

Context

Housing policy, practice, and research in post-war Angola

Angola's civil war left almost all its infrastructure, both rural and urban, in ruin. Peace in 2002 liberated financing for reconstruction, and the country's natural resources and booming economic growth attracted loans from both traditional Western donors as well as new emerging powers such as China, which offered deals with few strings attached. As the country's cities had rapidly grown during its war years, peace brought a strong public demand for urban renewal, basic public services, and housing for all. Post-conflict public policies committed to meeting these demands included the adoption of an official housing policy in 2006 (Resolution 60/06), which guaranteed the universal right to housing, followed by a Framework Law for Housing (Law 03/07), as well as programmes to provide 'water for all' and strategies to combat poverty, promote local development, and strengthen local government.

The housing sector was officially prioritized with the country's first National Urbanization and Housing Programme (PNUH), which was announced on World Habitat Day 6 October 2008, just after the country's first post-war elections, in a public meeting attended by UN-Habitat's then-Executive Director, Anna Kamujulo Tibaijuka, and long-standing President José Eduardo dos Santos.

At the time of the Programme's official launch in 2009, the Angolan Ministry of Urbanism and Housing estimated the country's shortfall of housing to be almost 2,000,000 units. Meanwhile, the National Institute of Statistics estimated that

90% of existing urban housing was substandard and needed substantial invest-ment to upgrade it to acceptable living standards (GoA, 2009). It was envisioned that by the next elections in 2012, PNUH would reduce housing deficits by at least 50% through an accelerated programme, using financing from the petroleum sec-tor along with credit-lines from China (Croese, 2012).

While the plan was to promote urban development (including slum renewal), the only clearly articulated targets were around housing unit numbers. The PNUH divided the responsibilities for meeting housing targets among a range of housing providers, with the state taking on 11.5%, the private sector 12%, cooperatives 8%, and (state-directed) owner-builders assuming the major share of 68.5% of housing to address the nation's unmet need for shelter. By 2012, little progress had been made in terms of implementation, and the dead-line was again extended to the following election of 2017. Meanwhile, the burden of Angola's accumulation of foreign debt from expenditures on hous-ing construction and expensive high-profile projects financed through Chinese and Israeli oil-backed credit lines became heavier in the face of steep eco-nomic decline due to plummeting oil prices from 2014 (Benazeraf & Alves, 2014; Macauhub, 2019). Further, highly centralized state structures meant that public programme implementation was often poorly coordinated with local government and lacked transparency. As a result, few targets were met and/or reached their intended beneficiaries.

Scholarly criticism of the governance and outcomes of post-war housing poli-cies in Angola has focused on lack of transparency around finance for housing construction, and the slum demolitions accompanying urban renewal (Rodri-gues & Frias, 2015; Gastrow, 2017; Waldorff, 2016). While such critiques are important, most of this work has focused on selected housing projects or specific moments in time. Moreover, the majority of this work was produced for the pur-pose of contributing to academic debates, rather than the practical improvement of the implementation of housing policies. In contrast, the work of DW is situated at the interface between research and policy.

Our research approach is premised on the principals of co-production, which can refer to partnerships or collaborations between the state and society in the realm of services (Ostrom, 1996), knowledge (Polk, 2015), or policies (Durose & Richardson, 2016), and with a view to producing more inclusive and sustainable outcomes. The need for and benefits of co-production in Angola emerges – as in many other places in the global South (Joshi & Moore, 2004) – in a context of weak state capacity. However, whereas in other countries grassroots-led co-production between state and society has represented a route to political power, influence, and transformation (Mitlin, 2008), civil society in Angola – with its legacy of long-term conflict and decades of authoritarian rule – remains relatively weak. As such, DW has played an important role in facilitating collaborations between state and civil society.

In the early 1980s, at the government's request, DW started working in Angola to assist in developing policies and programmes for human settlements and self-help housing. In the decades that followed, DW adopted a strategy of supporting and working together with Angolan civil society, community-based organizations, and local governments in areas ranging from infrastructure and basic services to community economic development, through research, practice, and advocacy on land titling programmes, water and sanitation committees, and micro- and housing finance (Cain, 1986; Cain et al., 2002; Cain, 2007, 2010).

Our research tools and methods include participatory mapping tools, GIS-enabled surveys, and data collection involving local government officials, civil society organizations, and community associations through training and capacity building, as well as the organization of Municipal Forums as spaces for deliberation. Much of the work at the community level engages individuals and communities that are often very vulnerable, naturally wary of any change, and likely to feel they lack the power to improve their lives. As such, trust building is a critical aspect and outcome of this work. Involving local municipal administrations and community associations in community research has contributed not only to better understandings of the intentions behind the work, but also to a local sense of ownership of the data and knowledge produced.

DW has integrated the approaches described earlier into our partnerships and collaborations with different state agencies in the monitoring of the implementation of global development agendas. In doing so, we seek to generate evidence that is co-produced and co-owned, and therefore capable of contributing to better policies and practices.

Monitoring global policy implementation in Angola

In 2006, UN-Habitat and the Angolan Ministry of Urbanism and Environment requested that DW lead the creation of the Angolan National Urban Observatory. This Observatory was one in a network of National Urban Observatories piloted to undertake work as part of the Global Urban Observatory (GUO), set up in 2001 by UN-Habitat, following the second UN Human Settlements Conference, or Habitat II. Taking place in Istanbul in 1996, the Habitat II conference had launched the 'Habitat Agenda', a collaborative approach to realizing sustainable human settlements and 'adequate shelter for all' through existing and new partnerships at the international, national, and local level (UN-Habitat, 1996). The purpose of the Observatories was to help governments, local authorities, and civil society organizations monitor the Habitat Agenda through the development and application of policy-oriented urban indicators and urban statistics. By integrating the targets and indicators of the UN Millennium Development Goals (MDGs) in this work, the Observatories could simultaneously inform the implementation of target 11 of the MDGs: to significantly improve the lives of 100,000,000 slum dwellers by the year 2020. A network of National Urban Observatories was piloted to undertake this work, creating local focal points for urban policy development, planning, and collaboration among policymakers, technical experts, and civil society. Local Urban Observatories were also created to coordinate capacity-building assistance and to compile and analyse urban data for national policy development (Ferreira et al., 2012).

As part of its inception, DW worked to build capacity at the Angolan National Institute of Territorial and Urban Planning (INOTU) and among provincial and municipal staff in the country's major urban centres in four provinces (Luanda, Huambo, Benguela, and Namibe). In the course of this work, DW built important partnerships with local civil-society poverty networks and community-based organizations to participate in data collection using MDG indicators. A number of important lessons can be drawn from this work. Most international agencies and many governments publicly committed themselves to the MDGs, which in some cases resulted in improved outcomes. For instance, the MDG of significantly improving the lives of at least 100 million slum dwellers translated into increasing the proportion of that population with secure tenure. However, aside from improving the lives of slum dwellers, the MDGs lacked adequate focus on urban issues, in part because of policymakers' then-common misconception that urban poverty was much less serious than rural poverty, and thus had little relevance to MDG achievement. The MDGs have further been criticized for being too narrow in focus, and too often determined by 'external' experts in a top-down manner, not reflective of local needs and priorities, and thereby producing unintended outcomes, especially for the urban poor (Satterthwaite, 2003; Meth, 2013; Fukuda-Parr, 2014).

Following our work establishing Angola's National Urban Observatory, the Angolan Ministry of Urbanization and Housing requested in 2015/2016 that DW lead the consultative process preparing the country's National Report to Habitat III in Quito, which would measure the country's achievements against commitments made to the 1996 Habitat II Agenda. A key finding in our analysis of the Habitat II Agenda process in Angola was that the MDGs' relevance for Angola's urban populations was compromised by inaccurate statistics, inappropriate criteria, and the use of unsuitable income-based poverty indicators (GoA, 2016a). These findings coincided with Satterthwaite's (2003) conclusions that MDG indicators were overly focused on deliverables from the national government – neglecting the investments and ingenuity that low-income groups and their organizations make. Monitoring efforts also were reliant on conceptually flawed indicators (especially the dollar-a-day poverty line), or ones for which the 'official' data was inconsistent or inaccurate (i.e., if an income-based poverty line was set too low, poverty would statistically disappear). In Angola, the validity of that ubiquitous indicator for measuring who qualified as income poor – i.e., the dollar-a-day poverty line – proved inappropriate for assessing the scale of urban poverty, as much of the urban population faces particularly high costs for non-food necessities as the combined result of being a post-conflict and resource-rich but highly dependent import economy (Soares de Oliveira, 2015).

While globally conceived indicators were measured nationally in physical terms, particularly regarding access to basic services, little attention was paid to the inequalities in power, incomes, and asset-bases that generally underpin the lack of those basic services. For example, access to water was judged only on the basis of distance to a well or standpipe, with no attention to water quality, ease of access, regularity of supply, or cost. The Observatory noted such issues in Angola, where there is a general lack of available data measuring things like who has access to 'safe water' or adequate sanitation. Further, the Observatory found that many urban dwellers who did live close to water mains had no means to utilize them, as waterlines bypassed them, being channelled to new up-market real-estate projects. Finally, impacts that were difficult to measure – such as more accountable local governance, protection of civil and political rights, and greater possibilities for community-designed, managed, and monitored initiatives – were neglected. Thus, MDG monitoring ignored realities like the fact that many of the poor in Luanda's inner city lived with the constant threat of eviction from the land they occupied for housing.

Fortunately, the post-2015 Sustainable Development Goals (SDGs) and the New Urban Agenda (NUA) adopted in 2016 were developed using lessons drawn from the problems encountered in monitoring the MDGs (Fukuda-Parr, 2016). This includes a more participatory approach to the conceptualization of the goals and agendas, and more qualitative targets and indicators through extensive consultations in the run-up to the adoption of the SDGs. While there are still challenges and shortcomings in both the SDGs and NUA (Klopp & Petretta, 2017; Caprotti et al., 2017), the SDG monitoring framework reflects a move to more adequate measurement of the implementation of urban policies and plans, while the NUA puts National Urban Policies centre stage in terms of achieving urban development that is both inclusive and sustainable.

Monitoring Angola's national urbanization and housing programme (PNUH)

In spite of the government's laudable and ambitions aims, the PNUH was initially developed without any plan for how to monitor and measure progress on its implementation. Moreover, the housing challenge was essentially seen as a numeric deficit, which would be solved once new houses were added to the existing housing stock, and with little regard for local realities and needs around the quality, access, and affordability of housing. Moreover, when the State's national PNUH programme identified four sectors as key actors in supplying housing, little information was available about the capacity and past performance of these actors. This was particularly the case for cooperatives and owner-builders, who together were tasked to deliver three quarters of the envisaged housing. Additionally, how these actors were to mobilize financing for housing had not been considered prior to launching the PNUH.

DW's work on the assessment of Angola's PNUH built on our experience of research co-production, considering the lessons from earlier monitoring projects, including the experience and shortcomings gleaned from the process of monitoring the Habitat II Agenda and the MDGs. To develop the framework,

DW quantitatively compared the results of PNUH-supported programmes (i.e., state, private, cooperative, and state-directed owner-builder efforts) with those of a slum upgrading component of PNUH's programme, as well as with owner-builder 'social production of housing'. This latter term is described by the Habitat International Coalition as 'all non-market processes carried out under inhabitants' initiative, management, and control, that generate and/or improve adequate living spaces, housing, and other elements of physical and social development, preferably without – and often despite – impediments posed by the State or other formal structure or authority'. In other words, builders who received no PNUH (state) support.[1]

Further, we developed the framework used here with the aim of going beyond a merely quantitative analysis, to gain a more comprehensive understanding around the beneficiaries of urban interventions, with a focus on the urban poor. Participatory research methods were crucial in this regard, and all research tools were developed and conducted in collaboration with local municipalities, civil society organizations, and community associations. In doing so, the methodology engaged both community members and municipal authorities in the co-production and co-ownership of data on their neighbourhoods.

Amongst the research instruments employed were a poverty scoring methodology and a housing client study, which are discussed in the following sections.

Methodology and tools

Poverty scoring methodology

An important dimension of the data collection was the measurement of poverty scoring that allowed us to identify the economic level of beneficiary families. In 2017, 58% of the Angolan population was living below the poverty line of US$1.90 per day (CEIC, 2018). The Traditional Poverty Line assessments used in the monitoring of the MDGs greatly overstated income poverty in rural areas, while understating it in urban ones. For our monitoring framework, we therefore wanted to use a poverty ranking system adapted to local conditions and reflective of a household's capacity to access housing and basic urban services such as water, sanitation, and transport.

DW collaborated in constructing a Poverty Scorecard, which is an easy-to-use tool for monitoring poverty rates and tracking changes over time in order to target services for the most vulnerable groups (Schreiner, 2015). Poverty scores vary from 1 (most likely below the poverty line) to 100 (least likely below the poverty line). Indicators are non-financial, including easy-to-validate household assets, housing conditions, and access to water and sanitation services. The scorecard's bias and precision are tied and weighted directly to indicators set by the National Statistics Institute in the Integrated Household Survey conducted in 2008–2009 with support of the World Bank and UNICEF (GoA, 2009).

Since 2015, community groups working with DW have collected scorecard question data on a biannual basis to monitor changes in local poverty indicators over time. The scorecard can measure individual households, or be aggregated geographically to assess a whole community's trajectory over time, into or out of poverty. Scorecard data can be mapped in relation to access to basic services such as water (Figure 7.1), and used in Municipal Forums and Councils, providing evidence for civil society and community organizations advocating for more equitable access to basic services and public investments.

Housing client study

DW also conducted a household client study to understand how clients from different sectors accessed and financed their housing. The household study assessed the level of urban basic services that each household was supplied with, and the mechanisms that families used to acquire these services.

Using questionnaires (which included the poverty scorecard questions described earlier), focus groups, and key informant interviews, the household client study was able to determine how the four PNUH sectors performed in delivering social housing for the urban poor. The methodology further provided social and economic data from questionnaires to help assess householder satisfaction, housing affordability, and level of service access.

In implementing the housing client survey, the research team enumerators (from both the community and local administration) worked with slum communities in Luanda to collect household data through the questionnaires using mobile-enabled Android tablets equipped with global positioning capabilities that can plot data in Google Maps. Such maps differ from paper maps in their greater spatial accuracy, permanence, authority, and credibility with authorities and communities.

Findings

In the following sections, we summarize the results of our 2016 analysis of the performance of the four housing sectors the PNUH was mandated to support (i.e., the state, the private, cooperative, and state-directed owner-built), and complement this with our research on interventions in the area of urban renewal and in-situ informal area upgrading, as well as on the social production of housing.

The public housing sector

Thanks to the PNUH, by 2016 the State had built 151,800 publicly funded units, mainly through contracts with foreign private companies, including the Chinese firms, CIF and CITIC, and KORA, an Israeli company. As part of the PNUH's public housing commitment, municipalities were supposed to build a total of 26,000 houses (200 houses per municipality in 130 districts). National firms and joint ventures were eligible to compete for the municipal sub-programme's public

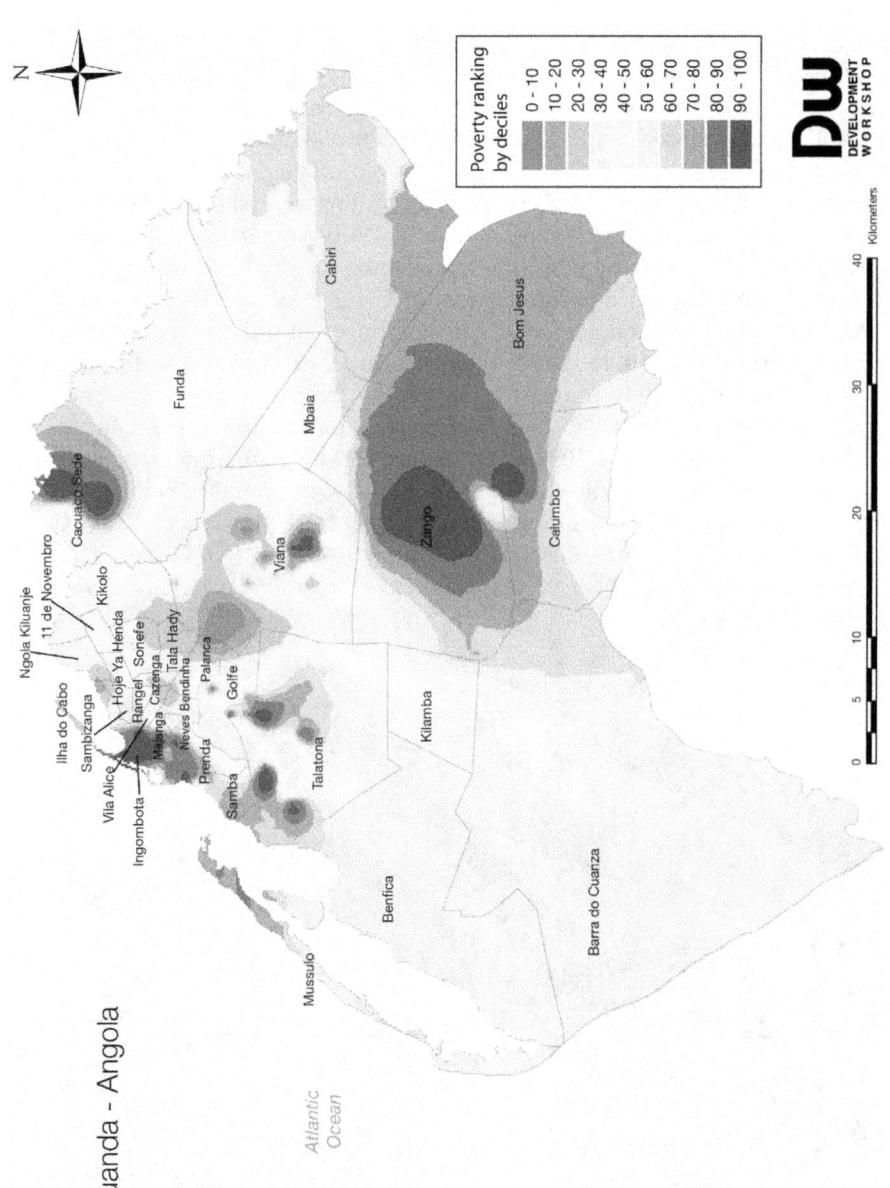

Figure 7.1 Schematic Map Indicating Levels of Access to Water Ranked in Deciles

Source: DW

tenders, but in the end, only about 10,000 units were completed, meaning that less than 7% of the publicly funded units were built by local companies.

The most significant state contribution under PNUH was in the construction of 'new urbanizations', mostly in the form of '*centralidades*', or public housing constructed on state land reserves. Each providing housing for at least 2,000 families (mainly intended for civil servants and middle-income clients), state-built *centralidades* or 'new town centres' were built by foreign firms in the five provinces of Cabinda, Uige, Huambo, Huila, and Namibe by the end of 2014.

The model for the *centralidades* was Angola's largest and most famous public housing investment: the Kilamba New City project, a mixed-use development built by CITIC, a major Chinese company. Delivering over 20,000 units of housing for more than 160,000 people, Kilamba was funded by Angola's first Chinese credit line for a purported cost of US$3.5 billion. Its first phase was completed in 2012 and included 750 apartment buildings, with initial selling prices from US$120,000 to US$200,000. In an effort to stimulate sales in early 2013, government introduced a subsidized 'rent-to-purchase' scheme, with an annual interest rate of 3%, and the cheapest units selling price reduced from US$120,000 to US$84,200. This scheme brought apartment ownership within the reach of middle-level civil servants with monthly salaries of US$1,500 or greater. With the introduction of successive subsidies however, any expectation of recovery of the state's investment in the PNUH by the sale or rental of housing was effectively abandoned (for more on Kilamba, see Cain, 2014; Cardoso, 2016).

Figure 7.2 Kilamba New City in Luanda, China's Largest Housing Project in Africa

Source: Moreira, 2012

Figure 7.3 Private Condominium Atlantico do Sul in Belas Municipality, Luanda
Source: www.wikimapia.org/p/00/00/54/61/45_big.jpg

The private sector

Although the private sector was envisioned as a key partner in the delivery of PNUH's national housing targets, a history of war and rigid economic controls meant that markets were still at an early stage of development. Private real estate enterprises and construction companies thus looked to the state rather than to markets for financing, focusing almost exclusively on the market's upper end, and whenever possible, entering into public-private projects on the condition that the state provide access to land.

The State's PNUH housing strategy specified that the private sector deliver 12% of the total targeted number of houses constructed. Under the PNUH, private-sector housing was to be financed via several mechanisms, including public-private partnerships, small-scale provincial and municipal home-building projects, and private contractor access to credit through Angolan banks, which could in turn draw financing from the Housing Development Fund.

Under the banner of 'Public-Private-Partnerships', the private partner takes the role of constructor and/or manager of state-financed projects. Government allocated a budget for the construction of 200 housing units for each of Angola's 18 provinces. Occupying land designated under the Land Reserve programme, these units were to be distributed to the various municipalities depending on need, and tendered out to local contractors.

Of the 120,000 dwellings that the private sector was supposed to build under the PNUH, only 12,756 units – 10.6% of the target – were actually constructed solely by private sector parties. Meanwhile, nearly 40% of the private sector target (45,600 units) was delivered through public-private partnerships or by contractors to provincial governments (GoA, 2016a, p. 73). The State also financed homes built by private foreign companies under the Programme; these units accounted for nearly 30% of the total private sector target, and though built by foreign companies, they failed to attract overseas direct investment (ODI).

Meanwhile, private financing focused on building the market's high end, rather than developing social housing. As a result, upper- and middle-class housing has been oversupplied, with many of these developments remaining unoccupied. Private banks remain reluctant to invest in the social housing sector without the protection either of a 'mortgage law' or transferable land titles to act as bank guarantees. The oversupply of high-end housing, which was often constructed with expensive loaned capital, has resulted in commercial banks taking ownership of much of this surplus unoccupied stock after investors defaulted on their loans.

Housing cooperatives

Housing cooperative legislation was drafted for the first time in 2010. It includes provisions for exempting cooperatives from paying any tax on their financial transactions, and requires state assistance in making land available from government-designated land reserves for housing with basic infrastructures properly installed, and swift issuance of the necessary surface rights, subdivision licenses, and construction permits. The draft law provisions preferential funding for cooperatives with at least 100 active members. The law further states that houses within the cooperative may be classified as individual or collective property, and that the prices of houses must correspond to the sum of the following values: cost of the land and infrastructures; cost of the studies and projects; cost of the construction and complementary equipment; administrative and financial costs related to the execution of the works. However, this legislation has yet to be implemented, as it lacked the publication of specific bylaws and regulations.

As a result, cooperatives were one of the weakest sectors in delivering housing units within the PNUH. By 2018, of the 80,000 units targeted for 2015, only 12,608 were built. This poor delivery was due to the fact that cooperatives providing low-cost housing require dedicated access to land and ongoing financing to succeed (Cain, 2017a, p. 12).

Housing cooperatives in the PNUH were not granted the promised concessions in relation to land, thereby creating a bureaucratic bottleneck that has resulted in long lead times in acquiring land. Inadequate training of cooperative members in leadership positions led to a lack of administrative and management capabilities in the processes and operations of housing cooperatives. Difficulties relative to access and mobilization of funds have been created by the following interrelated factors, such as unfavourable repayment period, the unwillingness of banks to grant mortgage loans, and the unwillingness of the National Housing Investment

Figure 7.4 Lar do Patriota, the Most Successful Housing Cooperative in Luanda
Source: www.wikimapia.org 1097180

Fund to provide loans. In addition, due to the failure to finalize the publication of the draft legislation discussed earlier, housing cooperatives do not yet qualify for tax exemptions or incentives, as they are still classified as business enterprises.

State-directed self-built housing

The state-directed, self-built housing sub-programme (*auto-construção dirigida*) was conceived as a key component of the PNUH, and more than two-thirds (68.5 % or 685,000 units) of the government's target of 1,000,000 homes was to be met through this modality. The programme promised to ensure the availability of affordable building materials so that homeowners in both urban and rural areas could construct their own homes. This programme's targeted beneficiaries were supposed to be owner-builders from low- and middle-income classes.

Of the total 685,000 units envisaged, over 60% (420,000 units) were to be built in urban areas. Planning to implement a total of 164 self-build urban municipal projects nationwide, the government was to supply all 18 provincial capital cities with infrastructure networks for water and electricity and community facilities, as well as a total of 100,000 hectares of land from state land reserves. The state-assisted self-build programme aimed to ensure the availability of construction materials (in the form of construction kits), and to provide architectural plans and technical guidance. Assistance and guidance from the state was to involve the provision of water and electrical infrastructure, formal urbanization plans, building plots with titled occupation documentation, house design, and technical support for construction. The programme also was to promote the use of local construction materials, to improve public health conditions through the installation of adequate sanitation, and to respect traditional aspects of architectural design and cultural values.

A variation on the self-build model that provides an alternative to delivering completed houses is the '*casa evolutiva*', or an upgradeable modular house that was piloted in a few communities. Here the state constructed the foundations, two divisions, and a sanitary block, and left the homeowner to further develop the house (i.e., build a kitchen, bathroom, and one or more bedrooms) when the necessary resources became available (Figures 7.5 & 7.6).

Implementation of the assisted self-help housing programme has been slow because of the lack of local capacity in the municipalities to issue the large number of land surface-rights titles and building licenses that the programme requires. Although 131,624 plots were laid out, by 2018 only 12,906 were built on under the PNUH framework, and few had received basic water services and road infrastructure.

In-situ slum upgrading vs urban renewal

The PNUH included an urban renewal provision to renovate ('*requalificar*') or redevelop *musseques* – the informal settlements that house more than half of Luanda's population – to promote the legal ownership of land, reduce densities, and improve housing conditions (GoA, 2016a, p. 49).

The '*requalificação*' procedure involves changing the status of the land from 'informal or illegal' into land with regularized tenure and basic services. Said to have been successful in Singapore and São Paulo, the strategy involves temporarily removing resident slum populations to a nearby site, and destroying existing housing to make space for the construction of new multistorey housing. The model is envisioned as a cycle of phased, sustainable actions that are self-financed through the sale of the land made available through the greater densification of occupation.

In late 2010, a Presidential Decree (266/10) established in Luanda a special 'Office of Urban Reconversion of the Cazenga Municipality and both Sambizanga and Rangel Districts' (GTRUCS) to pilot the *musseque requalificação*. Requalification also intends to consolidate and urbanize the *musseques*, incorporating peri-urban areas into the process by: legalizing already occupied land; conducting an economic valuation of *musseque* residents' homes; and installing missing public infrastructure and social services.

Under PNUH, the implementation of slum *requalificação* projects was envisioned as a public-private partnership, where private investors delivered the housing construction component, and government installed infrastructure. The GTRUCS Master Plan included the construction of water supply networks and roads, drainage for sewage, and public lighting and signalling. The plan was designed in accordance with international standards, with 55% of areas intended for housing, 30% for public roads, and 15% for social facilities and green spaces. The plan included building 4,038 dwellings, a mixture of houses and apartments.

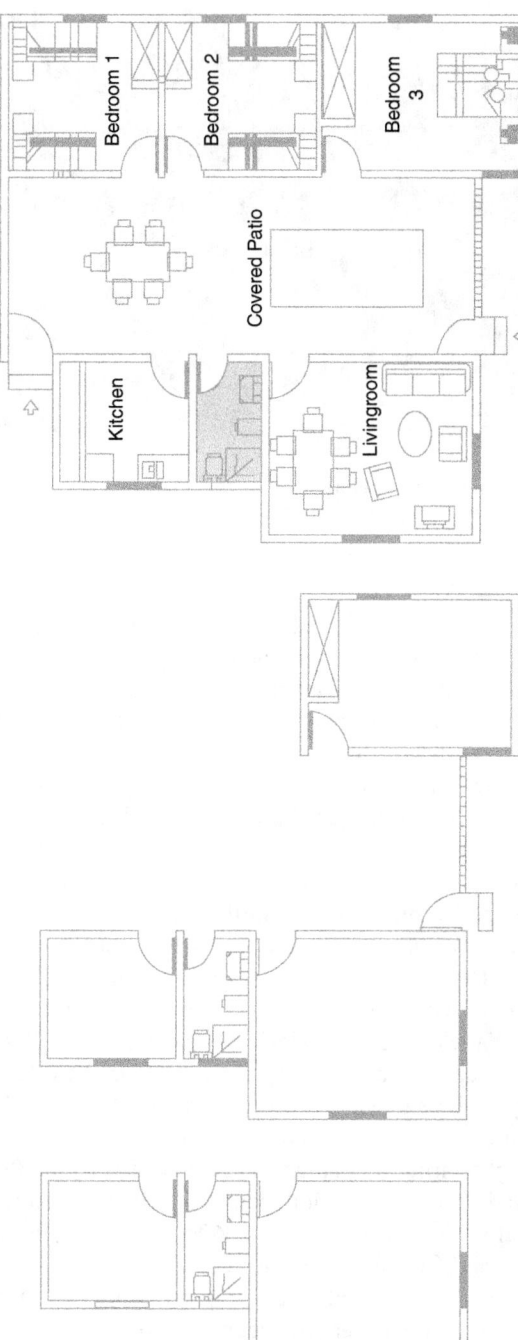

Figure 7.5 An Incremental Housing Plan (*Casa Evolutiva*) to Be Built in Phases

Source: Gameiro, 2010

Figure 7.6 Incremental (Upgradeable) House in Zango
Source: GoA, 2016a, p. 70

The reality of *requalificação* slum redevelopment, as seen in Luanda's old inner-city *musseques*, is that the approach has forcibly removed long-term residents, destroyed their housing, appropriated their land for new housing or commercial development, and permanently relocated them to the city periphery. The first and only *requalificação* project was implemented in Bairro Marconi in Ngola Kiluange District (Cazenga Municipality), using a public-private partnership with the Israeli company KORA. The project built 480 dwelling units in four-storey walk-up blocks in Bairro Marconi. However, as these units remained largely unoccupied by 2020, a housing client survey could not be conducted. It remains to be assessed if this *requalificação* model successfully provided the former *musseque* residents with improved housing conditions and at what cost.

Meanwhile in 2010, Brazilian advisors had introduced an alternative slum-upgrading approach. Focused on in-situ upgrading of urban infrastructure services and housing, the 'Favela-Bairro' model has been piloted by GTRUCS in two districts in Luanda. DW carried out a housing client study in the Tala Hady Barrio (Cazenga Municipality), where one of these pilot 'Favela-Bairro'-style upgrading projects was implemented.

A working-class neighbourhood in an area regularly affected by flooding each rainy season, Tala Hady's environmental conditions had deteriorated significantly since its original settlement in the late 1960s. The upgrading of drainage, road paving, and the provision of water and electric services were completed by GTRUCS without the displacement of existing residents. Utility service fees were introduced, with billing for water and electricity consumption on a monthly basis. Waste collection – made possible for the first time (even in the rainy season) thanks to improved access – was cross-subsidized through a surcharge on electricity invoices. In 2014, an urban real estate tax was introduced to generate local income for improving municipal infrastructure.[2] Tala Hady residents themselves financed and carried out the upgrading of their houses, which sometimes involved densification of use of the site. Improvements included the construction of backyard rental units, and the occasional vertical extension of a second floor.

Using the poverty scorecard tool, we were able to rank the Tala Hady neighbourhood population in order to estimate the affordability of this in-situ upgrading approach for residents. Most residents were shown to be lower-paid workers, with monthly household incomes between US$ 300–400, living close to or below the poverty line.

The social production of housing

Traditional building – construction by people undirected or assisted by the government's PNUH – continues apace in most urban centres across the country. That said, this activity largely depends on the informal sector for inputs of land, labour, and materials, and carries on without the benefit of subsidies, formal planning, or legal land allocations. Housing constructed with neither state engagement nor private sector investment remains largely unrecorded, and is poorly documented in Angolan official statistics. However, social production by owner-builders, or through the collective action of communities, accounts for a significant portion of all housing in Angola. Social production (by people or communities) may use informal sector mechanisms to acquire land and employ labour, but also sometimes relies on formal bank loans from consumer financing facilities, but these are not recorded as housing credit. Unable to access the lower rates usually applied to housing loans, owner-builders must pay the very high interest rates attached to such consumer loans. While foreign companies

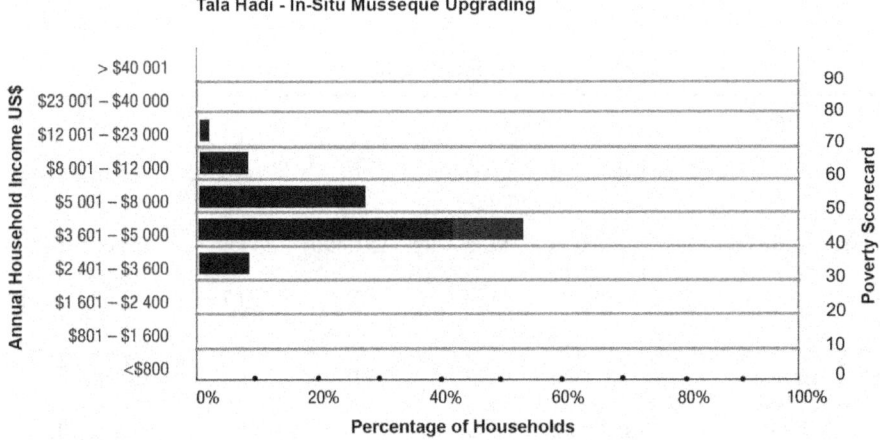

Figure 7.7 Ranking of Household Income in Tala Hady Barrio-Upgrading District

Source: Author

delivered most of the formal housing built under the PNUH, the social production of housing employs mainly local, small-scale builders and individual tradespeople. The Angolan National Housing Directorate estimated that each self-built house created 1.22 jobs, which means the social production of housing created 266,500 new jobs during the period from 2009–2015 (GoA, 2016a).

The National Statistics Institute demographic and census data estimates the total number of new households created during the PNUH period (2009–2015) at 428,426, of which nearly half were constructed through social production. In other words, housing constructed without the support of the Angolan State or private investors has delivered some 205,512 units, of which about 13,000 were built on land acquired from the state (Table 7.1). This number represents almost the same volume delivered by all other sectors combined (at 220,672 units).

Figure 7.8 Unassisted Self-Help, Owner-Built Housing on the Periphery of Luanda
Source: Cain, 2013, p. 25

Table 7.1 Showing the comparative performance of housing sectors

PNUH players	Planned targets		Achievements		Results against planned
	Units	Percentage of total	Units	Percentage of planned	
State public housing	122,000	12.2%	151,800	1244%	Exceeded target
Private sector	115,000	11.5%	45,600	39.7%	Disappointing results
Cooperative housing	80,000	8%	10,366	13%	Poor results
State-directed owner-built	685,000	68.5%	12,906	1.9%	131,624 Lots laid-out
PNUH total	1,000,000	100%	220,672	22%	33.9% if lots are counted
Social production			205,512		Unplanned

Source: Author's construct[3]

Analysis and reflections: who has benefited from PNUH?

Based on our assessment, the following findings can be highlighted:

- The state-built sector accomplished significant delivery of housing, exceeding its goal, but also consuming the majority of funds. Despite the 2007 creation of a Housing Development Fund (FFH) for 'all public, private, and cooperative entities that promote the construction of social houses and for citizens in general', the state ultimately consumed most of the earmarked public budget investments to build its '*centralidades*' or satellite cities.
- The private sector's results largely overlapped with those of the state, due to poorly articulated divisions of responsibility between actors in so-called public-private partnerships.
- The cooperative sector performed poorly.
- The PNUH's real failure was its lack of financing and support in land regularization for owner-builders, who were responsible for delivering about two-thirds of the PNUH housing, but achieved less than 2% of that.
- Finance from commercial banks proved difficult to raise for the private sector, cooperatives, and owner-builders alike. So far, banks have approved fewer that 10% of applications, mostly because they cannot provide loans to applicants lacking clear demonstration of land title.
- Aside from a few pilot interventions, the PNUH effort had little impact on informal settlements, or '*musseques*', where over half of Luanda's population resides.

We applied our poverty scorecard tool to household client surveys across all of the PNUH housing typologies studied, as well as residences benefiting from the in-situ slum upgrading programme, and housing built through social production (using non-state and/or informal-sector resources). Figure 7.9 maps the results of this analysis, demonstrating who benefits from state housing investments in Angola.

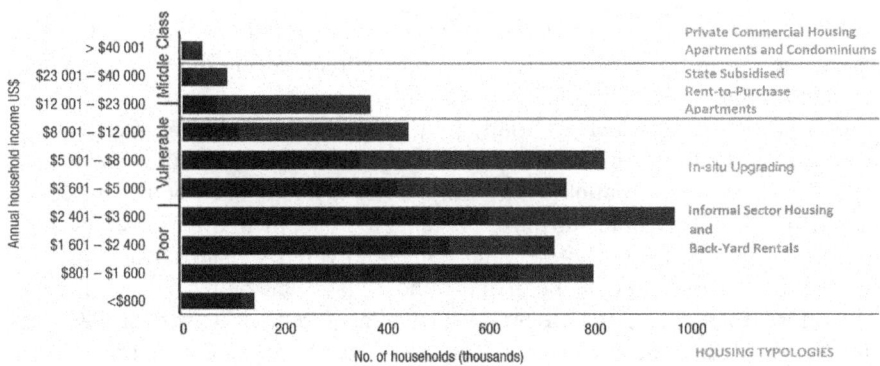

Figure 7.9 Ranking of Household Income Against Housing Typologies

Source: Author

Using the World Bank's ranking (2018) of the *poor* (those earning less than US$1.90 per day), the *vulnerable* ($1.90 to $11.00), the *middle class* ($11.00 to $110.00 per day), and the *wealthy* (above $110), the graph correlates those categories with our poverty scorecard's *decile* system, relating those rankings to probable annual household incomes.

The graphic demonstrates that the population benefiting from state housing subsidies built into the PNUH are almost exclusively in the top 30% of the wealth scale, all of whom are considered to be middle class or above. In other words, by 2016, the PNUH only reached a third of its 1,000,000 intended beneficiaries, and almost none of the bottom-of-the-pyramid target community. The few households that benefited from the pilot slum upgrading project in Tala Hady district could be classified as 'vulnerable'. Few if any families living below the poverty line benefited from state housing subsidies, and most of those depended on informal sector rentals or the social production of their own housing, using family or community resources.

While demonstrating that few of the urban poor benefited from Angola's major budget allocations to the PNUH, this research also draws attention to the Programme's failure to lay the groundwork to fulfil commitments made to the NUA's goal of building sustainable and equitable cities that leave no one behind. Even Angola's nascent housing construction sector seemed to have been 'left behind' in the PNUH. Indeed, our second major finding was that the international private sector was the major beneficiary of construction contracts from the Angolan State's PNUH. Despite its overwhelming construction needs after 27 years of war, Angola has failed to exploit its housing demand as an opportunity to develop competitive construction-sector expertise. Angolan firms could have benefited from government support to reach higher levels of performance; for example, being offered better access to credit, services, and training. Demands to use local contractors were made, but even on smaller projects this rarely happened. Meanwhile, government decision-makers argue that foreign firms are often more competitive in terms of offering better 'value for money' (Søreide, 2011). As a result, relatively little employment was created by the PNUH, as foreign companies brought their own skilled technicians, and government only belatedly set quotas for engagement of local companies (30% subcontracts), technology transfer, and national labour.

Additionally, despite being initially promoted as social housing, our research demonstrated that most of the housing built under PNUH was too expensive for the majority of the population. As a result, the state had to draw additional funds from its housing budget to subsidize the units to make them affordable, even for upper- and middle-level civil servants. State-delivered subsidized housing has satisfied an important segment of the middle-class and better-paid civil servants, offering a rent-to-purchase opportunity to acquire their units over a 20-year time frame. Meanwhile, a further subsidy embedded in the mortgage rate (3%, as opposed to the 15% market rate) ensures that the PNUH housing will continue to drain state budgets for years to come.

In sum, under the PNUH, the state reassumed its role as both developer and landlord (a position it had relinquished in the 1990s when attempting to privatize the housing sector), resulting in a saturation of the high end of the housing market, and a failure to deliver to the majority of the population at the 'bottom of the pyramid'. While the PNUH created high expectations among lower-paid workers and the economically active urban poor – all of whom hoped to benefit from subsidized social housing as their civic right – the housing shortfall still stood at 1,224,514 units in 2015 (GoA, 2016a).

Conclusions: towards a new approach to (re)building Angola's cities

With a weak culture of systematic evaluation of project performance after project completion, failure to draw lessons learned for future projects has become a pattern in Angola. DW's ongoing research in Angola seeks to redress this problem by partnering with communities and local government actors in the critical monitoring of the state's urban policies and programmes using co-production tools.

Having determined that an adequate monitoring framework needs to go beyond tracking housing delivery numbers, we more specifically wanted to measure the extent to which the implementation of the government's PNUH policies was addressing the housing needs of the poor. Additionally, given the PNUH's over-reliance on conventional housing solutions, we saw the need to examine how the state can better support the social production of housing, and also explore different means of improving informal settlements to make Angolan cities more inclusive and ensure that the urban poor are not left behind.

The dramatic fall of petroleum prices from 2014 resulted in a substantial contraction of the Angolan economy. The PNUH's continuing reliance on foreign contractors has contributed to Angola's US$43 billion debt, of which more than half is owed to China.[4] The housing contractor market's dependence on government contracts means that, with state budget cuts, payment delays have hit the private sector hard. This is particularly true for small- and medium-sized enterprises. It is clear that the government will be unable to provide investment and subsidies to continue building new housing in the same form and at the same pace as before. It is likely that the state will therefore withdraw from its position as primary housing developer, instead focusing on creating an enabling environment for the private sector and owner-builders. This must involve the reform and simplification of land administration (Cain, 2013) and the publication of legislation that would facilitate housing finance through a functional mortgage market (Cain, 2017b).

We found that the housing that is provided by owner-builders (i.e., social production) is financed by family members, employers, or personal savings. Land for housing is procured on the informal property market, disqualifying builders from receiving bank loans. Land purchases are normally recorded with documents or contracts that do not have the legal weight of land titles. Often owner-builders subsequently attempt to regularize their occupation through petitions to municipal or provincial government administrations, a process that may take years to success-fully secure legal tenure. In the meantime, housing is constructed incrementally and transacted through the informal market. A mechanism needs to be put in place to rapidly record, recognize, and legitimatize urban land occupations and housing construction that meets minimum standards, does not present environmental risks, and can be relatively easily provided with basic services. The research presented in this chapter provides evidence for civil society and consumer groups advocat-ing for a 'one-stop shop' to facilitate the formalization of informal housing in Luanda and other Angolan cities.

Angola's pent-up demand for housing means that the real estate market could still become an economic driver. Local construction companies securing more projects (as opposed to international developers) would represent a chance to increase employment figures. The potential for an increase in consumer pur-chases also holds promise for Angola's domestic industries. However, there can be no private real estate market without credit, and that credit needs to come from banks. According to the National Bank of Angola (BNA) data, commercial banks reject 86% of housing loan applications (Corrrêa, 2015). Without access to credit and the formal mortgage market, poor households will be forced to continue pro-ducing housing on their own, and they will be restricted to using their own savings and loans from family and friends.

Recommendations and additional research

Using sustained and co-produced research from the ground via our housing client study and poverty scorecard methodology, this study examined all sectors partici-pating in the PNUH, including slum upgrading and owner-builders, thus provid-ing a comparative framework to assess who benefits from the PNUH's different urban strategies. We hope that our results will feed into the Angolan public policy debate on how to best achieve global policy goals, and that the tools developed and utilized here will be employed in the ongoing monitoring of Angola's imple-mentation of these goals to help ensure that the urban poor are not left behind. Specifically, we note the following opportunities for improved policies and fur-ther research:

- Efforts to decentralize state power, finances and decision-making have accelerated since 2018. Although it is unlikely that local elections intended to create and empower new municipalities will take place as promised in 2020 (or before the next legislative elections of 2022), the future imple-mentation of the NUA will depend on the effectiveness of these theo-retically empowered municipalities in developing plans for urbanization; transparently managing land, housing, and public utilities; and finding a way for local citizens to participate in budgeting processes. Both to sustain themselves and to satisfy their constituents' demands, Angola's municipali-ties will need to be able to capture income through the offering of affordable urban services.

- Urban development and infrastructure for housing in Angola could be financed, at least in part, by capturing the increases in land value resulting from public investment in tenure regularization. Land-based financing is an opportunity for raising the revenue necessary to provide key public services and improvements in urban infrastructure and services. However, land information systems need to be strengthened and based on fiscal cadastres and valuation estimates. This means land information systems need to provide updated data on land occupation, use, and values. Our work has demonstrated that this is the kind of information that can be co-produced in participation with communities using innovative mapping tools.
- Urban land reform and the approval of legislation on mortgages that has been long stalled in parliamentary committees must both be key parts of a new approach to housing. Innovations in housing finance that are linked with land tenure security and accessible to lower-income groups (such as housing micro-finance) must be piloted, and funding mechanisms established to bring them to scale quickly.

Notes

1 See www.hic-gs.org/document.php?pid=2438
2 The Urban Real Estate Tax *'Imposto Predial Urbano'* was published as part of a tax reform under the Presidential decree N° 155/10 on the 28 of July 2010, but only enforced from 2014.
3 Based on data presented by the Ministry of Territorial Planning and Housing at the Consultative Council Meeting in Soyo, 12 April 2018.
4 The Angolan Finance Minister announced on 4th September 2018 that Angola's debt to China was US$23 billion.

References

Benazeraf, D. & Alves, A. (2014 April). *Oil for housing: Chinese-built new towns in Angola.* SAIIA Policy Briefing 88, pp. 1–4. Retrieved: http://urban-africa-china.angonet. org/sites/default/files/resource_files/saia_spb_88_benazeraf_alves_20140416.pdf

Cain, A. (1986). *Bairro upgrading in Luanda's Musseques.* Development Workshop, Luanda. DOI: https://doi.org/10.13140/RG.2.2.33424.51202

Cain, A. (2007). Housing microfinance in post-conflict Angola: overcoming socioeconomic exclusion through land tenure and access to credit. *Environment and Urbanization*, 19(2), pp. 361–390.

Cain, A. (2010). Research and practice as advocacy tools to influence Angolan land policies. *Environment and Urbanization*, 22(2), pp. 505–22. http://journals.sagepub.com/doi/abs/10.1177/0956247810380153

Cain, A. (2013). Luanda's post-war land markets: reducing poverty by promoting inclusion. *Urban Forum*, 24(1), pp. 11–31. DOI: https://doi.org/10.1007/s12132-012-9173

Cain, A. (2014). African urban fantasies: past lessons and emerging realities. *Environment & Urbanization*, 26(2), pp. 561–567. DOI: https://doi.org/10.1177/0956247814526544

Cain, A. (2017a January 10). *Cooperative housing sector Angola.* Centre for Affordable Housing Finance in Africa, Report 16, pp. 1–20. Retrieved: www.dw.angonet.org/sites/default/files/20170110__cooperative_housing_sector_angola.pdf

Cain, A. (2017b February). *The private housing sector in Angola: Angola's tentative development of a private real-estate market.* Centre for Affordable Housing Finance in Africa, Report 17, pp. 1–15. Retrieved: http://housingfinanceafrica.org/app/uploads/DWA_CAHF_Private-Sector-Housing-in-Angola_February-2017.pdf

Cain, A., Daly, M. & Robson, P. (2002). *Basic service provision for the urban poor: the experience of development workshop in Angola.* IIED Working Paper 8 on Poverty Reduction in Urban Areas, pp. 1–37. Retrieved: www.dw.angonet.org/forumitem/basic-service-provision-urban-poor-thhe-experience-dw-angola

Caprotti, F., Cowley, C., Datta, A., CastánBroto, V., Gao, E., Georgeson, L., Herrick, C., Odendaal, N. & Joss, S. (2017). The new urban agenda: key opportunities and challenges for policy and practice. *Urban Research & Practice*, 10(3), pp. 367–378. DOI: https://doi.org/10.1080/17535069.2016.1275618

Cardoso, R. (2016). The circuitries of spectral urbanism: looking underneath fantasies in Luanda's new centralities. *Urbanization*, 1(2), pp. 1–19.

CEIC. (2018 October). *Relatorio Economico de Angola 2017.* Luanda: Universidade Catolica de Angola.

Corrêa, C. (2015 September 25). Interview with Cleber Corrêa: an option for improving real estate credit. *Journal Expansão*, pp. 77–78.

Croese, S. (2012). 1 million houses? Angola's national reconstruction and Chinese engagement. In: Power, M. & Alves, A.C. (Eds.), *China and Angola: a marriage of convenience?* Oxford: Pambazuka Press, pp. 124–144.

Durose, C. & Richardson, L. (2016). *Designing public policy for co-production: theory, practice and change.* Bristol: PolicyPress.

The Economist. (2012 June 30). The oil money may start to trickle down. *The Economist* [online]. Retrieved: www.economist.com/node/21557811

Ferreira, A.C., Silva, L.T. & Ramos, R.R. (2012). *Urban observatories, tools for monitoring cities.* Conference Paper. Retrieved: www.wseas.us/e-library/conferences/2012/Algarve/EEESD/EEESD-41.pdf

Fukuda-Parr, S. (2014). Global goals as a policy tool: intended and unintended consequences. *Journal of Human Development and Capabilities*, 15(2–3), pp. 118–131.

Fukuda-Parr, S. (2016). From the millennium development goals to the sustainable development goals: shifts in purpose, concept, and politics of global goal setting for development. *Gender & Development*, 24(1), pp. 43–52.

Gameiro, A. (2010 October). Presentation at Dia International de Habitat, Namibe.

Gastrow, C. (2017). Cement citizens: housing, demolition and political belonging in Luanda, Angola. *Citizenship Studies*, 21(2), pp. 224–239.

GoA (Government of Angola). (2009). *Inquérito Integrado sobre o Bem Estar da População – IBEP.* Luanda: Instituto Nacional de Estatística. Retrieved: https://andine.ine.gov.ao/nada4/index.php/catalog/11/overview

GoA (Government of Angola). (2016a). *Angolan national report for habitat III.* Retrieved: http://habitat3.org/wp-content/uploads/Angola-Habitat-III-Final-Report-English.pdf

GoA (Government of Angola). (2016b). *Resultados Definitivos do Recenseamento Geral da População e da Habitação de Angola 2014.* Luanda: Instituto Nacional de Estatística.

Joshi, A. & Moore, M. (2004). Institutionalised co-production: unorthodox public service delivery in challenging environments. *Journal of Development Studies*, 40(4), pp. 31–49.

Klopp, J.M. & Petretta, D.L. (2017). The urban sustainable development goal: indicators, complexity and the politics of measuring cities. *Cities*, 63, pp. 92–97.

Macauhub. (2019 March 28). Angola plans to stop guaranteeing loans with oil. *Macau* [online]. Retrieved: https://macauhub.com.mo/2019/03/28/pt-angola-deixa-de-garantir-emprestimos-com-petroleo/

Meth, P. (2013). Millennium development goals and urban informal settlements: unintended consequences. *International Development Planning Review*, 35(1), pp. v–xiii.

Mitlin, D. (2008). With and beyond the state: co-production as a route to political influence, power and transformation for grassroots organizations. *Environment and Urbanization*, 20(2), pp. 339–360.

Moreira, P. (2012). Photo [Kilamba new city in Luanda, China's largest housing project in Africa]. *ArchiExpo* (e-magazine), reprinted with permission of photographer.

Ostrom, E. (1996). Crossing the great divide: co-production, synergy and development. *World Development*, 24(6), pp. 1073–1087.

Polk, M. (2015). *Co-producing knowledge for sustainable cities: joining forces for change.* Abingdon and New York: Routledge.

Rodrigues, C.U. & Frias, S. (2015). Between the city lights and the shade of exclusion: post-war accelerated urban transformation of Luanda, Angola. *Urban Forum*, 27, pp. 129–147. DOI: https://doi.org/10.1007/s12132-015-9271-7

Satterthwaite, D. (2003). The millennium development goals and urban poverty reduction: great expectations and nonsense statistics. *Environment & Urbanization*, 15(2), pp. 179–190. DOI: https://doi.org/10.1177/095624780301500208

Schreiner, M. (2015 December 15). *Scoring poverty for Angola.* Produced for Development Workshop and Chr Michelsen Institute. Retrieved: www.dw.angonet.org/content/research

Soares de Oliveira, R. (2015). *Magnificent and beggar land, Angola since the civil war.* London: Hurst & Co.

Søreide, T. (2011 November). Ten challenges in public construction CEIC-CMI public sector transparency study. *Angola Brief*, 1(19), pp. 1–4. Retrieved: www.cmi.no/publications/4288-ten-challenges-in-public-construction

UN-Habitat. (1996). *The habitat agenda: Istanbul declaration on human settlements.* Retrieved: https://undocs.org/A/CONF.165/14

UN-Habitat. (2014). *The state of African cities: re-imagining sustainable urban transitions.* Nairobi: UN-Habitat.

Waldorff, P. (2016). The law is not for the poor: land, law and eviction in Luanda. *Singapore Journal of Tropical Geography*, 37(3), pp. 363–377.

8 Conclusion

Towards a research agenda for knowledge co-production in Urban Africa

Sylvia Croese

This book brings together contributions from researchers and practitioners across Africa to provide insight into some of the continent's most pressing urban development challenges, including infrastructural inequality, affordable housing, climate resilience, and food security. The chapters show how African cities – ranging from small, peri-urban areas to entire mega-city regions – are at the coalface of such challenges. Central to all the cases is the disjuncture between policy and practice, often resulting from contrasting needs, understandings, and interests that guide the actions of both states and citizens. This disjuncture produces complex spaces and arrangements in which formal plans and policies are intertwined with informal actors and practices that are in turn strongly shaped by local histories and politics.

Taken together, the complex reality of contemporary governance in African cities has a daily impact on the degree to which cities and communities are safe, inclusive, resilient, and sustainable, and able to meet local and global urban development goals. The need for knowledge that engages meaningfully with this complexity and is capable of capturing the finer and often shifting grain of informal systems and actors is urgently needed to inform improved policies, governance, and urban development planning. By bringing together multiple actors and perspectives to examine and address these challenges and their different manifestations in eight African cities, the collection's authors created new spaces and entry points for knowledge sharing, production, and experimentation. This concluding chapter reflects and builds on those contributions, with the aim of outlining a research agenda to guide ongoing and future knowledge co-production in urban Africa.

Practising knowledge co-production in urban Africa

There is no single definition of knowledge co-production, and much of the literature on co-production still focuses on the co-production of services (Mitlin & Bartlett, 2018). Moreover, while there is increasing interest and work on transdisciplinary knowledge co-production, particularly in the field of (urban) sustainability, this still remains a novel approach to research in Africa, with the exception of

South Africa (Swilling, 2014).[1] As such, this collection's main purpose and contribution is to share its experimental practice of alternative and innovative forms of knowledge generation through co-production in urban Africa.

Most of the chapters in this volume follow a CityLab approach, broadly understood as the creation of deliberative spaces aimed at enabling dialogue between different urban actors and stakeholders. As such, many of the researchers conducted multi-stakeholder roundtables, meetings and workshops, municipal fora, learning labs, and policy dialogues. Other research methods included secondary literature review, participatory mapping, personal interviews, focus group discussions, GIS-enabled surveys, direct observations, as well as quantitative data-gathering methods.

To ensure the inclusivity and relevance of the research, all of these tools and methods included a vast range of stakeholders, from city and other (local) government officials, traditional leadership (chiefs), community leaders, and political party representatives, to local community organization representatives, business owners, and ordinary citizens, including youth. As a process-driven enterprise, the undertaking of urban knowledge co-production required not only the cooperation of stakeholders, but also their inclusion as equal research partners with invaluable perspectives. In most cases, the research also necessarily included activities ranging from community sensitization, stakeholder mapping and identification, and other preparatory meetings in the inception phase, to end-of-project stakeholder meetings and presentations as part of the research completion phase.

In addition to the chapters that focus on knowledge co-production within individual cities, a number of chapters focus on co-producing knowledge across geographical boundaries by comparing different cities within the same country (Chapter 3) or across national borders (Chapter 5). These comparative studies intend to offer yet another way of generating questions and insights to contribute to the construction of new 'South-South' knowledges, outside of the traditional paradigms of research practice and thought. While both singular (i.e., looking at one case city) and comparative modes of knowledge co-production offer productive avenues for rich insights into local realities, they are not without their challenges. The chapters here show that when working within a single local community, challenges related to (the lack of) trust between and among the varied urban stakeholders and complex local governance structures operating in that space can pose significant barriers. This dynamic was particularly notable in instances where power is practised and shared by numerous actors both in and outside of formal state structures (e.g., political parties and traditional authorities). Meanwhile, when engaged in comparative urbanism research, other practical challenges emerged, such as dealing with differences in definitions (e.g., of informality), expectations, and data sources and reliability from city to city.

Taken together, the chapters in this volume show the need for much more conscious reflection on the specific challenges involved in co-producing knowledge in urban Africa in order to come up with definitions and methods that are suitable and appropriate to Africa's context-specific local realities. In doing so, there is much to be built on in terms of the different exercises of adjustment and experimentation that the researchers in this book demonstrate to have undertaken in responding to and overcoming their respective sets of local challenges.

As the authors of Chapter 2 argue when writing about Lusaka's Soweto Market, the complexity of local governance structures has tangible consequences for the extent to which stakeholders can freely participate in (spaces of) governance, including spaces of knowledge co-production. Researchers thus must have the knowledge, intuition, and skills required to navigate and manage such spaces. As such, the ability to assess the degree of 'freedom' needed for participants to express themselves, and/or create conditions to facilitate the co-production process are crucial, and will mean different things in different contexts, as is also demonstrated in Chapters 4 and 6 (Thika and Kumasi).[2]

With these concerns in mind, the authors of Chapter 2 describe how they chose to 'separate political leaders from the administrative staff of the Lusaka City Council during the two CityLabs held on Soweto Food Market, in order for them to *engage more freely*' (my italics). Similarly, the authors of Chapter 4 on land sharing in Thika describe how workshop participants were chosen 'by gender and age, creating one workshop for women, one for youth, and one for men. The aim [being] to enable optimal engagement in a *free atmosphere*, and to better capture divergent and sometimes gender-specific tenure issues' (my italics). Workshop participants in Sepe-Buokrom in Kumasi, Ghana were similarly divided into groups based on age, gender, and power of authority in order for participants *to express themselves freely* (my italics). Despite these efforts, certain hierarchies persisted even within the groupings (e.g., 'queen mothers' within the women's focus group in Kumasi, and representatives of the chief in the men's group). That said, researchers continued to do what they could to ensure participants' comfort and ability to express themselves, as was seen in the Kumasi CityLab, where the local language (Twi) was used as the medium of communication during all focus group discussions at the community level for maximum participant involvement and understanding (Chapter 6).

The meaning and impact of such adjustments and interventions cannot be taken for granted, and depend on researchers being both in tune with local realities and flexible enough to adjust and switch gears when needed. There is a need for further analysis of the 'practice of best practice' as used throughout the continent, and the kind of tactical knowledge that underpins such work (Bulkeley, 2006). Such analysis would provide an important basis for further experimentation, learning, and theorization of alternatives to universal 'best practices' of knowledge co-production based on local experiences in urban Africa (Patel et al., 2015), as well as for a research agenda that can support and strengthen such endeavours.

Towards a research agenda

Existing practices of knowledge co-production in urban Africa show the importance of experimentation and innovation with alternative forms of knowledge generation. These are not limited to crossing societal, disciplinary, linguistic, sectoral, or geographical boundaries, but also include the use and mixing of new technologies to support 'citizen science' (West et al., 2020).

How can the experience gained, the knowledge applied, and the social capital built in co-production experiments by both researchers and co-production partners be harnessed? How can an explicit link to policy formulation and implementation be made? And how can sustained modes of collaboration be forged in order to build a lasting bridge between research and policy? These are some of the questions that we hope this collection catalyses researchers and urban practitioners to explore further.

Supporting the role and capacity building of researchers

Most of the contributors to this book have a vast wealth of knowledge and research experience, which we argue is a vital asset in navigating the complexity of knowledge co-production processes. Many of the authors refer to the importance of continuous engagement with stakeholders, as well as the neutral positionality of the researchers as partners, in order to build and maintain trust. The consequence of these deliberate efforts is the creation of an atmosphere conducive to participatory and inclusive dialogue (Chapters 4 on Thika and 7 on Luanda). In addition, the authors stress the ability to identify key actors with whom future partnerships could be developed (e.g., Chapter 6 on Kumasi) – a type of tacit relational knowledge that is acquired through years of experience and practice rather than the application of scientific or academic protocols.

How can such roles be better supported, and how can the knowledge created in these processes be captured and passed on to new generations of researchers? Importantly, the Centre for Urban Research and Planning at the University of Zambia (Chapter 2) and the Centre for Urban Research and Innovations of the University of Nairobi (Chapter 4) are members of the Association of Africa Planning Schools (AAPS), which intends to transform urban planning education and practice in Africa by equipping up-and-coming urban planners with the relevant skills and methodologies to address the challenges facing the African city. As demonstrated across the different chapters in this volume, this is crucial work – not only for research to more effectively contribute to participatory and inclusive community plans and policies, but also to strengthen the research-education nexus (Duminy et al., 2014).

Engaging knowledge co-production partners

The chapters in this book have illustrated the importance of relationship building and management in the knowledge co-production process. This not only was an essential research tool, but also in itself an important process that provided the researchers with deeper insight and understanding of the perceptions and experiences of research stakeholders.

The researchers in Kumasi, Ghana point to important nuances that were uncovered through the co-production process used in focus group discussions and stakeholder meetings, such as the community's diversified nature based on ethnic lines, apparent rivalry and tensions between local leaders, and various perspectives on the potential for and challenges to successful implementation of a Community Resilience Framework (CRF) for flood-risk management (Chapter 6). Consciousness of these nuances and the ability to engage with them carefully and constructively allowed the researchers to contribute to building awareness within the community of its own ability to take initiative independently of government action. That said, despite efforts to ensure a gender balance in stakeholder groups, the group composition in this research was overwhelmingly male, with females constituting just over one third of the participants. According to the authors, this is reflective of the male-dominated nature of Ghanaian culture, particularly in areas of decision-making. This observation raises questions around how such perceptions can be overcome, and how co-production processes can be more inclusive of gender and age, as well as political and religious beliefs.

Working with numerous partners builds greater and more nuanced understanding of the challenges faced by the different stakeholders. This is seen in the case of Zambian public servants who deal with the daily politics of urban markets, but also must strive to remain professional (Chapter 2) – an example that speaks to the plight of the countless public servants caught between the pressures emanating from failing market economy models playing out in constitutional democracies. The resulting conflicts and paradoxes of that dynamic are also noted in Chapter 5's comparative study of Johannesburg and Cairo, where 'on one hand, [there is] the need for cost recovery, and on the other, a constitutional pledge guaranteeing citizens the right to these services – [a situation that] has led to a number of court cases'.

In some cases, the political weight associated with key challenges can mean that government officials feel they need to withdraw themselves from the work, as experienced by the authors of Chapter 4 working on the 'the land question' in Thika, Kenya – a question that was considered 'too emotive to engage in during a campaign period'. In the same project, which examined the potential for land sharing in an informal settlement, the researchers also had to accommodate the high turnover of government officials, and the effects of shifts in political leadership on potential gains made under previous administrations. The tension between the long-term process of knowledge co-production and short-term political cycles represents an often unavoidable barrier to extending co-production models to regional and national levels, and putting results to action.

Such barriers also point to the necessity of taking things like political election cycles into account when planning research, and devising methodologies to engage high-level government officials and to mitigate against political influence. The case of Luanda (Chapter 7) is instructive in this regard. Working with both community members and local government officials through training and capacity building for data collection, this co-produced effort contributed not only to stakeholders having a better understanding of the intentions behind the work, but also to a local sense of ownership of the data and knowledge produced. Also seeking to fully engage focus group discussion participants in Kumasi, Ghana (Chapter 6), researchers note the positive impact of beginning all sessions with an audio-visual presentation of flood events, which moved participants to actively contribute to the discussions that followed. Whichever tools or methods were employed, all of the chapters in this volume repeatedly illustrated the vital importance of seeing co-production through to the end: that is, communicating and sharing research results as part of community and stakeholder engagement.

The research-policy nexus

One of the key questions underlying and unifying this volume is how co-produced research can be harnessed to inform both local and global development policies and agendas. Here we must take care to not blindly mimic global agendas – that is, simply transposing them to the local level – but rather to critically evaluate the relevance and utility of these agendas, and accordingly change and adapt them where necessary. To that end, as was revealed by some of the research here, co-production represents a useful tool to localize global development frameworks such as the Sustainable Development Goals (SDGs) and New Urban Agenda (NUA). Notably, several chapters revealed important gaps and shortcomings of global and local development agendas, by highlighting the importance of good land governance and well-functioning land administration systems (Chapter 4), spatial and intra-city inequality (Chapter 5), and the importance of assessing the extent to which existing urban policies do not leave anyone behind (Chapter 7).

In critically interrogating development agendas at the finer grain of local-level real-world application and through the lens of a multitude of stakeholders, all chapters underscore the importance of the negotiated co-production of policy interventions, as opposed to policies that are either imposed from top to bottom (or vice versa) without taking into account the full spectrum of urban actors, as well as practices and systems of urban informality, that operate in African cities on a daily basis. As such, the authors of Chapter 3 argue for the adoption of an integrative policy approach that necessarily considers and builds upon the existing ways in which the formal and informal are both connected and disconnected across three cities in Egypt. Similarly, authors of Chapter 6 stress the importance of Community Resilience Frameworks (CRFs) for understanding how communities at high risk of flooding effectively perceive their own adaptive preparedness within a sub-Saharan West African context, and thus can devise local adaptive responses and systems to flooding. The implication here is that such 'informal' locally implemented and owned systems can integrate with and supplement more formal government initiatives to collectively help Ghanaian flood-prone communities to meet global goals and targets on community resilience for disaster risk management and climate change adaptation.

In sum, much of the research from this volume both demonstrates the need and advocates for alternative policies that intentionally use the formal-informal interface as a key entry point to bridging the research-policy gap and advancing urban integration. However, understanding and mapping those entry points requires local knowledge, particularly of the informal, and we would argue that the acquisition of that knowledge is aided by co-productive methods and tools like the ones discussed in this volume.

Concluding thoughts

While interest in and experience of knowledge co-production in Africa is on the rise, it still remains a novel approach to research, and requires further support as well as theorization. The importance of such work cannot be underestimated, as when successful, CityLabs and other modes of knowledge co-production create important alternative spaces for knowledge-sharing, participatory planning, and urban governance, thus representing an important vehicle by which to bring the wider community together in understanding the urban challenges that beset African cities. The use of co-productive methods also offers the opportunity to incorporate the voices and perspectives of communities who have routinely been forgotten in the quest for one-size-fits-all technical solutions to development challenges. That said, CityLabs are but one method that can be undertaken as part of knowledge co-production, and researchers must continue to deliberately and methodically engage with communities and a wide range of urban stakeholders to generate the kind of knowledge that is required to disrupt the power imbalances that continue to be the hallmark of citizen and state relationships in African cities.

Notes

1 For a more detailed overview of knowledge co-production, see Chapter 1 of this volume.
2 Notably, out of the six different countries covered in this book, only two (Ghana and South Africa) were considered to be 'free' as measured by the degree of civil liberties and political rights by the US-based NGO Freedom House at the time of completion of the work in 2019. Zambia and Kenya are considered as 'partly free', while Egypt and Angola are considered 'not free'. See: https://freedomhouse.org/. By contrast, Chapter 5 on Cairo and Johannesburg, shows that different degrees of freedom can still result in similar outcomes for the urban poor, as in both cities 'mechanisms and modes of participation and engagement with the state are largely dysfunctional'.

References

Bulkeley, H. (2006). Urban sustainability: learning from best practice? *Environment and Planning A*, 38, pp. 1029–1044. DOI: https://doi.org/10.1068/a37300
Duminy, J., Odendaal, N. & Watson, V. (2014). The education and research imperatives of urban planning professionals in Africa. In: Parnell, S. & Pieterse, E. (Eds.), *Africa's urban revolution*. Cape Town: UCT Press, pp. 184–199.
Mitlin, D. & Bartlett, S. (2018). Editorial: co-production – key ideas. *Environment & Urbanization*, 30(2), pp. 355–366. DOI: https://doi.org/10.1177/0956247818791931

Patel, Z., Greyling, S., Parnell, S. & Pirie, G. (2015). Co-producing urban knowledge: experimenting with alternatives to 'best practice'. *International Development Planning Review*, 37(2), pp. 187–203. DOI: https://doi.org/10.3828/idpr.2015.15

Swilling, M. (2014). Rethinking the science – policy interface in South Africa: experiments in knowledge co-production. *South African Journal of Science*, 110(5–6), pp. 1–7, Article #2013-0265. DOI: 10.1590/sajs.2014/20130265

West, S.E., Büker, P., Ashmore, M., Njoroge, G., Welden, N., Muhoza, C., Osano, P., Makau, J., Njoroge, P. & Apondo, W. (2020). Particulate matter pollution in an informal settlement in Nairobi: using citizen science to make the invisible visible. *Applied Geography*, 114. DOI: https://doi.org/10.1016/j.apgeog.2019.102133

Index

ACC 6–7, 24
Accra 153–154; flood-risk management strategies in 165
adaptation: to flooding 156, 176–177; models 152; versus mitigation 152, 154–155; *see also* climate; community resilience; flood/ing
African Centre for Cities *see* ACC
African Urban Research Initiative *see* AURI
African urbanism/s 1, 37, 146
Africa's urban challenge 1–2, 4, 8, 214
agricultural land 44–45, 53, 55, 58, 65, 125, 130
Alexandria 9, 47–48, 55–58, 61–66, 70, 72–73, 76; formal-informal interface 55–57; *see also* borders, crossings, activities, and flows
Angola 11, 183–205; civil war 183–184; National Urban Observatory 186–188
AURI 2, 7–9, 12, 24, 76

backyard 120, 137, 144–146; dwellings 125, 130, 140, 199; rental 199; *see also* market
basic service delivery/provision 4, 9, 11, 20–21, 23, 26, 89, 93, 121–123, 134, 137, 166; exclusionary practices around 35; by municipal owned entities (MOEs) 121; by publicly-owned national holding companies 124
basic services 55, 97, 183, 196, 204; in Angola 183–184, 187, 190; in Cairo and Johannesburg 11, 134, 137, 141, 144–146; rights to access 83, 117; as a source of income 121; unequal access to 43, 45, 188; universal access to 117; *see also* constitutional rights to; housing; inequality

basic services and infrastructure 9, 11, 20, 113–115; in Angola 186, 194–196, 199, 205; comparative access in Johannesburg and Cairo 134, 137, 140, 143–145; in Egypt 43, 45–46, 55, 60–61, 65, 67, 69–70, 75, 122; as income source 121; in Kenya 82–83, 85, 87–88, 97; privatization of 114, 117–118
basic services and infrastructure in relation to inequality 11, 55, 113–116, 125, 137, 143–145, 147, 187–188, 208; spatiality of 113–118, 124, 137, 145–146, 208
basic services and infrastructure in relation to informality 67, 70, 95, 97–98, 115–118, 121–122, 134, 137, 143–146
'belting' 42, 46, 60
borders, crossings, activities, and flows 10, 47–48, 51, 70, 75; in Alexandria 57–58; in Cairo 53–54; comparative analysis of 61–70; in Minya 60–61; recommendations based on 70, 72–75; *see also* capital

Cairo 9, 11, 49, 51, 113–115, 141–147; comparative studies 76–78, 113–115, 212; fieldwork in 47–48, 118; formal and informal interface 43, 51; housing market 130; income and poverty 122, 124–125, 141–142; population and informality 122, 130; *see also* basic services; borders, crossings, activities, and flows; EMN; GCR; infrastructure
Cairo Laboratory for Urban Studies, Training and Environmental Research *see* CLUSTER
capital 103; access to 27–29, 31, 103; financial 28, 31; flows of 48, 54, 60–62,

For Product Safety Concerns and Information please contact our EU
representative GPSR@taylorandfrancis.com
Taylor & Francis Verlag GmbH, Kaufingerstraße 24, 80331 München, Germany